A Blossom at Midnight

A Blossom at Midnight

A.L. KNORR

USA TODAY BESTSELLING AUTHOR

Books by A.L. Knorr

Elemental Origins Series

Born of Water

Born of Fire

Born of Earth

Born of Æther

Born of Air

The Elementals

The Siren's Curse

Salt & Stone

Salt & the Sovereign

Salt & the Sisters

Earth Magic Rises

Bones of the Witch

Ashes of the Wise

Heart of the Fae

Arcturus Academy

Firecracker

Fire Trap

Fire Games

Legends of Fire

Source Fire

Rings of the Inconquo

Born of Metal

Metal Guardian

Metal Angel

Mermaid's Return

Returning

Falling

Surfacing

Elemental Novellas

Pyro, A Fire Novella

Heat, A Fire Novella

The Kacy Chronicles

Descendant

Ascendant

Combatant

Transcendent

The Scented Court

A Blossom at Midnight

A Memory of Nightshade

A Daughter of Winter

A Prince of Autumn

To learn more visit www.alknorrbooks.com.

Original Text Copyright A.L. Knorr, Intellectually Promiscuous Press and A&B Abilities Inc 2021.

The moral right of A.L. Knorr to be identified as the author of this work has been asserted in accordance with the Copyright, Designs and Patents Act of 1988. This work has been registered with Library and Archives Canada. Cover design and formatting by Damonza.

All rights reserved.

No part of this book may be reproduced in any form or by any electronic or mechanical means, including information storage and retrieval systems, without written permission from the author, except for the use of brief quotations in a book review.

All characters in this book are fictitious, and any resemblance to actual persons, living or dead, is purely coincidental.

ISBN 5x8 Paperback 978-1-989338-37-7

ISBN 5.5x8.5 Hardcover 978-1-989338-46-9

ISBN 6x9 Large Print Hardcover 978-1-989338-47-6

A brother is a gift of immeasurable value, and I have two. How rich I am, how blessed.

Preface

Before the veil between worlds was rent, letting human and fae traffic flow back and forth, the ancient fae kings and queens of Ivryndi were pure-blooded and powerful. Fae citizens were tethered to their monarch: the more powerful the sovereign, the more magic the citizens wielded. They were divided into courts by season.

The rend was repaired, and is now closed but to a few. However, the continent of Ivryndi was changed forever.

At the opening of our story, there remain only two fae courts that have maintained a perpetual season: Silverfall, the winter court, and Stavarjak, the spring court, both situated in the north. The other kingdoms have slipped into seasonal cycles that mimic those of Earth. Citizens of Solana and Rahamlar are a mix of human and fae, while the southern kingdoms of Boskaya, Archelia and Tryske long ago lost any magic they once had; their populations are predominantly human.

Over time, the courtly magic of some kingdoms evolved to accommodate Earthly plants and animals. Since fae species are generally aggressive (due to their magical nature), imported species had to evolve to survive; this birthed an alliance between Terran species and fae born with an inherent connection to the natural world; known as flora fae and fauna fae. It is their presence that allows Terran species to compete and thrive in the midst of vigorous fae species.

One kingdom has invested in these fae more than any other and become the wealthiest kingdom in Ivryndi as a result: the kingdom of Solana.

Prologue

It was early morning. So early that stars still lay across the velvet expanse, even as the sun hinted at the eastern horizon. Cows lowed from the pasture beyond the village. Cocks crowed. There were lights in a few windows, farmers preparing breakfast and getting ready for work.

Hanna opened the white picket gate in front of her neighbor's cottage. She shifted her basket of healing herbs and other supplies from the crook of one elbow to the other and let herself into the single-room abode without knocking, stepping quietly on the stone floor so as not to wake Marion. As she propped the door open to freshen the air, she noticed the flutter of an insect as it slipped inside. She'd deal with it later. Setting the basket on the worktable, she unloaded home-canned food, a small sack of flour she'd ground the night before, a bottle of fresh milk, a dozen eggs, a small box of salt and a few other basics.

The sound of a baby's coo from the bassinet in the corner made Hanna smile. With a glance at Marion's sleeping form on the single mattress in the far corner, Hanna went to the cradle to look at the twins.

They were perfect. Hanna felt herself melting as she took in their tiny, softly pointed ears. These belied a fae father, though Marion had never admitted any such thing to Hanna. One thing Marion made clear when she first arrived in Dagevli only eleven months ago was that she didn't welcome questions. An older, pregnant widow was not something the village was accustomed to having among their population, but the villagers had been welcoming enough to their newest member, probably due to pity. Hanna was secretly thrilled for her lonely neighbor. Marion hadn't been in Dagevli long but she'd already proven to be a good person to live beside. She wasn't nosy, she didn't hesitate to take care of Hanna's young daughter if Hanna needed to run an errand, and Marion often gifted them with loaves of her delicious berry bread. In their small community, helpful neighbors were a necessity of survival.

The twins each had a cap of dark hair curling around their wee fae ears, soft as duckling down. They slept wrapped up in one another and had often been found sucking on one another's chins. They were less than three months old and had been born on a rainy night with only Hanna in attendance. Marion had been grateful for the heavy downfall to drown out the sound of her difficult labor.

A small furry shape moved on the pillow just behind the girl's head, making Hanna start and suck in a breath. At first, she thought it was a hairy spider with a body the size of a teaspoon. Her heart hammered as she considered how to get the spider away without waking the baby. But the shape uncurled a wing and she realized with a breathless jolt of amazement that it was not a spider but a bat, no larger than the end of her thumb. It had shining ink-drop eyes and a furry brown snout. Fine rust-colored fur covered its wings. It blinked up at Hanna and then yawned, revealing pin-sharp, near-transparent teeth, as though it had every right in the world to be cozied up to the infant's warm scalp.

Hanna had not yet recovered from what the presence of the bat might mean when a butterfly fluttered over the children, as if materializing from the air. It landed on the boy's swaddling clothes and crawled along him until it reached his head. There it stopped, flexing its wings. It was a specimen Hanna had never seen before, and not like the flamboyantly colored insects that danced all summer over the gardens of Dagevli. The panels of its wings were as transparent as glass. Through them, Hanna could make out the details of the boy's hair. Framing each wing was a thin border of red-brown, and a dash of white decorated the tip.

Hanna's heart galloped. She had to wake Marion. This news was too lovely to wait.

Marion was a lump under her bedclothes, her breathing deep and even. With every exhalation, she loosed a small whistle through her nose.

Hanna put a hand on Marion's hip and gently shook her. "Marion, honey? Wake up, you have to see this."

Marion's breathing changed and her eyes slit open. She yawned. "Hello, dear. You're here early." She pushed herself up to sitting, her red and gray curls making a cloud around her head. She blinked blearily at the bassinet. "They were so good last night. Went right back to sleep after every feeding."

"That's wonderful," Hanna whispered. "And something else wonderful has happened. Come see."

Marion followed Hanna to where the twins lay sleeping but froze in her tracks when she saw the butterfly. Her face went the color of old candle wax, and she backpedaled with a moan. "No. No, no, no."

Hanna stared at her, confused, as Marion cast about the room as though looking for something she needed right that instant. She bent to retrieve a softcover recipe book from beneath her cooking counter and rolled it into a slender cone as she returned to the cradle with thunder in her face.

Stunned, Hanna almost moved too late. As Marion raised the rolled-up weapon overhead, Hanna dove in front of her, grabbing her wrist. "You mustn't!"

Marion went for the insect again. Her face crumpled, tears gathered in the corners of her eyes. "I must!"

Hanna panted with effort and spoke quickly, desperately. "You cannot. Eliminating them will only bring another. Dead familiars are quickly replaced, and killing them will hurt your babies."

"They're too young to know—" Marion sobbed.

"They're not. They're emotionally connected whether you like it or not. Kill the familiars and you'll hurt the children, and to what end? Will you kill the next one that comes along? And the one after that?" Hanna spoke gently now, seeing that her friend was distraught but coming to her senses. Hanna's hands were cold on Marion's arms from the shock of the mother's reaction.

"Them?" Marion lowered her rolled-up book, defeated, her tear-filled gaze combing Hanna's face. "I see only one familiar."

"If I let you near"—Hanna pulled the book from Marion's limp fingers, and her friend let her take it—"will you promise not to hurt them?"

Marion nodded.

Cautiously, Hanna stepped aside so Marion could approach

the babies. She was rocked to her core by Marion's murderous response to what most would consider to be a gift of magnificent proportion.

"A butterfly," Marion moaned, "*and* a bat." She covered her face. "I am cursed among women."

Hanna put an arm around Marion's shoulders, processing her strange words. She used the time it took to guide Marion back to her bed to search out the reasons why Marion might react this way.

"Just because they're flora fae doesn't mean they'll ever be Calyx," she said softly as she helped Marion lie down. It was the only conclusion Hanna could come to, that Marion was frightened her children might one day join the royal retinue. Many would give everything they had for this opportunity, apparently Marion did not share this view. But the chances were so slim, even for flora fae, that Marion's concern was greatly misplaced.

Tears leaked from Marion's eyes. She nodded, seeming to take some comfort from the words. "You're right, of course. Silly me. I'm so embarrassed. It was just a shock, that's all. A shock. Forgive me, Hanna."

"Of course." Hanna put a hand on Marion's arm. "There is nothing to forgive."

Marion lay her hand over Hanna's and gave her a grateful squeeze. "Thank you. You're too good to me." She rolled away and faced the wall.

Hanna could still hear tears in her voice.

"Just a shock," murmured Marion, sounding sleepy.

Baffled, Hanna straightened and looked from the babies to where their mother lay. "Marion, you must promise me you won't hurt them. I can't leave until you promise. Understand?"

Marion let out a long sigh. "I promise, dear Hanna."

"What do you promise, my love?"

"I promise I won't hurt my babies."

"And?"

"I promise I won't hurt the familiars."

Hanna patted her friend's shoulder again, trying not to think about what might have happened if Marion had discovered the bat and the butterfly while Hanna had not been there. "Good girl. Now let me see what I can rustle up for breakfast."

PART ONE

Chapter One

Jessica

"THAT'LL BE A penny for the berry bread and six farthings for the squash." Marion held her hand out for the coins from the blacksmith's wife, Shirri, as Jessica gathered the order. She weighed the sweet squash on the scales and deposited them into the burlap sack Shirri provided. She put the loaf of her mother's famous berry bread on top, so it wouldn't get crushed, wrapped in linen permeated with beeswax to keep the moisture out. As she did so, she felt Shirri's eyes on her, considering, judging. Jessica was used to this by now. One villager or another made an observation about Jessica's appearance every market day. She waited for the comments she knew were coming.

"How many summers have ye passed now, Miss Jessica?" Shirri took the burlap sack and held her other hand out for the change.

"Sixteen, Ma'am." Jessica's fingers flew to her hair, tucking and covering, making sure her ears were out of sight. She could feel Beazle—her tiny bat—as a warm lump inside her bun where her skull met the back of her neck.

"But she's a young sixteen," Marion added before shuffling over to help another customer.

Jessica endured the sweep of Shirri's gaze from her forehead to her hips. The rest of her wasn't visible to Shirri because she was standing behind the market table, but Shirri didn't need to see her legs to know that they were long. Jessica was getting tall. She hoped she was done growing; she was taller than many of the farm boys in Dagevli. Jessica knew what Shirri was thinking: Jessica looked older than sixteen, not younger.

"If you wore your hair down or in braids like the other girls, instead of like a widow, you might look closer to your age. You're a pretty thing"—Shirri's eyes crinkled at the corners—"more than pretty. Not beautiful, but different. Aye, there's something different about you."

Jessica had been called different so many times that she had to make a real effort to keep from rolling her eyes. Yes, people knew she was different. Covering her pointed ears was not enough to keep her faeness hidden. She held her breath, half hoping Shirri would ask her if she was half-fae so that her secret would finally be out in the open. But after another moment's observation, the blacksmith's wife only bid them good day and moved on through the market.

The shadows cast by the stalls and the shoppers had grown long, and the intense summer sun had lost its bite. Many of the vendors had sold out and were packing up their tables. Jessica and Marion had only a few small squash left and no berry bread except for a bit Marion had saved for a snack for their walk home. The crowd had thinned as the villagers thought about getting home to prepare dinner for their families.

Jessica waited in silent agony for her mother to signal that it was time for them to clean up too. Market days—which had been exciting in Jessica's youth—were now so mundane that she'd come to dread them. Even the weighty sack of coins dangling from her mother's belt wasn't satisfying anymore. Jessica went to fetch their mare from the market paddock.

"Come on, Apple." She clicked through her teeth in the way Apple recognized and the small gray pony emerged from the herd, the shortest of all the village ponies. Apple walked to Jessica with her head low. She was twenty-six and aging, but she belonged to the Fontanas and Jessica loved her, even if she wasn't the brightest pony. She was willing, and Jessica found that endearing. She led Apple back to where Marion rested under the awning with her walking stick across her lap. Jessica broke down their stall and loaded the cart with their scales, ledgers and moneybox. Together, they hitched Apple to their cart and left the town center, passing the pavilion and taking the high street home, trundling at a pace both Apple and Marion could manage.

"How did we do?" Jessica asked Marion from across Apple's mane.

"Well enough, my girl. Well enough." Marion's walking stick tap-tapped in the hard-packed dirt of the road; her other hand stayed on Apple's back for further stability.

They passed the Grein family who were also packing up their market stall. It took the Greins a lot longer since they sold wheat, oats, barley, rye and other grains. They had many barrels and sacks to manage. Their oldest son, Haft, was a well-built lad with nice green eyes. Jessica and Haft had been in school together until Haft's parents decided they needed him more at home. She smiled and he turned red to the roots of his hair. He made a gesture that might have been a wave. At a sharp word from his mother, he bent back to his work.

"Some girls are married by the age of eighteen," Jessica observed as they left the Grein family behind.

Marion slid her a sideways look. "And?"

"Some are even married by seventeen."

"So?"

"So, how am I supposed to meet men my age if you keep me occupied all the time?"

"Jessica, there is much wrong with what you just said." Marion ran her fingers through Apple's mane, untangling the knots. "First, there are no 'men your age.' Sixteen-year-old males are not yet men. Second, who do you imagine I am preventing you from meeting? Is there someone you think might be a good match for you?"

Jessica didn't even need to run her mind over all the boys she knew to answer that question. "No."

"And I can't keep you home long enough to learn how to bake berry bread properly, so I don't know what you mean when you suggest that I never give you your own time."

This wasn't entirely true. The Fontanas' market business took a lot of work, work that Jessica had to do since Marion didn't have the strength for it—preparing the earth after the last frost, planting, tending, weeding and harvesting. Jessica also foraged and made some coins that way, which meant she spent time in the woods and glades around Dagevli looking for wild edibles. The time Jessica spent foraging was her favorite, but it wasn't exactly free time. When she did have free time, she used it to climb the cliffs behind Dagevli for the thrill and for the view, but she wasn't liberal with her mother regarding her whereabouts. Marion liked Jessica to err on the side of caution.

"Anyway, why do you complain? You have everything you need." Marion produced a bit of wrapped beeswax cloth from her apron pocket and unfolded it. She offered her daughter a piece of berry bread but Jessica declined. She was sick to death of berry bread. In fact, she was sick to death of market days, sick to death of walking the stretch of high street between their cottage and the town center, sick to death of squash, sick to death of farm boys who were afraid to talk to her and sick to death of nothing exciting ever happening.

Yes, she had everything she needed, if all that mattered was a roof over one's head, clothing and food. But people had other needs, needs that were more difficult to define. Jessica chewed her lip, her fingers hooked in Apple's bridle, the pony's hooves clopping in a slow rhythm. While Marion waved to neighbors and greeted passing traffic, Jess became lost in her own thoughts. It wasn't that she wanted a husband, although one day it might be nice to marry. She only complained about it because that was the next thing on life's agenda for someone like Jessica, the next big event in the steady and relentless march of growing up.

But when Jessica scaled the cliffs, the ones Clair would never climb with her, she felt free. The desire to get as high as possible, to see as far as possible, drove her up and up and up, bare of foot and with her hair in a high bun on top of her head, her ears exposed to the world, though only the birds saw them. She climbed to get away from the cramps of her dying childhood. She yearned toward maturity as she yearned toward the sky, and adulthood. Independence. The horizon stretched out before her, seeming to go on forever, a hazy blur of color blending rolling field into forest. On clear days she could even see the clouds over Rahamlar, just a low smudge against the sky. In solitude, she could no longer pretend that a future in

Dagevli with a batch of children and a husband—loving though he might be—was enough for her. Need swelled in her bosom, an undefined desire for something more.

But for what?

She didn't know. She only knew that she wouldn't find it here, so close to home. She'd been to the borders of Dagevli, she knew every field, every tree, every rock. She'd even been to the neighboring village. What was beyond it? What was beyond Solana's border? What of the other kingdoms on the continent of Ivryndi? What were they like? What did the Ivryndian Sea look like, or the Valdivian Sea on the other side of the continent? She couldn't imagine looking out upon endless water, at a horizon that stretched out eternally. She would like to see that. She would like to climb higher mountains than the cliffs behind Dagevli. She could see the foothills of the Vargilath and had heard stories that it was a range of stunning blue mountains, very high and treacherous. She'd heard stories of herds of the giant horses of the Vargilath, with hooves like platters, whom no one could tame. She'd heard the older villagers talk of Solana City and its beautiful spires, marble streets, marvelous lights and university libraries. They said every Dagevlian should visit it once in their lifetime, but her mother had no plans to do any such thing. Marion was happy here, where every day was the same and the longest journey they ever made was to the neighboring town. Jessica had heard about bustling port cities along the coasts of Boskaya, full of curiosities. She'd heard of the faraway northern fae lands of Stavarjak and Silverfall, and the southern kingdoms of Tyrske and Archelia, which no one she knew had ever seen other than marked on a map. She couldn't see it all, but surely to see something foreign would do her good. Surely it would meet the need rising in her bosom that seemed only to grow day by day. She craved not just to know but to experience, and it would be nice to meet someone else like her, someone else with fae ears and creatures for friends.

She glanced at her mother as they drew close to the cottage, noting the increase of gray in Marion's hair. If Marion had her way, Jessica wouldn't even think about marriage until she was twenty, and up until that time she would be expected to continue on with life as it was. Seasons. Squash. Sameness.

They drew to a stop and unloaded the cart, carrying the broken-down tables, the empty baskets, the tools of their trade and the leftover squash to be stored in their proper places. As they worked in tandem to unhook the cart, Jessica's glasswing butterfly came fluttering around the cottage from the rear garden. She zigzagged, touching on a few blossoms before landing on the top of Jessica's head.

"Hello, Greta," she greeted the insect.

Marion's gaze lingered on the butterfly. Sometimes, her mother got a look in her eyes when she watched Greta floating around their property, a look Jess couldn't define. She used to think her mother wanted to hold Greta. The butterfly was stunning to look at up close. But when she would offer the butterfly to her mother on the back of her hand—Greta was more than willing to be held and admired as long as no one touched her wings—Marion would smile but decline. Jessica had long ago given up trying to understand Marion's reluctance to love either Beazle or Greta. She tolerated them because the familiars would never be separated from Jessica. Jess asked her mother once if she'd ever had a creature of her own. She got the idea that perhaps Marion had had an insect or animal friend and it had died, but Marion denied it, reminding Jess that she didn't get her faeness from her mother.

Jessica caught her mother's eye. "Before you met my father…"

Marion became still, as though bracing herself. She didn't like this topic, though she'd never explained why. She'd never even told Jess his name. But Jessica wasn't going to rehash that old argument; it clearly caused her mother pain.

"… did you ever go anywhere, or do anything… exciting or different?"

Marion took a moment to answer. Her eyes got that faraway look that used to frighten Jessica when she was younger, the look that made her feel forgotten. "My dear, I am in my sixty-fifth summer. When you came along, my miracle baby, I was forty-nine. Practically an old woman, even back then. I've seen more than I hope you ever see."

The pain that momentarily cramped Marion's face made Jessica suck in a breath, then it was gone. Her mother recovered the strength of her voice.

"The world beyond Dagevli will only disappoint you and put you in harm's way. Put it out of your mind. You have everything you need. Here, under my roof, you are safe. Stay as long as possible. Read as many books as you want and be satisfied with that. Books can't cut your throat while you sleep, steal your purse or betray you. Books can occupy you, keep you from making mistakes, and they can't break your heart." Marion slapped Apple on the rump. "Now go on, take this one to the paddock."

Jessica watched Marion's back until she disappeared in the front door of their cottage, bemused. Throats being cut? Purses being stolen? Her mother was exaggerating. Many Dagevlians had gone abroad to visit family or to do business, to bring back interesting treasures so they could sell them at ridiculous prices. They always returned unharmed and often with enchanting stories.

Apple tossed her head and bumped Jessica with her nose as if to say, *Haven't you forgotten something*? Jessica fished a broken carrot from her apron pocket. As the mare munched the carrot and Jessica led her behind their cottage, she marveled at how easy it was to make the pony happy.

As for herself, if all she ever did was stay in Dagevli and read books, brokenhearted was precisely how she would end up.

Jessica was wrangling her hair into a loose confection of curls when a pebble sailed in through her open window and skittered across the hardwood floor of her bedroom loft. She went to the window to see Clair standing in the flower bed beside the cottage, squirming and dancing in place like she needed the outhouse, her dark eyes lit up with excitement. Clair was Hanna and Tad's daughter and the best friend Jess had ever had. They were different; Clair was boy-crazy and dreamed of marriage and babies while Jess fantasized about getting as far away from Dagevli is possible, but the girls had lived side by side all their lives and cared for one another.

Clair's eyes shone up at Jess. "Come down! I have something to show you."

Jessica descended the ladder to the single room that served as kitchen, dining room, firepit and Marion's bedroom. Beazle was asleep in the rafters and Greta was in the front yard where her favorite flowers grew. Marion was in the squash patch. Jessica called to tell her mother that she was with Clair. She heard a reply but it wasn't anything she understood. Good enough.

Clair pulled her into a run toward the village center. It

appeared that at least half the town was milling around the vine-choked pavilion. People were talking and laughing, kids chased one another through the square, dogs nipping at their heels. A pair of oxen pulling a cart had been abandoned in a patch of wildflowers. A donkey brayed. Not until Clair pulled her through the crowd to read the notice nailed to the pavilion's post did Jessica understand the commotion.

There was to be a flower festival in Dagevli, hosted by a retinue from Solana City in eight days, including a parade, a banquet and a dance, all paid for by King Agir and Queen Esha as a reward for last season's exceptional harvest. But what held Jessica's attention to the announcement was the last part: *All children between the ages of ten and fifteen, who have a familiar or who exhibit the traits of flora fae, are invited to Discovery.*

Discovery—whatever that was—was hosted at the palace, which was enough to give her goosebumps. She'd heard that the palace was so beautiful that more than one peasant had fainted at first sight of it. Even if that was an exaggeration, it was understood: the palace was worth seeing.

"The Calyx." Clair grabbed Jessica's hand and squeezed so tightly she could feel Clair's fingernails biting into her skin. "We'll get to see the Calyx!"

Jessica searched her memory. "The flora fae who work for the queen, right?"

Clair pulled Jessica aside so others could read the sign. "I forgot, you weren't here for the last festival. Marion took you to Oubel, remember?"

Jess did remember; she had been eight when Marion woke her early and hustled her onto a loaded cart: supplies in cloth bags and filled with vegetables. They had trundled along the dirt roads all morning to reach the neighboring village of Oubel, where they sold their produce at the market. Jessica hadn't understood why they had to go to Oubel. They never had trouble selling at the market in Dagevli. She hadn't questioned it at the time, though, because to see another town was exciting.

Jessica replied, "I vaguely remember you saying there was a festival while we were away, but you didn't say much about it."

A look of guilt crossed Clair's face. "Mum didn't want me to go on about it, she was worried you'd be jealous. I remember wondering why your mother chose *that* day to leave."

"Did they invite children with flora fae traits to the palace back then, too?"

"Yes. But there wasn't anyone who qualified then, and there aren't any now either. If there was, we'd know." Clair sighed. "I can't wait for you to see them."

"Who?"

"The Calyx, of course; the flora fae." Clair's hands threaded together in front of her heart. "They are the most beautiful creatures you'll ever meet. They smell like heaven. They can do all kinds of magic, and they give away gold, too. You'll see for yourself in eight days. You'll love them." She looked wistful. "They kind of break your heart, though. The worst part comes after they leave. Life seems so dull, but while they are here, you'll think you've been reborn in a storybook."

As Jessica listened to the villagers describe the last festival to the children who were too young to remember or who hadn't been born yet, she was only half present. Those who had seen a flower festival described the event with unbridled joy. It sounded so extravagant that Jessica couldn't imagine it. If it was so wonderful and given free of charge as a reward for a successful harvest, then wouldn't every villager who contributed want to be there? Marion would never willingly give up a chance at free gold.

No sane person would.

Chapter Two

Jessica

Jessica found Marion in the backyard, singing and pulling up weeds. Marion was bent at the waist and, from the back, looked like nothing more than a woman's rump draped with green fabric. The bow of her apron perched on top of her waggling hips like a floppy bird. Her walking stick lay between the rows, just within reach. A small wooden cup in the shape of an acorn sat on a nearby stump between a pair of wicked-looking gardening shears and a short-handled trowel. The sun was four-fingers distant from the hills, which meant that Marion's acorn cup was not holding water. This could either work for or against Jessica. She contemplated her mother's backside and chewed her cheek, wondering how to approach the topic of the festival.

Marion had been strong and vigorous when Jessica was younger, enthusiastic about hard work, but now she usually left the more demanding labor to Jessica. If Marion was weeding, it was a sign she was feeling good. So maybe now was as good a time as any. Jess stepped forward and a twig snapped beneath her foot.

Marion straightened and turned, her cheeks flushed, her frizzy gray curls escaping from beneath her bonnet. She waved a cabbage moth away. "Hand me that trowel would you, dear?"

Jessica passed it and Marion took it, her hands covered in dirt and her nails black with soil. Aged though she was, Marion was a handsome woman, with large brown eyes and heavy eyelids that gave her a dreamy look. She had a wide mouth, was quick to laugh and had a pleasant, deep voice. If she wasn't drinking, she could hide her thoughts better than anyone else Jessica knew.

Greta fluttered to Jessica, landing on her cotton dress. The flowered pattern of her skirt was visible through the transparent panels in the butterfly's wings. Jess put her hand down and Greta crawled on. She lifted Greta to her hair as she wandered to a pea patch and picked a few pods.

"There's a notice at the pavilion." She hoped she sounded nonchalant. She certainly didn't feel it; her pulse was thready.

"Oh?" Marion grunted as she won the battle with a thistle. She tossed it into the wheelbarrow. Marion would be sore tomorrow if she kept on.

"You should let me do that."

"Just a few more minutes." Marion stretched her back, searching the garden for her next victim.

"We had a record harvest last year, so there's going to be a party." Jessica watched her mother's expression. There was a moment's hesitation, brief as a finch's chirp, but it was there.

"When?"

"In six days," Jess lied.

Marion clucked, reaching for her cup. "We're expected in Oubel in six days. Too bad we'll miss it."

Jessica played along. "We'll be in Oubel for the night?"

"All day. You loved it last time. You remember? We went to that pony race in the afternoon."

"But we'll be back the same day?"

Marion squinted at her. "Of course. We don't have gold for inns."

"Good, then we'll be here for the flower festival. It's not six days hence. It's eight days hence."

Marion's expression changed, moving into what Jessica thought of as her mulish face.

"We're not going to the flower festival, Jessica." Marion put down her acorn cup and attacked another weed.

Jessica's pulse quickened. "Why not?"

Jessica never used to ask why or why not. She supposed all kids went through that stage, but Marion's standard response of "you don't need to worry about it" had been intoned enough times that she hardly tried anymore. But she was older now. She deserved to know things.

"It's dangerous," Marion said with a grunt. Another weed went flying toward the wheelbarrow, landing on the grass beside it.

"It's a flower festival." Jessica was incredulous. "Is it dangerous in the way it's dangerous for people to see me with Beazle or Greta? Dangerous in the way it is for people to see my ears?"

Marion's look silenced Jessica. "I am your mother, and I forbid it."

Out of habit, Jessica picked up the weed and deposited it in the wheelbarrow. A breeze threw strands of hair into her face. She pawed them away, irritated. "But why? And why did you take me away to Oubel when the last one happened? Everyone loves these festivals. Not only does everyone love them, they only happen when there's a record crop, which is hardly ever. Clair will be there; Hanna and Tad will be there. The entire village. Everyone in Dagevli… except for us."

Marion sniffed. "I don't appreciate you playing tricks in order to get your way. We will have a nice time in Oubel. It will be a good day out. You'll see."

Jessica did not believe that her deceit was the reason for this. It had to have something to do with the announcement about children with familiars. "Is this about Discovery? Because if it is, only children aged ten to fifteen are invited." Jessica put her hands on her hips. "If you just don't want me to go because of that, then you've already succeeded, because I'm too old."

Marion's eyes widened fractionally, then she turned away, reaching for her cane. "That's enough, miss impertinence. Light the stove please, Jess. It's bath night."

Jessica took the narrow path back to the cottage, resisting the temptation to kick the wheelbarrow over as she went.

When Marion booted Jessica out of the house the next morning for moping, she went straight to the cliffs. Perched on a level, grassy section in the cliff face with her back against the granite, she gazed over the horizon. Thick condensation gathered over Rahamlar. A teacher had once told Jessica that it was thanks to the two deep rivers that converged there.

Beazle flapped around the cliff, nosing into cracks and crevices for bugs. He was usually asleep at this time, but he could feel Jessica's discontent. He flew away from her, ranging out over the forest.

Jess's vision flashed as she received an overhead view from Beazle. Clair was coming down the winding path leading to the base of the cliff. Jess whistled and Beazle zipped straight to her shoulder, then crawled into her hair. Jess began to descend.

A few moments later, Clair appeared at the base of the cliff with two baskets. She looked up, blocking her eyes from the sun. She pointed at the baskets.

"Coming," Jess called, though the wind tore the words from her mouth.

Rare and tasty pushrooms grew in the dark, damp undergrowth of prickly sheldie trees. There weren't many who enjoyed harvesting them, though almost everyone enjoyed eating them. The girls had found a large patch of them years ago and had sworn its location to secrecy so they could be the only ones to sell pushrooms at the market. Fried in a hot skillet with salted butter and herbs, they tasted a lot like steak. Thanks to their little business, they almost never wanted for pocket money.

Jessica descended, barefoot, taking the well-worn goat track she'd used a thousand times. Clair kicked Jessica's shoes over to her when she reached the bottom. She toed them on, brushing grass and dirt from her skirt.

"What's wrong with you?" Clair handed her one of the baskets.

Jess hooked it over her arm. "What makes you think anything is wrong?"

The girls walked away from the cliff and into the forest. "Marion almost bit my head off when I asked where you were."

Jessica grunted. "We fought. Kind of."

Clair's dark brows pinched. "About the festival?"

"How did you guess?" Jessica kicked a cone off the path.

Clair let out a long breath. "Is she going to take you to Oubel again?"

"Yes." Jessica pulled a face. "It's not fair."

Clair hitched her basket to the other hip as they ducked under the long fronds of preekness bushes. It smelled like dirty stockings, so Jessica held her breath until they were past the fae shrub.

"It's not just unfair, it's confusing," said Clair. "I don't understand why she would want you to miss it. Or miss it herself, for that matter."

Jessica was in the pitch of a heated inner battle. She was so well trained to keep her secrets that she half wondered if it might bring some kind of curse down upon her head if she spilled what Marion had always warned her to keep to herself. But rebellion and anger warred from the other side. Children with familiars were of interest to the king and queen, so what opportunity had she missed thanks to her mother? Whatever it was, she was too old to take advantage of it now, so what was the harm in attending the upcoming festival? For that matter, what was the harm in telling her best friend why? But then she'd have to show Clair her familiars, a secret that had been miraculously kept from everyone in town.

Clair had seen Greta flitting about their property, but Dagevli was full of beautiful butterflies for the glasswing to hide among. Greta was free to move about as long as she didn't interact with Jess while neighbors were watching. As for Beazle, he was a master at staying out of sight. He slept during the day and was nothing more than a tiny shadow at night. Hanna had kept her promise to Marion to never mention Jess's familiars to anyone, and that included Clair. If Clair had been a more vigilant type, she could have figured things out, but she was naturally unsuspecting. At times Jess found herself wishing Hanna wasn't such a woman of her word. She opened her mouth and then closed it again, unable to break her promise, even in anger. She reached up to make sure her ears were covered.

"It's not for me to say..." Clair began, then stalled.

Jess shot a weary look at her friend. "You *have* to say it now, Clair. You can't start and then clam up."

Clair spoke slowly, uncertainly. "You're just so risk-averse, such a good girl. You've always done what you're told, your whole life."

Jess's brow wrinkled. "Not always. Marion doesn't like it that I climb the cliffs."

"But you waited until she finally gave you permission before you did it. Remember? Because I do. We were ten. And there's other examples. You never raced Apple at the midsummer carnival, even though she was fast enough to win when she was young, because Marion didn't want you to fall and break your neck. But now Apple is too old and you're too heavy, so you'll never know if she'd have won because you never tried. And Marion never lets you come to the Rosebud Valley swimming hole with us. The hole is the best thing on a hot day, and you don't even know it. I mean, is it because you don't know how to swim? Or is Marion afraid you'll drown or something?"

Jessica could swim, but she wouldn't do it in public because it meant she could expose her ears. She might be able to keep her head out of the water, but Marion had warned her that kids tended to rough around. It was only a matter of time before someone dunked her. She would have loved to swim in the hole with the village kids her age.

"I just don't like swimming that much," Jess lied. "What are you trying to say, Clair?"

"Just this: at a certain point, you should stand up for what you want. Take a risk. Go anyway."

The idea made Jessica's stomach turn over. "You mean, defy Marion outright?"

"Yes. At what age are you old enough to decide for yourself?"

Jessica was quiet. What Clair was suggesting was just not done in Dagevli families. Parents had ultimate authority until children were married off. Law and order in the home was the reason Dagevli was successful enough to win a festival. Did Jess have it in her to show such rebellion? How would Marion react if she did?

They reached the pushroom patch. The soft amber tops glowed in the dim light beneath the shade of the sheldies. Pushrooms were so called because as they grew, they traveled along the soil, pushing tree droppings, needles and pebbles into little piles in front of their fat stems. Behind them they left little tails, like shooting stars. The girls knew to only harvest the pushrooms with tails longer than the length of their hand.

"Would you defy Hanna?" Jessica asked as the girls filled their baskets.

"Hanna isn't Marion," replied Clair. "My mother always explains why she disallows me to do things. Afterward, even if I don't agree with it, at least I understand it. Marion is notoriously private. I mean, Hanna is her best friend, but Marion won't even talk with her about her past, or why she came to Dagevli in the first place. She's never told my mother anything about your father. I mean nothing, even though my parents were the first people to help Marion when she arrived here. They only want the best for you and your mother, and Marion knows that. It's strange. It's like…"

Jess straightened, dropping three pushrooms into her basket. "She doesn't want to be known."

"Exactly. But why? Some people are just private, and I respect that. But with Marion, it's almost like she is ashamed of something."

Jessica shot a startled look at Clair. Marion was a proud woman. She didn't brag or swagger about town. She wasn't like that. She was just confident, self-assured. She said things with authority and always held herself composed. It was one of the reasons Jessica was afraid to cross her mother; she instinctively felt that Marion knew so much more about the world than she did. No matter what, Marion always knew best.

"Maybe it's me she's ashamed of," Jessica said, feeling Beazle squirm against her skull in reaction to Jess's discomfort at the idea.

Clair scoffed and rolled her eyes. "That's ridiculous. Why could she possibly be ashamed of you? You're hard-working, obedient, kind. You have a green thumb unlike anyone I've ever met. I mean, squash is squash, it's not that exciting, but you do grow the best-tasting gourds around. The village kids love you. Even the animals love you."

"Yeah, yeah. Okay. Enough already." Jessica dimpled and tossed a pushroom at Clair's head.

But Jess's smile faded as she returned to snapping off pushrooms. Clair only knew that Marion was reserved about herself and her past. She didn't know that Marion had made Jessica keep her half-fae identity under wraps her whole life.

Marion's simple explanation had always been that Greta and Beazle were small and vulnerable, that they might come to harm if the village kids knew about them, that they'd constantly badger Jessica to play with Greta and Beazle. And regarding

Jess's fae ears, they would draw attention that Marion didn't want on herself or her daughter, because it just wasn't anyone's business. But Jess knew the children in Dagevli would never harm her familiars, so that justification was thin at best. And while fae were uncommon in the small villages of Solana like Dagevli, they were commonplace in Solana City. Not only that, some flora fae were greatly valued by the crown. So what was Marion really trying to protect Jessica from? Was it really a matter of shame? And if so, why?

The girls returned to the village with full baskets, strolling arm in arm. The smell of fresh baking drifted on the breeze from the open door of Clair's house. Hanna's specialty was sourdough bread. Clair and Jessica stopped on the street outside Clair's cottage.

"Remember what we talked about," said Clair, facing her and making her stop. "Do it tonight, because the sooner the better."

Already, Jess's stomach felt like knotted fishing line. She practiced her words as though speaking to Marion: "I've decided to go to the festival. If you want to sell squash in Oubel, we can do that on another day, but I'm entitled to attend."

"That's right. And what else?" Clair put her hands on Jessica's upper arms.

"I work just as hard as anyone in Dagevli. I deserve to be rewarded as much as any other villager."

"Yes. And?"

Jess took a deep breath. Why did she feel so shaky? She could climb the most treacherous cliffs in the region, but just contemplating a confrontation with Marion made her knees feel weak.

"Not attending could even be seen as throwing King Agir and Queen Esha's generosity back in their faces. I'm a citizen of Solana and I don't want to insult them."

Clair nodded and let go of Jess. "Good. You can do this, Jess. I'll meet you after dinner, you can tell me how it went, and we can discuss what we're going to wear to the festival."

"Okay," Jess squeaked.

Clair left her in the street, skipping up the front walk and in through the open door of her home. Without her friend to encourage her, Jessica's bravado was already fading. She muttered her arguments to herself as she walked to her own cottage, feeling like she was going to her execution. Her mouth felt dry, but her armpits and the palms of her hands felt damp and clammy. Beazle stirred in her hair as Greta flitted across the fence to Jess's shoulder from the flower garden. Her bat dropped onto her shoulder, gave a squeak and then flitted off to hunt. Other bats were already swooping through the air, dipping and diving for insects so small that Jess couldn't see them in the evening light.

She sucked in a breath and marched through the open door of her home.

"Hello, Jessica." Marion was at the worktable, beating a lump of dough.

"Hello." Jess tried to smile.

"Looks like Clair found you." Marion nodded toward the basket. "That's a nice harvest you've got there."

It was an attempt at peace, but Jess knew there'd only be peace as long as Jess did what she was told.

Jessica set the basket on the table and fetched a square of cambric to wrap them in. Freshly picked pushrooms only stayed fresh as long as they were kept in a dry, dark place. She spread the cloth and poured the pushrooms onto it, then folded the corners over. She shoved the package into the back corner of the cupboard, her heart feeling like it was untethered and sliding around. She stood, leaning against the cupboard for support as she faced her mother.

"I've decided not to insult the monarch's garbage gifts… erm… I mean… to throw their… presents… into the rubbish bin."

Marion cocked an eyebrow. "Whatever that means. Hand me the rolling pin, please."

Jessica shook her head. "That's not what I—"

"The rolling pin, Jess." Marion held out a floury hand.

Jess retrieved the pin and brought it to Marion. Greta fluttered from Jess's shoulder, floating out the open window. Jess tried not to feel abandoned. Both Beazle and Greta hated confrontation, and they could feel one brewing.

"I mean, I'm just as entitled to rewards as any other Dagevlian." Jess's throat felt as narrow as a piece of straw. She went to the pitcher, poured herself a drink, and downed it, even though the water from the pump in the yard was much colder and nicer.

"You're entitled to what I say you're entitled to," replied Marion mildly, rolling over the dough with her pin and squashing it flat.

Jess watched the edges of the dough split as it flattened, submitting before Marion's practiced hand. She could relate.

Marion lifted the pin and pointed it at Jess. "If you keep going the way you're going, you'll be entitled to bed without dinner."

Jess gulped. Bed without dinner wasn't so bad. Her stomach might revolt against whatever she put into it anyway, but

Marion's face… the flinty eyes, the authoritarian composure and the utter commitment to maintaining sovereignty over her daughter and her house. It was the look Jessica had faced since childhood. Fear of that look ran deep. Jess closed her eyes and tried to think of all the advice Clair had given her, all the reasons Jessica had to do this now and not later.

"Hoo hoo!" a singsong voice came through the door. Hanna poked her head in, carrying a loaf of bread. She stepped over the threshold and Clair followed with a jar of homemade fruit preserves.

"Hello, neighbor!" Marion brightened. All signs of discipline vanished. "Come in. What have we here?"

"A loaf fresh from the oven, a pat of butter and moireberry jam that Clair made last week." Hanna and Clair set the food on the table just outside of Marion's ring of flour.

"How kind of you. Clair, I can't wait to taste your jam. Shall I boil some water for tea? It's past afternoon teatime, but I just bought some fresh bergamot earlier today and I've been dying to try it."

"That would be lovely." Hanna shrugged out of her shawl and draped it across the back of the chair.

"Jess, put the water over the fire, please, dear," Marion asked.

Jessica went out the back to the fire pit. Clair followed. Jess shot her friend an inquisitive look as she took a poker to the coals and stirred up sparks and embers. It wasn't strange for Hanna and Clair to pop by for a visit—they were over often through the week, just as Marion and Jessica visited them often in return. They'd been exchanging food and preserves for all of Jess's life. But these visits didn't usually happen so late in the day. Unless it was a holiday, villagers rose early and went to bed early. Clair just shrugged and made an *I don't know* face. Jess lay firewood over the coals and blew until it caught.

"Did you say something?" Jess whispered as the fire flared. She swung the kettle over the flames.

"Was I not supposed to?" Clair cringed.

Jess shot her a look of horror. Marion would be furious if Hanna let on that the girls had been conspiring against her.

Jess and Clair heard murmurs of their mothers talking and laughing. They heard mention of a new teacher, and something about an elderly couple who were finally selling off the farm where they'd raised ten children. As the water came to a boil, Jess began to relax. Maybe the visit was just a spur-of-the-moment thing and had nothing to do with Jess.

The water boiled and Jess carried the kettle into the cottage. Hanna and Marion sat at the table with teacups, a pitcher of cream and a pot of honey laid out. Jess poured water into the waiting pot, hardly noticed by Marion. Hanna smiled at Jess, her laugh lines crinkling. Jess smiled back. Hanna was like a second mother, her smile eased Jess's nerves.

"Cut some fresh greens from the salad garden for them, Jess," said Marion.

Hanna clapped her hands once. "Oh, thank you. I've been craving a herb salad lately. How did you guess?"

Jess took the shears they used to clip greens and left the cottage. Clair trailed silently after her.

The herb garden was far from the house, and as the girls trekked across the yard, they caught the word "festival." Jess froze and Clair walked into the back of her. The girls exchanged a wide-eyed look. Jess scampered through the garden, back to the side of the house then around to the front where the window was propped open. Clair snuck along the wall behind her, keeping low. The girls held their breath as their mothers' voices drifted to them from inside.

"I can't tell you how excited Finn is," Hanna was saying with a chuckle. "Clair has described it to him as a bedtime story from time to time. She is very clever in how she does it, making sure she describes his own reactions as a baby, since he can't remember it for himself. It's darling."

"Yes, well. I'm sure the children will have a lovely time," Marion replied over the sound of tea splashing into a cup. "Thank you again for the bread. You really do have the best sourdough in the village. It's our favorite. I'll be sure to save some berry loaf for you. I'm making an extra big batch this coming week to sell in Oubel."

There was a pause with the sound of a spoon tinging against glass. "Oubel? You haven't been there since… well, it must be eight years ago, because it was the same day as the flora festival last time." Hanna made a loud sipping sound.

"That's right, it was." Marion's tone was falsely wondering, as if she didn't remember herself that she had been away. "Isn't that funny. We're expected in Oubel again this time, as well."

"On festival day?"

"Mhmm."

"Surely you'll change your plans, though. Jessica didn't get to see it last time. It's so wonderful for the children."

"Well, perhaps if they'd given more notice. A week isn't much to go on, for a busy woman like me."

Jess shot a glance at Clair. Clair put her fingers to her lips.

There was a pause, then Hanna said, "I might know what you're afraid of, Marion." She spoke very gently, very sweetly. "I was there. Remember?"

Marion kept her tone cavalier. "I'm not sure what you

mean, Hanna. Gosh, is that the time? Jess will be starving. I'd better warm the pottage."

But Hanna didn't give up. "Please let her come, Marion. I know you're scared, but—"

"I'm not scared," Marion snapped. Then let out a long sigh. "I'm sorry. I don't mean to bark at you. You understand more about the situation than anyone else."

Hanna's tone was soothing. "I understand that you have a very obedient daughter who loves you very much and wants to please you, but who also wants more than anything to enjoy a day at the festival with her best friend. She deserves that, and whatever you're afraid will happen is just that… a fear. It's not real. Not anymore."

Marion was quiet for a long time.

"It's been sixteen years," Hanna added quietly. "You can't keep her socked away in a drawer forever."

Jess and Clair exchanged a confused look. Jess was sixteen and a half, so the only thing that fit this was Jess's birthday.

There was a weird sound, like a choked-off sob. This alarmed Jess more than anything. Hanna had just spoken and her voice had been calm and controlled. But Marion never cried. Ever.

Hanna went on. "My own parents were also protective of me and my brothers, don't forget, but especially me, as the only girl. I know a little of what Jessica might be feeling. When I left home, I wasn't on good terms with my mother. She tried to keep control over me, but I rebelled because I felt suffocated. We didn't speak for thirteen years. I don't want that for you and Jess. At a certain point, we just have to let our kids be free to live their lives. If we trust them, then they'll always come back to us, by choice, not because we compelled them to."

Marion took a breath. "You've never volunteered an opinion on the way I raise her before. Why now?"

Hanna took a sip and put down her cup. "Because, as you know, I respect you immensely. I wouldn't say anything unless I thought she might really be… suffering."

Jessica closed her eyes. Was Marion going to reproach Hanna for this? She was treading dangerous waters. But when Marion said, "Perhaps you're right," Jess's eyes flew open. She and Clair stared at one another. Clair covered a grin with her hand.

Hanna sounded relieved. "It will bring her so much joy. You'll see."

"Speaking of joy. Where are those salad greens?"

The girls bolted back around the cottage and leapt over rows of vegetables to the herb garden, Jess gripping the shears in her fist. Marion would wring her neck if she saw her running with scissors. They arrived in the herb garden and Jess began frantically cutting herbs and thrusting them at Clair. In lightning speed, Clair had an apron full of greens. They marched back to the cottage, sweating and puffing.

"What took you so long?" Marion speared Jess with a glance.

"Jessica showed me your prize pumpkin," Clair replied without missing a beat, her face flushed. "Guess the milk is working."

Marion gave Clair a bemused look but didn't say anything.

"Shall I make a salad with these?" Jess asked as Clair dumped the herbs on the worktable.

"I've got an idea. Why don't you bring your salad and pottage over to ours and we'll have a little potluck," said Hanna, getting to her feet.

Marion smacked the table with the palm of her hand. "A

wonderful idea. We can discuss what we'll wear to the festival. I have a new muslin that would look very nice as a bodice for Jess. There might just be enough time to whip it up."

Jessica's jaw dropped. Clair bounced up and down, whooping.

Marion smiled. Jess went over and threw her arms around her.

"Thank you," she mumbled into her mother's neck. "Thank you, so much."

Chapter Three

Jessica

The villagers of Dagevli gathered along the grassy flanks of the main thruway, the same strip of land where stalls were erected every market day. If some enterprising thief had wanted to plunder their homes and relieve the population of every gold coin or heirloom they held dear, the day of the flower festival would have been the perfect time to do so. Security was the job of their local knight and his men, but even they deserved a holiday. Jessica spotted a few of those men threading their way through the crowd or positioning themselves on knolls where they could see over the heads of those lining the street. Every face was lifted with joyful anticipation, everybody clothed in bright attire. Some wore the kingdom's sigil, a wreathed lion's head, over their hearts. Jessica and Marion stood with Hanna, Tad, Clair and Clair's brother, Finn. Finn, ten, slender as a stalk of summer wheat and just as golden, could hardly be held in one place.

Music could be heard from the south end of town where the retinue would enter, but it was not music Jessica had ever heard before. There were a few lutists among Dagevli's number, and one harpist, but this music carried a density and depth Jessica never knew was possible. It hushed the crowd to whispers.

Jessica felt a tug on her hand.

"Look." Clair pointed beyond the crowd to a copse of trees.

A young man stood in front of the trees, his dark eyes inspecting the scene with focused intensity. Even from a distance, Jessica could make out his fine clothing. It wasn't quite armor, as there was no visible metal, but it had the look of sturdy boiled leather. She couldn't make out anything below mid-torso, but Jessica suspected there was a weapon strapped to his waist.

"A Calyx guard," Clair whispered. "There's another one over there." She pointed toward the pavilion where a youth perched on the roof among the boughs of greenery. Her black hair had been fixed back from her temples in cornrows, her long braids cascading across her shoulders. She too had the intensity of someone on watch, someone who wouldn't be easily distracted. Jessica searched her for a weapon but the way she crouched among the foliage made it difficult to see.

"I thought the Calyx were only for entertainment," Jessica whispered, unable to tear her eyes from the young woman even as the music signaled the arrival of the royal retinue.

"They are. Those aren't flora fae, they're just guards. They're hard to spot at first, but when you finally see one, you see them everywhere."

Clair was right. Now that she'd had two pointed out, it didn't take Jessica long to spot more behind the crowd, up on rooftops and even in the trees. They were still and watchful, calmly observing. The Calyx must be very important to the kingdom to have such attentive guards, and so many of them.

When the first of the party came into view, the crowd seemed to hold its breath. Musicians in pretty garb—not unlike what the villagers themselves wore—came dancing along the dirt road playing instruments that seemed like magical talismans. The music swelled, the beat infectious and uplifting. Goosebumps lifted along Jessica's arms. Soon the villagers were swaying and clapping to the music. Children shrieked with exhilaration, unable to contain the emotions released by the newness and novelty of it all. Jessica could hear broken phrases from some of the adults around her: "… wait until you see…" and "… this isn't even the best part…"

Then the musicians were upon them, dancing through them, playing without missing a note or being out of step. There were wind instruments and stringed instruments, drums of all sizes and some obnoxious instruments made of shining brass that required the person playing to blow their cheeks out like a bullfrog. These made some of the children roll in the dirt, laughing. Behind the musicians came rows of organized acrobats in the blue-and-green livery of Solana. They tumbled and flipped, twirled and pirouetted. These were flanked by people with flowers woven into their hair and clothing. They carried baskets from which they tossed small gifts wrapped in blue cloth and tied with green silk ribbons. Others threw sweets twisted inside colored paper. Finn unwrapped one of the colored packets to find three coppers. He stared at them like he wasn't sure he could trust his eyes.

Jessica managed to snag some candy and pocket it, but none of the larger pouches came her way. Clair caught a shiny blue sack and opened it to discover a delicate brooch made of colored glass in the shape of a blue flower. In the center was the tiny figure of a seated lion in profile, made of tawny yellow and orange stones. Jessica felt a needle of envy pierce her heart. She had never seen anything so fine, and never dreamed of owning anything like it. Clair stuffed it away in her bosom for safekeeping. Villagers all along the way caught and opened gifts, popping sweets into their mouths. A few fights broke out among the children, but these were rapidly defused by members of the retinue who ensured that no child went empty-handed for long. They seemed even able to find adults who were less mobile or able to bend for gifts fallen into the dirt. Jessica watched in amazement as one of the basket bearers wove her way into the crowd where a disabled village woman sat on a tree stump with a patched blanket around her shoulders. In the distraction of the parade, none of the children at the front where the fetching was best thought to deliver something to her lap. But one of the royal retinue did, and of all the things Jessica saw that day, she thought that was the most magical.

When she saw the first of them, Jessica realized that a Calyx could not be mistaken for anyone else. He was a young man with tawny skin, dark eyes and long straight hair that gleamed under the sun and lifted in the breeze. He wore simple clothing, much like the villagers, but in Solana's colors and with the embroidered crest. He glided along the street like silk on the wind. A fragrance reached Jessica's nose as he spread the brown fingers of his elegant hand. Something misty and colorful spun into view, the head of a flower, but not one Jessica had seen in any garden in Dagevli, and the perfume was not one she could identify. The globe-shaped bloom spun and opened in the air. It was shaped like a water lily, only it contained silky yellow-haired petal-like bracts and dark leaves. The scent lifted heads and drew deep breaths from the villagers. Jessica's very bones seemed relieved of the burden of holding her together as the fragrance filled her senses. More misty blossoms were conjured from the fae's fingers, as light as dandelion fluff, to float on the air and slowly dissipate.

Another Calyx came through the crowd, a woman walking on bare feet in a gauzy dress that reflected sunlight in a spray, like a scatter of coins made of light. She was surrounded by acrobats and dancers, but she shone among them like a jewel. A new scent came with her, sweeter and with a touch of lemon. As she moved her arms, a spray of spinning blossoms filled the air. They floated above the parade and drifted over the villagers like butterflies. When Jessica reached out to hold one, it dissolved, leaving a damp patch on her palm that smelled of perfume. She pressed the wet patch to her neck and dabbed it on her upper lip, wishing it would never fade.

Each Calyx came with a new and diverting fragrance, each filled the air with unique ghostly blossoms. When Clair brought Jessica's attention to the ground, she saw that plants that had not been there before were now rooted along the roadside, their buds opening even as Jessica watched. She wondered if she might actually die from the pure beauty of it all. Dagevli had come alive with new and interesting flowers, the air rich and resplendent with perfume. Gifts filled the villagers' pockets and sweets melted on their tongues. Clair had been right. The Calyx captured every heart.

As the parade gathered at the pavilion and the villagers filled the town center in anticipation of a feast, Clair grabbed Jessica's hand and pulled her through the crowd toward one of the large white tents. Jessica looked back and caught a glimpse of Marion. Her mother smiled and waved, disappearing from view as the girls entered the tent, where the smell of flowers was replaced by the mouth-watering scents of fresh baking, herbed vegetables and roasted meats. They were welcomed by members of the royal staff; cooks and serving girls and boys dressed in blue-and-green livery and wearing adorable poufy hats. Tables upon tables of food had been prepared and Jessica thought the appearance of this food was another miracle of the day. Each dish was presented with edible decorations: fruit plates garnished with edible flowers, acorn cakes dusted with powdery sugars in delicate flower shapes and flourishes, green salads dressed with glistening oils and artfully sprinkled with toasted seeds. Every table was dedicated to a food group; the meats were separate from the breads and from the vegetable dishes and fresh, raw salads and sliced fruits. The dessert tables were astounding in form and fashion, where elegant cakes sprouted curling foliage and colorful edible buds. Delicate butterflies made of sugar perched on the tops of pies and pastries, while little candy ladybugs and sparkling beetles marched with sugary legs across glazed fruit and burnt butter crisps.

The girls walked up one side and down the other, mouths watering and eyes wide. There was no way they'd have room in their stomachs to try everything, so they took great pains in choosing what they wanted. The serving staff talked about their creations, asked the girls what they liked, about their favorite flowers, scents or colors. Each villager, whether they were old or young, wealthy or poor, was treated as the most important guest of the festival.

Jessica and Clair took their plates to a seat along the bench and were approached by serving staff balancing crystal decanters and elegant carafes sloshing with pretty liquids. When Clair chose blackberry wine, Jessica requested the same. Marion's love for fine wines had rubbed off on Jessica in some small way. She took delicate sips and closed her eyes to fully enjoy the sensations aroused in her mouth. As she chewed a forkful of buttery bulgur spiced with cinnamon and dried currants, she wondered if the courtiers who lived at the palace ate like this every day. She closed her eyes to soak in the pleasure of it.

Night had come. The banquet tent was aglow with smokeless candles and torches. Fireflies flitted over the tables, landing on hair and shoulders. Villagers and Calyx mingled, chatting and laughing. Music drifted through tent flaps that had been tied back with thick gauzy ribbons. Under the pavilion, people danced, burning off their food before going back for more.

Clair dragged Jessica toward a table full of sliced melon and piles of iced fruit, even as she protested that she was too full for anything more.

"I'm going to burst," Jessica laughed, a hand over her stomach. Not only had she eaten more than she ever had in her life, she'd also drunk too much. She felt overly warm, and a little dizzy.

Clair grabbed a plate, piling it high with yellow and pink melon wedges.

One of the Calyx passed Clair as she left the melon table. Jessica's breath caught as the female Calyx paused, looking down at her. She was a dark-skinned beauty with big hazel eyes. Her tightly coiled curls were festooned with blooms in a delicate shade of pink that matched her dress perfectly. A constellation of freckles danced over her cheeks.

"Well come," the Calyx said.

"Well found," Jessica replied, in the tradition of Dagevli.

"Are you enjoying the party?" She speared a piece of melon with a toothpick and held it out.

"Thank you," Jessica said, even though she didn't want the melon. She took it and chewed, hoping she'd be able to swallow it.

"I'm Aster." The Calyx popped her own slice into her mouth. "What's your name?"

"Jessica." Her stomach made an uneasy growl. She was thankful for the music to cover it up.

"Pretty name. You look fae. Are you?"

Jess froze, wondering if she could believe her ears.

Aster laughed. "I'm fae, so I know what to look for. Let me see your ears, then. You have glorious dark hair, but why hide your ears?"

Before Jessica could stop her, Aster tucked her hair behind an ear, revealing a pointed tip. "So fetching. Are you all, or half?"

Jessica's heart was pounding and she looked around the tent, hoping her mother wasn't watching from some corner. She felt winded. "Half."

Aster's smile was dazzling. "I'll see you at Discovery, then?" Her scrutiny deepened, her gaze flicking over Jessica's features and down her frame to her small bosom, then to her narrow hips, then back up. "How old are you?"

"Sixteen, too old for Discovery."

Aster held a plate of melon at an angle and juice dripped from it, splashing onto the floor. She righted the plate, blushing. "Woops. I see."

"How many Calyx are there?" Jessica put her finger under the hair in front of her ear to re-cover it, just in case Marion entered the tent. As she tugged on a strand, she felt Beazle move. It was time for him to wake up.

"Fifty," Aster replied, watching Jessica cover her ear again, a bemused expression on her face.

"But there are only ten of you here." Jess was astounded. There were forty more of these gorgeous creatures?

Aster nodded and popped another melon slice into her mouth, then held out the plate, inviting Jessica to take one. Jessica shook her head.

Aster swallowed her bite. "We get divided for these kinds of events. There are other villages deserving of a festival, too."

"But at the palace, you all perform together?" Jessica felt dizzy thinking about it.

"Mostly." She smiled. "Sometimes we can't all make it."

Over Aster's shoulder, Jessica saw the slender male Calyx she had noticed at the parade. He paused at the tent doors. His hair lifted in the soft breeze as he sent a blazing white grin at someone. One brown hand touched the tent fabric, holding it back for someone to pass inside.

"Who is that?"

Aster looked over her shoulder, then grinned at Jessica. "Do you find him handsome?"

Jessica felt heat rush into her cheeks. "All of you are handsome."

"That's Proteas. It's the flower magic, you know. That's what makes us beautiful. We don't look as nice when we first join the Calyx. It's the flora magic that enhances us."

"Really?"

"Really. It's a little sad, though. We are at our best when we are part of the retinue, but our charms eventually fade. It's the way blooms are, so it's the way we are. Ours is a passing beauty."

"You must appreciate it every moment, then," Jessica said, drinking in Aster's gorgeousness.

"That's precisely right. It's because the beauty is so fleeting that we value it so—"

Beazle crawled out of Jessica's hair. Jessica put a hand up to hide him, surprised he'd emerged at all, but it was too late. Aster's sharp gaze went straight to the tiny bat.

Her eyes widened. "You have a familiar, too?"

Again, Jessica was thankful Marion was not there, thankful Clair was caught up in her flirtation. She lifted a hand to Beazle to push him into hiding again, but he wrapped his limbs around her thumb. She turned her back so he was hidden from others in the tent. "This is Beazle. He's a secret and he knows it. I don't know why he came out." Maybe it was because Aster smelled so nice.

Aster set her half-empty plate on the nearest surface, never taking her eyes from Beazle. She put one hand over her heart. "Aren't you a handsome fellow," she breathed, reaching for him with her other hand. "May I?"

Jessica hesitated, but Beazle went for Aster, so she let him go. He preferred to cling to something, so he went for her index finger, threading one wing and a tiny claw between her middle and index.

"Please keep him out of sight." Jessica glanced around, but everyone was preoccupied with eating and chatting.

"Sure, although I don't see why. A familiar should be shown off for all to enjoy." Aster laughed as she turned her back to the people in the tent. "That tickles."

Beazle peered up at her, flicking his ears back, then forward, back, then forward.

"Oh, he is so sweet," Aster cooed. "Look at those eyes."

"He's showing off." Jessica was surprised by how good it felt that Aster appreciated Beazle.

"Well, it's working. I'm in love." Aster lifted her other hand to her hair where a butterfly clip sat in it.

Only when the butterfly moved onto Aster's hand did Jessica realize it wasn't a clip.

"This is Trea," Aster explained. "He's a *cyanea* butterfly." Trea was a mix of blue and purple, with squared-off wings lined with a darker blue. He was glorious.

Jessica's stomach tightened. "Beazle sometimes eats insects, even ones that are four times his size." Beazle would never eat Greta, but Beazle had never been around any other familiars, so she wasn't sure what he would do around Trea.

Aster laughed. "He won't eat Trea. Familiars don't eat other familiars."

Aster didn't seem worried, so Jessica tried to relax, taking in Aster and Trea with new eyes. They were just like her and Greta.

Aster seemed reluctant to hand Beazle back, but she did so as she lifted Trea back to her curls. Jessica lifted Beazle to her hair but he didn't want to crawl inside. He stretched his wings from his perch on her thumb, then fluttered over the heads of the diners and out the tent door. No one seemed to notice him go. It wasn't difficult for a creature no larger than a bumblebee to go around unnoticed. Jessica felt some of her tension drain away now that he was gone. She hadn't meant for her secret to get out—it had just happened.

"It's settled." Aster took her hand. "You must come to Discovery. That's where we test flora fae for magic, to see if they might join us. It won't matter to Ilishec that you're sixteen, not when he sees Beazle."

Jessica assumed Ilishec had something to do with recruiting the Calyx. "I'm pretty sure I don't have any magic. And even if I did, I don't think my mother will let me go."

Aster's smile dropped away. "Why not?"

"I wish I knew." Jess shrugged. "She'll be upset that you saw Beazle, and my ears. She's made me hide them both since birth."

Aster's expression was a mixture of horror and amazement. "Since… birth?"

Jessica nodded, feeling a tang of rebellious satisfaction. "I grew up thinking that my pointed ears were something to be ashamed of and my familiars should be kept secret. I didn't realize until now that lots of people admire fae with familiars, even envy them."

Aster looked at her with seriousness of a scholar. "Familiar…s?"

She nodded, on a confessionary roll. Aster already knew about Beazle and her faeness. What was the point in hiding the existence of Greta? "I have two."

Aster blinked. "No."

"Yes." She heard the pride in her own voice and thought that she shouldn't have had so much wine. It was making her boastful.

"But, this is—" Aster seemed at a loss for the right word.

Jessica lowered her voice to a conspirator's whisper. "I could sneak away to Discovery without my mother's consent."

Aster put her hand on her shoulder, moving fast, as if catching Jessica from falling over. "No, little love. Don't even dream of it. Ilishec wouldn't like that. He's not in the habit of taking fae from unwilling parents."

Jessica had been joking, but at Aster's reaction, an unexpected pang of disappointment took her breath away. In the last three minutes, she'd been identified as fae and Beazle had been held and admired by someone other than her, someone who had their own familiar, someone who understood her. The moment Aster told her not to sneak away without Marion's consent was the moment the desire she'd been lately trying so hard to identify came into sharp focus: she wanted to attend Discovery. She wanted to spend time with Aster, to meet Proteas and the other Calyx, to see where they lived and what their lives were like. Surely what she could learn from them would help her understand better what she wanted for her own life.

"What should I do, then?"

"Nothing." Aster's hand was still on Jessica's shoulder. "Don't do anything. Leave it to me. What's your mother's name?"

"Marion Fontana."

Aster nodded, then kissed her on both cheeks. Jess was suddenly drowning in the beauty of her fragrance.

"It was lovely to meet you, Jessica." Aster left her in a cloud of petal-soft perfume.

Jessica watched her leave the tent and disappear into the darkness, off to charm another guest with her presence. She felt dizzy and looked around for somewhere to sit. She lifted an arm and sniffed discreetly at herself. If part of being Calyx was smelling like flowers, she would never make it.

Sometime after midnight, Jessica left the dance floor where she and Clair and had been dancing with other village girls of the same age. She needed to find a bush to pee behind. There had been outhouses dug for the party, but as it got later, the outhouses began to smell in spite of the garlands of flowers that had been strung inside. As she emerged from the shrubs straightening her skirts, she enjoyed a view of the pavilion and open dance floor.

She'd caught glimpses of her mother throughout the day, mostly to be sure that she didn't look angry. But every time Jessica had seen her, Marion had been laughing with other adults and sipping from a goblet. She'd spotted her mother at the edge of the dance floor and had gone over to stand with her and listen to the music. Marion had put an arm around her shoulders. Jessica recalled a time when she'd looked up at her mother, but now she was taller than Marion. She'd wrapped an arm around Marion, squeezing gently, grateful that her mother had changed her mind and let them come. That had been around ten p.m. Jessica hadn't seen Marion in a couple of hours.

A cluster of musicians gathered to one side of the dance floor, playing jigs and reels. Many of the songs were country dances that the villagers had grown up with. Even older folk couldn't deny the music's allure. Villagers circled and clapped, laughing and red-faced with exertion. As the sky had darkened, more torches were lit, sending flickers of light across the smiling faces. Jessica had danced with nearly every member of the Calyx retinue and several of the musicians, but now as she stood back and observed the party, she couldn't see any Calyx. It was like they had melted away in the manner of their misty blooms.

The dining tents circulated with serving staff and villagers looking for snacks and drinks, but no Calyx were visible at the entrances. Jessica wandered to the nearest tent to look inside. The Calyx were easy to spot by their otherworldly beauty, they were always at the center of attention, but there were no Calyx inside this tent. She moved to the next, and the next, but there were no Calyx to be found.

"They've gone," came a voice from behind her.

Jessica turned to see a member of the serving staff balancing a mostly-empty tray of cheese on his palm. He had a good-natured smile and wore his poufy cap at an angle. His dark eyes twinkled. "Their duty ends at midnight. The rest of us are here until morning. They need a lot of sleep or they're useless the next day."

Disappointment welled in Jessica's heart. "Where did they go? Surely not all the way back to Solana. It's a day's ride from here."

"They have a camp at a secret location. Even we"—he jutted his chin to indicate his fellow servers—"don't know where it is. They rest and then return home early in the morning. Most of the guards have left, too."

Jessica frowned. She'd expected to talk to Aster again, perhaps after Aster had put in a word with Marion. Why else would she have asked for Marion's name? "I didn't get to say goodbye to Aster or Proteas, or any of the others."

"If they started that, they would never get out of here. They leave quietly so the villagers can continue their reveries without distraction. You're stuck with musicians and servers for the rest of the night. I know we can't compete with the Calyx, but..." He shrugged. "Are you having a nice time?"

"I've never had better." Jessica blushed at the insinuation that his company and that of his fellows was dreary next to the Calyx, which was only the truth.

"Good." He swung the platter toward her. "Cheese?"

She took a chunk and thanked him before he swept into the tent. Popping the salty cheese into her mouth, Jessica turned back to the dancers spinning in front of the pavilion. Now that the Calyx were gone, she became aware that her eyes were burning and she had the start of a headache. Staying up late was one thing, but staying up late after a full day of festivities and overeating and drinking was another. She marveled at the older villagers who were still going with apparently limitless energy as she strolled the perimeter looking for Marion.

As Jessica watched a cluster of adults at a nearby table, one of the men snagged a serving girl in voluminous skirts and a low-cut bodice. Pulling her onto his lap, he nuzzled into her neck as she squirmed and laughed and pulled away. She smiled and teased but kept out of his reach as she delivered drinks to the table. Another group flanking the dance floor stood talking and laughing boisterously. Jessica spotted Marion among this group, drawn by Marion's high-pitched cackle. Her mother only laughed like that after she'd had too much wine. Jessica knew her mother would be grumpy tomorrow and wondered whether she should drag her home.

As Jessica watched, a local widower named Otis who was usually reserved, swept Marion into a hug and turned her in a clumsy circle. Marion wasn't holding her cane and wine sloshed from her cup, spraying a red arc across the hem of another woman's dress. Jessica gasped. Not only did the widower seem oblivious to Marion's bad hip, but Marion also esteemed a good wine was as precious as gold and mourned any drops she spilled. Jess anticipated Marion would thrash him with a few choice rebukes, but to Jessica's astonishment, she only laughed and clutched Otis's shoulders. Jessica shook her head. She decided it was safe to approach, but as she did so, the man stopped spinning her mother to bow her backward over one arm and kiss her full on the mouth. Jessica froze, staring. She'd never seen Marion allow herself to be hugged in public by a man, let alone kissed long and thoroughly. Jessica felt unable to move her legs.

The crowd raised their goblets and shouted or whistled their approval. He stood Marion on her feet, her face flushed and her hair a frizzy corona around her head. Her lips were swollen and shining with his saliva in the torchlight.

Marion's gaze met Jessica's, and in the space between an inhale and an exhale, the two stared like frightened mice discovered beneath a bale of hay. Jessica's cheeks heated with embarrassment. To her further humiliation, Marion lifted an arm and swept it before her in a deep curtsy. She lost her balance and nearly fell but Otis caught her. Marion righted herself and beckoned to Jessica. "My baby girl, my beautiful Jessica." She crooned. "Come here, my lassie."

Jessica's face ignited. The adults welcomed her as she stepped within the ring of air laden with the sour scent of alcohol. One of them pinched her cheek like she was a plump toddler. She bore it patiently as Marion wrapped an arm around her shoulders and kissed her noisily on the temple, leaving a wet patch that Jessica longed to wipe away.

"Well, my darling?" Marion looked up at her daughter. "Happy? You got to see a flora festival after all, and wasn't it a spectacle?"

Jessica smiled. "It was wonderful. I'm tired now. I hear my mattress calling."

The adults laughed, but Marion nodded. "Find Clair and take her with you. What a good girl you are."

"Won't you come?"

Marion looked startled and then thoughtful, like it hadn't occurred to her to leave the party, but now that Jessica had presented it as an option, it was one she should consider seriously. She lifted a finger. "Why, yes. I do believe I shall. Come, daughter. Let us away, before the night's devilries wax strong and activities commence which shall spurn a fresh batch of fat-cheeked babes nine months from now."

"Spurn?" A lady in a tight red bodice laughed. "I think you mean spawn."

Marion didn't miss a beat. "That's what I said, spawn."

Jess shriveled inside. She hadn't seen Marion quite this drunk before. She didn't like it. Her mother didn't sound like herself. She extricated Marion from the crowd of merry villagers and got Clair's attention as she swung by on the dance floor, wrapped in Haft's arms. Clair kissed the farm boy's cheek and dismissed herself, joining Jessica and Marion in the shadows.

"Are you going home?" Clair's eyes glittered fever-bright in the torchlight. "I'm not ready to leave."

"Where's Hanna?" Jessica asked.

"In the tent. They just rolled out some pastries."

"Okay. See you tomorrow." Jessica kissed her friend's cheek and sent her back to the dance floor. Hooking elbows with Marion, she helped her mother down the street.

"Where's your cane?"

"Do you know..." Marion yawned. "I have no idea."

The party grew dim and the sound of night insects swept through the outskirts of the village. An owl called softly in the distant trees. By the time they reached the cottage's front steps, Marion's eyes were half closed.

Jessica was tired and thoughtful. The festival had been amazing, but she kept replaying the encounter with Aster. Was she going to talk to Marion at some point? How could she, now that the festival was over and Aster had to go back to Solana City? And how would Marion react if she learned that Jessica's secrets had gotten out?

"Well," Jess pronounced as they entered the cottage. "That wasn't so dangerous after all."

Marion went for the jug of water they kept on the table, drinking straight from the rim. She would have smacked Jess for doing such a thing. She let out a big, satisfied exhale, followed by a burp. "Oh, it's dangerous, girlie. Only we came home before the danger could get serious."

Realization dawned. She meant the Dagevli men deep in their cups.

Marion collapsed on her cot without taking the time to undress. She toed off her leather-soled dancing slippers and they landed on the wooden floor with a thud.

"Okay, but not quite a life-threatening danger," Jessica murmured quietly. The reasons Marion had kept her from the previous festival were hazier than ever.

Marion answered with a deep-throated inhale that was half snore.

Jessica drank some water, filled her cup again and took it up to her loft. She lay her clothing aside piece by piece, moving as though in a dream as she replayed the events of the day. When Beazle landed in her hair, she hardly noticed. He nuzzled her ear before flying back off into the night. She could make out Greta's shadow on the window ledge. Jessica blew gently on the butterfly, her way of telling the glasswing she loved her since Jess was a young child. Greta waved her antennae and fluttered to Jess's hand. Jessica blew on her again, and Greta waved her antennae in the flow. She flexed her wings, then fluttered to Jess's hair. Jess knelt on the floor and lay her elbows over the wooden sill, looking out over the soft knolls and dips of the fields behind the cottage. Further back, where the deep blue treetops touched the star-laden sky, a suggestion of taller, sharper peaks could be seen. Jessica fell asleep on the floor near her window, the sound of crickets in her ears, and the scent of night-blooming flowers in the air.

Chapter Four

Jessica

Jessica was tightening the leather thongs of her vest when she heard repetitive thumps drifting through her open window, broken by muttered curses. Greta clung to the window frame, antennae twitching. Running a brush through her hair, Jessica peered down into the yard. Marion had hung the frayed tapestry that served as a carpet over their laundry line and was beating it with an old walking stick that Jessica had thought Marion had thrown away. She must have dug it up when she couldn't find her usual cane. Marion's forehead glistened with sweat and moisture darkened the fabric at her underarms and between her breasts. With each strike, a dimple of fury cratered her cheek. With each backswing, she muttered some expletive under her breath that Jessica strained to hear. Marion had the most creative curse words. They were never as bad as the ones Jessica had heard farmers use, but they were often comical enough that Jessica wrote them down in a notebook for Clair. She plucked the notebook and a stub of a pencil from her dresser and returned to the window, padding quietly on bare soles.

Marion whacked the tapestry and drew back with a harsh intake of breath. "…chickenhearted foot-licker…"

A cloud of dust bloomed from the fabric and puffed toward the sky.

WHUMP! "…plague-ridden micro-phallus…"

Jessica scribbled greedily into her notebook.

WHACK! "…fusty, rumbumptious hedge pig…"

Jessica couldn't hold in her laugh.

Marion looked up, panting. Usually, she'd join in when her daughter laughed at her creative insults, but her face was full of thunder. She raised a finger. Jessica shrank back from the window and the finger but was too late.

"I knew we shouldn't have gone. Now look at the trouble coming. Right to our own doorstep, no less." Marion leaned on the stick and put a hand on her heaving bosom. She let out a high-pitched exhale of exhaustion and frustration.

Jessica peeked over the sill. "What trouble?"

"Never mind, you slugabed. You're chained to weeding this morning, young smarty bloomer. And this afternoon, take Clair and gather a crop of pushrooms—"

"We just did that. They'll go bad if we have too many."

"Then pick moireberries and I'll make a batch of bread for the market." Marion hefted her stick and drew back to strike, bracing her legs like a lumberjack. She'd hurt herself if she didn't let up.

"But market day isn't for three more days," Jessica protested. Moireberries went moldy if they weren't used the same day they were picked. Jessica suspected Marion's ploy was to keep her away from the cottage for the afternoon.

"The berries will last if I keep them in the cellar."

"But we're almost out of sugar."

Marion grunted. "I'll get some from the Solmans. I have to get fresh cream anyway."

Jessica considered this. "Who's coming, Mother? And how do you know they're coming?"

Her mother hissed like an angry goose and whacked the tapestry with frightening power. "A trifling prick-a-me-dainty, that's who. Never mind how I know. It's not your business, young lady."

Jessica withdrew and located a pair of socks. Greta fluttered out the window, headed for the garden. Beazle was hanging upside down in the rafter, his wings wrapped so tightly around him that he looked no larger than a rosehip. She went down to the kitchen where she splashed water in her face.

As she ate a bowl of warm millet with butter and salt and a sprinkle of dried fruit, Jessica observed the cottage. The furniture was pushed to one side, but there was a fresh bouquet on the table, the small library shelf had been cleaned and reorganized and crisp white lace curtains had been hung on the windows.

When Marion brought the tapestry inside, Jess helped her place it on the floor and they worked together to put the furniture back. All the while, Jessica's mind was tumbling. Whoever was visiting was unwelcome but important; they couldn't be simply sent away or ignored. They never had visitors so noteworthy that Marion banged out the rug and dusted every corner of the house. As her mother bustled around, Jessica formed a plan.

She put on her shoes and grabbed the berry basket from the cupboard. "I'll gather the moireberries now and do the weeding this afternoon." When it looked like Marion was about to protest, Jessica added: "I'll harvest them from Rosebud Valley. They get more sun and taste better."

This was a partial lie. The moireberries that grew near their cottage were just as sweet and juicy as the ones that filled Rosebud Valley, but the valley was past the north end of town and her mother knew that Jessica would have to walk for two hours just to get there and another two hours back. This did the trick, and Marion nodded, thinking that Jessica would be far away for most of the day.

"Take a water skin and some cheese with you. Grab an apple from the Grein's tree on the way."

Jessica packed her supplies while Marion swept the front walk. When Jessica said goodbye, Marion was furiously washing the front of the cottage and the windows. As dirty water and soap coursed down the plaster, the gray cottage was returned to its original color of pale blue.

Jessica walked in the direction of Rosebud Valley, but as soon as she was out of Marion's sight, she cut toward the narrow path the kids used to go down to the river. She harvested moireberries there, keeping an eye on the traffic passing back and forth along the road. Her basket was nearly full by the time she spied her mother striding purposefully toward the heart of the village, a bonnet covering her flyaway hair.

When her mother was out of sight, Jessica scampered home.

The cottage door had been propped open with a large stone. A sweet breeze flowed through the house from the open back door to the open front door and windows, filling the space with fresh air and earthy smells. The table had been draped with a cream-colored cloth and a nosegay of violets sat in the center.

Jessica took her shoes off and carried them and the berry

basket to the ladder. She ascended like she was made of mist. Her mouth felt dry, but she was more afraid of the visitor she might miss than of her mother's anger. She sat on the hardwood floor near the ladder with her back against the plaster wall and waited. In time, she heard her mother's footsteps. Jessica's butt ached from the hard floor but she dared not move and hardly dared to breathe. She could hear her blood rushing past her eardrums.

Marion bustled about and Jessica listened as crockery was pulled from cupboards and arranged on the table. Marion went to the backyard, probably to start a fire in their outdoor pit to boil water for tea. A short time after Marion had changed her dress and spent some time on her appearance, hoof strikes could be heard along the road. They came softly at first, then grew loud, along with the sound of voices. Jess tensed, desperate to see who was approaching, but if she got up and went to the window, her mother would hear her on the floorboards.

The riders stopped on the street out front. It was impossible to tell how many there were—maybe three, maybe six. Words were exchanged within the party; there was some laughter. Someone approached the front door. Marion hurried to greet them.

"Marion Fontana, mother of Jessica Fontana?" the stranger said, a young man's voice.

"Yes." Marion sounded breathless, almost penitent. "I received your letter, though I have no understanding as to why I've come to your attention."

"Honorable Gardener thanks you for your time," the man said. There was the sound of boots scuffing on the stone.

Jessica put a hand over her mouth. The royal gardener? This was Aster's doing.

There was no irritation in Marion's voice now. "He is most welcome."

Dying to see what was happening, Jessica slowly, slowly lowered herself onto her side so that her cheek pressed against the edge of the hole. The table came into view as well as part of a windowsill, but no people. Pulse skipping, Jess stayed like that, mentally begging her mother to move the guests to where she might catch sight of them. Another person entered the cottage and there was a rustle of fabric. Jessica tried to imagine her mother curtsying and failed.

"Lady Fontana," said a new male voice, this one older than the first. Jessica liked the sound of him immediately. "What a pleasure."

"Well come, Honorable Gardener."

"Well found, milady. Please, call me Ilishec."

Jessica bit her cheek to suppress a gasp. Ilishec was the person Aster had said wouldn't care if she was sixteen if he met Beazle. No one from the palace had ever set foot in their home before. No one had ever called Marion milady. The villagers of Dagevli didn't even know the etiquette for hosting a member of the royal household because it just didn't happen.

"I would like to introduce a member of my Calyx," said Ilishec. "This is Ruty Delacourt, from the kingdom of Boskaya. She's been a member of the retinue for seven years."

"Well come," repeated Marion.

"Well found," replied Ruty. "Call me Aster, please. We don't go by our birth names while we serve as Calyx."

Jessica's eyes stretched wide. She wanted to squeal. Her armpits felt damp and her pulse jigged and jagged.

"I recognize you from the festival. I have prepared tea,"

said Marion. "Although, I can hardly dare to imagine what has brought you back to our village, let alone to my cottage."

Ilishec moved to the table and partially into Jessica's view as he pulled a chair back and sat down. He wore a blue quilted vest with silver buttons. Over his heart was embroidered the lion's head sigil of Solana. When Ilishec sat, his head did not quite become visible, but Jessica caught a glimpse of a neat beard and long gray hair. Aster did not come into view as she took the seat closest to the kitchen. Marion slid across from Ilishec, her back to the ladder.

Marion immediately stood again. "The water is in the backyard, forgive me."

Ilishec made to say something but Marion was already to the door—even her limp didn't slow her down. He and Aster sat in silence as they waited. Marion returned and poured water into the cracked teapot. It didn't take long for the smell of bergamot tea to reach Jessica's nose.

"I'm sure you can imagine my curiosity," Marion said as she retrieved three mismatched porcelain cups.

"I met your daughter, Jessica, at the festival," said Aster. "By chance, is she nearby?"

"Jess is harvesting today and won't be back until evening. You'll miss one another, I'm sorry to say."

Jessica shook her head at the implication. It bordered on rude. However royal these guests were, they were not welcome to stay until Jess's supposed return.

"I understand." Ilishec was polite. "Aster explained to me that your daughter is half-fae, and that she has not one familiar, but two. Is that correct?"

There was a long pause before Marion answered. "Yes."

Jessica's eyes drifted closed. Just like that, her mother knew that she'd let her secrets out.

Ilishec waited for more information, but when none came, he prompted Marion. "What do you know about the Calyx, good lady?"

Marion sipped her tea and replied airily. "Not much. Of course, we witnessed them perform at the festival. Very enchanting."

Jessica pressed her lips together at her mother's deliberate aloofness.

"Thank you," said Aster.

"And we enjoyed the gifts they gave, of course. Our king and queen are very generous to their hard-working subjects."

"They are also generous to their Calyx," Ilishec added. "They would very much appreciate your ear, so that you understand what opportunity your daughter has."

Marion gave a tight, surprised laugh. "My daughter? Oh no, Jess wouldn't be interested in anything like that. She's much too attached to me to ever want to leave. She needs me and she's far too shy of strangers to move to the city—even Solana City, as beautiful as I've heard it is."

Jessica squeezed her eyes shut in mental anguish. Her mother knew how much she was craving adventure. Why was she claiming her daughter was too attached to ever want to leave? It was enough to make her clench her fists.

"Be that as it may, please hear me out." Ilishec waited for permission to proceed.

Marion sighed. "Suit yourself."

Ilishec waited as Marion refilled their cups. Jessica thought the fine handle of the cup looked odd in his weathered hands. The man was obviously not just a gardener in title.

"Children come from all over Ivryndi to take part in Discovery. We call it a day, but Discovery can take several days depending on how many children attend. I work with each child personally. Flora fae vary greatly in ability, and my objective is to get a glimpse of their natural talent."

"Jessica doesn't have any talent," Marion said, but quickly amended, "I mean magic. She has no magic."

"Even if she's never conjured a botanical, it doesn't necessarily mean she has no magic. Sometimes, in fact quite frequently, it just has to be coaxed into life."

Marion sounded doubtful. "I see."

"Most children are not invited to join the Calyx, as we have limited places available, because not only must they be exceptional, they must also complement the Calyx we currently have in the retinue. The children who are not offered a place return to their lives with some nice memories, and gifts." Ilishec paused, and when he spoke again, there was a smile in his voice. "I once heard that a mother purchased two strong Silverfall ponies with the gold her child brought home from Discovery."

Jessica suppressed a sharp intake of breath. The kind of gold that could purchase Silverfall ponies could also build an addition to their cottage, a private room for Marion, which she had long wanted.

Ilishec continued. "But for the children who *are* invited to join the Calyx, their lives change, and the lives of their families. Every Calyx is unique. Their capabilities vary as greatly as the blooms they produce. Their careers can last ten years, sometimes longer. By the time they retire, many of them have saved quite a fortune, but riches are not the most compelling reason to try for a position. The relationships they forge and the education they receive enriches their lives and informs the adults they become. You don't know me and I don't know you, but you strike me as a woman of substance. You have, if I am not mistaken, a strong sense of what is right and what is wrong, what is light and what is darkness. The Calyx are part of the light, and they bring that light with them wherever they go. To be one of them, even for a short time, is a gift of unimaginable worth."

Ilishec paused, perhaps waiting to see if Marion had questions. It was impossible for Jessica to guess at what her mother might be thinking, but Ilishec had struck Marion where she was weakest. She longed for a bigger cottage, finer clothes, new shoes every season, maybe even more than one pair, fresh paint for the walls, a carpet that wasn't so threadbare and meat for their meals. They weren't impoverished, but neither were they living in the lap of luxury.

Ilishec had also favored Marion with a compliment that did not seem like simpering flattery, while at the same time appealing to Marion's inner compass of truth. Whatever Marion's reasons for not wanting Jessica to attend Discovery, Jess hoped they had shrunk in importance next to the picture of privilege Ilishec had painted.

"Please consider allowing Jessica to attend. Discovery starts tomorrow."

Marion sounded strangled. "I cannot possibly have her there tomorrow, I'm sorry."

"If she and you are amenable, we would be pleased to escort your daughter to Solana this very day. She would have the king's own protection. She will be safe and well cared for. In the event she is not suitable for Calyx life, I will arrange to have her safely returned to you in a matter of days."

"Good lady, please consider it." Aster sounded so hopeful that Jessica's heart warmed. She saw Aster's dark hand reach over the table to lay over Marion's pale one. Marion did not pull back.

"I have never been happier. Our time as Calyx is not long. It's a phase that passes like a breeze. But already I am dreaming of my future, and my dreams are so much grander and more glorious than they ever were, yet they are not unattainable. But a little time, and I will be free to pursue them. In the meantime, my labor is not wearisome."

The table went silent.

Marion took a breath. "Well, I don't know. I-I suppose I could talk to her about it."

"That's all we ask," Ilishec said.

Jessica's stomach drifted like an autumn leaf descending. If Ilishec and Aster left, Marion could easily say nothing of this meeting to Jessica. She might pretend the visitors had nothing to do with her daughter at all, in which case Jessica would have to admit to eavesdropping if she wanted a chance to go. And if Jessica waited to admit her presence to her mother until Ilishec and Aster left, how would she contact them again if Marion remained against Jessica attending Discovery? She certainly wouldn't pay for an escort, nor would she take Jessica herself. Marion had expressed many times over the course of Jessica's life a disdain for city life and no interest in ever seeing any center of civilization larger than Dagevli itself. Jess had resigned herself to accepting that, due to Marion's prejudice, she probably never would see the city, at least not until she was able to make considerably more of her own income. These thoughts reared a panic so vicious and startling that Jessica's throat constricted, triggering a fit of coughing.

In a moment, Marion was at the foot of the ladder, looking up in alarm, her lips forming words that Jessica couldn't hear over her own body's attack. Tears leaked from her eyes as she gasped for air. She couldn't speak over the spasms in her throat. Marion's countenance flashed from ire to fright and she disappeared and returned with a glass of water, which she ascended a few rungs to deliver. The cool liquid slid down Jessica's throat, soothing the tickle. She finished the glass in a series of long swigs, then handed it down to her mother with a pitiful croak of thanks.

Ilishec and Aster appeared at the bottom of the ladder, peering up at her.

Aster smiled and waved. "Hello, Jessica."

Jessica grinned, her cheeks flushing as she wiped moisture from her eyes. "Hello, Aster. Nice to see you again. Didn't expect to see you here, in my own home. What a lovely surprise."

Ilishec rested his hands on his hips. "Miss Fontana. You've been here all along?"

She nodded and put her feet through the hole. She landed on the stone floor and dropped into a curtsy. "Forgive me, there is no excuse for my eavesdropping."

Marion's face was red as she held the empty glass. "My daughter knows better. I am horrified and beg you not to judge her too harshly."

"It's quite alright," murmured Ilishec. He bit the inside of one cheek and Jessica wondered now if he was trying not to laugh. "I suppose our proposal has come to an end, anyhow. At least you'll be saved the trouble of having to explain our visit."

"Yes." Marion fired a glare at Jessica that could have killed.

"I want to go," Jessica blurted. "I would like to go with you today, please. I don't need any time to think about it."

Marion paled. "Jess, dear, let's not be hasty."

"I am sixteen, almost seventeen, nearly an adult. Besides, you heard him. Most children don't get offered a place. I'll probably be back in a few days, but at least I will have tried."

Marion's lips compressed and her chest bounced as her fingers flew to cover her mouth. Jessica reached for her mother in alarm, realizing Marion was fighting back tears. Jess was stricken but resolute. She wrapped her arms around her mom. Marion hugged her back fiercely, every fear apparent in the strength of her arms.

"You're all I have, wee bun," she whispered into Jessica's hair.

"You'll never lose me, Mother." Jessica's heart soared, even as it bled from the anguish in her mother's voice. Marion's sudden display of emotion was astonishing.

"We'll take good care of your daughter, Mrs. Fontana," said Ilishec kindly.

Marion turned to the royal gardener, wiping her eyes with a corner of her apron. She kept one arm tight around Jessica's shoulders as she blinked back more tears.

"It's a great honor, Mrs. Fontana." Aster took Jessica's hand.

Jessica stepped closer to the Calyx, glorying in the feeling of Aster's hand so solidly wrapped around her own. She felt allied with them, as though she'd found her kin. She felt on the precipice of an exciting, far-flung adventure. Even if it was short, she wanted it dearly.

"Parents are welcome at the palace at regular intervals throughout the seasons if Jessica does get offered a place," Aster added. "I see mine twice a year."

Marion wiped her eyes, then propped both hands on her ample hips. Her body language signaled defeat, but there was a tiny smile lifting the corners of her mouth, even if her eyes were still leaking. That little lift at the corners of her mouth was all it took to send Jessica's heart winging.

Marion would let her go.

Chapter Five

Çifta

Çifta hauled the heavy wooden door of the manor closed behind her and slid the latch shut. The metallic clink echoed through the empty halls. The cityscape outside became muffled; the cries of seagulls, the rattle of wooden wheels on cobbles, the distant shouts of sailors and stevedores, the laughter and haggling of the crowded market—it all softened into the background. She looked down into the basket of fresh fruits and vegetables she'd purchased at the market. She'd bought too much again. When would she remember that the Unya household had dwindled from thirteen to four? She didn't need to buy so much produce; in fact, she didn't need to buy produce at all. Their cook would happily do it. Çifta just liked market day. It got her out of the house. She sighed and made her way toward the kitchen. Cook would just have to preserve the surplus… again.

Çifta stopped in the empty dining room to gaze at the Unya family's most recent portrait. Her heart gave an ache of loneliness and loss. The faces of her three older sisters looked down at her from the canvas. Their father towered over all of them, his bushy black beard an entity of its own.

Kazery's wife, Alana, had given him Una, Fetre and Gemma before succumbing to the illness which had plagued her lungs for years. Çifta had come afterward, from another relationship. Çifta's sisters had their father's dark brown eyes and their mother's strawberry curls. While Çifta's hair was the deep blue-black of Kazery's, her eyes were glacier-blue, the only such eyes in the Unya family tree. Where her sisters were freckled and pink, Çifta was porcelain. Sometimes she thought she looked more like a ghost than flesh and blood. People had commented since she was small that she was both striking and strikingly different. Kazery would only smile and say she was the love child of his widowerhood. Later, she learned to blush at this comment, but her father was never ashamed. Who could shame him? No one would dare reproach Kazery Unya, not even the king.

Çifta left the produce in the kitchens for Cook and made her way through the eerie halls to her suite. She was pouring water to wash her hands when the sound of the front door opening echoed through the manor.

"Çifta?"

She was surprised to hear her father's bellow. He wasn't due home until lunchtime.

"Here!" She splashed water onto her face and soaped her hands as he thumped down the hall. She picked up a towel and patted her cheeks dry, turning to the door. Kazery poked his head in, an oak of a man with a chest as large as a barrel. He smiled through his thick, black beard.

"Forget something?" She hung the towel below the ewer and basin.

"I have news that can't wait." He put a small package wrapped in thin fabric in her hand. It was closed with a shiny black bow.

"What's this?" She felt something small and solid inside, no larger than the palm of her hand.

"An image of your betrothed. It arrived this morning. That's why I rushed home."

She gaped. "My—"

Kazery chuckled. "Don't look so surprised. You knew it was my priority. I just didn't realize it was going to take this long to find the perfect match for you."

A tremor fluttered through her belly as she untied the ribbon. "Who is he?"

"Prince Faraçek, eldest son of King Osvitan and Queen Daryli. She's deceased, though, so you won't have a mother-in-law. That's a blessing in disguise, if my experience is worth anything."

Çifta stared at the small portrait in her palm, her mouth unfetchingly agape. She remembered herself and closed her lips, looking up at her father, wide eyed. "But… he's a prince?"

His dark eyes sparkled. "Are you pleased?"

Çifta dropped her gaze to the likeness of Prince Faraçek. He was very fae. This was most apparent by the sweep of his pointed ears—winged up and back from the sides of his head like the sails of the more exotic vessels in her father's fleet. Prince Faraçek looked out from a painting no larger than the bowl of a soup spoon, neither smiling nor frowning. He looked serious but content. He had a beard as dark as her father's, only Faraçek's was short and jagged around the mouth, more of a goatee. Çifta had always had a fondness for voluminous beards, since she'd never seen her father without one, but Prince

Faraçek's facial hair looked a bit like a clawed hand. His brows were thick and angled. His skin had a slight gray tinge, but his cheeks were rosy. He was not unattractive, but he looked nothing like the kind of man Çifta had always dreamed of marrying, and everything about him looked like it was carved from stone.

The match had likely not been easy to make. Çifta was not a princess; she was not even noble. What she was, was extremely wealthy. Some said Kazery Unya, the famous merchant and owner of Unya Trading, was richer than the King of Boskaya himself. Çifta knew it to be true because Kazery sometimes boasted in private.

Çifta realized her father was studying her face intently.

"Of course I'm pleased." Çifta threw her arms around her father's neck. It was a stretch. Kazery was six and a half feet tall.

He picked her up and hugged her, then set her on her feet again, his eyes bright. "Think of it, my minnow. A prince of Rahamlar!"

None of her three older sisters had such advantageous marriages. Una and Fetre would be happy for her, but Çifta suspected Gemma might be jealous. Gemma wed into the wealthy Hashe family, on the other side of Syrgana Forest where they controlled large swathes of agricultural land. It had been an advantageous match for the Unya family, expanding their business considerably, but Gemma's husband was almost thirty years her senior. The Unya girls were raised with the motto "duty above self," so Gemma never complained to Kazery or to any of her friends in Kirkik. But, behind closed doors, she cried to her sisters that she was doomed to the life of a nursemaid. Since then, and after bearing two sons and a daughter, Gemma had exploited the freedom her aging husband gave her to take a lover. Her husband knew he could not satisfy her and seemed willing to leave the task to someone else, but she had to be careful. Her husband's one stipulation was that she never allow her affair to be discovered. If she was caught, he would vehemently deny ever having given her such liberty. She would be set aside and disgraced, possibly even sent back home, though Çifta doubted Gemma's husband had the guts to do such a thing. It would anger Kazery, and his wrath was legendary.

"What did you agree to give them as a bride price?" Çifta asked. To catch a prince, Kazery must have offered an immense dowry.

"Gold, of course. Access to part of my fleet, aid if they need it and a trove of rare and valuable treasures from across the Valdivian." Kazery touched his youngest daughter's cheek. "It is fair, and in return your new family will allow Unya Trading access to the twin rivers."

Çifta better understood now why her father had made the match. She would become a member of the family that controlled the fastest and most direct trading access to the north, something Kazery had always wanted. The north-flowing Tamyrat and the south-flowing Tadylat were deep, fast-moving and smooth for something like a thousand miles. Rahamlar controlled both the gates and the tolls. They could charge what they wished for the use of these convenient byways.

For his part, Kazery Unya had made himself into a kind of king. Many sailors and soldiers swore fealty to him. He had conquered the life-threatening challenge of crossing the Valdivian Sea, a body of water supposedly riddled with sea monsters, and so vast that it took months to cross. He'd been rewarded a hundredfold as he brought foreign goods back to sell. When she thought of all he had done, maybe it made sense his daughter should wed a prince.

"What do you know of him? What is he like?"

Kazery's bushy brows pinched. "People say he is quiet and serious, but respected. He is nothing like his brother, Ander. Faraçek is the oldest of four but he'll never wear the crown. That's part of why they agreed to a match with us." He scratched his chin, his fingers disappearing into his beard.

"But he is eldest?" Çifta knew that some kingdoms were passed to the eldest child while others were passed to the favored child. Still others were given only to male children and excluded daughters unless no sons were born. She had even heard of an icy kingdom, beyond even Stavarjak, that was only ever ruled by a female, and Stavarjak had had the same queen for centuries.

"He took his appearance from his unseelie mother," said Kazery. "Rahamlar claims their strength comes from uniting human and unseelie. Their monarchs have intermarried for centuries, but it is law that the crown pass to human children first. Only if there are no human heirs can the crown pass to fae offspring."

"I don't understand. Wouldn't all the children be half-human and half-fae?"

"That's so with seelie-human children, my dear. But unseelie and human offspring are always one or the other, never a blend. Unlike you." He chucked her under the chin. He'd often told her she was a perfect mix of himself and her fae mother.

Çifta had never known or even seen an unseelie fae. They didn't seem to have any interest in visiting Boskaya, probably because it was dominated by humans and magic was frowned upon, but Rahamlar wasn't a lot different. Or so she'd heard. Their population was an unusual blend of human and fae whose magic had been bred out of them over centuries—such was the price of mixing.

Kazery peered at the portrait. "He has access to vast resources and a good army."

Çifta closed the locket, moving to the next task. "When do I leave?"

"When can you be ready? They are eager to meet you." Kazery moved toward the door, resting a hand the size of a plate on the handle.

"A week should be enough but I'll need extra time for the journey. I want to stop in Cardagenya for supplies, and then at Nasyk to see Gemma."

Kazery gave her a knowing smile. Their post at Cardagenya was out of her way and she could have anything she wanted delivered to Rahamlar, but her father knew that she loved to see and touch the newest textiles and fabrics in person, and visit Cardagenya's tiny bookshop. It sold the most beautiful embossed sketchbooks she had ever seen. They were made by hand in limited quantities and inventory never made it as far south as Kirkik.

Çifta went to her writing desk. She was a lover of list making and this list would be a long one. She'd have to pack her own things because she recently dismissed her personal maid after catching her bragging about the Unya family wealth in the marketplace, and hadn't yet hired a new one. Kazery could say what he liked in public, but the Unya family expected discretion from their employees. No point in hiring new help now. Çifta would acquire a maid after she arrived in Rahamlar.

Kazery was half out the door. "Very well, I shall send a letter. Congratulations, my dear."

She smiled. "Congratulations to you as well, Papa."

Kazery left Çifta to her plans.

But Çifta could hardly keep her thinking organized enough

to write the list. She kept returning to the portrait of the prince. Her thoughts went to the place that all young minds tread: the halls of hope.

Could she dare to dream of love?

She went to the wooden chest at the end of her bed where she kept a collection of old letters from her sisters, alongside sketchbooks and drawing pencils. The letters were wrapped in colored ribbons. Peach satin for Una, who was the luckiest in her match. She fell deeply in love with her lord almost immediately, and he with her. Soft lilac for Fetre, who married a courteous man with a stable full of racing horses that she doted on. And lemon yellow for Gemma, who had not found happiness in her marriage, but whose extramarital lover kept her pleasantly if illicitly occupied in haylofts, deep closets and quiet stairwells.

Çifta chose Una's letters and riffled through them, plucking out her favorite. She'd read them so often that she knew at a glance which ones would lift her spirits with stories of new love. Reading of another's good luck would strengthen her for the adventure ahead

Chapter Six

Laec

Laec woke when a booted foot nudged him off the porch and into the grass. The open bottle of wine he'd been cradling like a newborn spilled down the front of his tunic and one thigh. He jerked up to an elbow, bleary-eyed and blinking, his hair in his face. His head ached and the tumble had bruised him. Indignant, he clawed his hair out of his eyes and glared up at the backlit figure. Laec meant to say her name reproachfully but what came out was an inaudible slur.

Fyfa towered over him, hands on hips. "Get up. Wash yourself. You smell like the scum at the bottom of a wine barrel. You've drunk my stores dry, you've eaten my food and passed out on my porch for too long. Quit moping around." She bent at the waist and he glimpsed smug satisfaction in her face as she added in a low tone, "The queen wants to see you."

Laec bit back the retort he'd been mentally laboring to form and stared stupidly. "Queen Elphame?"

Fyfa straightened, her expression freighted with irony. "No, the Queen of Underpants and Stockings. Of course Queen Elphame. She's expecting you at court within the hour." Fyfa walked away in obvious disgust. She disappeared around her cottage and Laec could hear her murmuring complaints to Byrne.

Shame heated Laec's cheeks. He got to his feet, grasping at the porch to steady himself. So, the queen had taken notice of his lifestyle. Either that or Fyfa had complained and her mother had decided to step in. As much as he wanted to, Laec couldn't blame his friend. He could hardly stand himself these days, so why should he expect anyone else to? Fyfa and Byrne had been overly patient, expecting that any day now Laec would rouse himself from his slump and return to his usual clear-headed and irreverent self.

Laec wasn't normally so lazy. He didn't normally drink during the day, or even every night like many fae did, but somehow, he'd slid into a routine of indulgence that was proving difficult to break. There was no justifying his precipitous fall from grace. Daily he told himself that tomorrow he would climb out of this pit. Tomorrow would arrive, and he would ask himself why he should bother. What good thing was waiting for him at the top of the pit? Banquets, picnics, horseback riding, swordplay, running errands for members of the court, hunting, gardening. It had all lost its luster. What had seemed an enchanted life before Georjie now seemed dull and empty.

I'm depressed, thought Laec with chagrin. He stumbled into Fyfa's cottage and staggered to her bathing room. *And when I'm sober, I'm embarrassed that I'm depressed. I used to pride myself on being immune to such weakness.* He winced as the truth sliced through his mind like bright morning sunlight. He guzzled water from the copper tap and splashed his face, analyzing his reflection through bloodshot eyes. A face-washing wasn't going to do it, not for an audience with the queen. Laec stripped and bathed. He lathered himself with one of Fyfa's homemade bars of soap, his hair too. He scrubbed and rinsed, scrubbed and rinsed. Afterward he felt better, but he wondered if he was sober enough to walk through the castle doors in a straight line.

Toweling dry, Laec searched for clean clothes and found some folded on the chair outside the loft he slept in—whenever he didn't fall asleep on the living room floor or sprawled on the lawn. It was the same place Georjie had once slept. An annoying little voice whispered that that was part of his problem.

He made a mental note to thank Fyfa for doing his laundry, dressed and went into the kitchen to scavenge. There was fresh sourdough on the countertop, still warm from the oven, and cold butter in the ice cupboard. Laec helped himself to two slices of bread and butter and took a peach from the bowl on the counter and a handful of nuts. He felt ready to handle an audience with the queen now but already resentment burned in his chest. What right did Elphame have to interfere with his wallowing?

Laec left Fyfa's cottage, pausing on the porch. He could hear Fyfa and Byrne behind the house, laughing together, their drunken friend forgotten. His eyes drifted closed for a moment and he changed his mind about letting them know he was leaving.

I don't enjoy being sober, thought Laec as he strolled the path leading to the rear gardens of the castle. Being sober meant realizing fully what an ass you've been. It meant feeling that delayed sense of humiliation about things you did or said while you were not sober. Everything one *should* have felt while one was doing or saying the humiliating things came roaring in like a rabid animal.

Laec's head still ached. He was in for a reprimand, and he deserved it. Still, he was surprised that the queen would bother to involve herself. Laec was a courtier, but he wasn't an aristocrat—he was the offspring of a family that the queen had once been fond of. Being centuries old, Queen Elphame knew better the stock Laec had come from than Laec did himself. Maybe she felt she had to keep Laec straight from some misplaced sense of loyalty. Maybe Fyfa had complained about Laec using her cottage as a flophouse. That was probably it.

Laec wove his way through fae playing games in the gardens, drinking daisy wine from crystal goblets, listening to lutists and flautists playing spritely music, sitting on tree swings and whiling away the afternoon.

I'm not so different from these courtiers, Laec thought bitterly. *Just because I choose to drink by myself instead of in the queen's backyard with a bunch of popinjays and sycophants, I get reprimanded?*

Laec had worked himself into a state of pure rebellion by the time he entered the queen's reception hall. He took his usual place against the wall to wait for the queen to call on him, quietly fuming. His head was pounding and he wanted something to drink, but he kept away from the sideboards. Better not to smell of wine during his audience, especially when he'd taken such pains in the shower.

Queen Elphame was usually seated on the marble bench atop the dais while she held sessions, but she was not there today. Instead, she paced restlessly. A small wiry man in spectacles followed along behind her, short legs working to keep up with the long-legged queen as she dictated to him. She wore a close-fitting gown of pale green. Today, her hair was icy white and swept up in a mass of curls scattered with small green blossoms. The queen had different-colored hair every day, but she favored white above all. Many claimed she was the most beautiful fae to ever live, but Laec was immune to such beauty. He had long ago come to believe that her true appearance was most likely that of a crooked old crone with no teeth and a withered bosom. Why should he let her attractiveness affect him if it wasn't real?

Now that he was thinking about it, that was one of the things that had made Georjie so attractive. She had magic but not guile. Even better, she had chosen love over immortality. No one else Laec knew would ever make that same choice, least of all Laec himself. If Georjie had professed her love to him and asked him to leave Stavarjak and live in the earthly realm with her—in Scotland or her homeland of Canada, or anywhere else—he would have declined, in spite of his desire for her. But Georjie had—without struggle or a moment's hesitation—turned her back on immortality and opted to stay with Lachlan.

It wasn't so much the loss of Georjie's love that had sent Laec into the downward spiral. It was the mirror that Georjie had inadvertently held up by making such a choice herself. Against her conviction, Laec had compared himself and hadn't liked what he had seen. Laec certainly was not worthy of her. The fact that he'd treated her with such disdain when he first met her made this simple truth unbearable. Wine made it bearable, at least for a little while.

Laec let his memories torture him until the queen's violet eyes found him. Her gaze never left Laec as she ripped off a few more instructions to her secretary and then sent him away. Dispensing with the usual ceremony of having a guardsperson call subjects in an orderly fashion, the queen beckoned him with a sharp chin gesture.

Mutinously, Laec pushed away from the wall and ascended to the throne. When he reached it, Queen Elphame was no longer there. She had disappeared through a door at the back off the dais, leaving it open behind her. Laec slipped into the private chamber where the queen had resumed pacing.

The room bristled with carvings in dark wood: famous battles, famous lovers, famous fae inventors and poets. A new panel had been added since the last time Laec had been in this room. He recognized Georjie's visage and form, half carved, striking a heroic pose, one he was fairly sure she'd never struck. Curls of wooden shavings peppered the carpet beneath the panel. Carving tools lay against the wall. Another week or two and the black witch Georjie had destroyed would also appear in the wood. He struggled to pull his gaze away. No one would carve him in this room or any other. What had he ever done that deserved to be lovingly rendered in hardwood?

A semi-circular alcove with a padded bench sat beneath tall vertical windows. Outside, the glass was overladen with vines. Slender beams of sunlight filtered into the room. The queen went to this alcove but did not sit, instead she paced in slower, tighter circles. Her agitation was contagious.

He was supposed to wait for her to speak before he spoke himself, but he'd never been great at self-control or following rules. He settled his forearms into a barrier over his chest and glared. "What are you going to do, cut off my other thumb?"

She had punished him for helping Georjie steal something from her stores by cutting off his right thumb. The fact that the thumb grew back had not lessened the sting of his chastisement.

At his cheek, the queen cocked an eyebrow. "Why? Have you done something else to justify losing a digit?"

"There's no law against drinking too much."

The queen waved a hand. "That's not why I summoned you. Though I'm not impressed with your behavior of late, I am not your mother. If you want to spend a few decades drinking and getting fat, that's your choice."

Laec was surprised by how much this stung. Did the queen not care what happened to him, then? In some distant corner of his mind, he was aware of his hypocrisy and grimaced. Another reason to avoid sober self-examination for as long as possible.

"I have foreseen trouble for my cousin, Esha," the queen went on, still pacing.

Laec searched his memory. "The Queen of Solana?"

She nodded, her beautiful face pinched. Frustration stiffening every movement. "As usual, my premonitions are dark and vague. I cannot see the shape of this threat. I cannot tell if it is to her directly or to her kingdom, or perhaps to some individual in her care, but it is dark and it is persistent."

Solana was far away. It might as well be in another dimension. Laec's annoyance was supplanted by confusion. "What does that have to do with me?"

"I want you to go to Solana and present yourself to the king and queen, make yourself of service. Report any important happenings or developments back to me. Be my eyes and ears. I don't know if the threat is imminent or far off, but I would rather take precautions, and I cannot see well beyond our borders."

The queen could not demand this of Laec, she could only ask, since it meant Laec would have to leave Stavarjak's protective borders—and what magic he had—behind.

Laec had explored the hills, dales, forests and mountains of Stavarjak, but he'd never been outside it. Somehow, he found crossing the veil to Scotland less intimidating. The other kingdoms of Ivryndi had weak magic, if they had any at all, which meant the citizens lived hard lives. Laec was not interested in living a harder life.

"And if I decline?"

The queen's fine brows hiked up in surprise. "I thought you would want to go. Your uncle is the royal gardener," Queen Elphame reminded him, and added in a tone that suggested Laec should be more impressed: "He manages the Calyx."

Laec frowned. "I know."

Rather, he'd known about the royal gardener bit, but managing the Calyx was news. Laec's mother's brother, Ilishec, had gone to Solana City for a special occasion when Laec was a toddler, some event to do with Ilishec's kind of magic. He had liked Solana so well that he'd made a life there and eventually married a Solanan citizen. Ilishec and Hazel had visited from time to time while Laec was growing up, always during Solana's winters, but as a teen Laec had never paid much attention to his uncle's stories about gardening in Solana.

"I do not ask you this just for my cousin's benefit," Queen Elphame said, acknowledging the cynicism in his tone. "There is some reason you are supposed to go."

"What reason?"

Her eyes shuttered. "I can't see that."

Laec let out a breath. The queen did have some kind of foresight, and had used it to the benefit of herself and her kingdom for many centuries. The citizens of Stavarjak believed their kingdom to be the most beautiful, the safest, the richest, the most abundant and educated of all the kingdoms of Ivryndi, thanks to their queen. How much of that was true was impossible to know without going to see for oneself, but why would anyone bother? Further, the queen was also known to invent premonitions in order to manipulate citizens into doing what she wanted. She could just as easily be making it up as a pretext to exile Laec in a bid to break him of his self-destructive habits.

Or, she was telling the truth.

"Will you send me there with your…" Laec waved his fingers to indicate he was referring to Elphame's magic.

The queen shook her head. "You'll go there under your own power. Magic is not a crutch or a shortcut; it has a cost, and its value is high. You know this. I'll not waste it to save you a journey that will do you good. A fit fae like you should be eager to meet people, see the continent, learn about life elsewhere. It will make you strong."

"I am strong," Laec replied, insinuating that she meant physical strength when he knew better. Laec was lucky to have a naturally lean and muscular frame. Even his binge drinking had not yet marred his body, though it showed in the shadows under his eyes and the pallor of his cheeks.

Queen Elphame narrowed her amethyst eyes. "So strong you allow a pretty elemental you cannot have to send you into a spiral of self-loathing?"

"She had nothing to do with it," Laec lied, struck by Elphame's knife-like accuracy.

Ignoring that, Queen Elphame brightened. "It's perfect for you. I can already foresee that the journey will benefit you. It will build character. Go on horseback, book yourself passage across the Saltless Sea, enjoy the journey. If trouble finds you, so much the better to exercise your wits. When you reach Solana, there will be a lot to learn. Queen Esha will take care of you, and you will be free to be my eyes." She took on a faraway expression, chewing on a thumbnail. "Ivryndi has long been at peace."

"You say that like it's a bad thing."

She faced him. "Long periods of peace make both men and fae soft, ungrateful and unappreciative of their freedoms and wealth. New generations who have never known trouble are complacent and weak. Tyranny looms. It's a cycle as old as time and we are overdue. Like I said, I don't know if the risk is to Queen Esha alone, but it's rooted there in Solana, and it is destined to grow. Something is coming, maybe even all the way to Stavarjak. I do not wish to be caught unaware."

Throughout the queen's speech, Laec found himself warming to the idea. He'd once been useful and productive. He'd once made a routine of vigorous activity: riding, hunting, fencing, dancing. He was quite good with a sword. He'd fallen, but not so far that he couldn't rebound. Whatever the queen's premonition, she'd put Laec in front of it. It was an opportunity to make himself important, something that—when he wasn't intoxicated—actually meant something to him. Maybe he'd never be carved in wood or sculpted in marble, but he could make his mark, and in the process, he might locate his self-respect.

"I'll serve you in this matter, My Queen," Laec replied, concealing his enthusiasm. It wouldn't do if Queen Elphame thought that he thought she was doing him a favor. That would only mean he would owe her later. Better if he appeared to be inconvenienced for her sake.

Queen Elphame looked satisfied. "I'll send a letter to Esha ahead of you by bird."

Within Stavarjak, Queen Elphame did not need to resort to crows or pigeons to deliver messages the way other courts of Ivryndi did, but outside the spring court, the queen had no legal right to extend her powers.

"I will also send with you a list of items I would like you to ship back to me. I am low on some things that only Solana can produce." The queen found a writing tablet in the desk and began to scribble, using a flamboyant quill with a beautiful green feather. She paused to give Laec a sly look. "You will thank me for this assignment. I have heard that both the fae and the palace at Solana have beauty that rivals our own."

"You've never been there?" Laec was surprised, although maybe he shouldn't have been. Queen Elphame was a famous homebody. But she was so old that he assumed she'd had her fill of traveling many decades ago.

"Ivryndi was a different world the last time I ventured beyond our borders." The queen tore off the note and handed it to Laec.

He folded it and tucked it into his jacket. "Do you wish me to see you again before I leave?"

She returned her quill to its inkpot. Her movements were stronger now, more confident. Laec wondered just how much this commission meant to her; it was impossible to tell what anything meant to Elphame in comparison to anything else going on in her kingdom. "Yes. I will have one or two things I will give you for Esha, along with some gold for your journey."

"Very well." Laec dropped his chin. "Am I dismissed, My Queen?"

"Almost," she said, and he paused. "There is a mount in our stables who is seaworthy. His name is Grex."

"I know him." Grex was a huge black stallion that the stableman claimed had Vargilath blood in him somewhere far back. Laec didn't believe that for a second, but that didn't diminish the quality of the horse. Grex was intelligent, spirited and swift, but he was also calm, an unusual combination in a stallion.

The queen looked pleased. “Good. I’ll have the stablehands told to prepare him.”

Laec thanked her and left. He’d gone into the meeting tipsy, half-sick and dreading a reprimand. He’d left with an important commission.

As he passed a sideboard loaded with sparkling decanters filled with a rainbow of liquids, his fingers itched to hold a goblet. He paused and a battle commenced within. A battle he might have lost or might have won, depending upon his perspective. *Perspective is everything*, he thought as he poured a small glass of apricot liquor to celebrate his new purpose in life.

Chapter Seven

Laec

Laec pulled Grex to a halt at the crest of the hill they'd just spent two hours climbing. It could have been defined as a mountain, so steep and tall it was, but because it was covered in the soft fuzzy fae trees known as hylshe, from a distance the hill looked like a pile of green hair clipped from the scalp of a giant. Hair Hill, as it was known to the locals—though on maps it was called Okumak Mountain—was the southernmost landmark at Stavarjak's borders. The top of Hair Hill was where Queen Elphame's influence over Stavarjak's climate ended, meaning that as Laec descended the other side, the weather would turn bitter. It was not yet noon but heavy clouds the color of iron hung low over the landscape, blocking much of the sunlight.

A cold wind blew through Laec's tunic and drew a shiver, whipping his red locks around his head. He dismounted to free his cloak from beneath the rear fender of Grex's saddle. He wrapped the cloak around his shoulders and fastened it at the throat, then tied his hair in a low tail at the nape of his neck. Putting a hand on Grex's shoulder as the stallion nickered, he asked, "How about you? Do you need a blanket?"

But the climb had warmed Grex's body, and the heat of his muscles soaked into Laec's palm. He put his arms around the tall horse and pressed his chest against Grex's, letting the stallion's heat bleed into his torso. Warmer, he swung back into the saddle. As Grex descended the winding road, Laec felt the last of the magic of Stavarjak ease away. There would be no access to Earth from here on out, not that Laec needed to be able to visit the Terran realm, but knowing that he was that much further from Georjayna gave him mixed feelings. Laec had—in spite of his best attempts to keep his heart remote—fallen in love with her. Leaving Stavarjak was just what he needed. Queen Elphame knew it. Fyfa and Byrne knew it, and when he was sober, so did Laec.

Grex picked his way across the switchbacks, going east, then west as they worked their way down. Laec had ridden Grex before and liked the stallion, not just for his smooth stride but for the pitch darkness of his coat. Not a hair in the stallion's mane, tail or coat was anything other than the softest black, which made Grex both handsome and difficult to see after sunset. If Laec found himself traveling at night, which could easily happen when treading new roads, he could guide Grex into the trees and become nearly invisible. If trouble found him on a barren landscape, then he could rely on Grex's fleet and powerful legs. Failing that, and too far from Elphame for his magic to work, Laec had a sword, even if he'd not touched one lately. He shook off thoughts of being attacked and focused on the landscape. Laec couldn't yet see the strait, even from the heights of Okumak, but he expected to arrive at Ashtaraq by nightfall. He'd book passage, then find a stable for Grex and accommodation for himself.

When the pair reached the bottom of Hair Hill, the road widened and improved. Traffic increased as the forest terrain was broken up with patches of farmland and small villages. Crossroads became frequent. People were friendly, greeting those going in the opposite direction. When Grex passed a rumbling wagon full of brightly colored root vegetables with a young girl perched on top, she plucked a dirty carrot from the cart and held it out for Laec.

"For your pretty mare," the girl said sweetly, with the accent of those who'd been raised speaking the old form of Ashtaraq. Laec didn't correct the girl about Grex's gender, only thanked her and took the carrot. He brushed off the dirt and tucked the vegetable into one of the pouches hanging over Grex's withers.

By the time Ashtaraq came into view, there was a covering of snow on the ground either side of the road, which had turned muddy. Thin layers of ice formed over shallow puddles, cracking loudly under Grex's hooves, which he seemed to go out of his way to step on. Perhaps his way of alleviating boredom.

The small port city of Ashtaraq was quaint from a distance, and grubby close up. Steeply peaked roofs thrust crookedly into the sky like monster's teeth, and the smell of fish and animal dung tainted the air. The roads were slop. Laec didn't dismount until he'd reached the shores of the Strait of Ashtaraq. Here, a boardwalk kept things a little neater, but the place was a jumble of people and animals, fishmongers and ship makers, stevedores and women carrying baskets of vegetables or shellfish. There was a sense of urgency as the last of the day's light drained away. The shipyards and markets were closing, merchants dumping buckets of water across their flooring to wash away fish guts or sawdust.

Laec asked a boy where he might book passage across the strait and the young man directed him to a pub called The Parrot. "The captains gather there for dinner most nights," the boy told him in a voice that hadn't broken into manhood yet. "It's best to avoid the billets office where they'll charge ye twice as much."

Laec produced a copper from his vest pocket and flipped it at the youth, who caught it in the air with a grin. Laec went to the pub and dismounted, tying Grex in front of a watering trough at a respectable distance from three other horses. He went inside The Parrot. The wooden plank floor sagged beneath Laec's booted feet as he avoided the low-hanging lanterns strung along the soot-soaked ceiling. The smell of stale beer and salty meat washed over him as he combed the inhabitants for anyone who looked like a captain. Three respectable-looking fellows sporting impressive beards, and one vulturine, raw-boned and clean-shaven man sat at a corner table drinking watery-looking beer.

"Even', Captains." Laec offered a smile.

The three larger men mumbled a reply. The skinny man only took a sip from his mug.

"I seek passage across the Saltless."

The one with the copper tint to his hair bent his head back. "To which port?"

"I prefer Montyra, but I'll take any port along the southwestern coast."

The skinny man grunted. "I sail for Cardagenya in the morning. Ye're welcome aboard but I've no private berths left."

Laec glanced at the other captains with a hopeful expression.

The copper-haired one shrugged. "Sorry, lad. I sail for Rashampet in two days. No help to you, I'm afraid."

"Do you have room for a horse?" Laec asked the skinny captain.

"Is he seaworthy? I've no patience for the flighty ones. They disturb the other animals."

"Yes, sir. He's been on a ship before." In fact, Grex had been on several ships, but Laec hadn't been on anything bigger than a raft, a fact that Laec kept to himself. Volunteering his lack of sailing experience to these crusty old sailors wasn't a wise idea. None of the captains asked, probably assuming that, like themselves, sailing was a regular part of Laec's life.

The bony man said: "Then I've a stall for him and standing passage for you for five silvers."

Laec paid half the fare to the skinny one who, after introducing himself as Captain Dalel, pocketed the coins and gave him a handwritten ticket. Laec tucked it into a pocket and asked where he might find lodging. They gave him confusing directions to a stable and boarding house several neighborhoods away where he could also get dinner for himself, oats and hay for Grex, as well as breakfast. Laec thanked them and left the pub, bumping his head on a lamp on his way out.

Twenty-four hours later, Laec heaved into a gray, churning sea over a slimy railing. Hearty laughter from more than one sailor brought blood rushing into his cheeks, making his face feel like it was on fire in spite of the cold wind. Brackish seawater sprayed into his face and he squeezed his eyes shut as his stomach did another lazy roll. He wished he were dead. Laec had never felt worse and silently cursed Queen Elphame for suggesting the sea route. Going around the Saltless Sea would have involved braving the mountains of the Vargilath, but it would have been worth it. Oh how he longed for sturdy, stable land beneath his feet, the smell of grass and trees and flowers. He opened his eyes and watched the churning waves, taking deep breaths. He wiped his mouth and straightened, feeling only slightly less like throwing himself overboard. His mouth tasted like poison. He wondered how Grex was faring below decks and prepared himself to stagger to the nearest hatch and then tackle the set of slippery, narrow stairs.

"Not a seafaring fae, then?" came a friendly, feminine voice.

Laec turned his head slowly, hearing his own neck creak. Was this what it felt like to be old?

A young woman stood beside him holding a bucket with a ladle in it. Her feet were planted and her hips and knees moved like freshly oiled machinery as the ship rolled beneath her. She didn't grip the banister and none of the water in her bucket sloshed over the edge. She scooped some and held it out to him.

Gratefully, he rinsed his mouth, spitting over the side and being careful to turn his head so his spittle was carried away by the wind. He took another rinse, spat again and then swallowed the rest. He handed the ladle back. "Thank you."

"Take another," she replied with a smile. "Otherwise, next time you vomit, it'll burn something awful."

"The next time—" Laec put a hand on his mouth as his cheeks ballooned. He got himself under control, but only just. "I hit the burning point half an hour ago."

The girl wrapped one arm around the widest part of the bucket and held it against her hip as the other hand disappeared into a pocket in the front of her apron. She produced a kerchief and handed it to him.

Laec took it, thinking she meant for him to clean his face, but felt something solid tucked inside. Unwrapping it revealed half a green apple and a small white lump that looked suspiciously like sugar. Laec's stomach reacted at the sight of food and he handed it back with a grimace.

"Eat it. Even if you don't feel like it. The salt and apple together will calm your belly."

Laec gave her a doubtful look. "Truly?"

"Aye. Get it down and the worst will have passed."

Laec gingerly took a small bite of the apple and a lick of the salt.

"I'm Tarrin."

He swallowed down the first bite and took another. "Laec. Are you crew?"

Tarrin shook her head. "Captain Dalel would rather die than have a woman working on board. I make this crossing four times a year to visit my grandparents."

"By yourself?"

"Not at first, but now that I'm older, yes. The crew know me well. I'm in no danger."

Laec thought she couldn't be much older than eighteen but didn't say so. He was grateful for the water and the apple, but he didn't feel like socializing. "Thank you for the refreshment, Tarrin," he said, politely but dismissively turning back to the sea.

To his chagrin, she moved closer and set the bucket on the railing, holding it so it wouldn't fall over. She relaxed into an elbow like she was planning to stay a while. Tarrin's brown eyes flicked over his form and features with an intensity that made him look away. Her gaze dropped to his mouth. Her lips parted softly.

Laec groaned inwardly and took another bite of apple and lick of salt. He had to admit that his stomach was feeling a little better. He was grateful, but annoyed. Before Georjie, flirting was one of his favorite sports. Somehow, he'd lost the stomach for it.

"Where are ye from?"

Laec took his time before answering. "Stavarjak."

"I thought so. We don't see many fae on this crossing, but when we get them, they're from Stavarjak or Rahamlar, but you don't have the look of the fae from Rahamlar. You're a lovely pink color."

Laec popped the rest of the apple into his mouth and kept his gaze on the horizon. The clouds of yesterday had not broken that morning, nor all day, and now cloaked the moon. There was nothing to see. How Laec longed for a glimpse of land, or the flash of a lighthouse—anything that signaled civilization.

"I was born in Ashtaraq, but I live in Cardagenya now." She let out a dramatic sigh. Laec flashed a sideways glance at her and was horrified to see a dreamy expression on her features.

"What I really want to see—"

He closed his eyes. *Please don't start telling me your dreams. Please go away.*

"—is Solana. The Scented Court. Not that they'd let me in, but I'd love to see it, even from the outside."

He opened his eyes, almost telling her that was where he was headed, then clamped his mouth shut and looked away.

"I've seen paintings. They say it smells even better than it looks. The only reason I know that's true is because my father was there once. He's a mapmaker, you know, and a good one, too. He worked for King Armyn—that's the present king's father—to survey the gardens. He says he was only allowed to see half of what is there. The rest is kept secret."

"I thank you for the water, miss," interrupted Laec, intentionally not using her name, "but I find I'm not in the mood to talk. I'm sure you understand." He put a hand over his stomach and made a pained face, though he was feeling much better.

Tarrin looked hurt, then angry. "See if I bring you water next time you're hurling your intestines to the fish." She lifted her nose and flounced away.

Laec marveled that she was able to cross the seesawing deck with her nose so high in the air. He faced into the wind and closed his eyes. Peace at last.

His eyes popped open as a bunch of rowdy passengers crossed the deck behind him. One of them stumbled into him as the boat lurched, smashing Laec's tender stomach against the railing and bringing on a fresh wave of nausea. Laec used the railing to push back, sending the big man rebounding into his friends.

"Oaf!"

With a smooth step sideways, Laec managed to dodge the worst of the shove the oaf gave back. The man's friends didn't want to get involved, and continued on up the deck. Laec and the oaf contemplated whether the energy required to exchange blows was worth it. Laec's fist tightened but when the man snarled then left to catch up to his friends, he breathed a sigh of relief.

He made his way to the hatch to check on Grex. The stallion was munching hay and standing with a rear hoof tipped up on its edge like he was relaxing in a pasture rather than a damp stall on a heaving vessel. He paused in his chewing to blink at Laec with his big dark eyes, as if checking to see if his master was alright instead of the other way around.

Laec reached over the stall to stroke Grex's ear. "I'm glad one of us is seaworthy. If we had to cross water, this was the better route and a blessing in disguise. I might have expired before making it to Montyra."

He didn't stay long, as the nausea returned with a vengeance now that he was below decks. He fought the urge to gag and said a sheepish goodbye to Grex before staggering his way back up the stairs and returning to his place by the railing. His only comfort was another passenger, this one a tall scrawny boy, bending over the railing and yelling like a dragon at the sea as he lost his dinner. Laec hung his head over the side, closed his eyes and took deep breaths. When the nausea passed, he looked over at the boy, who looked back at him with a pitiful expression.

"I'd like to die now," the boy said.

In spite of himself, Laec laughed and the boy joined in with a guffaw of miserable hilarity that was quickly overtaken by a retch, which only made the two of them laugh harder. *What do you know,* Laec thought as his stomach revolted, *misery really does love company.*

Chapter Eight

Laec

Cardagenya appeared to be made of matchsticks and kindling. Laec's first thought, as he led Grex down the offramp and onto the long stretch of dock, was that all it would take was a spark or a more-violent-than-average winter storm to destroy it. Tall, narrow buildings with precipitous balconies clustered along the dock like mismatched books on a crooked library shelf. But for all the gravity-defying angles, asymmetric railings and warped staircases, Cardagenya was somehow still appealing to the eye—better yet, it was teeming with life. As the sun drifted toward the horizon, whistling lamplighters carried ladders and wick trimmers as they journeyed the streets touching fire to the charming, lopsided streetlamps and hanging lanterns. Wisps of smoke curled into the air, scenting the town with burning oil and settling a haze over everything. The amber glow warmed the shopfronts and alleyways, lit the interiors of pubs and shops and welcomed tired sailors and passengers to explore the depths of the narrow streets. Built on a hillside like many of the port towns along the craggy coastline, Cardagenya felt like a rustic, poorly built amphitheater. With its sweeping C-shaped port and undulating docks, Laec thought of a comb with missing teeth.

His legs felt weak from not having kept down much food over the last two days, but Grex took the dock like he'd been traversing slippery wood all his life. His hooves didn't so much clop along the planking as thud dully, leaving circular impressions in the spongy boards. Laec held Grex's bridle tightly, more to stabilize himself than to lead the stallion. When they reached the sandy road running along the coast, Laec savored the feeling of solid ground. The next order of business was food and lodging. Laec had never felt so hungry—a good sign.

He led Grex away from the harbor in search of a quieter area where they wouldn't hear the stevedores offloading and onloading cargo. Cardagenya—unlike Ashtaraq, he was told—didn't sleep. Laec guided the horse toward a sign in the rough shape of an arrow upon which the words "high street" had been scrawled in charcoal. Passing pubs, grocers, milliners' shops and a postal service, Laec's eye was drawn to a handsome building painted red with gold trim around the windows. Pristine glass had been installed along the front in straight frames. Through the window Laec could make out a neat counter with a clean-shaven clerk, and behind him, shadowy figures working at desks. It wasn't just the color of the building or the staff that drew his attention. The building appeared to be perfectly square, the only one among a profusion of off-kilter neighbors. Hand-painted signage above the door stated this building was the property of Unya Shipping & Trading.

The other characteristic that drew attention was the lineup of captains, which started at the clerk's desk and spilled out onto the street. These men—and one woman—varied wildly in appearance. Some wore fine, clean clothing with ruffles at the neck and ankles, while others wore boiled leather and visible weapons. All held paperwork and chatted amiably with each other. The reason for their affable mood was apparent: a pretty young woman in black breeches and a smart double-breasted jacket went down the line delivering steaming mugs of tea and a dollop of amber liquid from a silver flask for any who wanted reinforcement of the distilled kind. That was one way to show goodwill. Laec thought it was a clever perk to offer one's captains and mentally congratulated whoever Unya was for thinking of it.

A handsome horse-drawn carriage sat in the road, its shaft resting in the dirt waiting to be hitched to a pair of horses. The carriage was no peasant creation with crooked corners and wobbling wheels. This was a finely crafted conveyance with clean lines and decorative trim. Laec hoped for the occupant that the roads would be in better shape than the ones he'd taken to Ashtaraq. Trunks were piled on the roof and two men were loading more onto the platform behind the carriage body. Laec led Grex around the carriage but pulled up short when the door opened abruptly, almost smacking him in the nose. There was a rustle of fabric and a squeak as a foot depressed the carriage step, then the door closed again, leaving Laec chest to breast with the owner of a pair of startling ice-blue eyes and thick black lashes. Her dark hair flowed over her shoulders in long, loose waves. It was unusual for a noblewoman to wear her hair down, but she was young enough to get away with it. She wore a fine leaf-green dress, the square-necked bodice hugging her torso and waist. Her snug-fitting sleeves went all the way to her knuckles, leaving only slender white fingers poking out.

The warm scent of vanilla drifted past Laec's nose as she took in a sharp breath and stepped back to look up at him. "I'm so sorry. I didn't see you. I have to remember to draw the curtain back and look out before I open the door."

"That's... fine." Laec's mind emptied of all thought except that it would be rude to ogle the creamy skin of her décolletage. With great effort, he kept his eyes off her bosom and held Grex still until she'd gone around them toward the rear of her conveyance.

He heard her talking kindly with the men loading her carriage, giving instruction as to how she wanted her luggage stacked, and couldn't resist looking back over his shoulder. She stood at the rear corner of the carriage, the evening breeze tugging at her hair and dress. The last of the sun's rays kissed her cheekbone. There was something fae about her, yet as the wind pulled her hair back, he saw a delicately rounded ear. She caught him looking and he boldly held her gaze. A gentle smile lifted the corners of her mouth before she cast her eyes down, her cheeks flushed pink.

Laec faced front, unable to keep a smile from his own face. She was a beauty. Yes, he was recovering from heartbreak, but he was glad to see that not every female he met along the way was going to irritate him for not being Georjie.

Grex followed the high street as it switched back and forth up the slope. Quaint and crooked signs had been tacked everywhere: on lampposts, balconies, load-bearing beams and even on drinking troughs. Laec and Grex soon found themselves where the edge of town met a rocky outcropping. Beyond that, a sprinkle of low stars lay like freckles across the cheeks of the night. They walked along a dirt road lined with buildings until they found an inn with a stable called Pelargon's Billeting.

Once Grex was settled in a dry stall with fresh straw bedding and a dinner of oats and hay, Laec found a nearby pub that smelled more like savory food than ale. It was noisy and busy, but after locating a table that didn't tilt on uneven legs, Laec ordered a dinner of fish stew and rye loaf with a dish of butter he could slather generously on the bread. Halfway through dinner, he felt like a new person. With his belly full and the chill of his journey easing out of his limbs, Laec ordered a liquor made from a Terran substance called aniseed. There were no fae wines or botanical distillations of the kind he was accustomed to at home, so why not try something local? The liquor was overly sweet, but he finished half of it and enjoyed the heat soaking through the walls of his stomach. He paid the proprietor and offered his compliments to the chef before squeezing through the crowd and stepping out into the evening air.

As he was making his way back to the billeting house, he passed a mare loosely tied to a post in front of a low building with an assortment of handmade wooden items hanging in the windows. The horse was strapped with bulging saddlebags. A young man emerged from the building carrying a large bellows that looked freshly made. As he headed for the horse, she whickered nervously, ears flicking and eyes rolling.

"Steady on, Piglet," the boy said, trying to fix the bellows to the saddle as the mare danced sideways. She gave a squeal and kicked out with a hind hoof, which the young man only just managed to dodge. He uttered a curse as he jumped back.

Laec paused in the road. "Let her smell it before you expect her to carry it."

The youth looked up, startled. "Didn't see you there. Let her smell what?" He spoke with an accent like Tarrin's.

"The bellows. It's new, right? She's never seen it before?"

The boy frowned. "That's right."

"So she needs to understand it's not dangerous."

A skeptical look on his face, the boy approached the mare's head, the bellows thrust forward. She tossed her nose in the air, her ears pinned back.

Laec admonished, "Be gentle. She's spooked. Don't make it worse by shoving it into her face. You wouldn't like that. Neither does she."

The lad lowered the bellows and stood still. Blowing through her nostrils, the mare watched him for a moment before stretching her neck out for a sniff. After whiffing and nuzzling the bellows, she looked away, bored. The boy moved to the saddle and fixed the bellows with a lash. He looked over his shoulder. "Some kind of horse expert, are you?"

"Not really, no. They're just not all that different from us. We're afraid of the unknown too."

"Right." The youth stepped back and surveyed the saddle and bags with his hands on his hips. Standing like that, Laec realized how big and sturdy the lad was. He was clearly used to hard labor, even if he wasn't good at horses.

"How does it look?" the lad asked. "Think it'll all fall apart halfway between here and Solana?"

"Is that where you're headed?"

"Just to a village across the border. I'm delivering some things to my brother."

"She'll need some padding. Do you have a blanket for beneath the saddle? She might get sores otherwise."

The youth put his hand over his eyes and let out a long sigh. "Of course. What an idiot I am. Good thing I decided to do a dry run." He untied the bellows and set it on the grass before unstrapping the saddlebags.

"I wondered why you were saddling her at night," Laec

said. Most people didn't travel in the dark, not by choice. Every kingdom had its brigands and thieves.

The boy nodded, lifting the saddlebags off. "I leave at first light. I just got nervous about saddling her. She's not mine and horses don't like me much."

"Have patience. She'll get used to you." Laec started moving again. "I guess I'll see you on the road, then."

The lad straightened, his expression brightening. "You're going to Solana as well? It's my first time doing this route alone. I usually do it with a neighbor but he's not well at the moment, so I'm on my own with Piglet, here. We might be helpful to one another, companions on a journey. There's naught between Cardagenya and Nasyk but a few small outposts. Two is better than one, especially through Syrgana."

Laec hesitated, but when the young man held out a calloused, broad hand, Laec shook with him. "I leave at daybreak. I'm Laec."

"Dougal," replied the boy.

Laec gestured to his billeting house half a block away. "I'll meet you in front of Pelargon's Billeting then, at dawn."

"I'll pack lunch for two. My ma wins the prize for best butter buns every year at the harvest festival."

Laec smiled. "That's nice. See you in the morning."

"Good rest." The young man turned back to the mare.

Laec continued on to the billeting house where a soft bed awaited him. The sea journey was over. From here on out, it would be forests and dales and solid ground. If the boy turned out to be tiresome, Grex could easily leave Piglet behind.

Chapter Nine

Laec

The horizon was a jagged tree line against the dim glow of peach sky as Laec and Dougal left Cardagenya. In the growing dawn light, Laec saw why Dougal's mare was named Piglet. She was a strawberry roan, almost pink in color. The double-lane dirt road was hard packed and tacky, making the going easy. Winding through sparse forests of towering pines choked with fae creepers in bright pinks and oranges, the road meandered prettily through boulder-strewn forests interspersed with patches of farmland. A marble quarry loomed in the distance like a half-constructed pyramid. The sun reflected a white haze from the bright stone.

As morning drew toward midday, the traffic increased and so did Dougal's chatter. What began as questions Laec answered with one word to signal that he wasn't much of a talker became storytelling about Dougal's childhood with eight brothers. Being near the younger end meant Dougal's parents had exhausted the majority of their disciplinary energy and were indulgent, bordering on negligent. They turned their focus to the family's fishing business, letting the younger boys raise themselves and putting the older ones to work. Laec learned more than he cared to know about the peasant family who had been part of the Cardagenya community for so many generations that they were sometimes credited with founding the port town. Laec grunted at intervals and let Grex draw ahead of Piglet. Dougal finally fell silent and trailed behind, the steady clop of Piglet's hooves assuring that he was never out of shouting distance.

At early afternoon, Laec glanced back and saw that Dougal had fallen far enough behind that he'd joined another small band of riders and was waving his hands in the air and gesturing as he regaled this more attentive group with his stories. Laec smiled, satisfied, and faced front. Crossroads signaled villages in all directions. They continued southwest and anticipated the first sighting of a signpost that mentioned Solana's borders. As the forest thickened, the local farm and village traffic thinned. Dougal urged his mare to catch up, parting ways with the other riders.

Taking only a fifteen-minute break to water and feed the horses at a busy crossroads, they devoured the buns that Dougal had brought. Traffic approached from the side roads, but hardly any came from the way that Dougal and Laec were going. Laec wondered why traffic had thinned so significantly, then he saw the dense forest up ahead. The road thinned and became potted and rough as they passed into the woods.

The trees were extraordinarily tall with boughs that began over halfway up, leaving a widely spaced landscape of thick reddish trunks and a hilly forest floor carpeted with needles and cones. Birdcalls echoed strangely. Insects whirred and buzzed, surrounding the duo with an endless vibration of sound. An hour in, Laec glanced at the youth, saw creases marring his brow.

"What worries you?"

Dougal jolted, then looked embarrassed. "Don't much like close spaces."

"Close?" Laec made a show of looking around. Visibility surpassed two hundred meters. But, up ahead, the forest changed again. "This isn't close." Laec gestured down the road. "That's close."

"That's what I mean," murmured Dougal.

They passed into a forest of fat and knotty hardwoods which included Terran oaks and fae werlets. The werlets were slender and smooth, with silver-gray peelable bark used for papermaking in some places. The oaks were stout with rough-barked trunks full of holes and thick, far-reaching branches, gnarled like arthritic fingers. Together, the trees made a canopy that was so tight Laec wondered briefly if rain could get through. Somehow, it managed, because the forest floor was bright green and laden with moss. Space between the trees thinned and the atmosphere grew dark and humid. The air smelled of pondwater and algae; little green faemanders as well as a few Terran salamanders scuttled through the underbrush and along tree trunks. Birdsong became mournful. The road narrowed further, and the trees hung so low that, at times, Laec had to hug Grex's neck to avoid branches. Laec found the forest beautiful and strange. The weirdness of it doubled when the road began to meander nonsensically back upon itself in a tight, serpentine fashion, down into mucky areas and up over crests where the trees made tight tunnels. Piglet danced skittishly, her hooves sucking at a patch of muck. Dougal was white about the mouth and appeared to have aged a decade.

"Are you alright?" Laec asked.

"Aye," replied the youth in a tone that grimly expressed the opposite. "Have ye never heard the stories?"

"I'm not from here." Laec allowed Dougal and his mare to draw alongside on the narrow double-track.

"The sign that marked Syrgana Forest spoke only of the widely spaced pines. This part of it has no name." Dougal nudged the mare too close and Grex snorted at her. She danced away, tossing her head.

Laec bent away from the reaching branches of a fat oak. "No name? Why not?"

Dougal lowered his voice. "Truthfully, it probably has dozens by now, but whenever anyone puts up signs, they disappear." He seemed afraid to tell the story loud enough for the trees to hear.

"Someone takes the signs down?"

Dougal shuddered. "It's not just the signs. They keep trying to put this forest on maps, but those marks always disappear too. You won't see this place distinguished on any map anywhere, not the local ones or the continental ones. It's swallowed up by Syrgana Forest and defies any additional title."

Laec frowned. "Sounds like magic to me."

"Aye."

The pair came to a crossroad and drew to a halt, peering down the three options before them.

"There used to be a sign here," Dougal said, looking doubtful. "I always forget the way through this forest, must be the magic."

"Great," grumbled Laec. "How are we to know which way to go when the roads are so winding? We could continue west only to find ourselves turned around later, heading in the wrong direction." He could also admit that he no longer knew which way was north without a decent view of the sky. This was an unwelcome sensation, since Laec had an excellent sense of direction—so excellent that he never traveled with a compass in his own kingdom. He had, however, brought one with him on this journey, though getting it out meant he had to dismount and dig around in his saddlebag.

A blue-gray mist drifted along the road, creeping with wispy fingers. Ahead, the way was a little wider, a little mossier and a little less gloomy. If he could go based on feel alone, Laec would opt for straight, but traveling on feelings through a strange kingdom was not wise. He sighed and dismounted to unearth his compass.

From behind them came the loud retort of a branch cracking, followed by the snapping sound of smaller twigs. Then all went silent. Dougal's eyes went wide and Laec's hackles rose. He froze at Grex's side, hand jammed into his saddlebag. They listened for more but only a low whistle of wind sent mist swirling around the horse's hooves. Laec found the bag containing his compass. He upended the sack and focused on the swinging needle. It took a second to confirm that north was where Laec guessed it was, but it still didn't answer the question of whether the road that appeared to go west would indeed lead them west.

Keeping the compass in hand, Laec mounted. He nudged Grex forward. "This way."

He pulled up short a second later when the distinct sound of hoofbeats came from two directions at once. Piglet gave a high-pitched whinny of fright. Laec fought the urge to allow Grex to bolt at top speed down whatever path looked most appealing to the stallion. They had every right to use these roads. Laec vaguely wondered if bandits sheltered in these woods. He thought even thieves and pirates would find living here distasteful.

Riders arrived. Laec saw with some relief that they were

the same group of young men that Dougal had been talking to earlier. He put up a hand in greeting, but they were coming straight at him with no sign of slowing down. He yelled at them to stop. The first rider—a broad man with a day's stubble and a hood bouncing against his forehead—thrust out an arm that was as solid as a tree branch, striking Laec across the chest and knocking him from his horse. Laec landed hard in the mucky road, stunned, the wind whooshing from his lungs. Gasping for air, he was surrounded by the legs of excited horses. There was whooping and excited laughter as the attackers tried—from horseback—to liberate Grex of his saddlebags and saddle. Grex kicked out at them; his reins swung around like whips as he tossed his head.

Struggling for breath, Laec rolled, narrowly avoiding being crushed. He thought he could hear Dougal screaming but couldn't see the boy due to all the horseflesh. He scrambled for the closest ditch. He flailed for Grex's reins but missed, his vision blurring at the edges. As air finally swept into his oxygen-starved body, a set of boots landed hard on the earth, straddling him. He looked up into the wide face of a husky man with a patchy red beard just as he drew back a fist and slammed it across Laec's jaw. Laec's vision went black, though his hearing still worked. He was pummeled and searched; the bag of gold inside his pocket was taken.

"The compass, the compass," someone yelled, high-pitched and half-panicked. "He just had it!"

Laec's head spun as he tried to focus. How did these brigands know about his compass? This was the first time he'd taken it out. And where was Dougal?

It struck Laec harder than the fist across the jaw: that had been Dougal's voice.

He tried to summon defensive magic but failed, a bitter reminder of his vulnerability. He grappled, half blind and still not breathing well, as they pilfered from his clothing. Why hadn't he worn his sword at his hip? Properly, instead of in the scabbard under the fender of Grex's saddle? Stupid. He'd let his guard down.

Then a fresh wave of riders arrived. There was the squeak of a wagon wheel, voices shouting in a language Laec couldn't identify. More thugs? He felt as helpless as a baby, and wondered errantly if he was going to die.

His vision cleared to the sight of the one with the red beard mount Grex, who was now bareback. Laec rolled and bumped against a tree, using it to get his feet under him. There was a battle going on. What looked to be soldiers—not in full armor but each one with something armored on, a helmet on this one, a breastplate on that one—tussled with the brigands. The soldiers had swords but they were not drawn, instead fists flew and legs kicked. Men grunted and fought—some fell from their horses, either punched out of their saddles or bucked off. It was chaos. Dougal was across the melee, clinging to Piglet's side, barely hanging on as he grappled with a soldier who had him by the back of his shirt.

Beyond the chaos was a sight that made Laec wonder if he was hallucinating: The covered carriage from Cardagenya, drawn by two pretty chestnut horses, had stopped in the road. The boxes and trunks on top of the carriage had been covered with tarpaulin and belted down with thick leather straps. On top of the luggage, stooped to keep her head out of the trees, was the woman with the ice-blue eyes. She wore a tight-fitted blue bodice and layers of gauzy skirts. Her bosom was enhanced by a ribbon laced up in front. She shouted what Laec could only assume were instructions to her chaperones and guards, and potentially epithets at the brigands. She was yelling at the fighting group and waving a small pale fist, her eyes sparking with excitement and wrath. She did not appear to be frightened by the conflict unfolding between her carriage and where Laec stood.

A moment later, it was all over. The young attackers, overcome by the trained soldiers, to whom the action appeared to be a bit of fitness and frivolity, escaped the way they'd come. Their thundering hooves gouged holes in the mud and threw clods everywhere. Someone dropped Laec's saddle in the grass beside the road in his panic to get away. Soldiers gave half-hearted chase and soon turned back while others milled about in the crossroad, talking and laughing, wiping sweat from their faces. Dougal disappeared with the thieves, but not before he shot Laec a look of hatred. Had Dougal deceived him from the start, then? Or had the youth just seized on an opportunity to steal when he'd made acquaintance with the other riders? Laec supposed it didn't matter; still, shame heated his face.

Having rid himself of his red-bearded rider, Grex came cantering up to Laec. As he checked the stallion over for injury, the stallion's ears flicked forward and back, listening as the offenders retreated. There was foam at his lips, but he seemed otherwise unhurt. Laec murmured comforting words and straightened his bridle, then led Grex to where the saddle had been dropped. Laec checked his supplies and found that his compass was missing as well as his sword, and a sack of gold he'd hidden beneath the fender. He saddled Grex and led him to the party that had saved him, rubbing his jaw where he'd been struck. No teeth lost or bones broken, but he'd be tender for a few days. The guards looked at him with a pity that was annoying. He thanked them anyway.

The woman was on the ground, her hands on her hips. Her nearly black hair was tied back in a loose bun. "Are you hurt?"

Laec fought a sudden and powerful urge to crush her in a hug. He just smiled, wishing it was he who had rescued her instead of the other way around. "Only my pride."

She shook her head in disapproval, though not toward him, Laec felt.

"This is a famous trick pulled on foreigners. All the better if they can make you think that traveling together was your idea. I'm Çifta."

"Lady Çifta," said a guard standing behind her. He was tanned, scarred, and half an ear was missing. His dark blond hair was short and damp with sweat.

"I'm Laec." Laec couldn't divine whether Çifta was actually aristocratic or just rich. Should he address her as "Lady"? The guard had referred to her as a lady, but Çifta hadn't introduced herself with a title, and she hadn't given a last name.

"Nice to meet you. I'm sorry it wasn't under better circumstances. This"—she gestured to the guard who'd spoken—"is the captain of my escort, Endyr." She smiled at Endyr but gestured at Laec. "This is the man I almost bashed in the face with my carriage door back in Cardagenya."

Endyr acknowledged Laec. "You're welcome to travel with us if you find it convenient. We are going to Rahamlar."

"I'll stay with you until the road breaks for Solana, then," Laec replied. "Thank you."

"Good." Çifta turned away, but instead of getting into her carriage, she mounted one of the other horses which had been saddled with a sidesaddle, an invention Laec hadn't seen since he was a boy. She had a soft accent and rode sidesaddle—she had to be from a southern kingdom.

The men resumed formation. Laec mounted Grex and let the party pass by before falling in behind them. To his surprise, Çifta brought her bay alongside Grex. Two of her guardsmen guided their mounts into the trees and waited for them to pass, then fell in behind them.

"Where are you from?" Çifta asked.

"Stavarjak. You?" Laec let his reins rest on Grex's withers so he could rake his hair back and fix his tail.

"Kirkik. Do you know it?"

"Yes, though I've never been." Kirkik was another harbor city, like Cardagenya and Ashtaraq, but much wealthier than either, and used as a naval and military base by the King of Boskaya.

"You've mud on your back," Çifta pointed out.

Laec did his best to dust himself off.

Çifta watched him with an open expression. "You're fae."

"Yes."

"Me too. Well, half-fae, though I've no magic. I've heard the Stavarjakian queen has strong magic. Is it true?"

He gave a grim smile. "It's true. Too bad it doesn't reach this far. I would have been able to defend myself from those thieves."

Her brows arched. "You have magic?"

"Not this far from home, unfortunately. We Stavarjakians do not have much reason to venture from court. I knew my magic would wane but underestimated just how much. It is… humbling."

She laughed. "You'll have to learn the way of steel or you might not make it back. Why did you leave?"

Laec didn't disabuse her of the notion that he was not trained to use steel; after all, she hadn't seen him with a blade in his hand, much to his chagrin. "My queen sent me to aid her cousin, Queen Esha."

"Aid her how?"

Laec was surprised by how little her inquisitiveness bothered him. He generally disliked chitchat. Somehow, with this woman, it was nice, comfortable. "I suspect I'll learn that when I arrive. I have not been useful at court lately, so Elphame saw fit to make use of me abroad. And you? Why are you traveling to a foreign kingdom?"

Her petal-pink lips closed for a moment and she looked away, as though wondering how to answer. "I have a commitment in Rahamlar that my father arranged."

"And who might he be?"

Her gaze swung back to him, watchful. "Kazery Unya."

It took a moment for Laec to recall why the name was familiar. "That's why your carriage was parked in front of the Unya Trading office."

"Yes."

"And you've been sent to Rahamlar on business for your father," Laec concluded.

"Something like that."

She seemed hesitant to say more and Laec didn't push. They rode on in silence for a while. As the group traveled through the mist-laden, shadowed tunnels, Laec mourned what had been stolen from him. He comforted himself with the knowledge that everything would be replaced when he reached Solana. A growling stomach drew him back to the present.

Çifta broke the silence. "We plan to stop at my sister's estate for the night. It's just beyond Syrgana along a side road. It's beautiful, with large orchards and a very old manor. One more added to our party would be welcome. They have plenty of room." Laec was about to decline when she added, "I do hope you'll join us," in such a sincere tone that he stopped himself.

He gave her a nod. “Thank you for the invitation. I accept.”

Çifta’s smile widened. “Good. We should arrive just before dusk. I’m starving.”

Chapter Ten

Jessica

"Promise me you'll write." Clair drew Jessica in for a hug and squeezed her hard. "Ooo, I'm so jealous and excited for you!" When she drew back, Jess was astonished to see her friend's eyes glistening with moisture.

"I'll most likely be home in a few days, Clair."

"Maybe." Clair smiled through her tears. "But maybe not. If not, I expect letters. Maybe I can even visit you at the palace one day." She glanced at Hanna, who smiled and nodded.

Clair visiting Jessica at the palace seemed so far removed from reality that Jess could only stare at Clair, trying to imagine it. She shook her head, laughed, and hugged Clair again, her heart full of mixed emotions: hope, excitement, doubt.

After Jess said goodbye to Hanna, Tad and Finn, Marion walked her to the road with an arm around her, to where Ilishec's group waited. Jess had no luggage, so she used an old carpet bag that had been under Marion's bed for years. It was strapped securely to a saddle. The bag contained only one other dress, the dancing slippers she'd worn to the festival, a bonnet, a book and a small sack of coins. Since the party had only enough horses for Ilishec, Aster and their escorts—three guards, one woman and two men, all dressed in dark green boiled leather vests—Jessica shared Ilishec's mount. She settled in behind him and waved goodbye to her neighbors and Marion as they moved away.

Ilishec's mare had such a smooth gait that at first Jessica barely needed to hang onto the royal gardener for balance. Beazle nested in Jess's hair and the rocking sent him straight to sleep. Greta perched on top of her head. When there were fragrant wildflowers in the ditches, she fluttered along beside the road. The party stopped every hour to allow Jess to stretch her legs, but when she figured out that they were only stopping for her, she insisted they continue without breaks. Three hours later, she finally murmured to Ilishec that she needed to get down. They stopped at the crest of a hill and the guards positioned themselves with a view of the road, as well as the fields to the left and the forest to the right.

As Jessica stretched, the shadow of a large bird skimmed across the landscape: a bird of prey with golden feathers and a hooked beak. It swooped low over the party, stretching a pair of wickedly clawed talons. The bird angled itself on a rapid downward trajectory, banking toward one of the guards. Its talons swept forward and opened menacingly. Jess gasped, but the guard only lifted his forearm to receive the bird. He wore no protection against the raptor's long, sharp talons aside from his tunic sleeves. As the hawk folded its wings, the guard reached into a pouch and took out a piece of meat, which the bird snatched up. Two more filets disappeared before the magnificent bird stretched its wings and took to the air once more. The guard noticed Jess's open-mouthed stare. A dimple appeared beside his mouth as his mount danced in a half-circle.

Jess lost sight of the hawker's face as Aster handed her a water pouch. "Her name is Ferrugin," she said. "The hawk, I mean. And he is Regalis."

"Was he at the festival? He looks familiar."

"That's right."

Jessica tried to smile at Regalis, but the guard had his gaze on the sky. Jess took a drink, stretched again, then settled behind Ilishec once more.

The cool light of early autumn dusted the valleys with a soft haze of gold as they crested the last hill before Solana's outer gates. Ilishec stopped his mount to allow Jessica to take in the view. Her first sight of Solana City made her forget to breathe. A high wall encircled it with a blue-gray ring of stone. Behind the wall, tiled rooftops and colored spires peeked shyly or thrust themselves mightily into the sky where the first stars had begun to appear. A series of bells rang, high and cheerful. Far from the front gate—with what seemed like miles of city between the updrawn portcullis and itself—stretched the towers of the palace. Arched windows reflected the sunset, making the castle glimmer like a polished jewel.

"Welcome to Solana City." Ilishec urged his mount forward. "Beauty is our strength."

"Beauty is our strength," murmured the guards and Aster in a quiet echo.

They passed through a long, low valley populated by travelers on foot and horseback, some leading oxen pulling carts. Joining the flow, they slowed only when they walked beneath the yawning and toothed gates. No one stopped them, but Jessica counted no less than fifteen guards observing the traffic.

Their guards exchanged friendly words with the soldiers at the gate, and more than one addressed Ilishec with a respectful nod and the simple greeting of "Gardener." No one noticed her, seated behind him with her arms wrapped around his waist. Jessica's neck was sore from twisting her head to the left and the right, but she couldn't stop gawking around like a toddler.

The sounds of the city were unlike the sounds of her village. Dagevli was quiet by comparison, even on market day. The dirt roads muffled the sound of animal hooves and people didn't need to shout to be heard. But the moment they passed into the city, a cacophony barraged Jess like a volley of arrows. She shrank against Ilishec's back, a little intimidated. Horseshoes struck against stones, dogs yipped like street gangs arguing over territory, children laughed or cried while parents commanded, comforted or berated. Birdsong came from everywhere in every key possible, while a breeze picked up banners and flags, whipping them through the air with loud snaps. Every noisy thing seemed to echo off every solid thing, magnifying the symphony to a point where Jessica had to try not to clamp her hands over her ears. No one else in the party seemed bothered by the din.

They wound their way through the stone and marble streets, roadways deeply gouged from centuries of wagon wheels. Jessica realized she'd never be able to find her way back to the front gate without help. In places where the way was narrow and the buildings high, she even lost sight of the palace itself.

When the road became a shallow set of steps, the horses mounted them without trouble. These stairs took the party to a new height where tiled terraces and rooftops descended to the city gate far in the distance. When they arrived at the closed palace gate, they had to wait until the bolts were drawn back. The nondescript side door that opened to receive them was barely wide enough to fit a single rider. They emerged in a small and tidy courtyard. Jess's back, hips and legs ached. She watched eagerly as the guards and Aster dismounted and disappeared into what looked like a hole framed with ivy, leading their horses. Ilishec helped Jess down before leading her and his mare through the doorway into a second courtyard, this one milling with people and animals. Stable boys and grooms wearing blue-and-green livery materialized, lingering at bit and bridle. They held the horses until the saddlebags were emptied or removed, then led them away toward the stables.

While Ilishec was in conversation with one of the stable hands, Regalis led Jessica to a simple wooden bench. There was no sign of his hawk anywhere. Jess wanted to ask him about Ferrugin, but she was too tired.

"Aster will take you inside." Regalis patted her shoulder and left her there.

Jess sank onto the bench, grateful to be off the horse. Jessica winced as her thighs spasmed. The horses and the guards melted away. The shadows were long against the dirt of a nearby paddock and the cobblestones of a walkway which wound around the base of the palace.

Aster came over and helped Jessica to her feet, noting how stiffly Jessica moved. "Poor thing. I've forgotten how difficult my first long ride was. Come on, I'll show you where you'll sleep tonight."

"Where did Ilishec go?"

"Don't worry, you'll see him again tomorrow." Aster took Jess's elbow. "You can lean on me."

Embarrassed but too tired to protest, Jessica let herself be helped. They entered a hall flanked by furniture and closed doors, then mounted a set of spiral steps. The climbing improved the feeling in her legs as blood flowed again. Torchlight illuminated the carpeted way with a steady amber glow and Jessica wondered why the firelight didn't flicker. Aster paused at a wooden door with a hand-painted sign fixed to the gray planks, reading "Guest." The letters were beautifully flourished with small pink blossoms inside the "G" and at the base of the "t."

"Are you hungry? I can have supper sent to your room if you're too tired to come down to the hall."

Jess gave Aster a weak smile. "I'm more tired than hungry. If I don't lie down, I'm going to fall down. I'll be fine after a good sleep."

Beazle crawled out from her hair and flitted to the window ledge where he sniffed at the air. Greta fluttered to perch on one of the bedposts. Jessica collapsed on the bed, barely looking around.

"It's a little stuffy in here." Aster set down Jess's bag, then opened the shuttered window to let in fresh air. Beazle fluttered out into the evening. "This will be your room during Discovery. I understand you already have a few neighbors, but we expect a few to arrive tomorrow."

"How many?"

"I don't know. I don't actually have anything to do with Discovery. I only got involved because I wanted you to have a chance."

"Thank you." Jessica lay back against the pillow. The straw-stuffed mattress felt much the same as her own at home, only this one was larger. The feeling of laying out flat on her back with her legs stretched out was beyond glorious. She let her eyes drift shut for just a moment. Aster said something else, but the sound of her voice only sent Jess straight into the arms of sleep.

Chapter Eleven

Jessica

She poked her head out her bedroom door in the morning, hoping to find Aster. The hall looked larger and more colorful with morning light blasting in through the windows. Greta perched on Jessica's shoulder, but they'd left Beazle sleeping in the rafters. Distant voices lured them toward the stairs where a stained-glass window centered with a wreathed lion let in colored shafts of light. A pageboy wearing the Solana livery sprinted to the landing.

He waited for her, sunning her with a sweet smile. "Good morning, Miss Fontana. I've come to bring you to the hall to break your fast."

"Who are you?"

"I'm Graf, Miss. Follow me." His skinny, hose-encased legs took the steps back down in a flurry. They emerged on a busy hallway, humans and fae going in both directions. Everyone looked like they had somewhere to be. Graf and Jessica joined the flow and the smell of food grew strong. Jessica's mouth watered. After having gone to sleep without dinner, she was starving. Graf led her into a large hall where he directed her to help herself from the tables laden with food. What looked like hundreds of people were eating and chatting in groups of various sizes, with plenty of empty tables to spare. A high ceiling of thick wooden beams held banners and bunting in Solana's colors. Along the stone walls lay thick colorful tapestries, all depicting scenes of nature. Calyx picked from plates of food piled with colorful fruits and edible flowers. Servers carried carafes of colorful liquids, both opaque and transparent, and went about filling goblets.

But most astonishing was the presence of birds, insects of all kinds and mammals. Bees, moths, butterflies, wasps and hornets were everywhere. Colorful beetles trundled across the tables or perched atop hair or shoulders. Birds zipped around or perched on tapestries or sconces. A marsupial with a ringed tail scampered by Jessica's feet, playing with a smaller rodent with tiny ears and an excess of fur between its elbows and knees. Utterly enchanted, Jessica wanted to examine every creature. Greta joined a host of butterflies gathered around trays of fruit, potted flowering plants and pools of nectar.

Jessica looked for Aster but didn't see her. Feeling shy, she turned to speak with Graf, but he'd disappeared. She went to the nearest table and began to gather fruit, cheese and a couple of hard-boiled eggs.

"Leave room for the pastries."

Jessica turned. A boy with vibrant red curls stood there holding a plate of food, smiling at her openly. "I'm Oren."

"Jessica. Are you here for Discovery?" Jessica picked up a pair of silver tongs and piled strawberries on her plate.

He replied in an accent so thick it could have been speared

with a fork. “I arrived three days ago. I’ve already seen the gardener. You?”

“I arrived last night.”

“So you haven’t had your Discovery yet.” Oren fell in step beside her as they looked for a space to sit.

“No. What was it like?”

They found a clean table and sat down across from one another. “It was easy. I’ve been able to conjure flowers since I was eight so I didn’t have any trouble. My Discovery barely lasted twenty minutes.”

Jessica’s eyes popped. “Lucky you. Where’s your familiar?”

Oren gestured to where the majority of butterflies had gathered. “She’s over there by the fruit, the oversized yellowjacket. Her name is Jalla. Where’s yours?”

“Beazle, my bat, is upstairs sleeping and Greta is with the butterflies. She’s a glasswing.” Jessica speared a berry. She closed her eyes as the sweet juice refreshed her throat.

“You have two and one is a girl?” Oren shoveled a forkful of scrambled eggs into his mouth. “First time I’ve met someone with a familiar of the same gender—didn’t know that could even happen.”

“Really?” Jess felt uneasy. It probably wasn’t good to be so unusual, although she wasn’t sure how knowledgeable Oren was. He had the same farm-kid innocence as Jess herself. “Do you know many flora fae?”

“My whole family is fae, but I’m the only one with a familiar, so no. My village did have someone who went on to be Calyx once, but that was before I was born.” Oren shoved another bite of egg into his mouth. He ate just like the farm kids back home, fast but with obvious enjoyment.

"Do you know how many are here for Discovery?" Jessica asked between bites.

"So far, including you, there are a dozen hopefuls, but I heard a few more are yet to arrive. Only four positions are open"

A slender male server came over with a tray of juices. "Blueberry juice, melon puree, sour cherry, orange or lemon? Or I can have something made special for you?"

Jessica asked for the cherry and Oren took a mix of lemon and orange. When the server moved away, she asked, "Is all this just for the Discovery? Or is it like this every morning?"

"I think every morning is like this. All three of mine have been. I heard that when you become Calyx, they test you to see what kinds of foods your body likes best, since everyone is different." He lowered his voice. "You see the Calyx with the white hair and really long neck? Behind you to your right."

Jessica casually turned and spotted Proteas first, the handsome long-haired Calyx from the festival. The woman sitting beside him looked like she might provide illumination in the event no other light source could be found. Jessica faced Oren so she wasn't caught staring, though she badly wanted to ogle. "I see her."

"That's Gardenia. She has a special green drink made every morning, served in a special cup. If she doesn't get it, she gets emotional. *Gardenia* are fragile and finicky, so that means she is too. Or that's what I've heard." Oren stabbed a disk of sausage. "I eat everything. Nothing changes my mood."

"Maybe if you become Calyx, that will change." Jessica looked around. It wasn't difficult to spot the Calyx. Their features were exaggerated: Their eyes a little too big, eyelashes a little too long, hair a little too thick and shiny, movements a little too graceful and voices a little too musical. Meanwhile the hopefuls in the room could easily be mistaken for humans if their ears weren't visible. Some of them had spots on their skin or scars. They walked normally, not with a floating precision and grace. Some hopefuls had frizzy hair or dark circles under their eyes.

As Oren and Jessica talked about their home villages and their familiars, another flora fae entered the hall. Not a Calyx, from the look of her dull complexion and tired eyes—she had the bearing of a queen, though, and entered with her head up like she'd lived at the palace all her life. She had pale skin, dark hooded eyes and nearly black hair.

"Who's that?" Jessica asked. "A hopeful?"

Oren grimaced into his food. "That's Kei. She had her Discovery the same day as me. If you want to know what she's capable of, just ask her. She'll be happy to tell you. She'll also be happy to tell you that your ditch-loving weeds stink like ragwort and your species is about as valuable as pond scum." He looked at Jessica through his lashes. "Not my favorite person I've met so far, in case you can't tell."

Kei made eye contact with Jessica and subsequently lifted the tip of her nose, as if she detected something nasty smelling in the air. Jessica smiled at her. A smile given rarely failed to return a smile back, but Kei looked away. She ignored the tables of food and headed for a group of Calyx sipping from elegant goblets. She squeezed herself between Gardenia and Proteas.

"She's already so at home." Jessica felt a tingle of nerves in her belly. "Like she belongs."

Oren took a bite of toast. "Yeah, but it's not up to her, is it? It's up to the king and queen, and the gardener."

"Well, she might have some really rare, impressive talent."

"She might. Discovery is private, so who knows. But Kei

made sure that I knew that there were no other Calyx in the retinue right now that could bring up her species. She figures her spot is watertight." Oren's expression didn't hide his disdain.

Jessica made a thoughtful sound and sipped her cherry juice. "Maybe she's right."

Oren looked thoughtful. "Ilishec said that flora fae are not selected based on how fragrant or flamboyant their blooms are, but how they fit into the retinue overall. Meaning, they don't want duplicates and they don't necessarily just want the brightest colors or the biggest blossoms."

Jessica set her goblet down, thinking that made some sense. She doubted she'd be able to conjure anything at all. If Oren had been doing it since he was eight, surely Jessica would have done it by now.

"Have you brought up anything yet?" Oren asked, as though he could read her thoughts.

She shook her head.

He grinned. "I wouldn't worry. You have two familiars. You're sure to bring up *something*, and if you're not able to access the magic yet, there's no one better suited to help you than the royal gardener. He's been doing this for years and seen all kinds."

Jessica appreciated his positivity but figured he was mostly just being nice. "It's kind of you to be so encouraging."

He blushed. "When is your Discovery?"

"I'm not sure. Maybe today, but no one has told me anything. What are you going to do now that yours is over?" Jessica took a bite of a butter-soaked waffle.

"Explore the palace grounds, visit the stables. I like horses. They have some rare Terran breeds here. If I don't become Calyx, I want to be a breeder."

Jessica hadn't a clue what she wanted to do but it certainly didn't involve farming squash. "Sounds like you've got yourself all figured out."

"I've loved horses for as long as I can remember. Do you know the difference between a horse and a donkey?"

Jessica thought about it. "Horses are prettier."

Oren nodded. "Yes, but it's more than that. Horses will spook when startled, but otherwise they're fearless. They'll ride straight into a battle with no concern for their own welfare. A donkey will never do that. A donkey has a very keen sense of self-preservation. Horses are incredibly noble."

"A willingness to self-destruct is noble?" Jessica took another bite of waffle, her gaze wandering to a Calyx with a mantis on his shoulder that looked like she was made out of brown leaves.

"Of course! Battles change the course of history. Battles free the oppressed, unseat tyrants and protect laws that benefit the common people. They'll do the opposite, too, of course, but that's why every kingdom needs an excess of horses, not just warhorses but ponies and draft horses, too." Oren's eyes were bright, his tone enthusiastic.

"So if you don't get offered a place, you'll pursue your passion," Jessica said.

A red curl fell over his brow. "Yes, but there'll be time for horses later on. If I get offered a place, I'll be happy. I'll save enough to start my own stable. Maybe they'll let me work in the stables here, just as a hand, so I can keep learning. What about you? What do you want?"

She put down her goblet. "Before I heard of the Calyx, I thought maybe I would learn illustration and become a scribe, or mapmaking. Something that's useful and means I can travel. But now, there's nothing I want more than… this." She gestured to the room. "I love flowers, I always have, so the magic excites me—but more than that, I want to learn about… everything. Life. There has to be more to it than the change of the seasons, getting married, having babies. I want adventure, knowledge, to be inspired."

"You sound like my older sister," said Oren. "I bet you'd get along. She wants to be a fabricator."

"A fabricator of what?"

"You know, people who take drawings of inventions from Earth and try to recreate them. She's already fabricated something called a telescope that's supposed to magnify the stars so you can see their details."

Jessica gasped. "Does it work?"

Oren laughed and shook his head. "No. In fact, I couldn't see right for a few minutes after I looked through it. But she's only fifteen, so she's got time."

Jessica liked listening to Oren talk about his family and his hopes. He reminded her of a deep river with a gentle current. He pointed out a few of the other fae he'd met: a quiet boy named Tom, three girls from the south and a young boy from Stavarjak who had prominent ears who claimed to have seen the horses of the Vargilath, whom Oren spoke of in reverent tones.

Their dirty plates and goblets were soon whisked away and the number of breakfasters dwindled. As Oren and Jessica decided they'd go to the gardens and see if they could find Ilishec, Aster appeared.

"The gardener will see you in one hour, Jessica," Aster said, her eyes shining. "Come on, I'll take you to the hothouses. You don't want to be late. Hello. Who are you?"

Oren held up a hand in greeting, cheeks reddening. He opened his mouth but nothing came out. He had spent breakfast talking Jessica's ear off; now he couldn't introduce himself.

"This is Oren," said Jessica, after a long beat of silence.

"I'm Aster. Please to meet you."

Even Oren's ears were red.

"Do you want to come with us?" Aster asked him.

He nodded, and a moment later, Jalla zipped over and landed on his shoulder. She was a handsome wasp, with bright yellow stripes and big ink-drop eyes.

Jessica waited for Greta, then followed Aster out a rear exit.

They entered a courtyard and passed beneath the arches of an old stone aqueduct draped with ropy vines. Broad gardens opened before them with winding pathways going every which way, between patches of glistening lawn, ponds and brooks. Trees towered in the distance. Aster told them to wait outside a rustic building of gray timber beams with tall windows. This was Ilishec's workshop, she told them, and he'd be out to meet with Jessica soon. They sat on a marble bench and watched as Greta fluttered among the flowering hedges. Jalla buzzed away.

"I didn't know yellowjackets were pollinators," Jessica said.

"They are, but not as much as other insects. Jalla likes nectar and sugary foods, but she also eats grubs and beetles."

"That's the same as Beazle."

Oren switched the subject back to horses and Jessica only half-listened. Her belly grew tight with apprehension. What if she couldn't perform, even with Ilishec's help? What if she conjured some horrible plant of no value? Was it possible there were plants of no value? In Dagevli, the villagers cursed aggressive species. If not held in check, these weeds would strangle the precious fruits and vegetables they worked so hard to grow. What if Jessica could only conjure invasive botanicals no gardener would want? As she sat waiting, her anxiety grew.

When Ilishec emerged from the workshop and beckoned to

Jessica, she hopped up like she'd been struck by lightning. Oren had been midsentence and stopped talking abruptly. He took her fingers, squeezing them gently. "Good luck."

She thanked him and went to join the gardener.

"Ready?" He seemed so calm.

"I'm nervous," she croaked.

"And thirsty, from the sounds of it. Come on. Let's get you a drink. Nothing is more restorative than a cool glass of water."

Jessica hoped he was right because her knees had begun to tremble.

She followed him into a bright airy space with two big worktables and a lot of cupboards. Every surface was covered with something: books and scrolls, candles and tapers, potted plants, terrariums, pots of soil, gardening tools and measuring sticks, watering implements and a lot more she couldn't identify. It was not a greenhouse, exactly, but it had the feeling of one. The place smelled of vellum and minerals and dirt. Ilishec left the door open and air flowed through another open door where Jessica could see a hallway lined with wooden paneling.

The gardener went to a marble sink where water flowed from a copper tap wrought in the shape of a hummingbird. He filled a glass and handed it to Jessica. "Have you ever conjured anything green before?"

"No, but I've never tried." Jessica gulped her water down and handed the glass back. "Thank you. How do I start?"

"It's not difficult for a flora fae with the ability. Just quest mentally into the soil and will life to come forth." Ilishec gestured to a pot. "Give it a try."

Jessica's stomach shrank with doubt but she focused her gaze on the rich dirt, visualizing some tender shoot poking up from the surface. The dirt did not change. She closed her eyes and mentally asked something to grow, but when she opened her eyes, there was still nothing.

"Relax," said Ilishec. "It shouldn't be a strain."

Jessica blew out a breath and dropped her shoulders. Placing her hands on the table either side of the pot, she tried to forget that she was being watched. It was just her and the soil. Minutes passed. The bottom of Jessica's feet felt itchy. She squirmed but ignored the desire to bend over and scratch them. She narrowed her gaze by tightening her eyes, forcing her peripheral vision to become blurry.

"Where are your familiars?" Ilishec's voice broke her concentration.

She looked up. "Beazle sleeps during the day, but Greta is outside. Should I get them?"

Ilishec looked thoughtful. "Don't wake Beazle, he won't be at his best. But get Greta and we'll see if that makes a difference."

Jessica went outside and called her butterfly. The glasswing fluttered over, landing on her shoulder. Jessica returned to the worktable to try again.

"Let's see if we can make something grow," she told Greta, who was walking along Jessica's arm and flicking her antennae. Jessica focused on the soil and commenced all the same tactics she had tried before Greta had joined her. She let out a sigh and closed her eyes, laying her palms flat on the soil. She could feel nothing. When she'd exhausted everything she could think of and felt a little annoyed at the gardener for not giving her any help, she looked at him, defeated.

To her chagrin, he laughed and patted her shoulder. "Don't look so upset. I have a feeling about you. Will you meet me back here at midnight and bring Beazle with you?"

Ilishec didn't seem nearly as frustrated as she felt, and that frustrated her even more. "You think that will work?"

"I do. You have two familiars, but only one of them can be your true companion in magic. You've just demonstrated that it's not Greta."

Jessica blinked at him, jolted. Ilishec's words seemed so harsh, she wished he hadn't said them in front of Greta. She put her hand to her glasswing and Greta crawled onto her knuckles. "That… doesn't seem right."

"I know you love her, and she loves you, that will never change. What I've told you is not a shock to her. She is already aware that she is not your true familiar. She is happy to be with you all the same. She'll never leave you."

Jessica watched Greta flex her wings open. "But, if she's not my familiar, why is she with me?"

Ilishec took a moment before answering. "I'll explain that after we complete your Discovery."

Jessica worried her lower lip with her teeth.

"Don't be anxious," he told her with a chuckle. "It doesn't help."

"That's it?" She tried to keep petulance from her voice and didn't entirely succeed. "That's your advice."

"My dear, I've been doing this for many years. Are you going to trust me, or doubt me?"

Jessica blushed. "Trust you."

"Good. And are you going to trust yourself, or doubt yourself?"

She said what she felt he wanted to hear. "Trust myself."

"Also good." He waved her toward his open door. "I'll see you at midnight."

Chapter Twelve

Çifta

Gemma's plump elbows rested on the stone sill of the second-floor window of her bedroom where Çifta and Gemma had been catching up after dinner. She was indulging in her favorite sport of people-watching. When she'd married the elderly Hashe and moved to his estate, she'd claimed a bedroom for herself that was perfectly positioned to look down into the busy courtyard. Çifta was sitting cross-legged on Gemma's bed, leaning against a pillow set against the headboard, laughing as Gemma—her ample bosom resting on the windowsill—gave a running commentary about the goings-on in the courtyard.

"There's my dashing husband, stooped of back and with mismatched socks, bless him. He's got a bottle of wine tucked under his jacket, which he and the bookkeeper will polish off as they review the week's expenses. He doesn't know that I know that the accountant's office is where the majority of our spirits go to die, but it's better he doesn't realize that he married a snoopy wife."

"Just an adulterous one," Çifta injected with a laugh.

"Yes, well, lucky for me, old Mr. Hashe would rather I'm kept occupied than taking note of his less admirable habits. You see that box in the rear pocket of his trousers?"

"No, I can't see anything from where I'm sitting."

"Then let me describe it. It's small and square and hand-carved and it contains a very expensive substance known to induce an altered state. He's addicted to faerie wort. I keep telling him it'll kill him one day, but what do I know? I'm just the silly young wife." Gemma turned back to the window. "And there goes Endyr. Not the brightest guard in Father's ranks but definitely one of the bulgiest."

"Gemma!" Çifta blushed and covered her eyes. "Have you no shame?"

"No. You should know that by now. Shame is the enemy of fun. Haven't you figured that out yet? Did I ever tell you that I went through a phase when I was about eight or nine when I made an academic study of the bulges in men's pants—the ones in the front, not the back—trying to figure out what they were hiding and why they varied so much in size?"

Çifta had forgotten how much Gemma could make her blush. She still found it amazing that they were even related. "You did not! And you can't tell they vary in size when they're all covered up."

"Want to bet? I whittled it down to an art. Bulges can be misleading. They look big when they're actually small because the tip of the business sits where it can make a little tent, which looks like it's packed full but really it's mostly air."

"How did you know it was mostly air unless you were—"

"Spying?" Gemma waggled her eyebrows. "Because I was spying. The reason Father moved some of his men from the east wing of the manor to the west was because I'd winkled out all the best spyholes." She looked suddenly serious. "I wonder what kind of goodies Prince Faraçek is hiding inside his bottoms. You'll have to write and tell me."

Çifta choked and reached for the glass of water on Gemma's bedside table. "I'll do no such thing. You're terrible."

Gemma put on a look of false offense. "These things are important, little sister. This is the man you're going to spend the rest of your life with. He'd better have the goods to make you happy. If he doesn't, then he'd better be man enough to admit it, like my dear Hashe, and let you sort out an alternate source of happiness."

"A young prince would never be as generous as your old man," said Çifta. "And even if he was, I don't have it in me for improper dalliances."

"You say that now," Gemma warned, "because you're a virgin and you don't know what you'd be missing. Stop thinking about what's right or what's wrong in love and passion. Life is short. Sometimes you just have to have the guts to go after what you want." Gemma arched a blond brow and pursed her cupid's-bow mouth. "I did, and things turned out alright for me." She turned back to the courtyard and took a breath. "Oh, hello. Who is this fellow? Well, well. Speaking of bulges—"

Çifta thought she knew who Gemma was talking about. "Does he have red hair?"

"Hard to tell in the torchlight but it looks that way. Goodness, what a stallion."

"I'd tell you his stallion's name is Grex, but I have a feeling you aren't referring to his horse."

"No, I wasn't. Is he one of Father's new men?"

"No, he's a loner we came across in Syrgana. We got him out of some trouble. He'll travel with us as far as Solana."

"He's gorgeous. Is he approachable?"

"What do you mean?"

"I mean… does it seem like he'd be open to an invitation to become better acquainted with a plump naked lady in a hayloft?"

"Isn't one lover enough?" Çifta felt a hint of annoyance. Sometimes Gemma didn't know when to quit.

Gemma shrugged, her gaze still outside. "Percy is lovely, but a pass for one is a pass for a dozen, as far as I'm concerned. Estate life is boring. I miss Kirkik. I have to get thrills where I can. I wonder why he's not wearing a shirt."

In a moment, Çifta was off the bed and crowding her sister at the window. Gemma was right. Laec stood in a pair of breeches and nothing else, not even boots. His broad shoulders and pale skin were dusted in torchlight as he wrung out wet fabric. His saddle and bags and other gear sat on a low table near a trough, items set out in rows, like he was taking inventory. The muscles of his back flexed as Laec shook out and then hung the tunic over a rope strung between two posts where a pair of socks had already been strung up.

A warm feeling pooled in Çifta's belly. "He got muddy earlier. He was also robbed. I guess he doesn't have a spare outfit."

"Lucky for us."

Çifta barely heard her sister's comment. Why did she find even the sight of Laec's naked feet arousing? She should look away, she should retreat, leave Laec to do his laundry and sort his tack without being spied on, but she felt rooted to the spot. He was so… beautiful. He had all the features of a man at the height of maturity, plus something more, something Çifta could only credit to his faeness: The slightly too-long eyeteeth, the violent shade of his hair, the naked look of appreciation he'd given her in the streets of Cardagenya. Even now, remembering that look made her stomach float. How could he have such an effect on her? They'd only just met. Did he also feel the magnetism between them, or was she just being a silly, naive girl? He might even have a woman back in Stavarjak.

If Laec knew he was being watched, he didn't show it. A couple of guardsmen came over and began to talk with him. He stood with his weight on one hip, so casual, so confident. The way he moved his hands when he talked was mesmerizing. Çifta hadn't spent much time around fae men, all of her father's men were human, but meeting Laec made her wonder if all fae were so self-assured. He was accustomed to having magic. Was that what made him dauntless and unabashed? Even after he'd been beaten and robbed, he'd carried on with his day as though not much had happened. He'd admitted to feeling humbled, but he hadn't acted embarrassed. Maybe, back in Stavarjak, he was used to such clashes.

"—tongue back in your mouth." Gemma bumped Çifta's shoulder.

Çifta yanked her gaze away. She felt another flare of annoyance, but it wasn't at her sister, it was at herself. What was she doing? Drooling over a stranger when she was set to meet her own betrothed in the next day or two? And a prince, besides. A prince who was leagues more fae in appearance than Laec. She hoped she'd feel half this attracted to Faraçek. She went back to the bed but didn't sit down, instead she began to pace, until she felt Gemma's eyes on her, then she stopped and forced herself to sit. "What?"

Gemma narrowed her gaze. "You like him."

"I only just met him."

"Time isn't always a factor in attraction. I'm your sister. Your secret is safe with me, just like I know mine is with you."

"I don't have a secret, and I don't know anything about him."

"Is he nice?"

"He's… direct but aloof."

"Hmm. Is he single?"

"I don't know," Çifta cried, exasperated. "It doesn't matter. After tomorrow, I'll never see him again. I'm betrothed."

"You can dissolve it."

That brought Çifta up short. "What?"

"Father built an escape clause into the agreement." Gemma's look turned sly. "He didn't tell you? I shouldn't be surprised."

Çifta was astounded. "No. How do you know that?"

"It was my idea. I made him promise that whoever he betrothed you to, he would negotiate an eight-week window so you could get to know your fiancé. If you write to him that you're unhappy with the arrangement for any reason, he is within his legal right to dissolve it. If the deadline passes and you *are* happy, then the marriage will be ironclad and the bride price will be delivered. The terms are why it took so long for him to find a match for you. Not a lot of families would agree to such a clause. A canceled betrothal means rumors, and no one important wants to deal with those."

Çifta could hardly find words. "But I… You didn't… None of you had such a clause."

Gemma came to sit by her younger sister, tucking her skirts up under herself. She took Çifta's hand. "Things turned out okay for me because my husband doesn't want to be bothered trying to keep me satisfied, but when I first got here, I was miserable. Miserable and angry."

"I remember." Çifta had the letters to prove it.

"I was angry with Father for hitching me to a man who already had one foot in the grave. I understood my duty, so I didn't complain, but deep down, I felt betrayed. I thought he loved me more than that."

The urge to defend Kazery rose in Çifta's breast. "It's complicated with Father. He's risked so much to get where he is. We've all benefited from that. It's only fair that we shoulder some burden, too."

Gemma's marriage, like Fetre's and Una's, had increased the family's revenues by orders of magnitude. Çifta's would as well.

"Yes. I know. Duty over all." Gemma's mouth flattened. "I was still upset. I'm still not happy that he made the match for me that he did, but it helps that I have some freedom. I didn't want the same thing to happen to you. It's a testament to how much he loves you that he agreed."

Çifta squeezed her sister's hand. "Thank you. I've never received a better gift."

"You're welcome. I hope that Faraçek turns out to be everything you want, but if he's not, promise me you won't settle just to make our father happy. We're rich and powerful enough. We don't need Rahamlar in our pocket. Promise me that you'll take into consideration the rest of your life?"

Çifta hesitated. These were just the kind of words Kazery despised. Still, it warmed Çifta's heart that Gemma would have her happiness foremost in mind.

Gemma pushed her. "Don't just promise for yourself. Promise for me and Una and Fetre. We would have loved to have had a choice."

"I get that, and I love you for it, but I also promised myself that I'd go into this marriage with a positive and hopeful outlook. I can't greet my future husband thinking that I might need a way out. We weren't raised to give up."

"I'm not telling you to give up. I'm just telling you to be careful. That's all."

Çifta kissed Gemma's cheek. "I promise."

The first sound to wake Çifta was one of Gemma's maids stirring up embers in the fireplace with a poker. The second sound was thunder. Lightning flashed, illuminating the tapestry hanging near the door: a still life of a table laid out with an abundance of food.

Çifta sat up and stretched. "What time is it?"

The maid looked up from arranging logs over the coals. "Not yet six, milady. It will be a very wet day today. I heard you were planning to leave early, but you might consider delaying. The road to the main throughway will be a mud pit. I saw your pretty carriage when you arrived yesterday. Those wheels won't make it through."

Rain spattered against the windows, gently at first, then harder. Çifta dressed in one of her simple traveling gowns, wrapped herself in a shawl and toed into a pair of shoes. She grabbed the smallest of her sketchbooks, picked out three pencils, and headed down to the dining hall. The old windows rattled, pummeled by huge droplets, and the smell of eggs and bacon made Çifta's mouth water. She put a hand over her belly, feeling it growl.

The manor was built in the old style of large families, with a smaller dining room for private events, and a larger main hall with high ceilings and many tables where anyone from farm hands to ladies' maids and soldiers came to eat. Through an archway and three steps down was a large kitchen with many ovens, a fireplace, worktables and sinks. Bakers and cooks bustled about, turning scones and fresh pastries out to cool. Covered dishes sat in a row along one of the tables in the large hall. Çifta jumped out of the way as a cook carried a platter of steaming tomatoes by and deposited them into one of the dishes.

It was early, but the place was already busy.

Çifta said hello to Gemma's husband, who introduced her to a couple of local farmers there to discuss the turnover of land. As she filled a plate with scrambled eggs, toast and broiled vegetables, she overheard conversations about a new well being dug, a pair of foals that had recently been born and a leak that needed to be fixed in one of the sheep barns. Having come from a large manor that was almost always empty, Çifta found the atmosphere of the hall comforting. Even topics about troublesome things had an air of measured calm, and most faces were smiling.

Çifta found space to sit near the fireplace and left her heaping plate and her sketchbook on the table. She went to a sideboard where three copper teapots sat steaming. Each teapot sat on top of a second pot filled with water. Beneath the second pot sat a cylindrical reservoir with a latch on the side. As Çifta was sniffing, trying to discern what she was looking at, a maid appeared.

"Excuse me, milady." She carefully wielded a large set of tongs. She unlatched the door in the side of the cylinder and deposited hot coals beneath the kettle.

"That's ingenious," said Çifta. "Where can I buy one?"

The maid closed the door with the tongs. "There's a man that makes them in a village near Rahamlar. I saw you sniffing the pots." She pointed to them in turn. "The far one is mint, these two are black but this one has steeped for longer. This one is red and very strong. Don't forget to add water."

The maid moved away and Çifta selected the red tea, filling a cup with half the strong brew and half hot water. As she picked up her cup and turned, she almost ran straight into Laec. She gasped and kept the hot tea from splashing him by grabbing the cup, which singed her fingers. She put them in her mouth as a reflex.

"Good morning," she mumbled over her fingers.

"Morning. Sorry. Did you burn yourself? I shouldn't sneak up on people like that. Bad habit from my youth."

"Don't worry." Already, the pain was fading. "Sleep well?"

Laec nodded. "You?"

"Very. I was exhausted, and now I'm starving. Bring your breakfast? I'm sitting there." She gestured to her plate. She explained what she'd just learned about the teas to him, and took her cup to sit down.

As she reached the table, Gemma rushed up to her, rubbing at her hair with a towel. She was bundled in an overcoat and wearing muddy boots. She held a basket over one arm. "Good morning. Did you sleep well?"

"Yes. I didn't realize you were up," Çifta said. "Have you been outside? In this?"

Gemma's cheeks were flushed with pink, her eyes bright. "I love the rain. I've been down the road to the Brands farm. Mrs. Brand went into labor last night and the midwife could use a hand. I just came back to get some herbs." Gemma lifted a hand to wave at one of the maids. "Sorry about the floor, Misti!"

The maid waved at her with a smile, as though telling her to go.

"Should I come?" Çifta knew nothing about childbearing but felt she should offer.

"Thank you, that's kind. But no. We can't fit any more people into the room, anyway. I wanted to tell you that the roads will be horrible and you're better off waiting until tomorrow to leave."

"Yes, I've been told."

"Good." Gemma kissed her cheek. "There's new kittens in the barn. Have a nice day. See you when I'm back."

Çifta smiled as she watched her sister bustle away, all purpose and action. It was nice to see how well Gemma had warmed to country life, even if her marriage wasn't ideal. Çifta sat down and tucked into her breakfast. By the time Laec took the seat opposite her, she'd already wolfed down half her eggs and a piece of toast.

He speared a baked mushroom cap brimming with cheese. "Was that your sister?"

"Yes, she's helping a midwife down the road. She says the road will be bad. She's the second person to tell me that this morning." Çifta took a sip of the red tea. It was bitter and just as strong as the maid had said it would be.

"Can your business in Rahamlar wait a day?"

"Yes. One day won't make a difference. I'll talk to Endyr. It will make Gemma happy if we delay."

"You and Gemma are close."

"Yes, although I don't see her much now that she's married. I have two other sisters as well. Una and Fetre have the same hair and eyes as Gemma. They look like triplets."

"You and Gemma don't look much like sisters." Laec cut a long strip of bacon in half.

"That's because we have different mothers. My father's wife, Alana, died before I was born."

"He remarried, and that's where you came in?"

She sipped her tea, smiling at him from over the brim. "Not quite. These days, my father leaves the sailing of merchant vessels to other captains, but before I was born, he traveled a lot. Journeys were long, especially the ones that crossed the Valdivian."

Laec looked impressed. "I don't know anyone who has crossed the Valdivian, or the Ivryndian for that matter."

"My father was the first," Çifta said with no small amount of pride. "He returned home with a baby." She pointed at herself. "I was less than a year old, so I don't have any memories. My earliest memories are of my governess—and my older sisters, of course."

"Has Kazery told you about your mother?"

Çifta stirred her tea and blew off the steam. "He says she was beautiful and kind. My father told me that he wanted to bring her home to Kirkik, but she wouldn't have survived the journey, and she had family she didn't want to leave. Shortly before my father was due to leave, she became very ill. She convinced my father to take me, to raise me and give me the kind of life she knew she never could. She died a short time later."

"That's very tragic."

She set down her cup. "Not really. I mean, yes, it's tragic that she wasn't around to be my mother, but I don't remember her, and I had a wonderful childhood. I wouldn't trade my sisters or my father for anything. I have a portrait of her packed in my things. I look at it sometimes, but it's not painful. It's a bit like looking into a mirror, actually. Except for these." She touched her round ears. "I never grew up around fae. I feel as human as human can get."

"I could have guessed from your eyes that you are half-fae. Not many humans have eyes as pale as yours, but there is a whole nation of fae that have them. I'm surprised that Kazery brought you back from across the Valdivian. I would have guessed your mother was Silverfae."

"As in, from Silverfall?" Çifta cocked her head. "The nation north of yours?"

"That's the one. We don't mix much. We like it warm and they like it cold. But I've met my share of Silverfae, and they all had icy eyes. Some of them have irises as white as fresh snow."

This wasn't something Kazery had mentioned to Çifta before. "Huh. Maybe my mother came from a line of migrants."

"Maybe."

Çifta noted the slash between Laec's brows. "Why do you frown?"

"It's just that Silverfae don't migrate. There may have been an outlier or two over the centuries, but Silverfae are notorious homebodies. We from Stavarjak have that in common with them because we're weaker away from home."

"Maybe that's the reason my mother wasn't strong, because she left Silverfall. Or maybe she was the descendant of a Silverfae who crossed the Valdivian and never went home again." Çifta took a bite of broiled tomato.

"Yes. Perhaps." Laec still looked doubtful but didn't argue. He gestured to the sketchbook at her elbow. "What's that?"

"Oh. I like to draw. I try to sketch something every day if I can. I've been doing it since I was a little girl, but I've done it more since my sisters left home. I have a library full of sketchbooks back in Kirkik."

"May I?"

She pushed the sketchbook across the table. Sliding his dirty plate to the side, Laec pulled the book close and flipped it open. It opened to the sketch of a woman's face.

"It's Gemma!" He flashed a surprised look at Çifta. "You've drawn her perfectly. You're a master."

Çifta laughed. "Thank you. I guess I should have some talent. I've been doing it for long enough."

A maid cleared away their breakfast dishes, leaving their tea.

Laec flipped the page over, careful not to smudge the art. "And this is the mare you were riding yesterday. You really captured her, even the expression of her eyes."

Çifta sat quietly as Laec looked through her work. She had been shy about it when she was young, but she'd gotten over her bashfulness a long time ago. Most visitors who came to the family manor in Kirkik, or the summer home in the foothills, were treated to a viewing of Kazery's favorite drawings. He was proud of Çifta's ability and took the opportunity to brag about her whenever he could. She'd grown accustomed to compliments and knew she had skill, but she didn't do it for the attention. Sketching calmed her. It pulled her mind away from anything that might be troubling her, at least for a little while. It was an escape, as she zoned into smaller worlds. She'd long ago discovered that entire universes existed in the small things that people mostly ignored in daily life: a butterfly sipping nectar, the tender sprout of a new plant as it unfurls from the soil, even the way rain carved shapes in the road held fascination for her. She noticed things that others didn't. For instance, the way that Laec's smile went up higher on the left side of his mouth than on the right, and the little scar just under his eyebrow, and the other scar beside his eye that folded into his laugh line when he smiled. His gaze was one thing—that of an old soul—but his jaw and lips belonged squarely in the camp of youth.

She studied him while his eyes were on her work. Her fingers itched to pick up a pencil and sketch him while his lashes lay over his cheeks like that, and while the light from the fire played over the bones of his face and his long red hair.

"You don't miss much, do you." Laec glanced up. His expression changed when he saw the way she was studying him. Their eyes met and held for a long moment. The corner of his mouth twitched and he looked down again, flipping over to the drawing of a sunflower.

"No," she said softly. "Not much." She got the feeling he didn't miss much either, but rather than observing the world like an artist, he weighed it for meaning, like a fortune hunter pans for gold.

Why was her heart beating so fast? She looked at the remaining tea in her cup and set it away. She felt flushed with warmth and let her shawl drop from her shoulders. "How about you? Will you carry on with your journey in this rain?"

He glanced up briefly. "Grex gets surly in the rain. Hates mud. If I'm still welcome to stay, I'll wait until the road dries."

"Of course you're welcome. Since we have all day ahead of us… would you allow me to sketch you?"

He looked surprised. "Why?"

"Why not? I have to sketch something or someone. It's a daily ritual," she replied, even as she thought: *Because you're the loveliest mix of opposites I've ever seen. Warm, yet flinty. Sweet, yet dangerous. Mischievous, yet conscientious. Confident, yet subdued. And there's something else. As though—very long ago—you were a feral creature.*

He looked doubtful. “If that’s what you want, I suppose. I am good at sitting still.”

She beamed. “That’s music to my ears.”

Chapter Thirteen

Jessica

Jessica arrived for her Discovery a few minutes early, holding a blinking Beazle in her hand. The tiny bat was hungry, but Jessica made him understand he was needed and could hunt after they were finished. Greta was in her hair, refusing to stay behind.

Ilishec came down the garden path holding a pendulous lantern containing a soft amber ball of light. He wore a simple tunic belted at the waist and a pair of loose, mid-shin-length pants. He led Jess past his workshop to the adjacent building and through the hothouse door to where the air was humid and intensely fragrant.

Jessica's hair clung to her neck as her skin became instantly damp. She shadowed Ilishec down a long central aisle. Boxes of freshly churned soil lay in rows on the ground. Glass panes high above them were propped open and fresh night air drifted in, cooling Jessica's cheeks. She took several deep inhales. The air smelled so good. What was it about night air that was more delicious than day air?

Ilishec set the lantern on a side table and reached for a small box fastened to an iron rib of the house. He touched it and that same amber illumination appeared in the bellies of a dozen lanterns hanging from the ceiling.

Jess brightened. "It's magic?"

Ilishec approached a box of soil, rubbing his hands as if to warm them. "Not quite magic, no. It's one of the more useful technologies Solana has developed. Did you notice the large open rose window on the front of the palace when we came into the city?"

She wracked her memory but shook her head.

"Look for it next time. It's difficult to see from palace property. It gathers and channels the energy that powers our lights and other things throughout the city. The palace itself was built to hold and distribute the energy through its columns and piping, but its reach is limited. That's why villages like yours don't have this power."

Jess was quietly astounded. "If we built a rose window, could we attract this energy too? Our villagers would love the convenience of lights you can turn on with a simple switch."

Ilishec raked his fingers through the dirt, loosening it. "It's not my expertise, but I believe the architects who do this can only erect these energy-channeling buildings in certain locations. You can ask one of the carpenters we have on staff if you're curious. Let's focus on the task at hand, shall we? Just the way we discussed earlier today, I want you to focus, but I also want you to put your feet in the soil. Where are your familiars?"

"Beazle is there." She pointed to the upper boughs of a tall flowering shrub. "Greta is…" She put her hand up to her hair to discover that the glasswing had taken flight without her noticing. "… somewhere nearby."

"That's fine. Now, it's important you block out all other thoughts and distractions. Take your time. Don't allow my presence to pressure you. Pretend you're alone. It's just you and the dirt." Ilishec stepped out of Jessica's line of sight.

She took off her slippers and stepped into the nearest box. The soil was cool and soft and was as pleasant as dipping one's feet into a freshwater brook. She felt rather than saw Beazle flutter about near the glass ceiling. She closed her eyes, picturing life as a green light all around her, lining the stem of every plant and the curve of every leaf. She imagined speckles of light inside the soil under her, glimmering like constellations. She imagined she could feel energy humming through the soles of her feet from the dirt, warm and tingly. She imagined the air filling with floral perfumes and ivy wending itself around every pillar.

"Jessica." Ilishec's voice broke through her fantasy. "Look."

She opened her eyes, the little hairs of her body spindled to standing. The box she stood in was full of plants. Small pink and white flowers with bright yellow centers carpeted the soil at her feet. Layered over the edge of the box and across the floor was a vine with heart-shaped leaves and ghostly white blossoms shaped like little trumpets. Clustered in a corner were hardy, upright flowers with tubular yellow heads. And there was more, species she had never seen before. A heady fragrance filled the air. The pride she felt at having successfully conjured them was quickly overshadowed by surprise. "But there's so many!"

Ilishec helped her out of the box. "Let's identify what you've grown, shall we?"

The gardener knelt to smell and inspect each plant. "These little ones"—he touched the clumps of delicate daisy-shaped blossoms with short stems—"are called *erigeron*, or daisy fleabane." He plucked one and handed it to Jessica. "Every Terran plant has multiple names. You'll learn more about that in your classes if you are offered a place."

"I've seen this before." Jess held up the flower. "It grows in ditches back home."

Ilishec scratched his chin, nodding. "Yes, it's a hardy type that prefers to be left alone."

"So, it's a weed?" Disappointment pooled in her stomach like cold water. She looked around. "In fact, they all look kind of weedy."

"Even if they are weeds, don't think they aren't of value. You've brought up a lot here. You're very prolific, which is unusual for a flora fae. The majority conjure only one genus, one species, or one subspecies." Ilishec illustrated with his hand that genus was higher than species, and subspecies was below both of the other two. "I've even met fae who can conjure only one varietal, meaning they control a single minor species subdivision. Don't worry about the jargon. It's not important right now. My point is that you appear to be among a rare group who can conjure multiple genera. Nine, if this collection is complete. What we can learn, should we get the opportunity to work together, is just how deep within each genus your talent runs."

Jess felt a little dizzy. "Meaning?"

"For example." He gestured to a tall patch of tiny yellow flowers on long stems. "You can bring up *solidago*, also known as goldenrod. But *solidago* comes in one hundred and twenty species. Perhaps we'll have a chance to answer whether you are capable of bringing up all one hundred and twenty species, or only this one. Or perhaps forty or fifty of them."

"That sounds like a lot of work."

Ilishec grinned. "It is."

Jessica gazed at the overflowing garden box. "What else?"

"I see the beginnings of *datura*, not to be confused with *brugmansia*. I see *ipomoea alba*, or moonflower. I see *caprifolium*, or honeysuckle, which is partially responsible for the lovely perfume we're smelling right now. I see also *atropa*, *cleome* and *cestrum*, the latter of which also goes unofficially by the name of jessamine." He plucked a cluster of tubular flowers that looked almost black. "It's hard to tell in this light but these are an unusual shade of deep scarlet. They're very attractive in daylight."

Jess held the flowers to her nose. The scent was green and heady. "So nice." She could hardly believe she had brought these flowers into existence.

Ilishec got to his feet and fetched the notebook from the workbench. He opened to a blank page, hovering the pencil over the page, then paused, seeming to rethink what he was doing. He closed the book again. "I'm quite excited to sketch these, but I think given the late hour and the poor lighting, it will be a better task for tomorrow."

"You have to draw them all?"

"Not necessarily me. I work with several artists who help us keep up to date with all the documentation." Ilishec helped her to her feet. She found her slippers and put them on.

They admired the box of plants for several minutes.

"Well, you've done it. Congratulations."

"Thank you. Why did it work at night, but not during the day?"

Ilishec's expression became cautious. "Because of Beazle. He's nocturnal." He ran a hand through his hair and let a long breath out through his nose. "Now that we have finished your Discovery, I have a duty to explain something to you, but please understand that I would much rather your mother had told you this before you and I ever met."

Jessica went still. For some reason, she feared what he was about to say. It was going to be something bad—she could feel it in her bones. Beazle, responding to her unease, flapped around overhead before landing on her arm and clinging to the fabric of her sleeve.

Ilishec put a steadying hand on her shoulder. "I could tell when I met you and your mother that she has never told you that you were born with a twin. I am sorry to be the one to upset the apple cart, but knowing this is critical to understanding your magic."

Her jaw went slack. "A… twin?"

She immediately knew that Ilishec was telling the truth. So much of her life suddenly made sense where it hadn't before. She loved Greta dearly, but she and Beazle understood each other without having to guess at what the other was thinking. Her mother's distant relationship to Greta and Beazle made more sense now too. Greta must remind Marion every day that she'd lost a child.

"Why…" Jessica whispered. "Why didn't she ever tell me?"

"I can't say, but now that you know, I hope the doors of communication between you and your mother will open fully. I would have asked her permission to tell you but there wasn't time to get her alone, and I have a feeling if I did ask, she would have said no. Whatever her reasons are for keeping your twin a secret, they're wrong, so in this case it's better to ask forgiveness than permission. We have to understand who you are. That is critical to categorizing you properly."

"So, Greta belonged to my twin." Her heart felt sore and swollen. Her sinuses tingled with tears.

"Yes, and because she's female, it means your twin was male."

A storm was brewing in Jessica's body. Her skin was covered with goosebumps. She was silent for a long time.

Ilishec removed his hand from her shoulder but inspected her face. "Are you alright?"

She wasn't, but there was nothing the gardener could do about it. Jessica needed to be alone to process what she'd just learned. She moved to a topic that was less prickly and confusing. "Does this mean I won't be able to conjure plants in the day?"

"Not at all," the gardener said. "Now that we've opened the tap, so to speak, you'll be able to conjure any time you wish, and you'll learn to feel the differences between the species and grow plants with specificity and at will. As for why you needed it to be dark to find your powers, that is very simple. All of the species you've brought up attract bats. That's their commonality."

Jess thought this made sense too, but she was finding it difficult to focus. As much as she enjoyed having the gardener all to herself, she really needed to be alone.

Ilishec took note of her distraction and headed for the box that powered the lights. "Come, it's past time for bed and you've earned a good sleep. The day after tomorrow, you'll be required to show your talents to the king and queen, so you'll need your rest. Tomorrow, you'll meet with the tailor. She'll measure you and make a costume for your presentation."

Jess felt so unprepared to digest this information that it bounced off her. Her response was a feeble "Okay."

The gardener powered off the lights and she followed him out of the hothouse. It was a wonder she made it back to her room with her mind barraged by a torrent of questions. She had been born a twin! What had happened to him? And why had Marion kept his existence a secret from her?

Jessica emerged with Beazle snuggled in her hair the following morning to find a young woman standing quietly beside her door. Jessica, mid-yawn, came up short just before treading on her. "Oh! Good morning."

She wore a cream-colored sleeveless tunic pinned at each shoulder with a glossy, lacquered brooch in the image of a violet. Her long dark hair was parted down the middle and combed straight back behind her ears. Tiny violet earrings no larger than peas sat in her earlobes.

"Morning, Miss Fontana." The girl dipped a curtsy. "I'm Gabrielle, your couturière. You can call me Gaby. I'm to take you to Moth—uh, the Tailor's Den to be fitted for your presentation tomorrow. It's important that we dress you to show off your magic and your beauty. If you want to be offered a place here, the first impression must be perfect." Gaby paused and then added, "After you break your fast, of course. The Royal Tailor, Olinya, is waiting for you. Whenever you are finished eating, I will escort you to her."

Jessica's stomach was a jumble of knots. She'd hardly slept. She'd imagined how the conversation about her mysterious twin might go between herself and Marion a thousand different ways as the moon traveled across the sky. She'd still been turning the problem over in her mind when she opened the window to let Greta out at dawn to forage in the garden. Jessica was at a complete loss in coming up with a good enough reason to keep such a secret. If she wasn't offered a place here, the moment she arrived home, she intended to sit Marion down and not let her rise until she'd explained every last detail about her twin. If she was offered a place, she'd have to write a very serious letter asking her mother to come to the palace to explain herself, though how she would word it was beyond her. Would she tell her in a letter that she knew? Or was it better to just ask her to come and tell her in person so she could see her reaction? Maybe Ilishec would help her figure out what to do.

"I don't think I need breakfast," she told Gaby. "You might as well take me to this Olinya right away."

Gaby grinned. "Excellent, Miss."

Jessica followed her down a wide hall filled with portraits and sculptures. They turned down another corridor, and another, and another, until Jessica felt they must have crossed half the palace. At last they climbed a set of sweeping steps and came to a large gallery with many windows. An army of forty or fifty people labored in this space. They worked alone at sewing machines, or clustered around tables in small groups conversing with a passion that made it apparent they cared greatly about their work. At least twenty long tables were positioned throughout the room, and at the end of each table were the kind of dummies that Jessica had seen in the tailor's shop in Dagevli. Each dress form wore a different creation, many only half-finished: gauzy dresses with diaphanous skirts that sparkled, close-fitting military-style jackets with shiny buttons, form-skimming dresses of exquisite lace overlaying richly colored silks, simple tunics in fabrics so light they moved when someone passed in a hurry. Shoes, boots and slippers of all colors and materials lay scattered around and cobblers tinkered at their molds.

Gaby was several meters ahead when she realized Jessica had stopped and was staring around. The couturière returned, a smile lifting the corners of her mouth. "This is a whole new world for you. Isn't it marvelous?"

"It's… I'm—" Jessica was lost for words, but she finally found her legs again as Gaby nudged her along. "I suppose these tailors and cobblers make clothing and shoes for the king and queen?"

Gaby laughed and a few of the workers looked up, dewy with sweat. Jessica spied a man with strange headwear; a band of leather hugged his cranium, and from the band a spindle like an arm bent in front of his face. Fixed at the end of the spindle was a pair of spectacles. He grasped the spectacles and pulled them in front of his face as he bent to focus on his work.

"These workers are solely for the Calyx. The royal household is outfitted by another group, on the other side of the palace."

Jessica almost tripped. "But… there are enough workers here to outfit an entire city."

"Not the way we do it." Gaby led Jessica to another set of steps. "The Calyx are famous for a reason. We are part of that reason."

Jessica couldn't comprehend what Gaby was saying. She'd seen the Calyx perform—ten of them, anyway. They were outfitted nicely but their clothing wasn't much different than that of the villagers they were sent to entertain. Surely this army of craftspeople were bored and listless most of the time? Surely it wasn't a full-time occupation to outfit fifty fae?

When they reached the top of the steps, Jessica's wonder only increased. Bolts of fabric arranged by color filled endless rows of shelves. A group of young people dressed similarly to Gaby milled about at worktables. Oren perched on a stool near one table, deep in discussion with one of the workers. They were bent over some paper, the worker sketching while they talked. At another table was Kei, laughing with her own retinue of workers. She positively glowed to be at the center of such attention.

"Come." Gaby led Jessica toward a carpeted section surrounded by mobile, free-standing mirrors. A dais occupied the middle where people being fitted could see themselves from any angle.

A striking woman emerged from behind these mirrors. She saw Gaby with Jessica. "My darling, here you are to meet Olinya."

When Olinya smiled, Jessica understood at once that she was Gaby's mother. The two shared identical features, only, Olinya's years showed on her face in a network of fine lines. Her hair was just as dark as her daughter's and fashioned similarly with a part down the center, the two sides combed back and tucked behind the ears. Olinya came straight to Jessica and took her hands, inspecting her with a little smile. "Oh yes. We shall have fun with this one, shan't we?"

Gaby momentarily disappeared, then reappeared with a little notebook. She held it open for her mother to see. Jessica made out drawings done in colored pencil of blossoms and plants. It took her a moment to realize that the drawings were all sketches of the species Jessica had brought up the night before.

She gaped. "How did you—?"

Olinya interrupted her. "Quite a variety we have here. Nothing too opulent or flashy, low maintenance, sturdy, fragrant, and oh—" She arched an eyebrow. "A couple of noxious genera as well, I see. This should be fun." Olinya made a flippant gesture and Gaby withdrew the notebook.

Jessica was made to stand on the pedestal in the middle of

the room. Olinya gave off two resounding claps and stepped back. Eight girls, all dressed like Gaby but with differing colored belts and brooches, closed in around Jessica. Two of them manipulated her limbs to take measurements while another two recorded everything. Two had sketchbooks and stood back, laying down a flurry of sketches. Meanwhile, Olinya gave instructions to Gaby and the last girl, making gestures toward the bolts of fabrics. The girls made notations, then rushed off together.

All this for someone who hasn't even won a place in the retinue yet, thought Jessica.

When her measurements had been taken, the workers vanished. Olinya crooked a finger and Jessica followed her to a worktable where stacks of books of massive proportion sat in towers.

"Let's discuss your hair. Should you join the Calyx, you will find that the majority of parties you attend here will require you to wear your hair up. It allows us to show off your blooms in more artful and appealing ways. However, for your first presentation, I recommend you wear your hair half down." She put her hands in Jessica's hair and began to work with it, brow tight with concentration. When her fingers brushed against Beazle, Olinya snatched her hand back with a yelp. She splayed a hand against her ample bosom in a comic parody of shock.

Beazle emerged, tottering sleepily along Jessica's shoulders before winging his way to the ceiling.

Olinya burst into laughter. "Oh, he gave me such a fright. What's his name, my dear?"

"Beazle, Ma'am."

"Call me Olinya, darling." She scanned the rafters. Beazle was so small it would be impossible to spot him unless he was flying. He'd hidden himself so he could sleep in peace. "He can't stay up there, my dear. I have a fortune's worth of materials in here and it will not do to have bat guano landing at random."

Jessica blushed. "Beazle knows better than that. As long as he can get outside, there's no need to worry." She gestured to the row of windows where several were open.

Olinya smiled. "Very well. I'm afraid I haven't much experience with mammal pollinators, and the few I have encountered were inclined to make messes."

"Does Beazle need to attend the performance tomorrow?" Jessica felt borderline nauseous when she said the word "performance."

"Of course, the royals. They will want to meet him. But if you're asking whether he will require an outfit, I'm pleased to inform you that the answer is a hard no. We stop short of the ridiculous here." Olinya winked. "But only just."

She eyed Jessica's locks with dramatic dubiousness. "Now, promise me you haven't hidden any other rodents in your hair. We have a lot to do and only a day to do it in."

Chapter Fourteen

Çifta

As they drew near to the crossroads, and Çifta saw the signposts up ahead, her heart felt heavy. She and Laec had spent the entire rainy day together, playing games, talking, eating and visiting the barns to view the livestock. Rain hammered the barn roof as they cuddled a new batch of kittens and watched foals and fillies frolic in the wet grass beyond the big open door. They fed apples to cows, and even watched the birth of a calf in the dairy barn. By day's end, Çifta reeked of manure and had to order a bath. She slipped into the hot water feeling deliriously happy and wishing she could go on living this kind of life, as long as Laec was there too. They had ridden side by side from the estate, talking and laughing the whole time.

They saw the place where they were to separate at the same time and fell silent. When Laec mumbled something, she had to nudge Caramel closer to Grex and ask him to repeat himself.

"I said, it feels like I've known you forever."

Çifta felt momentarily winded. "And here I thought it was just me."

Laec shot her an open look. "Will your business in Rahamlar keep you long? You could visit Solana City afterwards. it's only a little out of your way back to Kirkik."

Shame burned in Çifta's gut. She found it hard to look at him. "I would love to visit Solana City one day, but I have no plans to leave Rahamlar. It will be my new home. I'm betrothed to the prince."

"I see." His expression snapped shut like a flytrap plant.

The shutters that fell over him caused a physical pain in Çifta's heart. She felt like she'd just watched a turtle retreat into its shell. "I'm sorry. I should have told you sooner. I didn't expect us to become… friends."

Laec waved a hand but didn't look at her. "No, no. It's none of my business, and I'll probably be too busy at the Scented Court to show a tourist around anyway. Some friends are for a lifetime, some friends are for a short time."

His words stung.

"You would be welcome to visit me in Rahamlar." The moment she said it, Çifta regretted it. How would she know if he would be welcome? It wasn't her kingdom yet. She sounded naive, even foolish. Whatever bond she and Laec had developed in the short time they'd known one another, if allowed to continue unchecked, would cross the line from friendship to lover in short order. She'd lost count of how many times she'd thought about kissing him the day before. She couldn't allow their relationship to continue. Doing so would be stupid and risky. Further to that, unlike Solana, Rahamlar was not a tourist destination. Even if she had never met Laec, she would love to visit the city of the Scented Court. But people only visited

Rahamlar for trade or business. While she'd heard it was not quite ugly—because it was very green thanks to the rivers—it was crude and brutal in its architectural style, and the citizens reflected that style in their culture.

Laec chuckled. "I'd have to come over that." He pointed at the huge mountain looming straight ahead of them. A giant of the Vargilath range, the rugged peaks thrust into the sky, shrouded with clouds. The distance on a map between Solana and Rahamlar was short, but in reality, the journey from one to the other was arduous, steep and cold.

He added with a sly look that made her pulse speed up, "Also, somehow I don't think your prince would appreciate my visit."

His acknowledgment that their friendship might threaten her marriage did strange things to Çifta's emotions. So he did feel the same as she. It made her simultaneously feel like she was floating but also on the edge of tears.

"I'm sorry," she whispered, but Laec was looking at a flock of vultures feasting on a carcass, and didn't seem to hear her.

Çifta's retinue drew to a halt at the crossroad, rather than turning and carrying on without stopping. It made her blush when Endyr glanced at her, then looked away, waiting for her to give the signal to carry on. How could he tell that she needed a minute to say goodbye to Laec? Was she really such an open book? That wasn't good. She needed to grow up. She needed to keep her feelings private and behave properly, not like a wanton peasant with a crush.

Since the previous morning, she and Laec had spent almost every waking moment together. Çifta had watched for Gemma's return so she could spend time with her sister, but Gemma had come home from the birth too exhausted to even eat. So when

Gemma went to bed, Çifta joined Laec for the evening meal. It had felt so natural that they be together. Of course Endyr had noticed, and so had the rest of her father's men. She was just thankful that they were loyal. They wouldn't sink so low as to spread rumors. Some of them had been in her father's employ when she was a baby and viewed her as a surrogate daughter. She did wonder if Endyr might report to Kazery her behavior with the red-headed fae male, just as a matter of duty. She hoped not, but there was nothing she could do about it now.

"Good luck," she said to Laec as they came to a standstill. She wanted more than anything for them to dismount so they could hug. But Laec made no move to dismount, so neither did she.

"Good luck to you too, milady." Laec gave her a polite smile as he fingered his reins, appearing eager to move on. It was the first time he'd called her milady, and not used her first name, since they'd met in Syrgana. "I hope your marriage to the prince is happy and prosperous."

"Thank you. I hope you enjoy the Scented Court." She hesitated, wishing there was some way she could show him how much it was hurting her to say goodbye. Finally, she said simply: "I'm glad we met."

He nodded politely, saluted Endyr, then nudged Grex. As he began to canter down the road to Solana, Çifta found it difficult to tear her eyes away from him. She took some satisfaction in observing that Grex had no apparent problems cantering in mud, in contradiction to what Laec had told her the morning before. She wondered if Laec would look back, maybe even wave. When he didn't, she nudged Caramel.

"Move along," Endyr called to the men.

The carriage wheels groaned as they rolled through the

soft earth, but the rainwater had drained away, so there was no getting stuck.

Çifta took a deep breath, feeling the humidity increase as they traveled. She thought of her sketchbook, tucked away in a trunk. She had done three different drawings of Laec. Yes, maybe some friendships were meant for a short time, but it was comforting knowing that she could gaze at his likeness whenever she wanted and remember the rainy day they'd spent together.

Part Two

Chapter Fifteen

Laec

THE ROSE WINDOW and turrets of the palace made Laec stop and stare. Glassless and empty, yet somehow not appearing incomplete, the rose window seemed lit with a hue of gentlest blue. Standing with his tired feet on stones that leached the heat of the day into his soles, Laec felt something; not a tingling, not quite a hum, but a soft resonance. Grex felt it too, tossing his head and whickering. The stallion nuzzled Laec into motion and the pair continued to the gates, where Laec presented the ring Queen Elphame had given him. Her seal granted him immediate entry. The guards even wished him a good evening.

Laec wondered at the organization and civility of it all. Queen Elphame's kingdom was beautiful but in a wild, untamed way. A sense that life could not and should not be too manicured, too civilized or organized pervaded every event, every banquet, even the clothing. The fae of Stavarjak liked to wear eccentric embellishments: huge feathers, strange leaves, dried insects, fake fruit.

Here in Solana—the city, at least—the outfits had meaning and practicality. It was easy to see who served the castle and—most of the time—in what capacity. Solana's green-and-blue livery with white trim, and the wreathed lion's head sigil, was apparent in some way or another on palace staff, stable hands, servants and guardsmen.

Horses and dogs—some pulling carts overflowing with goods—funneled left where a downslope led to the stables. Beyond that, a training ground was just visible. A horse lifted its tail and made a deposit on the cobbles of the courtyard, and almost before the load hit the dirt a stable boy leapt into the fray with a shovel.

A groom too young to grow a full beard greeted Laec and offered to take Grex. Laec gave him some instructions and let the boy take the bridle. He stroked Grex's nose so the stallion could smell him.

"I've fresh oats and some carrots with his name on them, sir," the boy said with a serious and respectful air. As Laec gave Grex into the boy's care and turned toward the palace, he heard the boy murmur to the horse in a gentle tone.

Laec climbed the slope to the open courtyard.

"May I offer my assistance, sir?" A pageboy in livery, who couldn't be more than twelve, dropped into a bow he appeared to have learned recently.

Laec smiled. "Probably. I'm to present myself to Queen Esha but I'm unsure of where to go."

The boy's little body seemed made of wires as he nodded, eager to help. "Follow me, please."

The boy kept just below running speed and led Laec across the courtyard, down a long walkway and through a garden where women harvested fragrant herbs. Small white butterflies flitted everywhere as the women quietly sang together. The pageboy led him into the palace and down a series of long passages, none of which were straight. Laec wondered if the architect had any sense of economy of space.

The pageboy stopped at a set of steps and gestured that Laec should climb them. "The queen's attendants will see to you, Sir Laec. I'm not permitted to go any further." He scampered off.

Laec trekked up the stairs and found a long row of windows overlooking the city. A woman met him at the top. She showed him where he could pour himself some cold water and disappeared to relay the news to a superior.

A night caller announced the time, and some blocks away another echoed him. A sense of stillness came over Laec. He could see why people who came to Solana didn't like to leave. Many who visited made applications for residency but only those with some skilled trade or resources that could be put to the kingdom's benefit were accepted.

Laec had no desire to leave Stavarjak, the balmy highlands where Elphame reigned was his home, but he saw no harm in taking note of the practices perfected here that might benefit his sometimes-chaotic kingdom. Seelie fae were good-natured but resistant to being organized or keeping to a schedule. Laec himself grated against it but could see the benefits of it around him now and mused that perhaps it was something to be desired. Stavarjak's castle was pretty, but it was also bizarre and nonsensical with strangely decorated rooms, disparate and illogical pockets of magic and disarray among the servants and staff. At times, it seemed like there was no one in charge, and if things were done properly, it was a miracle to be celebrated with reveling and pilfering from the kitchens.

"Queen Esha will see you in one hour."

Laec turned to see the same maidservant as before. She had two others with her. One of them took the empty cup from his hand with a curtsy.

"Perfect." Laec was dusty and smelled of horse and sweat. The servants here were so well dressed and clean that they made him feel self-conscious, even though he, as a courtier and guest of Queen Esha, was above them in the hierarchy. Laec took off his cloak and rolled it, tucking it under his arm. "Might it be possible to have a bath before I am presented to the queen?"

"Certainly. We have been instructed to give you the Violet Suite."

The Violet Suite had, unsurprisingly, violets painted on the ceiling. Open windows overlaid with a gauzy curtain let in night air that smelled like jasmine and wisteria. While Laec settled his things and took off his traveling clothes, one of the maids filled the tub in the adjacent bathing room. Before Laec was finished cleaning himself, a male servant came into the room with a tray of fruit and juice. Laec ate, washed and put on the best clothing he had brought. He shrugged into the tunic and frowned down at it. He'd forgotten this one was a little itchy. Nothing to be done about it now. He emerged to find the same male servant waiting outside his door.

"I'll take you to the queen." The servant dipped his chin, then turned to lead Laec down the corridor.

Stopping outside a set of double doors, the servant rapped and a moment later they were let in to a room that smelled like lilies. The chamber was a parlor, but it wasn't quiet or relaxing; rather, it seemed full of people reading while sunk into the plush furniture, playing a piano in the corner and chatting by the windows. A group of children were being taught to make letters and illustrations. At least three small dogs lay about the place. A puppy lay curled up on a cushioned stool at the feet of a woman in a diaphanous gown. She sat on a couch with a small girl tucked into her side. The girl had a picture book open on her lap.

"Laec of Stavarjak," the servant announced.

She looked up with a smile. "Laec Fairijak?"

He bowed. "Your Majesty, it's an honor."

She held a hand out and he dropped a kiss on the back of her small-boned wrist.

"I was expecting you yesterday."

Laec straightened, studying this queen. How different she was from his own. Queen Esha had large eyes, a short cap of curly dark hair and was much tinier than Elphame, who was willowy but very tall. Where Elphame oozed power and ethereal authority, Esha looked like a woman who enjoyed mothering and quiet fireside chats. She held herself with a quiet elegance.

"I had some trouble in Syrgana," Laec explained.

Queen Esha gestured that he should sit on the chair across from her. He did, explaining in understated terms that he'd been set upon by brigands and then rescued by a passing group of soldiers. Queen Esha listened quietly, concern etched on her features. The little girl looked up from her picture book as Laec talked, to stare at him with open curiosity.

"But you are seelie," the little girl exclaimed when Laec got to the place where he'd been rescued. "Do you have magic?"

"This is Princess Kara," said the queen. "My daughter."

Laec made to get up and greet her properly, but Queen Esha indicated he shouldn't. "Please, dispense with formalities unless we are in public. They are so tiresome."

Laec might have considered the group in the room to be public, but none of the others had paid him any more attention than a cursory glance.

To Kara, he said, "I am seelie, that is true. I was born in Stavarjak. Do you know where that is?"

"In the north," said the princess in a soft tone. "Where it is supposed to be colder than here but it is warm instead."

He nodded. "The magic that makes it warm is the same power that I have access to while I'm there. It all stems from Queen Elphame. In the same way that you share your mother's blood, I share Elphame's magic."

"My mother's cousin."

Laec nodded. Queen Elphame called Esha cousin, but the actual connection was nebulous, given that Elphame was centuries old. The two queens were blood, that was all that mattered to Elphame. "Yes. But the difference is that no matter where you go, you'll always have your mother's blood in your veins. When I go far from Elphame, I no longer have her magic."

Princess Kara looked up at her mother, and Queen Esha nodded. "It's true."

"Why do you leave, then?" The princess looked puzzled. "Did you do something wrong?"

It took Laec a second to recover. "Not really, no. We just sometimes have responsibilities that take us beyond our borders. I am sent to be of service to you. So here I am."

"Thank you," Kara said.

"You're welcome." Laec thought he'd never been so politely spoken to, nor spoken so politely to anyone as this before. He tugged at the neck of his dress shirt, hoping that not all Solanan people were so well mannered. Laec could play civilized for a while, but the longer he did it the harder it got. Constant courtesy made him want to rip off his shirt, dance around half-naked and barefoot, then sucker punch someone and blame someone else, just to see if it might liven things up.

The queen stood Kara on her feet and told her to join the group making letters. The princess waved a shy goodbye to Laec.

Queen Esha allowed concern to show in her brown eyes. "While you are most welcome—and I know Ilishec will be especially pleased to see you—Elphame did not really explain why she sent you in her letter."

Laec spread his palms. "I can't add much. Queen Elphame has foreseen some trouble for Solana, though not the shape or source of it. She knows not whether it concerns you individually, or the kingdom as a whole. She dislikes… not knowing things."

"I remember," Esha murmured.

Laec cleared his throat. "I was not being useful in Stavarjak just now, so she asked me to come, and to keep her apprised of any developments. That's all I can tell you."

Queen Esha dimpled. "How intriguing. Were you from another kingdom, I'd label you a spy."

"Yes. I'm sure you would." Laec couldn't deny that's what he was, in essence—a spy who had announced his presence openly. But Elphame loved Esha and had only good intentions for Solana. Neither he nor Esha herself could doubt that.

"Hmm." Esha pursed her lips. "Were I less fond of her, I might feel insulted at her poking her nose into our affairs. But Elphame's knowledge and talent are not inconsiderable. If the legends are true, my cousin was there when all the courts were divided by seasons, instead of by politics and economics. She is a living icon, a symbol of a bygone age. I am happy she is on my side. It's very kind of her to care, and you may tell her I said so in your first report."

"Yes, Ma'am." Laec sometimes forgot that his queen was a legend. He knew her too well. But Esha was right. Aside from

Silverfall—a winter court—Stavarjak was the only kingdom in Ivryndi to have maintained a perpetual season, and that was a result of Elphame's presence.

"You are invited to attend the banquet we will host the day after tomorrow. We will be initiating the newest members of our Calyx. I will introduce you to my husband and the Scented Court, but I'm sure you will want to see your uncle and aunt before then. If you wait in the hall a moment, I'll have someone escort you to Ilishec's workshop, though I warn you, he'll be busy."

"I shall endeavor not to be underfoot." Laec bowed.

The moment he was out of the parlor, he loosened the ties at his neck, scratched beneath his shirt, and went to find his uncle without the help of an escort.

Chapter Sixteen

Çifta

Rahamlar's fortress sat on wide, rocky land between two rivers, perched between two iron gates like a fat toad. The gates reached into the bottom of the freezing depths, allowing no traffic to pass through unless the toll was paid. Control of these two arteries had made Rahamlar rich, though one might never guess at the wealth by looking at the fortress itself. Behind its stone walls, green and slimy with algae, nestled a collection of buildings like the misshapen eggs of some great seabird.

The prow of the fortress hung over the river like a jutting beak, but what sailors saw as they approached the gates was only the nose of the great beast; the rest was swallowed by twisted trunks and hidden by foliage. Condensation covered everything. Moisture-rich lichens and mosses coated every stone wall and the base of every tree. The air grew dense and wet, making Çifta's hair curl and cling to her forehead. Her skin felt dewy and her clothes felt cool and damp. Insects chirped and frogs sang from the ditches. What had started as flat, easily traversed roads became rocky, slippery and uneven. Caramel's shod hooves slipped over the smooth stones rising from the road like breaching whales. She guided the mare to walk along the ditch where there was tacky earth to be had. Her escort soon followed suit. Their single-file line of riders had to slow to allow the carriage wheels to roll over the rocky terrain.

An arch appeared over the road and a figure sat on horseback, swathed in shadows. He exchanged words with Endyr then led them over a bridge and beneath a portcullis. The horse's hooves were muffled on the soft wood of the bridge. The party emerged in a dry gravel courtyard with a mostly open view of the sky. Dogs scampered around, sniffing at the newcomers as they dismounted, before a command from someone had them running with their tails tucked. Human and fae alike went this way and that, carrying tack or tools. A few stopped to observe the newcomers before carrying on their way.

A young woman in a black dress appeared in a window overlooking the yard. She wore a lacy veil over her forehead, not quite covering her eyes. She didn't smile but she waved to Çifta immediately, which Çifta returned. The woman disappeared from the window. Çifta checked herself, combing her fingers through her hair, wondering when her betrothed would appear. Aside from the woman, the only Rahamlarin citizens she could see were servants, soldiers or stable boys. A stable boy took Caramel's reins from Çifta.

Unease crept under her skin. She didn't like the fortress, its dampness, its ironclad clouds or the expressionless faces of the men working in the yard. She told herself she had a young bride's nerves and it was normal not to like a new environment. It was normal to feel alone. She had to give herself time. The bad feelings would pass—they always did.

The young woman in black materialized from an open door on the ground floor. She crossed the courtyard at a fast walk, dodging traffic. She opened her arms to Çifta and the women exchanged kisses.

"You are even more beautiful in the flesh." The woman's eyes shone as she combed over Çifta's face and form.

Çifta felt herself flush and some of the tension went out of her body. The woman had the faint grayish tinge to her skin that Prince Faraçek had. She looked younger than Çifta, barely out of her teens. "You must be Princess Serya?"

The woman smiled, but her eyes were sad. "That's my elder sister. I'm Princess Isabey. I'm to welcome you and get you settled. I'm sorry my family is not here to greet you. Please don't think badly of us. We are very out of sorts. We tried to send a bird to let you know what has happened, but maybe you were going through Syrgana at the time. Birds get disoriented in there. Our crow returned with the message intact. They're usually very good finding their addressee."

"I detoured from the route to visit my sister. What's happened?"

Isabey's chin wobbled. "My older brother died five days ago. The whole kingdom is in mourning. By the time we tried to alert you, you were on your way. I'm sorry."

Shock made Çifta's body go cold. "Prince Ander? How?"

Princess Isabey set her fingertips gently into the corners of her eyes, dabbing at tears. "A horrible, stupid accident. A snake spooked the prince's horse. He was thrown into a quagmire and couldn't be saved."

Çifta gasped, reaching for Isabey's arms, her heart aching for the woman. "No."

The princess's hands came up to settle on Çifta's elbows. The women clutched each other. "Yes. Prince Faraçek was with him when he died. I have that small comfort to hold on to. At least he wasn't alone."

Çifta stared at Isabey, hardly seeing her anymore. Her betrothed had just witnessed his brother's death. He would be traumatized, heartbroken, grieving. "I shouldn't have come," she whispered.

Isabey's grip on her tightened. Her expression grew fraught. "Please don't say that. You are a beam of light. Yes, we are in mourning, but your presence will soften this crippling blow, give our people something to look forward to, even if we can't celebrate your betrothal yet."

Isabey's words were as kind as her character. Çifta clung to that, hoping Isabey had not spoken out of misplaced naivete.

"Come. I'll show you to your rooms and you can rest and prepare to meet our family." Isabey tucked Çifta's hand beneath her arm, like the girls were old friends.

Çifta's men were taken to where they could wash and eat and rest while the horses were freed from their tack and turned into stalls for feeding and grooming. Çifta's luggage was already sitting on the ground, ready to be relocated to her suite.

Grateful for Isabey's warmth, Çifta let the princess lead her inside. They commenced a dizzying journey through a maze of narrow passages with low ceilings. Sputtering torches in iron sconces illuminated the hallways poorly. They passed a busy kitchen smelling of grease and smoke and yeast. They passed countless closed doors and some open ones showing dark chambers with heavy, dark furniture. Çifta already missed Kazery and the bright halls of her own home. Duty pushed her fears down deep.

Isabey told her where the halls led and what the different wings of the fortress were used for. They climbed stairs, and with the advancing height, the air grew sweeter and fresher. Reaching a landing, they heard birdsong through a small open window. A breath of cool air lifted the sticky hair at Çifta's forehead. She closed her eyes and inhaled. There was beauty here; she would find it.

A flash of his face rose in her mind, like a sudden spring storm. Sharp angles, fierce red hair, too-sharp eyeteeth and large questing eyes. Her heart throbbed and she pushed Laec's face away. He belonged firmly in her past now. Reflexively, Çifta squeezed Isabey's arm. Her cheeks heated and she was glad that Isabey couldn't read her mind.

"Are you alright?" Isabey looked at her with concern.

Çifta smiled. "Just tired from the journey."

"Of course. And here I am, dawdling you along. We can save the rest of the tour for later. Your room is close." The princess pushed through an arched wooden door with a small judas window. "Here we are. I hope you'll be comfortable."

"Goodness, did this room belong to a giant?" The room was cavernous, but it wasn't for the lack of furniture. A large four-poster bed dominated the room, with spindles thicker than a man's waist and a mattress Çifta would surely get lost in. It had to have been built in the space because there was no way it would have gotten through the door. There was a fireplace, and an adjoining chamber with a huge porcelain tub and matching washstand. Two wardrobes sat along the far stone wall with a warped mirror in a large oval frame between them. The depth of the windowsill matched the length of Çifta's arm. She doubted that she'd be able to reach the latch without laying on her belly. At least the window was open.

"It's a bit masculine, I know. All the royal chambers are big like this." Princess Isabey looked worried. "You don't like it?"

Çifta laughed. "I'll get a good walk every morning just crossing from the bed to the window."

A knock on the door made them turn. A woman in a black dress and a veil fixed to the crown of her head entered with a pronounced limp.

"Lady Çifta." The woman held her hands out, palms up. "Welcome."

The brunette hair peeking from beneath the veil was the same shade as Isabey's, though this woman's eyes were a stormy blue, and her complexion lacked the gray tint. Çifta dipped into a curtsy. "Princess Serya, it's a pleasure to meet you."

The elder princess took Çifta's hands and squeezed before letting go. "Your arrival is a much-needed balm. I'm sorry you've not come under happier circumstances. Princess Isabey has told you of our tragedy?"

"I am so sorry." Çifta felt embarrassed for the bright greens and yellows of her dress. Even her homespun traveling cloak had merry red trim and birds embroidered along the chest. She looked garish next to their mourning gowns. "As soon as my trunks are brought up, I'll change. Your loss is my loss."

"Thank you. You'll want to send a letter to your father to let him know of your safe arrival. You'll find paper and ink in the desk, as well as sealing wax. When you're ready, a servant will show you to the aviary. Please allow Isabey or myself to give you a tour of the fortress when you've rested. It's very easy to get lost. I'm certain you've never been in a castle like Rahamlar before."

Çifta shook her head. Her life had been kept to the manor in Kirkik and the Unya's winter home in the balmy lowlands beneath Boskaya's capital city. "I would appreciate a tour very much."

Isabey said, "It's a necessity. Think of Rahamlar not as one big fortress but as many smaller ones. Each one is built upon beds of rock that vary in height. You'll tire quickly moving through the stairs and passages, but you'll find your legs will grow strong."

Çifta recalled Princess Serya's limp and turned to her. "How do you manage?"

There was a look exchanged between the princesses before Çifta realized that she'd said something rude. Her hand flew to her mouth. "I am sorry. Damn my ignorance."

But Princess Serya only smiled. "Was my condition not told to you, then?"

Çifta shook her head. "I thought it an injury. I beg your pardon. I have shamed myself, I didn't mean—"

Serya put up a hand, a queenly motion that suited her. It was authoritative but not unkind. "Don't fret. I was born this way. I manage well enough. There is nothing wrong with what matters most: my mind."

Çifta was too embarrassed to speak. She was grateful for the distraction when her trunks arrived. Two fae men carried a tall stack of wooden boxes into her room. They both had long sharp ears and wore matching brown livery with a small bird embroidered over the chest. The women stepped out of the way to let the men pass.

"Against the far wall," Princess Isabey directed.

They were the first of a steady stream of powerful-looking fae guards carrying Çifta's personal items. They moved with single-minded efficiency that Çifta found intimidating. Their faces were expressionless, impassive. As the last of the trunks were delivered, Princess Serya dismissed herself, leaving Çifta with Isabey.

"I'll have your bath filled. Do you need anything else? If you can't wait for supper, I can arrange for some bread, cheese and wine?"

Çifta shook her head, feeling panicky as Princess Isabey moved toward the door. She'd be left alone with her thoughts in this huge, foreign room. *What a wonder,* she thought, *I felt less terrified in the middle of an eldritch wood full of brigands than I do here, behind thick stone walls filled with allies.*

"When will I meet… him?" Çifta asked, fiddling with the clasp on her cloak.

Princess Isabey hesitated. "I'm not certain. I'll find out. It won't be long, I imagine."

"Alright. One more thing. Is there a girl who might assist me? My father should have mentioned that I no longer have a lady's maid."

"Of course. Yes, I believe he did. I'll send Eda with the water. She's a sweet girl, quiet and polite. She'll be yours to command." Princess Isabey gave Çifta a final smile and backed out of the room.

When the door closed, Çifta found writing paper and ink. Sitting at the large desk near the window, Çifta considered what to say to her father. Should she describe the damp strangeness of the place, or the cool detached nature of the guards? A shiver walked over her and she closed her eyes. Complaining was unladylike and would only make her father unhappy. She focused on describing the warmth of the sisters who had welcomed her, her excitement to be introduced to the prince and the vastness of her chambers and sturdiness of her furniture. She described the dense forest, the deep rivers and the busy courtyard and the unusual fortress. Çifta signed the letter and sealed it.

Eda made her entrance as Çifta was struggling to rekindle the fire with damp wood. The maid was as quiet as Isabey had said. Her round cheeks were childlike, but her eyes were watchful. She filled the tub with hot water, and emptied it when Çifta was done bathing. After helping Çifta dress, Eda went about unpacking Çifta's things. It was apparent to Çifta within a few minutes of meeting Eda that the maid likely wouldn't become a friend. Eda's skill was efficiency. All of Çifta's things were hung, folded or wrapped in paper and stored in the drawers. Eda retrieved fresh reeds for the floor and sprinkled them throughout the room to freshen the air. Eda's quick fingers plaited Çifta's hair and knotted it back before fixing her black mourning veil in place.

"I never imagined I'd need to wear the black so soon," Çifta said as Eda pinned the veil in place.

"Yes, milady," said Eda.

To Çifta's dismay, the maid's eyes misted up. Eda brushed at the moisture and turned away. She took a breath and turned back to her work, but it was obvious that she had tried to keep her emotions under control.

"You were fond of the prince," Çifta guessed. "I'm very sorry for your loss."

"Thank you." Eda gave a sad smile. "We all were, milady."

"And were Prince Ander and Prince Faraçek also very close?"

"I think so, milady. They rode together often. Prince Ander was special to everyone." The girl retrieved black fingerless gloves, helping Çifta wriggle into them. She turned Çifta's hand palm up and laced the gloves tightly into place, leaving Çifta's slender fingers peeking from beneath a fringe of lace.

"Prince Faraçek must be devastated."

"Yes, milady." Eda didn't raise her eyes from her work until she was done.

Çifta observed herself in the glass. What she saw sent a shiver down her spine. A pale face starkly contrasted by the folds of the veil falling alongside her cheeks. Eda had fixed the mourning veil perfectly, which meant it covered Çifta's dark hair and stopped just over her brows, leaving her bright eyes to peep from beneath the fringe. While in mourning, a woman was not to brighten her cheeks or lips with stain or to darken her eyes with kohl. She was not to show her hair to any great advantage and her décolletage was to be covered to the neck. Çifta's face hovered above a shadowy figure. She looked like an apparition, and a frightened one.

Maybe Eda recognized her despair, or perhaps she really believed her words, but she finally ventured an opinion. "Milady looks properly grieved."

"Yes," replied Çifta softly. "I do."

What a way to start her new life: as a woman swathed in coal and ashes, with no blood in her cheeks and no joy in her eyes. She turned to Eda, fortifying herself to face whatever awaited her. "Will you take me to the aviary before we go to the hall? My father needs to know I've arrived safely."

"As you wish, milady." Eda curtsied and led the way.

What Çifta really wanted to do was crawl under the massive quilt and go to sleep, hoping for pleasant dreams. Surely, when she awoke, she would feel better.

Chapter Seventeen

Jessica

Guards in ceremonial armor stood either side of the doors leading into the Grand Hothouse, waiting to usher Jessica through. Birdsong filled the air. Butterflies and bees flew everywhere. This greenhouse was different than the others, more elaborate and set apart on the huge palace grounds. Curved copper ribs, green from years under sun and rain, held glass panes in irregular shapes, like the panels of Greta's wings. She'd learned that, in fact, a butterfly's wing was the precise inspiration for the design of the panels making up this greenhouse. The Grand Hothouse was the place flora fae made their presentations, where Ilishec showed off his recruits and acted as mediator, highlighting their abilities against the talents already harnessed within the present Calyx. Already, the king and queen had seen presentations by eighteen flora fae. Jessica was the last.

The instinct to bolt back to the safety of her bedroom was nearly overwhelming. But Ilishec was behind these doors. His presence would calm her, and he wouldn't let her embarrass herself. Jessica kept the posture of someone relaxed, simply waiting her turn. She kept her nerves in check by examining the creation Olinya's team had dressed her in.

Handmade leather sandals hugged her feet and crisscrossed her calves to her knees. Soft pink daisy heads in a sturdy, sparkly fabric had been sewn at some of the places where the ties crossed. The tender pastel color had been painstakingly matched to her dress, which was a simple shift but made of so much fabric that when Jessica first tried it on and spun in a circle, it had flown up to chest height. A green sash cinched the dress in at the waist. A cluster of lacy moonflowers had been sewn to the right shoulder, then fastened to her left hip. More of these flowers were fixed in Jessica's hair.

Olinya had thought it would be nice if Beazle made himself a home inside one of these flowers, but he preferred Jess's hair to the lace and kept crawling out. Greta had settled on her one bare shoulder and hadn't moved from that spot. Jess's half-bun was held in place by a glossy green hoop encrusted with tiny daisies. When she was dressed, she felt like a princess, albeit a very nervous one.

When the guards opened the double doors, she lifted her head and stepped over the threshold. Shafts of broken light filtered through the panels onto a garden of knee-high ferns. Ilishec waited for Jessica amidst a clutter of pots and flowerbeds, some of which held only dirt, while others overflowed with plants. Ilishec was dressed simply and cleanly in a belted tunic with the lion's head crest over the chest. Instead of sandals, he wore shiny boots over soft leather leggings. His long gray hair was tied neatly back at the nape of his neck.

Jessica's first look at the royals made her blink. They wore no crowns or fancy jewels, and their clothes were beautiful but not majestic. The king held a scroll open on his lap and the queen sat so close to him that it looked like they could be one body with two heads.

Behind them sat several Calyx, including Aster and Proteas, who greeted Jessica. She felt herself relax as she returned Aster's smile. To see the Calyx looking so at ease made Jess feel at ease herself. This performance had a more casual feel than she'd been anticipating, and she was relieved.

"Jessica Fontana, from Dagevli Village," Ilishec said, holding a hand out to her.

She curtsied the way Gaby had shown her. She'd been told to address the king and queen only after they'd spoken to her, and to address them as Ma'am or sire. When the king heard the introduction, he looked down at the scroll.

"Welcome, Ms. Fontana." Queen Esha had a long neck and high cheekbones and the shortest hair Jessica had ever seen on a woman: just a close-cropped cap of dark curls. It made her brown eyes look big and showed off the little black pearls in her earlobes to charming effect.

"Thank you, Ma'am," Jess replied, thankful her voice had come out smoothly.

Ilishec explained: "They are finding your village on a map. They like to know where the flora fae come from."

Jess nodded. Her fingers trembled in Ilishec's hand and he gave her a reassuring squeeze.

The king looked up. "Dagevli is famous for squash?"

She took a second. "Yes, Sire. Also root vegetables: beets, carrots, potatoes and turnips."

Queen Esha said something softly to her husband and he bent to listen and nodded in agreement, looking pleased.

"Your parents are farmers?" Esha asked as the king set the scroll on the marble bench beside his hip.

Ilishec released Jess's hand and she put them behind her back and stood with her shoulders straight. "My mother is a gardener. I can't tell you anything about my father."

The king's brows arched. "Nothing at all?"

"I know that he died before I was born." If Jess had felt bolder, she would have told them that her mother had moved to Dagevli from a different village. Marion kept no portraits or drawings of her father. Jessica had once asked Hanna about her father, whether she'd known him, but she said that she didn't, given that Marion had arrived in Dagevli as a widow. Jess couldn't bring herself to say much more than a sentence at a time; surely the king and queen of Solana didn't wish to hear some long, drawn-out story with no real information in it.

"May we meet your familiar?" The monarchs stood, the king holding the queen's hand as they stepped off the dais.

Ilishec stepped to Jess's side. "She has two."

"The gardener has explained that you had a twin." The queen's eyes widened. "What happened to him?"

"I don't know, Ma'am." Jessica's cheeks flushed with embarrassment. Would they hold her ignorance about her own family against her? More likely they'd hold it against Marion, which was only fair.

The monarchs stared at her for a moment, then the queen, mercifully, spotted Greta and pointed. "I see the butterfly, there."

"This is Greta." Jess gestured to where the glasswing sat on her shoulder, flexing her wings prettily, as if she knew she was on display. Jess had no doubt the insect knew that these strangers were important.

"But her wings are transparent," Queen Esha breathed, touching the king's shoulder. "Look."

King Agir, who was tall and deep-chested, bent for a closer look. He knew better than to touch Greta, Jess noted with relief. Butterflies were so fragile that an innocent stroke would pull the tiny feathers from their wings.

"Beautiful," the king said. "And the other?"

Jess tucked her head so the bun on her crown was more visible. She could feel the bat move. "Beazle is up top, there."

Queen Esha gave a gasp of delight. "But he is no bigger than a moth!"

"Beazle is a bumblebee bat," Jessica said.

"The world's smallest mammal," Ilishec added.

"But also a pollinator?" the king asked, then answered his own question: "He would have to be, to have bonded with a flora fae."

"Look at his little snout, how sweet." The queen lifted a hand. "May I?"

Jess bent her knees to make the crown of her hair easy for the queen to reach. She was several inches shorter than Jessica, her limbs as narrow and as fragile looking as a fawn's legs.

Beazle allowed himself to be held. When the queen held him in her open palm, he yawned and blinked at them, then crawled to her thumb and hugged it. The queen looked delighted.

Jess thought suddenly that she could easily love these monarchs. If they could appreciate the tiny miracles of Beazle and Greta, then being loyal to them would come easily. She began to understand why villagers spoke of the Solanan monarchs in adoring tones. They seemed like regular people.

The queen put Beazle back on Jessica's head with reluctance.

"Jessica is able to bring up multiple species. She is broadly talented, but it remains to be seen how deep that talent runs."

Ilishec moved toward a collection of pots filled with soil. "Now that the introduction is out of the way…"

Jess turned to the empty pots as Beazle settled into her hair. She realized then that the other pots scattered about the marble floor of the presentation area were filled with species that the flora fae who had come in before her had produced. This gave her a jolt, as she saw some very unusual botanicals: a flamboyant lily that was such a dark shade of purple it was almost black, a cactus covered in thick silver hair and a fantastic bush full of massive purple-red blossoms so heavy they drooped.

She had a bad moment when she was convinced nothing was going to happen. She wished she'd had weeks to prepare, not just a few hours. But the moment passed and she exhaled, visualizing moonflower. Shoots emerged as the magic flowed through her and the plant grew. It snaked sideways to crawl over the edge of the pot, a vine with heart-shaped leaves. Buds formed, then burst open with white moonflower blossoms. By the time the moonflower vine was mature, Jess's forehead felt damp. She moved to the next pot and worked at bringing up honeysuckle. The queen and king moved along with her, following her progress without commenting. A few of the Calyx had gotten out of their seats and stood at a respectful distance.

Getting into the rhythm of it, she moved from one pot to the next, to the next, feeling the variety in the magic as she brought up *cleome*, then *datura*, then *cestrum*. She worked until she had filled nine pots with her plants. When she stepped back, breathing fast, the fabric in her armpits growing humid, the monarchs clapped politely. The Calyx joined in.

Jess couldn't tell if she'd impressed anyone. Certainly, looking at her plants next to the others, hers seemed drab. The goldenrod and fleabane were downright weedy. What she was capable of would amaze her mother and Clair and everyone else back home, but here among the Calyx and flora fae from all over the continent, she was not special. She felt suddenly that she had failed, and worked hard to keep her expression neutral. Desire for a place among the Calyx lanced her heart with such ferocity that she sucked in a breath, but there was a strong possibility that this was as close as she would ever get. But how could she go back to Dagevli to sell squash? How could she go back to playing human? She belonged here more than she'd ever belonged among the farm children back home. She felt her hands tremble and clasped them behind her back, threading her fingers. She felt Beazle stir and then move to her shoulder where he nuzzled her neck. Greta fluttered from Jess's shoulder to her forehead, where she clung licking Jessica's salty skin.

The queen smiled as the applause dwindled. "Beautifully managed."

The royals turned away, talking quietly together as they moved among the plants, discussing them, bending to smell them. They hadn't scented any of Jessica's flowers. Surely that was a bad sign?

Ilishec put a hand at her lower back and steered her for the door. "Well done. You are dismissed."

The Calyx began to mingle with one another among the plants. They seemed so unaware of their breathtaking beauty, their dreamlike gestures, of how they filled every room with intoxicatingly beautiful fragrance. Jessica felt tears at the corners of her eyes as she put her back to them and walked for the doors. She felt that if she was not offered a place among these fae, and in the court of these gentle royals, she would probably die of a broken heart.

Jessica found Oren waiting for her on the lawn outside the palace doors. A series of stone walls and arches separated large angular sections of land that Ilishec had designed over the years. Birds, butterflies, bees and other insects and animals populated the gardens and filled it with a hum of life.

"You look nice." Oren held out his hand and Jessica took it, hoping some of his calm would soak into her. He pulled her toward the stepping-stones leading around the side of the palace to another building Jess had never been inside. "Are you nervous?"

"Extremely." She cleared her throat and found a lower key to speak in. "How about you?"

Oren shook his head. "I'm not expecting a place. I'm already back home in my mind, helping my father plan next year's crop. We have twin foals."

As they walked, Jess thought how much Clair would like Oren. He was like the farm boys that populated Dagevli. Strong but slender with rough, calloused hands. Holding his hand was like grasping a chunk of limestone warmed by the sun. Most farm kids got progressively darker as the summer wore on. By the time the harvest season struck, Dagevli was filled with kids in a rainbow of sun-kissed shades running from golden to black. Oren was pale with constellations of freckles dusting his cheeks and the tops of his shoulders. His gray-green eyes were warm and his hair had a personality all its own. Jess found Oren adorable. It wasn't difficult to believe that he could conjure flowers. From the few male Calyx she'd met, they had a gentle streak that lacked in most men nearing their physical prime. Just the fact that he was holding her hand without pretense or expectation was unusual.

"I don't think I'll get invited either," said Jessica, "but I'll be sad to go home. I'm meant for this."

Oren grinned down at her, the corners of his eyes crinkling. He seemed so much older than fifteen. "If you're meant for it, then you'll get invited."

"I suppose." Jess had doubts. She felt like she was meant to have a father as well, and that hadn't worked out.

A group of flora fae milled around in front of a glass-domed building with its roof open to the sky. Colorful hummingbirds zipped from the open roof to descend to where their fae companions mingled. The hopefuls trickled inside, subdued and serious. A group of females, all with the kind of beauty that inspired artists to paint, watched as Jess and Oren came up to the door.

Jess resisted the urge to put her gaze on the ground. She felt no hostility from the Calyx, but the intense scrutiny was uncomfortable. She felt they formed an exclusive club, one they all knew many desperately wanted to join but would be found unworthy.

A butter-blond with a wide mouth and an athletic figure stared openly at Jessica. She found courage and didn't look away and the Calyx broke into a grin so wide and full of mischief that Jess couldn't help but grin back. A fat, fuzzy bumblebee as big as an acorn droned over to land on the blond's head. She lifted a hand in greeting, no higher than her waist. It couldn't be mistaken for anything other than a subdued but friendly hello. Jess lifted her own hand, just at the wrist, in return.

After that, several of the Calyx took on open, warm expressions. They followed Oren and Jess inside where marble benches had been set in a half-circle. A set of arched steps crossed over a pond, and it was these steps the gardener mounted. Everyone found a seat, the Calyx gravitating to one side of the room and the hopefuls to the other.

"As many of you will know, I'm not big on ceremony," Ilishec began. "This event is always short and a little bittersweet. I want to thank you for attending my Discovery and giving your best. You are all in possession of rare and valuable talent. Though we only have four places to fill, I hope that those of you who leave here find ways of developing your gifts while you have them."

The thought that she'd one day lose her gifts unsettled her. She'd only just discovered them and was excited by the thought of seeing what else she might be capable of. That they would vanish one day was distressing.

"Those of you who are not offered a place will be compensated for your time. Please see my wife, Hazel, and her assistant, Lotus, over there near the palms afterward."

Ilishec's petite and slightly dazed-looking wife stood next to a much taller, dark-skinned Calyx woman with shining black pupils, angular features and willowy arms. In a soft pink dress and black hair swept up in a topknot, she looked like a creature from a dream. The largest wasp Jessica had ever seen sat on Lotus's forearm, flicking his wings. She could hear the buzz from where she was sitting and could even see the villainous stinger. She shuddered and looked away. She'd never been fond of wasps or hornets.

Ilishec continued, "If I call your name, please rise and come to me. Kei Ashkan, Tom Hiller, Oren Jils and Jessica Fontana."

The room sat quiet for several seconds as the names sank in. How quickly Ilishec had said them! Then the Calyx burst into polite applause. A few of the flora fae joined them, but others, including Oren and Jess, sat in stunned silence.

Oren nudged her. "That—He said our names. We're invited."

She found her legs and let them carry her through the stream of flora fae heading for Hazel, dreamlike. The gardener had already descended to the floor and stood waiting. Kei and Tom had joined him. Kei was openly beaming while Tom looked as dazed as Jessica felt. Tom's familiar, a red-and-brown moth with a complicated wing pattern, clung to the front of his linen shirt just under his collar. Kei gave a shrill whistle that startled several in the room. A long black wasp with a jewel-like abdomen buzzed to her and disappeared against the black of her hair. She wore a bright red lip stain and a tight red dress. The outfit screamed for attention.

Ilishec offered each of them a hug. Kei clung to him with her scrawny, pale arms like he had saved her life. When the gardener hugged her, Jessica understood why. She felt safe, cared for, and her trust in him grew. She wondered if this was how Clair felt about her father, Tad.

As the rest of the fae trickled from the hothouse, Ilishec produced four small scrolls and handed one to each of them. "You don't need to sign them now, but I would like them back before breakfast tomorrow. If you decide to decline for any reason, then it will give me an opportunity to extend the place to someone else before the other flora fae go home."

Kei untied the leather thong and unrolled the short scroll. "A contract?"

"That's right. It states the terms of your placement, including the terms of your royalties for any products you contribute to the manufacture of during your time with us. You can choose to receive payment once per quarter—some Calyx do this as they have families in need back home—others opt to take their earnings when they depart, using the palace coffers to keep it safe. You are paid in two ways; one is a percentage of products sold, the other is by earning gifts from courtiers. You are not permitted to solicit these gifts. They must be given freely."

"I don't understand." Tom lifted a troubled gaze to the gardener. "I don't know how to make anything other than shoes. My father is a cobbler."

Kei snorted and Tom flushed.

Ilishec's tone verified Tom had not been stupid to ask, which cut off Kei's laughter. "Helping you develop your gifts is my job. We don't know yet what you are capable of, but no Calyx has ever left Solana City empty-handed. The contract also states that your place cannot be given away to any new flora fae, no matter how spectacular their skills. Your place here is stable. However, there are breaches in contract that will render our agreement void. They include: abuse of anyone in the royal household, treason or treachery to the crown, theft and falsehoods. My Calyx are beautiful on the outside but must endeavor to be beautiful on the inside as well."

Jess thought the look Ilishec gave Kei as he delivered these terms had a hint of warning. The smile slid from Kei's face and she pressed her lips together, casting her gaze down.

"Excuse me, Gardener." Oren put up a finger. "How do we know when our term here is done if we don't break any of the rules?"

Ilishec put his hands behind his back. "The career of a Calyx, if not cut off prematurely, follows what we call a bell curve. You arrive a young teen, some even younger. As you mature to adulthood, your powers will grow. At some point, they will peak. Many Calyx peak around the age of twenty-five. Others have gone on to the age of thirty. Once you reach your peak, you can maintain it for a while with hard work, but inevitably your talents will decline until they disappear altogether, leaving you open to move on to the next phase of your life. The career of a Calyx is not always easy, but it is enjoyable and rewarding."

Tom and Kei were staring at the gardener with a species of muted horror. Oren nodded like he'd understood all of it already.

"Our powers disappear?" Kei said with open shock.

Jess was surprised that she knew something Kei didn't. The girl seemed so know-it-all.

"It sounds horrible because you're just falling in love with your abilities, but trust me, the vast majority of Calyx are ready to let their talents go when the time comes. This is a phase, not unlike that of a well-bred racehorse, if you'll pardon the comparison."

Jess had a sudden realization. "*You* were Calyx?" She glanced pointedly at Ilishec's rounded ears.

Ilishec smiled. "When flora fae lose their magic, their pointed ears soften. The appearance of a flora fae fluctuates with the magic, as you'll see. I joined when I was eighteen and left when I was twenty-four. I loved my time as part of the retinue, but I've never once regretted leaving.

"Your powers waned at twenty-four?" Jess felt cold. If she followed this same timeline, she only had seven years left.

"Yes, but I was ready for it because I wanted to marry. Don't worry, the decline of your gifts helps to prepare you to move on. It's not as traumatic as it sounds—for most, anyway. The other matter is that of your names. Calyx take on a name which helps us easily recall which botanicals you work with. For instance, Kei, since your gift lies in the family of *paeonia*, you might want to go by Peony. Oren, since you can bring up snapdragons, you could go by Snap."

"I like that," said Kei.

Oren shrugged. "If that's part of the rules, sure. I'll go by Snap."

"What about me?" Tom looked perplexed. "I don't want to be called Erica."

Ilishec smiled. "Your species is also known as heather. I propose you take the name Heath."

He relaxed. "Okay."

Ilishec turned to Jess. "Since *cestrum* is also known as jessamine, and it's close to your own name, why don't you go by Jessamine? Unless you'd like something different?"

Jess thought she'd have a hard time answering to Honey, or Goldenrod, or Cleome. "I like Jessamine, and Jess for short. Easy." But she had a much more troubling question growing in her mind. "What about our familiars? When we lose our powers, do we lose them too?"

"I'm afraid so." Ilishec understood the impact his answer would have on her and put a hand on her shoulder.

She had to sit on the edge of the pool. Oren sat beside her. Tom and Kei stood by the gardener, taking this in with expressions of unease.

Jess looked at the floor and concentrated on breathing. She felt like she'd walked into a door… hard. She lay a hand over her stomach. Beazle felt her distress and crawled from her hair and onto her shoulder. She felt Greta crawl along her neck. She lifted a hand and Beazle went into it, wrapping his limbs around her thumb. Greta followed him. Jessamine looked down into Beazle's tiny, sweet face, and at Greta's delicate transparent wings. Beazle blinked up at her with that wild intelligence in his eyes that she so loved.

"It cannot be," she murmured. Moisture welled along her lower lids, blurring her vision.

Ilishec sat beside her. "It's one of the crueler facts of the life of a flora fae."

Jessamine couldn't form a reply. Cruel didn't begin to cover it. *When I lose Greta and Beazle, I might also lose myself.*

Chapter Eighteen

Jessamine

Jessamine sat at the small desk beneath her window, a quill in her hand and open ink bottle nearby. She had already penned a letter for Clair, getting the easy one out of the way first.

She'd written "Dear Mother," at the top of a fresh page nearly twenty minutes earlier. When she'd sat down, there'd been daylight and Beazle had been nested in her hair, but now the horizon was a soft inky blue. A dim glow of amber light lit the lowest part of the sky over Solana City. Voices peppered the night, gardeners sharing a drink in a gazebo near the tool sheds. They sounded at ease with the world, settled in their lives.

Jessamine had had a wonderful day. Olinya had draped her body with the most luxurious, exquisitely textured and richly colored fabrics, unlike anything Jessamine had ever seen before. Fabrics that glimmered with silver or gold thread, fabrics so soft that she felt bereft when they'd been removed from her skin, fabrics so light they floated on still air. When a style and fabric had been decided upon, with Jessamine giving in to Olinya's expertise, Jessamine had gone to the hall for lunch, yet the food was almost tasteless. She was torn between savoring the delights of Solana Palace and thinking about how she would word the letter to her mother, since she would not be back in Dagevli anytime soon. While being fitted, while eating and while practicing the conjuring of her blooms in the hothouses and gardens, she had mentally penned at least a dozen letters.

Dear Marion, I found out today that you've been lying to me my entire life.

Too accusatory and cold. No good. Marion likely had an excellent reason for keeping Jess's twin a secret. Even if Jess couldn't fathom what that reason could possibly be, she didn't want to risk embarrassing herself or sending Marion into a rage. Try again.

Dear Mother, I hope you are well. I have a surprise for you: I'm a member of the Calyx! Looks like I have magic after all, the finding of which unearthed another surprise for me as well: I had a twin! Imagine my shock, my chagrin, my… dare I say it… dismay that you've kept this from me.

Hmm. Too excited, too cavalier, too trite. Perhaps a letter designed to get Marion here in the flesh so Jessamine could corner her and force her to talk.

Dear Mother, Solana City is everything a young person dreams of. Why did you never bring me? Ah, but I'm here now, and I've found my place in the world, the place where I belong. You can no longer put off a visit, for your daughter has become a member of the Scented Court. I'll expect you at the initiation ball and banquet, after which I will personally show you around…

Ugh. So formal. Marion was her mother. Why write to her like she was a diplomat?

She had a right to know about her twin. Marion was secretive, not stupid, and Jessamine was a member of the court now. The faith placed in her by the king and the queen and the gardener inspired in her a desire to behave like one.

She took a breath and put her quill to the paper, letting the words spill onto the page.

Dear Mother,

I realized today that I've never written you a letter before. I've never spent time enough away from home to warrant it. How intertwined our lives have been. I can imagine how you've been faring without me. I hope you've hired Haft or Sam to help you with the squash. You know they love to help. Also, you will put a big smile on Clair's face if you have Haft in our patch on a regular basis.

While I only rode through Solana City and caught some glimpses of life here from the back of Ilishec's horse, I have had more time to enjoy the gardens of the palace and have had time with Ilishec to find my magic. It's there. It was not difficult to tap into, actually, and has been inside me all along. It took a couple of tries because the first time Beazle wasn't with me (it was during the day), only Greta was. When I couldn't conjure anything, Ilishec told me to meet him at midnight and to make sure Beazle was with me. That time, it was easy, and I brought up nine different species. Ilishec says that is unusual, even if they are mostly weeds. Some flora fae are "deep" while *others are "wide." I guess I'm a "wide" one. No jokes about my hips, please.*

With these things now said, I can't avoid the main point of this letter: I need to understand what happened at my birth. Ilishec has explained that Greta is not my true familiar, and that the only way I can have two familiars is if I was born a twin and my twin passed away yet their familiar stayed behind. Maybe I've always felt that something was missing and yet never knew what to attribute this hollow feeling to. Now I know, but I only have more questions.

I would prefer to talk about this in person. In fact, I found out several days ago about my twin but I put off writing because I believed I would be home soon. But a miracle has happened. I have been given a place among the Calyx. I am Calyx! So I won't have time to come home for many months. Even the midwinter festival, while a holiday for everyone else, is not a holiday for the Calyx.

There is to be a banquet and a ball to initiate the new Calyx (there are three others besides me) and begin the new season. Family is invited. Into the very heart of the palace! While I know you're not enamored with city life, you must come for the party. The initiation ball is the only one that family members of Calyx are invited to, the whole year long. Even the midwinter one is not open to outsiders.

I am told by the palace courier that my letter will take a day to arrive in Dagevli. If you have your reply in the post before seven the following morning, then I'll have your letter in my hand by sundown that same day.

Most important is my need to understand what happened to my twin and why you've never told me about him before. Until I see you, my imagination will spin stories.

I am waiting for your reply.

Love, Jessica (Jessamine is to be my name at Court)

She put down her quill and sat back. It would have to do. It was polite and mature and the opposite of how she felt. She felt like throwing a tantrum, or at least throwing a candlestick. What right did her mother have to keep a fact of such enormous and personal impact from her?

She squeezed her eyes shut, halting the direction her thoughts were taking her in.

She changed into her sleep clothes as the ink dried, then reread the letter, folded it and sealed it with wax. She had been given her own wreathed lion's head seal which would give speed to any letter she wrote. Toeing into her slippers, Jessamine took the letters down the hall to a post box which funneled all mail to the ground floor where it would be collected early the following morning, before she was even awake. She listened for the sound of them hitting the bag at the bottom, and then returned to her room.

Chapter Nineteen

Çifta

Çifta's first view of Faraçek was of his back. He stood waiting under a tree in a courtyard garden.

"Under normal circumstances," Isabey said, keeping her voice low as they paused at the garden's entrance, "you would be presented with great ceremony at a ball. You'd be seated side by side so you could talk. You'd be able to dance with one another. But—"

Çifta touched Isabey's forearm. "Please don't worry. I understand. The usual traditions are not observed during mourning. It is the same for my people."

Isabey looked relieved and brushed at her eyes. "I can accompany you. Or if you wish, Eda can stay with you. One custom of propriety is that you are not permitted to be alone with one another upon first meeting."

Çifta nodded. She felt some relief that she wouldn't meet Faraçek alone. "You can both come, if you like," Çifta replied, feeling idiotic, like she was inviting them on a picnic.

"If it makes no difference to

you, I will leave you with Eda, then," said Isabey. "I am anxious to attend my father. His heart is in ribbons. Forgive me."

"Not to worry," Çifta said, finding a smile. Isabey and Serya had taken her to meet King Osvitan on the evening of her arrival. He was bedridden, and just managed to hold her hand as he unofficially welcomed her to the family. His eyes were red and glassy, his hand shaky. It was apparent he didn't have much time left. Çifta watched Isabey leave, feeling sorry for the girl. She'd lost her brother, and she'd soon lose her father. Çifta couldn't bear the thought of anything happening to Kazery, but her father was a trunk of a man, powerful both physically and in his character. His health should not decline for many years to come.

Çifta headed across the lawn, hearing the swish of Eda's skirts as she followed.

The situation felt wrong. She wished she'd received the message they'd tried to send to her. She would have returned home, delayed the betrothal. Had Prince Ander not died, she and Faraçek would have met with pomp and joy. There should be a party where she would be introduced to the nobility, those she hoped to call friends. Instead, she was an afterthought. Worse, an inconvenience. She pushed aside the ungrateful thoughts. She hadn't known Ander, but these people had—and they'd loved him. She told herself to be strong. This was how the die had been cast. There was no good to come of wishing it different.

Faraçek turned at the sound of her approach.

Çifta hoped he couldn't hear how the beating of her heart doubled. His shoulders were wide but not deep, his limbs long and his waist narrow. His face was angular, almost sharp, his eyes as black as tar. His skin had the same grayish cast as Isabey's, but where the princess was flushed, Faraçek was pale. His hair was long and black, tied neatly at the nape of his neck. At his forehead was a sharp widow's peak. His ears were knives. They more than anything took Çifta's heart to a gallop. His portrait had been altered to make him appear less unseelie, but Faraçek possessed every unseelie feature she'd ever heard of, to the extreme. The only exception being long black talons. She supposed she should be thankful for that. Though Faraçek's nails were darker than human nails, they were not sharp. He was beautiful in his own fierce way, yet a chill swept up her spine.

"My Lady." His voice was deep and distant.

"My Lord." Çifta curtsied. She rose and put her hand in his.

His fingers were cold and grasped hers gently. His eyes combed her face, lingering on her hair, her lips, at her neck. "At last, we meet. I regret the timing."

"Your loss grieves me."

"Thank you. It is a far cry from what I would have liked for us." His gaze flicked to Eda, standing quietly back.

She had turned three quarters away from the couple and pretended not to hear them.

He raised his voice. "You may go."

Eda hesitated. She'd been assigned duty of chaperone, but what could a lady's maid do against the authority of a prince? Çifta held her breath, expecting the girl to protest.

Eda curtsied deeply, keeping her eyes focused on the ground. "Yes, Your Grace." She headed toward the fortress without looking back.

Faraçek tucked Çifta's hand under his arm. "Let's walk."

He took her toward a garden planted at the base of a slope where brick paths wandered between patches of shrubs. Çifta found herself struggling to keep up with him. Shortly, she was panting.

"Tell me of your journey."

She took a deep breath. "We had some excitement in Syrgana and acquired a traveling partner until the crossroads. Otherwise, it was uneventful. I stopped overnight at my sister's estate."

"Where is that?"

"Not far from the crossroad to Solana, near Mosdac Valley." Çifta described the estate and manor to him.

Faraçek asked her to expand about the events in Syrgana, so she described the fight, explaining how they'd helped a traveler who'd been attacked, but left out Laec's name and the fact that he'd spent a night at her sister's place. Her instincts screamed at her not to bring Laec to Faraçek's attention. If she did, the prince would surely sniff out her inappropriate feelings. Maybe she was being paranoid, but she didn't know this person and she didn't feel safe enough yet to test the truth with him. She hoped that in the future, she could tell him everything.

While she talked, she felt Faraçek's attention drift away from her, that he was politely pretending to listen. She let her story dwindle. When she stopped speaking altogether, she was dismayed to find that he did not prompt her to continue. Soon, it seemed like he'd become unaware of her entirely. When she could stand his vacancy no longer, she gently squeezed his arm.

He looked down and slowed his pace, for which she was grateful. Awareness returned to his features. "Forgive me. My mind is elsewhere."

Çifta responded timidly. "Of course. Your brother…"

Faraçek's hand tightened over hers as they followed the stone path. "It weighs heavily on me."

Çifta allowed Faraçek to lead her up and down, over curves and dips. It was said that the only flat surface in Rahamlar were the floors and courtyards. Çifta was beginning to discover just how true it was.

She tried and failed to sense Faraçek's mood, his feelings about her. He was a locked vault, distant, even alien. She fought back waves of dismay. Was he always this serious and withdrawn? How much of his reservation was grief? When she got to know him, would they laugh together?

A yellow butterfly fluttered in front of them along the path. "Oh, how dear."

"Sorry?" Faraçek looked down.

"The butterfly." Çifta gestured to where it had landed on a squash blossom. "It's so beautiful. I've never seen one like it in Boskaya. What kind is it?"

Faraçek looked deeply mystified by this question, almost shocked, like she'd asked him to take off his own head and throw it over the garden wall. "How would I know that?"

Çifta felt his response like a punch in the gut. Pointing out tiny miracles in the natural world and responding enthusiastically when they were pointed out to her was an expression of love in her family. "I just thought… since you grew up here…"

"I have more serious matters to spend my time on." He looked away. He seemed disappointed, even weary of her.

Çifta's mind spun like a dust devil. Doubt worried at her like rat's teeth. What should she do? She was almost his. The union would raise the Unya family's status, give her father access to routes of trade previously closed to them. She had to make this work. Dreams of love drifted away like smoke from a censer. So, maybe they wouldn't fall in love, but surely they could develop a partnership that was pleasant and productive. Surely that much could be forged.

"Perhaps, one day," she said, "we can be friends, if you do not find yourself attracted to me—"

Prince Faraçek made a sound at the back of his throat. She couldn't tell if he was laughing or choking. He stopped her, putting his hands on her shoulders. His gaze didn't so much meet hers as clash against it.

"I've never been one for flattery." His gaze consumed her the way wildfire consumed dry underbrush. "But anyone can see that you are attractive."

Çifta gulped. Where had this passion come from? One moment he was as cold as a glacier, the next his eyes were boring through her. "Thank you."

"I doubt we shall have a problem in our bed. At least, none on my account."

This speech put her into a state of shock. That he could so casually mention the physical relations that would come months down the road, when the period of mourning was over and the marriage ceremony completed. But his words were only the beginning of her stupefaction, for now he was bringing his face to hers.

She froze like a rabbit scenting a predator. His odor came into her nose, strange and earthy, with a hint of something she'd smelled before but could not name. At a loss to do anything else, she made herself pliant and let herself be kissed. He was her betrothed, after all. His arms stole around her, pulling her against him. She felt the solidity of his body and the questing of his lips. When his tongue invaded her mouth, she gasped and broke away, suppressing a shudder.

A flash of ire came over his features but was quickly replaced with concern. "My lady? Are you unwell?"

She had the impression of a very tall, very heavy block of

stone, one that might fall and crush her. She took a step back but the ground tilted. She would fall. She reached for him, the only steady thing nearby.

He clutched her and held her upright. "You *are* unwell."

"I'm just tired—" She was both grateful for his solidity and repelled by his touch. What was wrong with her?

"The journey was long," he said. "Shall I carry you?"

Without waiting for an answer, he swept her up in his arms. Çifta gave a soft cry of surprise as her feet left the ground. Her arms reflexively wrapped around his neck. His strange earthy scent swirled around her, making her feel like she was amidst a thick fog. It stole her usually sharp vision as well as her thoughts. She wondered if she really was ill. She felt like she'd had too much wine. Over Faraçek's shoulder, she spotted a set of tall, slender mushrooms beside the path that she hadn't noticed earlier. They were charming orange cylinders with blunt tops, a kind she'd never seen before. Çifta tried to focus on them, and not the dizziness she was feeling. She could draw them; that would make her feel better.

Faraçek mounted the steps to the fortress as though he carried no burden at all, hugging her to his chest like she was an infant. His apparent concern made her regret her unpleasant thoughts and assumptions. Her dizziness faded as Faraçek took her to her suite of rooms. By the time they arrived at her door, Çifta was feeling painfully embarrassed.

"I'm myself again," she said, trying to let him know he could set her down now. "I'm not sure what came over me."

Holding her with one arm, Faraçek let them into her chamber. He lay her on top of the coverlet.

Çifta felt well enough to get up, but she could hardly spring back to her feet like a new daffodil after he'd gone to all the effort to carry her here. She tried to relax against the mattress, but she couldn't take her eyes off him.

"Shall I send for something? Broth?"

"That's alright. I already feel so much better. I am embarrassed."

"You are obviously weakened from your travels." He moved to the door. "I will ask… your maid…"

"Eda," Çifta supplied.

He nodded. "I will ask her to come to you."

Çifta didn't have time to form a reply before the door shut. She stared at the fabric draped over the four columns of her bed, the frolicking birds and leafy ferns. Her heart was pounding and her body was a cocktail of adrenalized emotions. She put a hand over her racing heart.

What just happened?

Çifta had never been kissed before, let alone carried by a man, other than her father when she was a little girl. It hadn't been anything like what she'd imagined a kiss to be. There had been something strange about it, not just the fog that had come over her. His tongue. She put her fingers to her lips, then poked out her tongue and touched it to her salty fingertip. It came to her. Though his lips had been warm, his tongue had been cool. She shuddered. That was it. A kiss that might have otherwise been nice had instead been jarring and strange. Was it an unseelie characteristic?

She'd stepped into a betrothal without any understanding of the creature she was to wed. The prince's inhumanity was so much more apparent in person than it had been from his portrait, even though the painting had shown his unseelie features. Çifta rolled onto her side, reliving the kiss over and over. If his temperature had matched hers, might she have liked it?

She couldn't say. She wondered if her father might have reconsidered the union if he'd known how strange the prince was.

Feeling much better, she got up and retrieved her sketchbook and colored pencils from her desk. Sitting in the light coming through the window, Çifta flipped to a clean page. As she selected a pencil and prepared to sketch the mushrooms from memory, the pages flipped themselves back to the most recent drawing. Her heart gave an ache as Laec gazed back at her. She stared at the sketch, feeling unable to turn the page and put him out of sight.

Chapter Twenty

Jessamine

Jessamine, Heath, Peony and Snap met outside Ilishec's workshop for orientation. Aster and three other Calyx—one of whom was the friendly butter-blond—waited with the gardener for the new Calyx to arrive. Ilishec paired them so each new member had an experienced Calyx. When the blond stepped to Jessamine's side with an air of ownership, introducing herself as Rose, Jessamine was flattered. Jessamine was spoken for, Aster went to Peony. Proteas went with Heath, and a Calyx named Anthurium paired himself with Snap.

Ilishec told them to meet back at his workshop in four hours, where they would have lunch together. As the teams scattered, Rose took both of Jessamine's hands. "What would you like to see first?"

To be under the intense gaze of such a stunning creature left Jessamine tongue-tied. Rose, like all the Calyx, was astonishingly beautiful, but though many Calyx were beautiful in a waifish, ethereal way, Rose embodied feminine sex appeal. Her wide expressive mouth was naturally red, her cheeks flushed with pink. Her eyes were the clear blue of a summer sky, and her hair a vivid blond. Her proportions approached the ridiculous, but while she projected all the devastating confidence of a woman who was fully aware of the power of her beauty, she had also an athleticism that lacked in most of the other females. Add to all that a mischievous impishness and one simply wanted to stare at her for longer than was polite.

When Jessamine failed to answer in a timely manner, Rose pulled her into Ilishec's workshop. "Let's get the library and classrooms out of the way first, since they are nearest."

Something sweetly scented and citrusy drifted past Jessamine's nose as they passed through Ilishec's workspace. She closed her eyes and breathed it in. It took a moment for Jessamine to realize that it was Rose she was smelling.

"That's one of the reasons I chose you." Rose looked back over her shoulder. "Everything you're thinking is written on your pretty little face."

This statement astonished Jessamine. "Truly?"

The Calyx dimpled. "One of my favorite jobs is to show around new Calyx, especially when they're from small, remote villages. It reminds me of how I felt when I first arrived. The novelty of the opulence does wear off, after a while. Through you, I can relive it."

Jessamine could not imagine ever growing so accustomed to the wonders of the palace that she felt bored by them.

A fat fuzzy bumblebee buzzed over and landed on Rose's cheek. She pointed to it. "This is Bombini by the way."

"He's very handsome," said Jessamine.

Bombini buzzed his wings a few times and then droned away as Rose was showing Jessamine what was behind a set of sliding doors: a collection of books, scrolls and illustrations protected under clear materials that Rose called vapor barrier. Jessamine could access all the information; she just had to make sure that whatever she took out was put away, and nothing was to leave the workshop or the library.

Behind another door was a cool, humid cave with a pool of still water. The stone walls were covered with mosses, lichens and colorful algae. In the pool bobbed a variety of water plants. The whole room smelled sweet. Jessamine wished she could spend more time in the moss cave, but Rose told her there was too much to see.

"The gardener will let you spend as much of your free time in there as you want or in any of the hothouses, but right now you're on palace time." Rose pushed through another door to a circular room filled with wooden desks and worktables. It smelled of paper and must, old books and an unidentifiable blend of floral scents. Scattered throughout the room and in the library beyond it were Calyx, either studying by themselves or with a teacher. Rose lowered her voice to a whisper as she led Jessamine through the study hall. "You need to spend twenty hours per week in study for the first six months. You'll choose your subjects, and most of them are privately taught. Sometimes you'll get put into a small group if the class is popular."

"What kinds of subjects?" Jessamine whispered, resisting the urge to drag Rose to a slower pace.

"All kinds of things. Languages, geography, history, dancing and etiquette, philosophy, botany—and nomenclature, of course. In later years, you can request a tutor for subjects you want to pursue after you leave here. Things that will help you be successful in the outside world, like architecture, education, the sciences, horticulture, animal husbandry, millinery and tailoring, engineering, trade. Whatever you want. Later today, Ilishec will take you through the subjects and you can select some."

Jessamine's mind whirled. How she would ever narrow her options down to fill only twenty hours per week seemed impossible. She was interested in everything and anything that had not been offered to her by the humble teachers of Dagevli.

They took a plain stone passage that meandered past a courtyard where a group of musicians played. Calyx were being instructed by a slender, elegant man in the chorography of a country dance.

"I know that dance," Jessamine said to Rose.

"I'm not surprised. They're learning it so they'll be able to dance with the villagers in Clover, a town north of here. Before we do country festivals, we're taught the local customs and are fitted for clothing that won't intimidate the villagers. You'll learn the palace dances too. When we perform at banquets in the palace, you'll be fitted for the most beautiful and expensive costumes you've ever dreamed of. Some of the dances are very energetic and challenging, and the Calyx are expected to be the best."

Before Jessamine dreamed up more questions, Rose led her past kitchens where the scent of fresh bread overpowered the smell of Rose's natural fragrance. They stopped at a bright room with a tall ceiling. Servants bustled about carrying bundles of herbs and baskets of fruits and vegetables. They operated strange silver machinery from which spewed fresh juices.

"Here is where your custom elixirs will be made." Rose waved at a sweaty but smiling woman who wore a white cap.

"That's Ms. Tierney. You'll spend time with her this afternoon so she can learn what your body likes. Then she'll develop several recipes for you so you don't get bored, because you'll drink one of her creations every day, sometimes three times a day during the high season. They help to keep your body and your magic in peak condition."

As Jessamine gaped, Rose ushered her past the elixirs kitchen, through more palace halls and up a set of stairs. As Jessamine kept pace with Rose, she got hopelessly lost. Rose showed her more than one ballroom from the balcony level, a theater, a throne room, more libraries and parlors as well as a council room where the monarchs discussed policies, laws and foreign relations. Some rooms were empty and others were busy with finely dressed people of all ages. Everyone looked so civilized and behaved with elegant manners. Rose explained these were courtiers. Some of them lived at Solana year-round while others came from abroad for the summer season. There were nobles from every kingdom of Ivryndi except Silverfall.

"Our job is to use our gifts to entertain these aristocrats, both during banquets but also during the week. You'll be scheduled to do rounds. During rounds, you'll spend most of your time in the gardens, either walking or riding. That's where the guests expect to find Calyx. You'll learn how to maintain relationships with them that are both intimate yet distant."

Jessamine's head whirled. "How? Those are opposites."

Rose smiled. "It is a delicate art to make a courtier feel like they are special, but to make it clear that we do not welcome any physical relationship beyond dancing. The gardener will have already told you that physical relations between the Calyx and guests are forbidden."

Naturally, she would be forbidden to consort with the aristocracy, but how she might fend off a guest without offending them was a mystery.

"Are the guests told of this rule as well?" Jessamine asked as they descended a set of busy marble steps.

"It's understood," said Rose, but she lowered her voice and added, "though I've heard that the gardener has had to clarify this rule in private for more than a few foreigners. As you can imagine, many of them want to get their hands on us. For the less genteel guests, I have also heard that to 'bag' a Calyx is something to brag secretly about among their own courts."

Jessamine was horrified. "Don't they know how much we stand to lose?"

Rose shrugged. "Do hunters care about the fox kits or fawns they orphan? They might pretend to be refined while they are here because Solana is unusual and prized in all of Ivryndi, but a snake cannot shed its fangs. It can only hide them."

At the look on Jessamine's face, Rose's laugh tinkled out. "Don't worry. You'll be equipped with everything you need to brave the gauntlet of palace life. Come on. We'll cut through the gardens and go to the Perfumery. It's my favorite place."

The gardens they passed through had a different feeling to the ones nearest Ilishec's workshop and the hothouses. Paving stones cut in simple and perfect shapes made paths that meandered all over the place. Manicured topiaries, hedges, borders and trees were the pride of the palace gardeners, Rose explained. Color-coordinated beds of plants graced the spaces between the walkways and led to pavilions and quaint pergolas where musicians played. On the grass, a bevy of young children in bright summer clothing were being taught dances by a Calyx. People in astonishing hats and tailored outfits strolled arm in arm, observing the fish in the ponds and the birds in the hedges.

Rose picked up the pace, making it apparent to all who glanced their way that they were on a mission. Rose greeted those they passed and Jessamine tried to mimic her warm but closed tone.

Through a narrow passage draped with grapevines and fragrant *wisteria*, Rose led Jessamine until they reached a wooden door painted purple. Rose put her hand on the silver handle but didn't push through. She looked at Jessamine. "This is one of the secrets that the Calyx are required to keep. You are not permitted to tell outsiders any details about what you're about to see. People know that Solana is famous for its perfumes, but production is a secret. Telling is treason because it could put the Calyx in danger. Do you understand?"

Jessamine nodded.

Rose looked satisfied. "You've already signed the contract, so you are bound. I just wanted to remind you." She opened the door. The scent of flowers grew strong. A wall draped with flowering creepers surrounded a large grassy area with equipment unlike anything Jessamine had seen before. A group of Calyx were engaged in various activities. Dressed in minimal white outfits that made Jessamine blush—she'd never seen a bralette or shorts smaller than a pair of bloomers worn in public before—the Calyx all glowed with sweat.

A pair of male Calyx wearing small white shorts used wooden paddles to bat a ball back and forth over a low woven fence. A larger group seemed to be rotating around a circuit that required them to pull their bodyweight off the ground repeatedly or to lift heavy stones and carry them from point to point.

"What are they doing?" Jessamine was trying not to stare—but failing.

"Making sweat."

"But, why?" What struck Jessamine as the strangest was that they weren't doing any real work. Farm hands back home worked hard like this, but they're always doing something productive. Pulling weeds, picking stones, swinging scythes, bundling hay, breaking horses.

"It's the beginning of the perfume making process. Do you see the pretty buildings back there?" Rose pointed to a glass dome and the connected long, low building with vertical windows. That's the Perfumery. When we've worked up a sufficient sweat, it is harvested in the dome."

They skirted the Calyx and Jessamine took deep breaths of the fragrant air, trying to pick out individual fragrances. Passing into the glass dome, Jessamine's jaw dropped again. In the middle of the room stood two nearly naked, very sweaty Calyx. They held their arms out and stood with their eyes closed wearing expressions of serene contentment. All over their bodies fluttered tiny colored lights as well as butterflies, moths and bees. The lights and the insects landed on the sweaty skin and crawled around for a while, before departing through another archway which led to the long, low building.

"But those are fae!" Jessamine cried, amazed. The tiny colored lights were also known in Dagevli as the wee folk because they never grew any larger than a droplet of water. Jessamine had seen the wee folk in the wild many times, but never in an organized effort like this one.

"Yes. Sometimes they help, but unlike the familiars who are trained to do it, the wee folk only harvest when they feel like it. I think they take part just for the fun of it. No one here will ever hurt them or destroy their habitat, so they feel safe. Many of them are born here, in our own hothouses. They grow up around this process."

"No one would destroy the wee folk around Dagevli either," replied Jessamine.

"Of course. Solana is the safest kingdom for fae. There are other places that are not so kind to them."

This sounded unbelievable to Jessamine. She couldn't think of any reason why anyone would want to hurt the wee folk. But Rose was talking again.

"They harvest the sweat and deposit it in vials which then go through a refining process. The end result is a pure, stable, long-lasting perfume, which gets shipped to shops all over the continent. If you get good at making scents, and people like the brand you as an individual produce, you can make a fortune." Rose had a look of smug satisfaction. "I can make sixty-eight distinct perfumes. Mine are among the most expensive available."

"Sixty-eight?" Jessamine was astonished.

Rose put her finger over her lips and pulled her through the archway to the refinery. "Try not to disturb the process. When you first learn to stand for the harvest, it tickles like crazy. If you can train yourself to think of other things, then the tickling stops, but if we interrupt them, they won't be happy with us."

The long, low building was full of rows of glass tubes. Insects and wee folk bearing sweat entered these fine tubes and flew along them to where the payload was deposited into small clear vials with delicate words painted on their sides. The majority of the vials were empty, but as Jessamine watched, the steady flow of sweat-carrying traffic buzzed through the tubes and deposited sweat into two vials—sweat from the two Calyx in the dome.

"You can only produce the scent of one genus at a time," Rose explained, "so even though I can produce sixty-eight different fragrances—and I'm working on more—I can only do one kind per session. The more sweat sessions you do per week, the more you have to sell. The more scents you produce, the higher the chances you have of making a popular fragrance that people will pay a lot of money for. Trends come and go, but I'm lucky because rose is always popular."

"How do you control what kind of scent you're making?" Jessamine asked, tracing the little colored lights and fluttering insects as they flowed through the tubes like blood through arteries.

"That's what Ilishec will help you with, along with other things. What are your fragrant species again?" Rose's blue eyes trained on Jessamine.

Jessamine had to think. "I bring up honeysuckle, *cleome* and moonflowers..."

Rose brightened. "Honeysuckle is lovely. If I were you, I'd start with that one."

"I'll try." Jessamine felt overwhelmed. "How long did it take you to make your first perfume?"

"A few days," Rose replied. "But it took a few weeks to make a product good enough to sell."

"How often do you do these sweat sessions?"

"Sometimes multiple times a day. I want to buy my parents a villa on the coast and start my own textiles mill."

That explained Rose's athletic shape. Jessamine knew that hard work resulted in a strong body. Though she'd never seen anyone do activity solely for the purpose of getting sweaty, she supposed she'd get used to the idea.

"What happens next?"

"The chemists collect the vials when they are full. They have another place where they do the refining. There is a shop outside the palace where the public can buy our perfumes. I'll show it to you on a day when we are allowed an outing."

As they left the Perfumery, Rose counted on her fingers.

"You've seen the places where you'll spend most of your time when you're at work. You've been to Olinya. You've been to the elixirs kitchen. You've seen where your lessons will be, the library and Ilishec's workshop. You've seen the public gardens and the ballrooms. Would you like to see the stables? You can ride during your free time."

Jessamine's thighs and hips had only begun to feel normal again. If she rode more often, then it wouldn't be painful anymore. Jessamine told Rose she would like to see the stables.

"Right. We only have a half hour, so let's run." Rose laughed and looked back at Jessamine. "You can whip up your first batch of serious sweat!"

The hall of tailors bustled with preparations for the banquet. A line of mirrors and vanity tables had been set up facing the windows where the Calyx could get ready. Pots of soil—some empty, others already filled with botanicals in full bloom—perched prettily on each table.

Jessamine sat between Rose and Aster and copied them as they brought up full-grown plants and clipped fragrant blooms to festoon their hair with. There was no face powder, kohl or lip color. The Calyx were expected to show off the beauty of their faces as they were, without synthetic stains or colorants. Most of the energy went into updos and costumes.

Jessamine studied her face after her hair was set with white honeysuckle and pale pink evening primrose. Her face was attractive; a dimple graced both cheeks when she smiled, and her eyes were a pale gray. She had been called fetching since she was little, but sitting between Aster and Rose—Calyx nearing the height of maturity—she felt like a toad between two swans.

"Do you have any family coming?" Aster asked as she perfected the positioning of the flowers in her hair.

"I don't know. I invited my mother but haven't received a reply yet." Jessamine felt nervous when she thought about the reasons her mother's letter could have been delayed… or not written.

"I bet she's here already, and she didn't write because she wanted to surprise you." Rose dimpled in the mirror at Jessamine.

"I bet that's just what it is!" Aster grinned.

It was exactly what Jess was hoping for. She smiled at her friends, feeling lucky that these two fae had taken a liking to her. Perhaps they were right and Marion, even now, was entering the ballroom, eager to see her daughter perform, and even more eager to talk with her afterward.

In the afternoon of her first day, after spending one hour with Ilishec and learning how to conjure only honeysuckle blossoms by subspecies—a task that required intense mental energy the first time, but got easier each subsequent time—Aster took Jessamine to an artists' studio that occupied one of the turreted towers. Artists had erected easels or had their work laid out flat on broad tables beneath bright lights. Some worked in watercolor, others in oil paints or with brightly pigmented oily chalk. Cubby holes and shelves were filled with every kind of substratum an artist could want, from handmade paper, to stretched canvas, to wood, plaster or sheet metals.

Aster introduced Jessamine to a skinny artist with a large nose and a prominent Adam's apple named Auvo Fetekey. Auvo was a serious, quiet seelie with silver hair that flopped over his forehead. Thick-lensed glasses perched on the end of his nose. He tilted his head back a little to see through his lenses as he sketched a nosegay sitting in a delicate vase on the table.

Auvo turned eyes the color of new grass on Jessamine and examined her with such intense scrutiny that she felt suddenly shy. He took her by the shoulders and made her stand in the light coming in through the opaque windows. He turned her face this way and that, examining her bone structure, her features, her coloring, until his gaze finally caught on her eyes. He gave her a brief, close-mouthed smile and tapped both of her shoulders in an awkward gesture that she thought was supposed to be congenial.

He said: "Welcome to the Calyx. Let's record your image, then." He released her and took up a graphite pencil and a blank sheet from a nearby stack. Auvo began to sketch her, looking up and then down and up again as his graphite raced over the page.

"All Calyx change while they're in the retinue. As your magic waxes, your appearance will take on the qualities you see in mature fae such as Lotus or Delphi."

Jessamine remembered Lotus but didn't know Delphi. Still, she wasn't sure exactly what qualities Auvo was referring to. She grasped on the most obvious visible features these Calyx had.

"You mean my eyes will get bigger?"

"Keep still, please." Auvo adjusted his glasses and tilted back his head to examine her. "It's a little different for everyone and depends on the species you're connected with, but your eyes will likely get bigger, yes. It's a way of taking in more sunlight. You may or may not get longer limbs, some do, some don't, but for sure your skin will become uniform. Your lip color will settle into a distinct hue. The shade of your eyes will probably change, your hair will thicken and your nails will become as shiny as the surface of a still pond at noon."

"How poetic," murmured Aster.

"Do you disagree?" Auvo asked her as she leaned on the worktable and stole peeks at his sketches.

"No. You are right, all of that happens. But I think artists notice the subtler shifts that we don't see in ourselves."

Auvo looked smug. "Yes, the artist's eye is unmatched. Even the smallest change will not be missed by me; the way the bones shift minutely to give an ethereal appearance, the brow bone and chin might sharpen or lengthen, or shorten, if that is what is called for. The neck usually elongates and the shape of the skull becomes more uniform. I've seen the most misshapen head become beautiful, with smooth curves. Noses can change too, but the biggest difference is usually inside the eyes." His pencil flowed over the paper.

Jessamine longed to lean forward and take a look. "Is this your career, then?"

Auvo nodded. "The royal artists do this full time. We are busy chronicling the Calyx, but we often get commissioned to do work for the courtiers, especially for those who live abroad. Everyone likes to have a portrait made at some point or another. Some want one every year."

Aster added: "But with the Calyx, it is more scientific. Yes, we like to record the changes of all the members, but we also have mathematicians who record the changes that happen within your structure."

Keeping her lips as still as possible, Jessamine asked, "And when the magic wanes? We go back to the way we looked before?"

Aster glanced at Auvo and he shrugged. "More or less, yes. Some features don't fully return to their previous state because the Calyx come to us quite young, some before puberty. All faces, Calyx or not, change significantly between the ages of ten and thirty." He turned his sketches toward Jessamine for her to see. "We have made a start."

Jessamine was amazed. He'd rendered her likeness four times over in slight marks of graphite. Auvo had captured her profile, a dead-straight view, a three-quarter view, and closeups of her eyes, lips and nose with straight lines and dots placed on them as though they'd inspired a constellation.

"You're amazing!"

A few artists looked up and smiled. A couple of the Calyx turned to see who was speaking and were told off by their artist for moving.

Auvo smiled. "Solana takes only the best."

"Where are you from?"

"Stavarjak. I used to make portraits for Queen Elphame. Eight years ago, Ilishec invited me to do a temporary placement. I just never left. Of course, he knew that I would never leave. Most of us don't." Auvo shrugged and went back to his drawings. "Solana is the best-kept secret in all of Ivryndi."

Jessamine sat for Auvo for an hour and let him create a bounty of sketches. He would then work from the sketches to create an official portrait that would go into the archives. She would have another one done in six months. Depending on how fast she changed, she might have one made every year, or every eighteen months. Aster explained that when she first arrived, she changed so fast that she had had portraits made every three months for the first four years, and after that it slowed to once every year.

When Jessamine had asked to see them, Aster took her to the archives on the level below the studio, where there were fewer windows and less humidity. Encased and alphabetized portraits trapped between transparent barriers hung on hinges one after the other. These could be flipped through at the viewer's leisure, just like an enormous book. Jessamine hardly recognized Aster's first portrait. Her face was soft and rounded, her cheeks fat, her forehead pimply, her eyes closer together and smaller, her nose upturned. She was cute, but nowhere near the extravagant beauty that she'd become. They flipped through a series of portraits rendered in watercolors which displayed soft but unmistakable changes that had occurred throughout Aster's time as Calyx. Jessamine wondered how she might change and how she would feel about it. Would Marion recognize her? What would Clair think?

"Do you ever worry about losing the beauty you have now?" Jessamine asked as Aster sealed the archives room shut.

"Sometimes. It is nice to be admired, but I look at it as a passing phase. It motivates me to develop other skills not related to physical attractiveness. I figure if I value my beauty too much, when I lose it, it will hurt more, so I want to cultivate other values."

Now, seated between two stunning flora fae prepared for a party, Jessamine looked forward to seeing what changes the magic would bring over her. When they rose, they moved like water nymphs. When Jessamine rose, she bumped the table and knocked over a half-full glass of water.

Rose gasped and Jessamine apologized and began to mop up the spilled water with a kerchief.

"No, it's not that." Rose looked down at herself, troubled. She put a hand to the strap of her gown. "My mother's brooch. I pinned it here, yesterday. It's gone."

Her gaze combed the desk and the floor. Jessamine bent to help her search. Aster shook out articles of clothing, lifted hair tools, books and other belongings scattered about.

"When do you last remember seeing it?" Jessamine asked.

Rose paused, intense concentration marring her forehead. "Yesterday. Oh, we don't have time for this."

Already, the flutes had sounded twice. On the third trill, they were to proceed to the hall and be ready to perform.

"We will have to look for it afterwards," said Rose, but Jessamine could see how much it pained her.

"Is it valuable?"

"A little, yes, but it has been passed down in my family for more than two hundred years. I'll be sick if I've lost it."

It amazed Jessamine that neither Aster nor Rose seemed to betray any thought that they considered the brooch might have been stolen. No one but Calyx or tailors used this hall, she realized, and no Calyx would risk expulsion by stealing.

The flutes gave the final trill and the Calyx swept toward the door, giving kisses to their personal tailors and to those who'd made them look so beautiful.

Thoughts of Rose's missing brooch evaporated as Jessamine went to the front of the line. This was her debut—along with Peony, Heath and Snap. The first ball of their lives as Calyx meant there would be no hiding behind the more experienced fae. They would be the first to perform before the king and queen and the entire Scented Court.

Chapter Twenty-One

Laec

Laec—at the end of the head table—couldn't put his finger on the atmosphere in the hall. Stavarjak's banquets and balls felt like a raucous party, with plenty of wild laughter and frenzied dancing. Here, the hall was hushed with anticipation. Two aisles ran through the banquet tables, leaving a large empty intersection. There were no place settings yet, only goblets and glasses. There was no food, servants with food, or even the smell of food. Those pouring drinks for the guests were dressed in the plainest livery Laec had ever seen, brown upon brown.

The ceiling was a long arch of opaque glass letting in shades of twilight. Chandeliers and sconces cast a diffused amber glow, making everyone's skin look ageless.

King Agir and Queen Esha occupied the center of the head table and had the best view of the hall. The head table formed a semicircle so all guests seated there could see one another. Laec had met some of the courtiers but not all, and had been surprised when given a place of honor. He hadn't had the chance to brand himself as a troublemaker yet. To Laec's right was the end of the dais and a set of steps leading to the ballroom floor. To his left were two empty chairs. He wondered who was late and peeked at the name card on the plate beside his: *Lady Lecta.*

Positioned throughout the room were pretty terracotta pots filled with soil. More planters containing only dirt were hung along the walls and from overhead beams. Depressed into the floor were long, narrow troughs of earth. These reservoirs filled the hall with the scent of earth and mulch.

As Laec wondered what was next and how peculiar it was to smell dirt before a meal, a set of huge double doors at the end of the room swung open. Music filled the hall as four beautifully dressed Calyx swept into the room, two boys and two girls.

A voice at Laec's elbow made him turn. A woman slid into the chair beside him, her lined face done up with makeup and gray hair piled on top of her head into a cascade of curls. Her eyes were lit up. "The first four are new, just selected. This is their first banquet." She held a gloved hand out. "Lady Lecta."

He grasped her fingers. "Laec. Pleased to make your acquaintance."

The first four Calyx moved to the outer edges of the room, each at the end of an aisle. They looked barely into their teens, and very nervous. Even from where he sat, Laec could see the glistening of sweat on the red-headed young man's brow. The two women were both dark of hair but with entirely diverse features. The thin one with blue-black hair had cat-like black eyes, while the other had tawny skin and hair the color of dark chocolate.

As the music swept through the hall raising goosebumps, the four Calyx moved their arms with the music. At first nothing happened, but when tendrils and leaves began to emerge from the pots in one quarter of the room, the audience applauded politely. The plants matured before the audience's watchful eyes, bursting with greenery, buds, then flowers. Laec recognized heather as it was conjured by the lad with the brown hair while the other Calyx held elegant poses, like statuary. A pleasant scent filled the air. Laec felt a wave of homesickness. Heather grew everywhere in Stavarjak. When the heather plants had matured, the flora fae came to rest in a thoughtful crouch, waiting. Attention turned to the girl with the tanned skin and pale eyes. The pots near her filled with trailing tendrils. There were whispers throughout the room and Laec wondered what everyone was talking about.

But when Lady Lecta leaned over and whispered, "Night jasmine?" her eyes still trained on the flowers, he realized people liked to guess the botanical before it reached full bloom.

The scent in the hall sweetened as small whiskery white flowers matured.

"I was wrong. It's honeysuckle. How lovely." Lecta flipped open a handheld fan and wafted the air around her face, making her curls sway.

The audience made sounds of appreciation as they took deep inhales. Those near the pots plucked some of the blossoms and tucked them into their hair or held them for their neighbor to get a better sniff. The female Calyx who'd conjured the honeysuckle bowed and retreated. She came to stand behind the other male who was finished. The only clue that she'd done anything impressive at all was her bosom heaving beneath her bodice.

The Calyx with hair brighter than Laec's moved less gracefully than the others, but the crowd laughed with delight when bright snapdragon plants suddenly appeared out of the soil, popping up so quickly they seemed to burst, rather than to creep as the other plants had done. The snapdragons gave a subtle scent that could not overpower the honeysuckle. Laec marveled that he could smell either, being so far away from them.

The snapdragon conjurer moved to join his friends, leaving attention to fall on the cat-eyed female. She walked forward with a regal air, possessing the room in a way those before her hadn't. She moved her limbs slowly and gracefully, walking the aisle with her arms wide, her fingers beckoning. To Laec's surprise, goosebumps sprang up on his arms in response to her performance, and she hadn't even conjured anything yet. She had such gravity, such confidence. How was it possible that she was new? As she passed her empty pots, her plants came into fullness, a wave of botanical life answering to its master. Thick bushy leaves filled woody stems and—with a flourish, a pirouette, and the dramatic tossing back of her head as the music reached a crescendo—they burst forth with hundreds, maybe thousands of bright pink peony blossoms. The scent of peony dominated the room. Many guests stood and applauded, a few even whistled. The enormous blooms were quickly harvested and given out as the woman curtsied and bowed, then retreated.

The music changed and beautifully dressed Calyx, stunning with the natural beauty of flora fae in their prime, poured into the ballroom from all directions. These were older than the first performers, and far more celestial in their presence. Some of them, Laec guessed, had to be closing in on thirty.

What followed was a performance unlike any Laec had seen. Not only were the remaining pots filled with blossoms of all kinds, but even the air was filled with images of blossoms which hovered and floated. Bees and butterflies fluttered and buzzed prettily from blossom to blossom. Laec recognized lilies, roses and birds-of-paradise, but there were many botanicals he'd never seen before. Oohs and aahs of pleasure filled the hall as the scent of rose came. As the scent of rose died, the scent of lily followed. Rather than one generic floral bouquet, each fragrance was given its own time to be experienced and appreciated. How this magic was achieved was the gift of the experienced Calyx retinue, and the audience clearly loved it. Some left their seats to touch the floating images. These would disintegrate against the skin, leaving perfume behind to be dabbed on necks and wrists. Laec saw some guests making notes on pads of paper or napkins.

"What are they doing?" Laec asked Lecta.

"Marking down their favorites. The shops in Solana always run low on stock after every banquet." Lady Lecta explained that these well-trained Calyx exerted precise control that took practice to master. They knew when to diminish their scent and allow another to fill the air. In this way, the guests would never be overpowered. The new Calyx were not yet capable of such control which was why they went first.

Laec felt his stomach growling. He wondered how the guests would manage to eat amidst the smell of so many flowery perfumes.

The hall was overcome by blossoms, vines, leaves, boughs and creepers. They covered almost every surface, giving the impression that the guests were more outdoors than in. As the performance moved into its denouement, the plants did not age, wither or die; instead, they receded as though going backward in time. Blossoms closed up and shrank. Stems and leaves diminished, retreating to a size much more appropriate for a banquet. What remained was a modest collection of bouquets and potted greenery, and no overpowering fragrance.

As the Calyx retreated, everyone stood to applaud.

Lady Lecta leaned toward Laec. "They'll rejoin the banquet, but they'll change out of their performance clothing first. You can talk to them if you like."

The flutes trilled again.

Servants swept in carrying plates and platters of food. The hall filled quickly with the mouth-watering scent of fresh-baked breads, juicy meats and savory vegetable dishes. The head table, to Laec's surprise, was served last, so he and Lady Lecta made polite conversation as they waited.

"In Stavarjak, the royalty is served first," Laec said.

Lady Lecta waved her fan into her face. "Not so in Solana. The king and queen carry on the tradition of the days of Erasmus. It is a reminder that a monarch is there to serve the people, not to overpower or tyrannize."

Laec watched as people talked, laughed and ate. He wondered if Queen Elphame would feel any shame when he relayed this backward tradition to her. He'd never encountered any aristocrat or royal who would deign to be served last or who wanted to be considered a servant to their people. He decided it was clever because it increased the love and loyalty of the people. Even so, it was still a strategy. Laec couldn't believe anyone would do anything out of pure altruism, least of all a royal.

As food was brought to the head table, Laec noticed a servant wearing livery that did not match the others. He did not carry any food or drink as he slipped in to stand behind the king. He looked serious. When the king noticed him, he gestured for the young man to approach. They exchanged some quiet words. The king turned to talk to Esha, his expression concerned. No one in the banquet hall noticed except those at the head table. Queen Esha whispered to the man on the other side of Princess Kara, over the child's head. He whispered to the woman on his right, and so on until Lady Lecta turned to Laec. "Rahamlar's king-in-waiting has died."

Laec absorbed this. "What was his name?"

"Prince Ander. King Agir and Queen Esha traveled to Rahamlar when he was born to celebrate the princeling's birth. They have not seen him since then, so they don't know him well. He was beloved. This is a hard blow for them."

"Was he recently betrothed, by chance?" Laec's pulse picked up speed at the thought of Çifta. Not even officially married and already a widow. He wondered if the prince had died before or after Çifta had arrived at her new home. What a shock for her.

"Yes, I believe so, which makes it only more tragic." She sighed and took a sip of her wine.

"What happened?"

She put down her goblet. "A riding accident. It's not widely known yet, but I heard just before I arrived in the ballroom that the young prince was thrown into a quagmire. When they found him, it was too late."

Laec was surprised. Royalty rarely went anywhere without guards to keep them safe. "He went alone?"

Lady Lecta spoke from behind her fan. "No, he was with his brother. They make a game of losing their guardsmen. It is said that when the guards arrived there was no sign of the king-in-waiting, only Prince Faraçek in horrible despair."

Laec shuddered and took a sip of blackberry wine. "What are the obligations of King Agir and Queen Esha under such circumstances?"

Lady Lecta gave a delicate shrug, making the jewels at her throat sparkle. "I'm sure they will seek counsel—a precedent that might have been set in the past. If there isn't any, then they will make one. They're fastidious about foreign policy."

A shape appeared in Laec's periphery.

"Little Princeling!" Ilishec's eyes sparkled as he clapped a hand on Laec's shoulder. "Already plying your charms on our most eligible lady?"

Laec grinned wolfishly, even though Lady Lecta was probably twice his age and he had no interest in her. It was always better to flatter in new company.

Lady Lecta laughed and stood to embrace Ilishec. "I hardly recognized you. You've grown so old and fat."

Ilishec slid into the empty seat on the other side of Lecta, laughing. Ilishec had indeed aged, but Lecta's teasing was clearly sarcastic, because the gardener had only grown more handsome with time. Ilishec was thick with rounded muscles. His silver-streaked hair was tied at the nape of his neck and his skin was golden brown and spoke of hours in the sun. The deep lines at the corners of his eyes belonged to a man who smiled a lot.

Lady Lecta turned to address Laec. "Are you a prince in Stavarjak, then? Forgive me, I didn't know."

Laec shook his head. "No, my lady, it is a nickname. One that long ago passed from memory."

Ilishec laughed again. "He *wishes* it passed out of memory."

"But it is a compliment, no?" Lady Lecta shifted as a servant set a heaping plate of food in front of the gardener and another poured his wine. They fussed and fawned, asking Ilishec what else he wanted. He was a clear favorite among the staff. He repeatedly thanked them before they backed away.

Ilishec turned to Lecta. "Laec was a fussy child, eating this but not that, wearing silk but not wool, riding only dark horses, not whites or grays. His hair had to be cut to show his jawline, and heaven forbid he get too much sun and turn the red brassy, even at the age of six."

"Surely not." Lady Lecta's eyes widened.

"All true, and still true today," Laec said shamelessly. "I drink only blackberry wine, no water. All of my clothes are lined with silk and I wash my hair every other day, no more, no less." Laec flipped his hair in an exaggerated fashion. "I carry a chest with twenty of my favorite colognes wherever I go, and my nails are buffed to a shine on the daily."

Lecta laughed aloud, but at a look from the queen, she smothered it. Laec sat back in his chair, quiet. Lady Lecta appeared appropriately chastened.

Ilishec looked blank. "What did I miss?"

Lady Lecta's fan snapped open and she spoke through the side of her mouth. "Prince Ander died. An unfortunate accident."

Ilishec stopped chewing. It took several long seconds before he rediscovered the use of his jaw. "I'm shocked. He was a young man. Hale and hearty, I'm told." Ilishec glanced at Princess Kara fondly. "Sadly, accidents can and do happen to anyone."

The banquet tables were being cleared, and many of the guests had left to change into their evening clothes. The head table finished their meal and servants arrived to make changes. Comfortable seating and smaller tables were to replace the dining table so smaller groups could visit and watch the dancing. Lady Lecta excused herself and left the hall to change. Ilishec and Laec walked together to the open doors.

"They've put me in the purple place," Laec said.

Ilishec looked bemused, then understanding came. "Oh, the violet suite?"

"That's the one."

The gardener smiled to a passerby who congratulated him on the performance, then returned to his nephew. "I did not have time to ask you before: why did you come? Do not mistake me, my lad, I'm glad to see you but no citizen of Stavarjak leaves without a good reason."

"What was your reason?" Laec asked as they left the banquet hall, closed in by a perfumed crowd.

Ilishec looked surprised. "I came for Discovery, I thought you knew that. Was I mistaken that you were a child of enormous ears? There was nothing your parents could keep from you."

"You weren't mistaken, but my enormous ears only worked for things that had to do with me."

"Of course, how silly of me." Ilishec laughed but it passed quickly and his brows tightened. "Is there some kind of trouble? Some issue in the family?"

Laec explained why Queen Elphame had sent him but left off that he'd been drinking and moping, and his opinion that the queen had gotten rid of him as much for his own benefit as for hers. It would be better for Ilishec to think well of him.

"How intriguing," the gardener said when Laec had finished. "I haven't been under Elphame's influence since I was seventeen but I always thought she was a touch melodramatic. Solana is the most peaceful and stable kingdom in all of Ivryndi. Even great fae queens can be mistaken."

Laec just smiled. "Let's hope so."

Chapter Twenty-Two

Jessamine

Everywhere she looked were admiring faces, though none of them were Marion's. Jessamine's anxiety came back with teeth. As she tried to imagine the reasons for her mother not having written back, her stomach tied itself into knots. When Ilishec pulled her aside and put his hands on her shoulders, telling her to relax, she realized that she simply had to put the subject of her mother aside for now or risk making a poor showing at her own initiation ball. She promised Ilishec she was fine, but on her way back to the dance floor, she scooped up a goblet of wine and took three long swallows. After that, she began to enjoy herself.

She whirled about the room with courtiers and nobles, and everyone knew the dances. She danced with handsome young aristocrats who liked to spring her across the floor like they thought they had to cover every corner. She danced with kind elderly men who held her gently and swayed docilely, keeping within a few square meters and chatting with her all the while. She danced with stoic upright men who didn't talk but executed the steps with technical perfection, keeping their eyes focused over her head. If she herself hadn't yet learned the dance, then she gave the lead fully to her partner and did her best to cover it up if she fumbled.

The Calyx did not dance with one another. In fact, they hardly spoke to one another except in passing. To all outward appearances, they were guests as well, but this was an illusion. They were there to make the party lively, to make guests feel appreciated, to listen and submit positive and polite responses on whatever topic the courtiers wished to discuss. Calyx were not to give strong opinions or disagree on any matter. Discretion and tact were part of their art. Jessamine understood now why the Calyx were educated in many different subjects. It was not required that they be experts in anything except the management of their botanicals and fragrances, but it was expected that they could converse with any guest on a great range of topics. Jessamine listened to a breeder talk about bovine stock, then a shipbuilder about the magnificent and coveted timbers of Boskaya, then a young noble with impressive sideburns and muscular calves about swordplay, mathematics and the constellations. Throughout it all, she was expected to maintain the appearance of devoted attention and respectful interest. The majority of the guests seemed to want to talk about themselves, so it took her by surprise when an older gent with a stooped posture and kind eyes said: "Tell me, my dear, is it very difficult?"

She felt Beazle stir in the base of her half updo. It was getting late and he was waking up. She made a mental note to go to the balcony between dances so he could fly into the night sky without having to flit over the heads of the dancing guests. Insects were welcome; bats… she'd forgotten to ask Ilishec about. In the meantime, she struggled to understand the question. "Is what very difficult, sir?"

"Bringing up your pretty plants. Yours was the honeysuckle, if I'm not mistaken."

"Oh." Jessamine realized he was talking about her magic. "It was difficult the first time, but not anymore. Not when I'm concentrating on one species at a time."

The man's bushy brows jumped. "You have more than one species? I thought each of you mastered only one."

"Some of us, yes, we master only one. Others have more."

The man's eyes took on an interested shine as a hopeful look dawned on his face. "You only conjured honeysuckle during the performance, right? I should very much like to see your others."

Jessamine ran her mind over the instructions she'd received. This kind of request was welcome, since it's what the Calyx were best at. Some courtiers even came to the ball fresh out of the bath and without perfume, so they could ask their favorite Calyx for a mystic bloom to perfume their skin with. "If you like."

He stopped them mid-dance and looked at her with a keen, expectant impression.

"Oh. Now?"

He hesitated. "If it's convenient?"

Jessamine couldn't help but laugh. "Sure, no problem. I just need soil."

"There?" He pointed to the troughs lining the wall where some irises grew, but there was space that Jessamine could fill. They went to the trough and Jessamine knelt. The man bent at the waist, putting his hands on his knees, watching with the intent of someone almost frightened to miss any detail.

Jessamine brought up a sprig of *cleome*, enjoying the way the man held his breath and then gave a cry of appreciation when the blossoms burst open. She found another empty patch and raised a cluster of daisy fleabane.

"Oh, bravo, my dear." The man actually clapped his hands together with delight, like a child. "How droll. How absolutely charming."

Rose went by arm in arm with two handsome courtiers and winked at Jessamine.

Jessamine smiled at her friend, remembering that she'd promised Rose she'd help her look for her missing jewelry after the ball was over. She moved her hand to a new patch to raise a stem of *solidago*. As the stem stretched upward and the clusters of yellow flowers burst open, Beazle shifted against her skull. With a squeak, he emerged from her hair and flapped away.

"Cute little fellow," the man said as he ducked out of the way.

But Jessamine couldn't answer because she'd lost sight of the ballroom. Her vision went dark, and she had to reach for the edge of the pot to keep herself steady. A vision unfurled before her. She was flying, first over a balcony full of people and then out over the palace gardens. She felt dizzy as she swooped toward Ilishec's workshop and straight in through an open window.

"My dear?" The gentleman's voice came into her ears, but distantly, like he was a dream.

The room was in shadow, but moonlight cast long diagonal beams across the stones. She dropped down toward a table, then beneath it, before coming to land on the floor. There, lying in front of her on the stones, was a silver brooch holding a cluster of seed pearls in the shape of a white rose. She gasped.

As quickly as the vision had come, it vanished. Jessamine blinked rapidly as sight returned to her. She tried to stand but fell back to the floor, nearly knocking into the elderly man's legs. She felt dizzy and put a hand to her head. Her pulse was racing. She'd seen Rose's brooch and she knew exactly where it was.

"Are you alright?" Her dance partner's brow furrowed with concern.

She let him help her stand. "I'm so sorry. That's never happened before."

The Calyx were not to be a cause for concern to guests; that was definitely forbidden. She gave him a wobbly smile and pitched her voice low. "Yes, I'm fine. I just remembered something important. I'm terribly sorry, but would you excuse me? Please forgive me."

"Of course, my dear. Thank you for humoring an old fellow." He gave her a shallow bow.

She curtsied and headed to the nearest exit. The music and noise of the ball grew dim as she passed the balcony where courtiers and Calyx drank and talked at little tables. Crickets sang from all over the gardens, filling the air with night music. The sky was a spray of glimmering stars. Jess paused, looking for Beazle, but he wasn't in sight. She carried on, single-mindedly focused on retrieving Rose's brooch before someone else found it.

Ilishec's workshop was dark and quiet. The door was closed but unlocked. She knocked out of politeness but went straight in, and directly to the worktable. There on the floor, hidden in shadow, was Rose's brooch. She snatched it up, straightened, then bit off a scream.

There was a dark silhouette in the doorway.

She put a hand over her pounding heart. "Who's there?"

It was a small woman, that much was clear from her silhouette. She moved into the moonlight.

Jessamine let out a sigh. "Hazel. You frightened me. Is everything okay? Why have you left the ball?"

"What ball?" Ilishec's wife leaned on her lion's-head cane. She wore a beautiful gown of deep red and her hair had been decorated with white blooms. A pouch dangled from one wrist, festooned with flowers. She was clearly dressed for a party.

"The… party in the ballroom. The initiation ball."

Hazel's blank features transfigured with sudden understanding. "Oh! Yes. I only came down to fetch something for Ilishec. And you?"

"I came to find my friends jewelry. She dropped it here accidentally and I know she's anxious to get it back." Jessamine showed Hazel the brooch.

Hazel's gaze flicked from the brooch to Jessamine's face. She seemed to be searching for something she'd lost as well, but a thought, not a physical item. "You left the ball to retrieve it now? How strange. Why did you not get it for her before the festivities began?"

"I didn't know until now that this is where she left it." Jessamine was mystified herself. "I… we… suddenly knew where it was. It *was* a bit strange, actually." She hadn't been with Rose when the brooch had been lost, so how had Beazle known where it had fallen? He must have seen it earlier while he was separated from Jessamine, and chosen that moment to share the information with her. Maybe he'd just woken from a nap and thought of it, but it was still unusual. She'd seen through his eyes many times, but only in real time. He'd never shared information in a vision like that before.

"My dear, how did you come by the knowledge of its whereabouts?" Hazel seemed suddenly serious.

"I-I can't explain it. I was conjuring blooms for Sir Edund, and then…"

"You saw it in your mind?" Hazel offered.

Jessamine nodded. "Exactly. I think my familiar—"

Hazel held out her hand. "Best give the brooch to me, dear one. I'll return it to Rose. Keep to yourself the event that led you to it. Share it with no one."

"But—" Jessamine hesitated. "I would like to give it to her myself."

"My dear girl," Hazel said, sternly but not unkindly, "Rose will ask you how you found it and your explanation will raise curiosity. Far better for me to give the trinket back and explain that I discovered it when I came down to retrieve a book for my husband."

Jessamine felt a cool finger trace up the back of her neck. "I shouldn't tell anyone?"

"Precisely. You are to discuss it with my husband before anyone else. He is your master in all things." Hazel's hand was out, still waiting for the brooch. She seemed to recognize Jessamine's concern. "Some fae have abilities outside of growing plants and making fragrance. It's rare, but it does happen. Until these abilities are classified, they need to be kept secret."

Reluctantly, Jessamine handed the brooch over, too uneasy to do anything else. Hazel was, after all, the gardener's wife. She'd been here nearly as long as Ilishec himself and surely knew as much as he.

"Go back to the ball, dear. I'll follow shortly."

Jessamine retraced her steps to the ballroom. Almost immediately, she was invited to dance by a sweating nobleman who appeared to be having the time of his life. She stepped into his arms and he swept her away, but Jessamine kept an eye on the doorway the whole time. True to her word, Hazel returned. She floated across the room toward a group of courtiers talking with Ilishec. She looked neither right nor left, nor made any apparent sign that she was looking for Rose.

Jessamine kept half of her concentration with the vigorous dance partner—who whirled her around the floor like a small tornado—and half on Hazel, wondering when the lady would look for Rose. Rose was not difficult to spot. She hardly left the dance floor, for she was popular among the guests. Not only did she smell intoxicatingly fragrant but, being in her prime, she glowed with exquisite beauty. Even the moths and butterflies were attracted to her. If anyone wanted to find her, they need only look where a pillar of pretty insects fluttered in a column. Rose would be directly beneath it.

Jess assumed that Hazel didn't want to interrupt Rose in her duties. Still, as the song broke and partners were changed, Rose took a break for a drink. Hazel still made no move to find Rose. Six more songs passed and Jessamine grew concerned. Rose had taken several short breaks. Hazel could have easily delivered the brooch by now, yet Hazel did not move from Ilishec's side. She didn't appear to be overly engaged in conversation either, she just looked from face to face, appearing at times to be listening and at other times to be daydreaming. From time to time, Ilishec would put his arm around his wife and kiss her brow. At these moments, she would give her husband a loving look. Then he would resume conversation and she would resume daydreaming. Jessamine felt perplexed. Why should Hazel delay?

Another four dances passed before Jessamine resolved to

approach Hazel. Perhaps if she were in the woman's line of vision, Hazel would be reminded. Perhaps the woman simply didn't realize how important the brooch was to Rose; after all, she had referred to it as a trinket.

Jessamine filled a goblet with a pink punch floating with mint leaves and carried it over to the clique Ilishec was entertaining. She made sure to stand in Hazel's line of sight. When Hazel felt Jessamine's eyes on her, the woman looked at her. Jessamine gave a little wave and a hopeful smile. Hazel smiled benignly back, gave a wave, and then returned her attention to the group. Jessamine moved a little closer and continued to look meaningfully at Hazel. When Hazel looked again, Jessamine waved again and then beckoned.

A serene smile on her face, Hazel came toward Jessamine. "My dear?"

Jessamine kept her voice sweet and quiet. "I was just wondering if you were planning to return Rose's brooch. She doesn't look upset right now because she's working, but she was very worried before the ball began. It will make her so happy."

Hazel's fine brows drew together. "Brooch? What brooch, dear?"

Jessamine went cold. It hit her like a splash of water in the face: there was something very wrong here. Was Hazel faking ignorance so that she could keep the brooch herself? Surely not. Thievery was a serious crime. Surely Hazel, the famous and beloved gardener's wife, would not be so bold?

Jessamine was searching desperately for a response when Hazel gave a jolt and her expression abruptly changed. "Brooch!" She clenched a hand around Jessamine's forearm, causing some of her punch to slosh onto her hand and the floor.

Hazel put a hand to her forehead, then to her chest, then to her hips as though looking for a lost pocket watch. She looked at the red sack on her wrist, reached in and retrieved the brooch. "Thank you for reminding me." She sent a quizzical look at Jessamine. "Who did you say it belonged to?"

"To Rose, Ma'am." Jessamine shook the punch off her hand.

Hazel scanned the dance floor, located the butterflies over Rose's head, then set off at a fast pace, straight through the dancers.

Jessamine watched, bemused and relieved, as Hazel tapped on Rose's shoulder mid-dance. Rose and her partner stopped dancing and turned to look at the tiny woman. They were out of Jessamine's hearing range and partially blocked by couples going by, but she was able to see Rose's expression as her gaze fell on the brooch. A look of amazed delight overtook her. She fell on Hazel with enthusiastic hugs and kisses, making Hazel and Rose's dance partner both laugh, utterly charmed. Jessamine watched with a smile on her face but an ache in her belly. She had found the brooch—she wished she could have had the pleasure of returning it to her friend. She sighed. Rose had her heirloom. What did it matter how it was returned to her?

A voice at her shoulder drew her attention. "May I have this dance?"

Jessamine set her goblet on the nearest table and took the hand of a handsome fae gentleman with bright red hair flowing over his shoulders. "It would be my pleasure, Lord…"

He gripped her fingers with an impish smile. "Name is Laec, but I'm no lord, and I don't dance like one either."

Beazle came swooping over and plopped on Jessamine's chest. He climbed up her curls.

Laec's gaze flicked to her familiar. "There's a bat in your hair."

Jess smiled. "This is Beazle."

Laec withdrew his hand, holding it close to his chest in a parody of fright. "Does he bite? I've already been nipped by a ladybug."

"Only if you're a bad dancer."

He reached for her hand again. "In that case, I would deserve it." Laec led her to the dance floor as the symphony began a new tune. "But there's no danger of that. I just hope you can keep up."

Without thinking, she replied: "Try me, old man."

His jaw dropped with a playful sound of indignation. She mimicked him, then Greta landed on her forehead.

Laec pointed. "There's a moth on your face."

Jessamine laughed again, stepping back into the opening position. Already, the weirdness with Hazel was a distant memory. "Her name is Greta, and she is a rare species of *lepidoptera*."

"If you say so. Let's go, then, moth-face." Laec bowed, a challenge in his grin.

She curtsied, and away they went, with her glasswing clinging to her eyebrows and Beazle swaying from her hair. Jessamine had never been happier.

Jessamine was awake before the roosters began their crowing competition. She always slept with her window open so she could enjoy their rough cries. This morning, though, she hardly heard them. The moment she opened her eyes, she relived the most startling and intriguing event of the ball. Not the performance, not the banquet or the dancing, not even Hazel's odd behavior, or the fun she had dancing with Laec could top what she'd observed toward the end of the evening.

She had been standing by one of the tables laden with fresh food. Aster was nearby, drawn to the fresh fruit. They heard the disturbance before they saw it, when a hush came over the crowd. The symphony faltered and resumed, faltered and resumed, as though the musicians had lost their place in the music and were fumbling to retrieve it. Dancers stopped to gape at the doorway between the tables of food. Aster and Jessamine turned to see what was causing everyone to act so strangely.

She nearly jumped into Aster's arms.

A blue-black panther rippling with muscle and with eyes the color of lemon rind stalked into the hall. She was sleek and beautiful, moving with restrained power. Jessamine had only ever seen such an animal in drawings but those, she realized now, had been a poor substitute for the real thing. This animal was massive. Her long, tubular tail twitched back and forth at the tip. She paused between tables and lifted her head, taking no note of the dancers or musicians. Her nostrils flared and she gave a purring bark before strolling lazily to where charcuterie had been laid out, caring not a bit that she had an audience. When the huge cat tumbled a platter of meat to the floor with an enormous paw and began to feast on the spillage, the symphony stopped altogether. People moved to get a better view of the animal, now gobbling up their midnight snack.

She dropped to her haunches as she ate. Jessamine heard a rumble that reminded her of the barn cats back in Dagevli, only much deeper, like distant thunder. She couldn't tear her eyes from the beast and half wondered if she'd had too much wine. But no, everyone else was seeing this vision too, and some people didn't even look that shocked—although no one seemed to know what to do.

Then a young man dashed through the doors and skidded

to a halt, looking frantically around. His hair was sweaty and standing up in all directions, just as blue-black as the cat's. Stubble darkened his angular jaw and the muscled column of his throat. He spotted the cat, then stood with his fists on his hips, his face in a scowl, his elbows thrust out to the side. He was ruggedly dressed in quilted brown breeches and a loose oat-colored tunic with a thick worn belt and dirt on one sleeve. Whoever he was, he hadn't meant to come to the ball.

The panther looked at the young man, a pile of red scraps between her enormous paws. She licked her lips, revealing a frightening set of teeth. Her whiskers flicked and she gave another raspy bark, trailing off with a playful, rumbly purr. Jessamine got the impression that she was laughing. The young man gave a silent and indignant command, pointing out the door with a straight, stiff arm. Scooping up a final mouthful, the cat stalked toward the young man, chewing as she came. As she padded past him, the young man faced the crowd. He gave a close-mouthed smile that did not meet his eyes, bowed mockingly, his arms swept out to the side, and stalked out after the cat.

The ballroom was quiet for several long seconds. Then servants flew into action and began to clean up the mess and take the soiled scraps away. The symphony started up again and, after some exchanges about what had occurred, the dancers filled the floor again, carrying on with the party as though nothing had happened.

Snap materialized at Jessamine's elbow. He took a plate and absently stacked it with berries, spilling a few back on the table. "Who was that?"

"I've no idea. Aster?" Jessamine was still too shocked to even think about food.

When it didn't seem as though Aster was in any hurry to explain, Jessamine took Aster's plate away. "Could we trouble you for a minute?"

Aster took her plate back, whispering, "You've met a Fahyli already. Why are you so surprised?"

"I have?" Snap spilled another couple of raspberries.

"Not you. Jessamine." Aster kept her back to the crowd as she speared melon slices onto her plate.

Jessamine took Aster's plate again, the melon sliding around. "Fa-hee-lee?"

Aster sighed and took her plate back once more, glancing over her shoulder. "Stop that. You're supposed to save questions like these for your free time. The Fahyli are the crofter's charges. The guard with the hawk who escorted us here, Regalis, he's Fahyli."

"I remember him." Jessamine recalled the way the man's predatory bird had dive-bombed him and then landed on his arm at the last second to be fed hunks of raw meat.

"Right. He was named for his familiar, *buteo regalis*, a species of hawk, just like you were named for one of your botanicals. We're flora fae, they're fauna fae. We have pollinators, they have mammals. We serve the Scented Court under the Honorable Gardener, they serve it under the Honorable Crofter. That was Panther and his familiar that you just saw, stealing our food."

"How do they serve?" Snap moved closer to Aster, abandoning his plate beside the berries he'd dropped.

Trea fluttered over from the direction of the nectar table and settled on top of Aster's curls. "They do all kinds of things: scouting, translation, security. I don't really know everything they do. It's not my business. Calyx and Fahyli only cross paths when the Calyx need to be escorted somewhere for a performance. Our territory is the East Keep, theirs is the west."

Jessamine's mind's eye filled with the big black cat. "So… that huge animal was a familiar?"

Aster took a bite of honeydew. "I can't remember her name, Felicia or Fus… something, but it's easy to remember his, of course. Panther isn't the most social of the Fahyli, but they're all kind of aloof like that. They're not courtiers. They don't learn to dance and they don't come to balls. They're like the blacksmiths or the woodworkers—" She faltered.

Ilishec was striding over, a serious look on his face. Aster moved a few steps away while Snap and Jessamine snatched up their plates and began to build piles of fruit.

"Need I remind you of your duty to keep your attention on our guests?" Ilishec took a plate from the stack and began to spear strawberry halves one at a time onto it, addressing Aster. "These two"—he nodded toward Jess and Snap—"are wet behind the ears, but you should know better."

Aster flushed. "Yes. Sorry, Gardener." She moved away, gaze on the floor.

Guilt speared Jessamine. "It wasn't her fault."

"We badgered her to explain the cat." Snap was frantically picking up the pile of berries he'd dropped. "Very sorry, Gardener."

"It won't happen again," Jess added.

Ilishec gave a curt nod. "Being a successful Calyx requires focus. Don't forget why you're here. You can talk about unrelated things on your own time, if it's so interesting, but I encourage you to focus on your own business."

She and Snap meekly agreed.

"Then back to work with you," Ilishec said, not unkindly.

"This is your initiation ball. Make me proud. Show the court that we were right to choose you."

Jessamine noticed a few of the Calyx watching this exchange, but when courtiers took notice that discipline was being given, the Calyx distracted them by asking them to dance. Ilishec moved away, his features once again fixed into a pleasant smile. Jess and Snap exchanged a sheepish look, then arranged their own faces with gracious serenity and went into the crowd in search of dance partners.

The ball ended soon after.

Jessamine got out of bed and let Greta out into the early-morning light. She rested her chin on her arms as she looked out into the garden. Birds twittered and flew in happy loops. Jessamine wondered if Regalis ever had to worry about Ferrugin hunting the songbirds that populated the palace gardens. Jess longed to learn more about the Fahyli. And to see that big cat again, the shining fur that looked soft to touch, the powerful muscles rippling under her hide, the huge paws that made no sound on the parquet flooring.

A tap came on Jessamine's door and she opened it to see Snap's keenly energized features on the other side. He was wearing the clothes he'd worn when she first met him: a plain-woven shirt with green patches at the elbows and a pair of thin leather pants worn at the knees.

"You're up early," she said with a yawn.

"We have half an hour before we're expected for breakfast. Want to visit the West Keep? See if we can spot any Fahyli?"

Jess was galvanized. "I'll be right there."

He waited for her to dress, then they slipped outside into the quiet of the early morning. Only servants were up and about, carrying folded linens and piles of laundry, firewood and trays of crockery.

Beyond the stables were a collection of buildings which were part of the West Keep. This was where the men-at-arms, stable hands, grooms, metalsmiths, blacksmiths and ostensibly the Fahyli had their domain. They followed a stone wall along a gently sweeping hill until it rounded a curve, and soon they were out of view of the stables. There, Jessamine conjured a *datura* tree, the biggest she'd ever made, by far. She and Snap climbed high enough to peer over the stone wall.

The sun's rays had just begun to filter across blades of grass, clusters of weeds and shrubs, a trickling stream and patches of bare ground. In the distance, and too much in shadow to make out clearly, were small outhouses, buildings and other structures. From the door of one of the long, low outbuildings emerged a shape. It took a moment for the creature to come into the sun, but when it did, it was anticlimactic: only a dog. Small and sleek with a white coat and a black muzzle, it snuffled through the grass.

They watched for as long as they dared, but saw only more dogs and a few birds, some of them quite large and dangerous looking, but no fae or humans. As they made their way back to the East Keep, Jessamine felt disappointed. And yet, there had been something odd about the animals they'd seen. It took her some time to piece together what it was. There had been a crow, but only one, no more, when crows usually traveled in company. There had been one hound dog, though they usually hunted in packs and were trained and housed and fed in packs as well. These animals had also appeared to be perfectly comfortable with one another. So, did that mean they were familiars of the Fahyli, then? Unsure of what they'd seen, Snap and Jessamine agreed to keep their little quest a secret, and returned to their rooms to change for breakfast.

As Jessamine was closing her door for the second time that morning, one of the palace staff approached.

"This came for you." The girl bobbed a curtsy, holding a little tray with a letter sitting on it.

"Thank you." Jessamine smiled as the girl flushed and scurried away. Palace staff were not required to bow or curtsy to the Calyx, but many of them did anyway. Jessamine found it both uncomfortable and endearing. She retreated to her room and opened the letter as she sat on the edge of her bed.

> Jessica,
>
> Congratulations are in order. I don't mind admitting the truth: I am heartsick. At first, I didn't know how to respond to your letter. I've read it several times every day since the day I received it. I was torn between asking you to come home, and surprising you by attending the ball so I could see you in your glory, with your faeness on display for all the world to see.

Jessamine sucked in a breath. So her mother had thought about doing exactly what Aster and Rose had thought she might. Somehow it made Jessamine feel better knowing that Marion had considered it.

> But I resolved long ago to never visit Solana City again. I have my reasons. I will eagerly await your next visit home, at which time I promise to tell you everything about your twin. I am not, and have never

been, ashamed of you. I hope you know that. I sought to protect your identity for reasons I'll also share in person. I'll not deny that you were born with a brother, but I'll not say more in writing. Please do not think poorly of me. I have been selfish, I know, but only because of how much I love you, and because of how much I've lost in the past. You are everything I have in the world. Nothing means anything if you are not in my life. But, in your absence, Hanna has helped me to understand that you must be free to live as you wish, free to make your own way, and she reminds me that you are more likely to visit often if you embark upon this adventure with my blessing. So you have it. Though I'll never think of you as Jessamine, take my blessing with you as you are initiated into the Scented Court. Dagevli is abuzz with the news, and I daresay you should not publish widely when you plan to visit unless you want to be mobbed by the village children. I have only a little advice, and that is keep yourself to yourself. Privacy is worth more than you can possibly know at your age. Focus on your work, be the best that you can be. And visit your mother often. She is waiting for you.

With all my love,

Marion

PS Haft frequents the squash patch often, you'll be happy to know, although I suspect he spends more time flirting with Clair than he does weeding. If you haven't yet received a reply from Clair, blame Haft.

Jessamine brushed a tear away, her heart full of mixed emotions. Marion had given her blessing, and she'd admitted the truth about Jess's twin. The tone of the letter was softer and more diplomatic than Marion's usual, Jess had Hanna to thank for that, but it had achieved the same result that might have been achieved by the demanding tone that Jess was accustomed to. Jessamine wouldn't learn anything further about her twin, not even his name, until she made time to go home.

Chapter Twenty-Three

Çifta

Four days after Çifta's arrival in Rahamlar, Çifta wondered when she'd see the prince again. She hadn't even run into him in the hall, any of the many parlors, or the main banquet hall. Since she'd arrived, she'd taken part in two mourning visitations with the Queen-in-Waiting Serya and Princess Isabey. These entailed standing in the courtyard and greeting citizens who came bearing gifts for the royal household in a display of sympathy and solidarity. Rahamlar's subjects came in all sizes and shapes, human and fae, rich and poor, pulling rickety carts or riding in fine ones. They'd given all kinds of items, from sacks of potatoes (with the burlap dyed black) from the poorest of them, to a fine hand-crafted pocket watch with the prince's likeness engraved on the inside. Çifta had worn the same black dress and the same veil every day. She wondered how long she was expected to wear the same gown, dusting it with cleaning powder every night in an attempt to absorb sweat and body oils, to keep it fresh. She finally asked Eda if she could find her another or have a second one made. The girl had agreed to ask the household tailors, but Çifta had yet to hear more. Every afternoon, tea had been laid out for Çifta in a parlor overlooking the Tadylat. Sometimes Princess Isabey joined her, other times there were a few courtiers milling about and having quiet conversations, but never Faraçek.

Dinners were either taken alone in Çifta's room or in a loud dining hall filled with courtiers who all knew one another. She made lists of the names of those she met and noted some distinct feature so she could recall them, but none of them were as warm and hospitable as Princess Isabey, so Çifta sought the younger princess's company whenever she could.

On her fourth afternoon, as a thunderstorm closed in over the city, Çifta went down the hall to Princess Isabey's room to see if she would be interested in a card game that Çifta had brought with her from Kirkik. As she approached the door, card deck in her pocket, she heard hushed voices.

"...landed beside me. Right where I had been walking," said Princess Serya.

Çifta froze, her knuckles halfway up to rap on the door.

Princess Isabey answered, "Couldn't it have been an accident?"

"The stones and mortar of Rahamlar do not just come loose, dear one. And even if they did, this stone was far too large to fall on its own. I'm telling you... it was pushed."

Isabey sounded terrified, her voice high and childlike. "But who would do such a thing?"

The queen-in-waiting let out a long-suffering sigh. "My dear, you are too sweet. Have I not taught you anything? What must we always ask ourselves?"

"*Cui bono*… but I refuse to believe—" Princess Isabey cut herself off.

Had they heard her? Heart in her throat, Çifta rapped on the door just before it opened.

Princess Serya looked out at her, a false smile on her face. "Lady Çifta, are you well?"

Princess Isabey opened the door wider. "Hello."

"I was just wondering, because the weather is so frightful," Çifta said, showing no sign that she'd overheard anything, "if I might interest you in a game of sneak, since our afternoon visitation has been canceled."

"Sneak." The princess glanced at the queen-in-waiting. "I don't think we know that one. Do we have that game?"

"I brought it with me from Boskaya. It's a card game. I'd be happy to teach you."

"That sounds fun," replied Isabey, brightening.

"You two enjoy," said Princess Serya. "I'm not feeling myself just now. I think I'll lie down for a little while. Perhaps I'll see you at dinner." The queen-in-waiting brushed by Çifta with a gentle touch on her shoulder and headed to her suite. With a final smile, she disappeared inside.

"Is everything alright?" Çifta asked, as she and Isabey walked to the parlor together.

"Oh, yes." Isabey hooked her hand under Çifta's forearm and pulled her close. "Very well. I actually love thunderstorms. Don't you?"

Çifta shivered and pulled her black shawl up around her shoulders. "Sometimes, I guess."

"Come on. I'm a very quick study, and I love games." Isabey took Çifta's hand and picked up the pace. "It's freezing in the halls today. An afternoon in front of a crackling fire is just the thing I need to forget all my troubles."

And, for a little while, the card game made Çifta forget her own, too.

Chapter Twenty-Four

Laec

Though the morning's sunshine filtered in through the oval windows of the noble's breakfast room, a subdued energy settled over the room. The king and queen nibbled from their plates and talked quietly. Lady Lecta and other courtiers sat at the oval table in the center of the room, quietly eating and sipping fresh-squeezed juice from crystal glasses. Laec went to the sideboards where a sumptuous breakfast had been laid out. As he piled fruit, pastries, eggs and sausages onto a plate, Ilishec entered. He greeted everyone and joined Laec at the food.

"Uncle," Laec murmured.

"Nephew," Ilishec replied. "Have you caused trouble already? Why is everyone so grim?"

Laec spoke out the side of his mouth. "I found them like this. I think they're hungover."

He waited for his uncle to fill a plate and then they sat together at the central table. The door opened again and a large man Laec had never seen before came in. He wore workman's clothes: a vest of black leather, a thick belt, leggings tucked into sturdy boots. At his shoulders, rustic brooches held a black cape in place that swayed as he walked. His arms were bare and crisscrossed with scars, his eyes somehow both sleepy and wary, and deep lines bracketed his mouth. Short dark hair stood this way and that. Laec thought he looked like a warrior. A glance at his fingers revealed that he did not wear any rings, not even one such as Ilishec wore, bearing the wreathed lion's head.

"Who is that?" Laec nudged Ilishec, who had just bent to take a bite.

Ilishec glanced up, his gaze earnestly fixed on the man who was now approaching the king and queen. The monarchs sat up straighter when the man bowed and greeted them. The king beckoned for Ilishec to join them. When Ilishec got up and Laec followed him to the monarchs' table, Queen Esha invited them to sit. The large man had just pulled a chair back and sat, far enough away to make it clear he was not there to eat.

"Gardener." He nodded at Ilishec. His voice was like gravel.

"Crofter," Ilishec returned. "We don't often have the pleasure of your company at breakfast."

"As you might guess, what brings me isn't good news." The crofter turned his attention to the king and queen.

"Don't make us wait, Ian." The king settled his hands beneath the table.

The crofter frowned. "There was a skirmish at a border town last night."

The queen gave a small gasp. "Was anyone hurt?"

King Agir's expression was flat. "I'm not surprised. I expected there might be trouble."

"Yes, there were injuries. No deaths. But several families

have lost their homes. They were burned, their crops destroyed and their animals stolen."

"Our border patrols could not warn us in time?" The king's brow furrowed.

The crofter dropped his eyes, as though squirming mentally, though his body was still. "Nothing was reported, my king, I regret to say. There were no Fahyli posted there last night, only soldiers. Our ranks of fauna fae have thinned, meaning individuals have to cover more and more territory. When the scuffle took place, they were elsewhere and arrived too late to prevent it."

"Are you telling me our soldiers cannot be relied upon?"

The crofter thought about this. "Perhaps. This will serve as a wakeup call. I warned Bradburn that Ander's death might trigger unrest, but we have had peace for so long that we hardly know what an enemy looks like. In any case, we were taken unaware."

"Is that why Bradburn isn't here to report this himself?" Disappointment was palpable in the king's tone.

"He is on site at the moment, my king. He will report to you directly as soon as he returns."

"But it is the job of Rahamlar to keep the raiders in check," said the queen. "They've done so for decades. The last time there was trouble at our borders, I was just a young girl. I hardly remember it."

The king templed his fingers over his half-eaten breakfast. "The whole kingdom is reeling. We must send a message of solidarity which will also remind them of their duty to us."

Ilishec straightened. "Solidarity, my king?"

King Agir nodded and now so did the queen. "Along with our offer of assistance, we will send a retinue of Calyx."

Laec looked from the monarchs to the gardener and back again, trying to discern the wisdom of this strategy. This was a beautiful kingdom, but strange. Queen Elphame's answer to a skirmish at her borders would be swift and violent, not a perfumed parade.

"The Calyx, my king?" The crofter sounded hesitant. "Will they welcome flora fae to pretty their halls at this time?"

Laec's pulse sped up. They were talking about sending a retinue straight into the heart of Rahamlar to perform in the midst of the fortress… for the citizens of a kingdom who had just ruined a border village. His palms felt damp, and he wiped them on his thighs. Was this foolishness or was there some clever tactic here?

"There is never a bad time to bring the warmth and beauty of nature to grieving souls." Ilishec's gaze sharpened. "We can be a balm to our neighbor. I am sure they will take comfort from our visit. This is the correct strategy."

"Is it?" Ian frowned.

The king punctuated the air with a finger. "We need to show them that we, too, valued Prince Ander's life. What softens the sting of grief better than understanding that you are not alone in it? And what better way to remind them of our presence and our value than to share the beauty of our most symbolic blooms? You excel at enriching our lives, dear Gardener. I have faith that you can also soothe our neighbors, soften the blow of their loss. Not with frivolity, but with solemnity and dignity."

The gardener let this sink in. "I see, yes. The tone must be mournful, sympathetic, a requiem."

"Precisely. You understand." The king nodded. "Should the situation be reversed and our own daughter have passed so suddenly and tragically, pride forbid, then we would receive such a gift with gracious thanks. Would we not?" He looked at Esha.

Esha shuddered and she put a hand over her heart. "Pride forbid, of course we would."

Ian shifted in his seat. Laec wondered what he was thinking. "We have not sent Calyx to Rahamlar since the birth of Prince Ander, twenty-four years ago."

The queen glanced at her husband and back at the crofter. "Were there problems?"

"No, they were cared for and appreciated," the crofter admitted. "However, that was during a time of celebration. The prince had just been born. Even Queen Daryli was in an uncommonly generous mood."

"The Calyx trust us not to lead them into danger." Ilishec looked from Ian to the king and back again. He looked eager to prepare for the assignment, but when the Calyx left Solana, their security was out of Ilishec's hands.

"There need not be danger," the king said, with a glance at the crofter. "Ian will arrange the security. Enough to ensure safety, but not so much to make them feel untrusted."

The crofter gave a nod that suggested he would do as asked but wasn't necessarily in agreement with the idea. "I can provide protection, as you wish."

"I'll go as well," Laec said.

The king looked at him as though seeing him for the first time.

Queen Esha leaned toward her husband and whispered, "Stavarjak. Remember?"

The crofter's lips twitched and he looked at Ilishec. "One of yours?"

The gardener smiled. "My nephew."

Laec dropped his chin in deference. "Please, let me make myself of service. It's what Queen Elphame sent me for."

"Queen Elphame?" Ian's expression came alive with the first real emotion he'd shown since he entered the room: a mix of surprise and confusion. "And do you come with her authority and power as well?"

All gazes fell on Laec. He answered with confidence he didn't quite feel, but if he appeared confident, then maybe he'd instill some. "I am to be her eyes only. For now."

"It's up to you, Ian," said the king.

The crofter let out a breath and scratched along his jaw. "If Queen Elphame wants to babysit us, who am I to deny her? If you agree to place yourself under my authority for the entirety of the journey, and follow my orders, you may come."

"No problem," Laec replied smoothly.

"I'll expect you at the West Keep tomorrow at dawn, then."

"How much time do you need to prepare?" the king asked Ilishec.

"The musicians already know the mourning songs, but I need time to select the appropriate Calyx and work out the performance with them. A month would do nicely."

The king and queen exchanged a displeased glance.

"But three weeks is manageable," Ilishec amended. He looked at Ian. "I suppose that's enough time for you?"

The crofter's mouth twitched. "You worry about your part of the assignment, Gardener. When you're ready, we'll be waiting. As always."

The king clapped once. "Then its settled." He turned to Esha. "My dear, will you arrange for the procurement and packing of gifts?"

"Of course. But what about the villagers?"

"We will take care of them, too, of course." The king said to the crofter, "When Bradburn arrives, we will discuss how best to help them rebuild. In the meantime, will you arrange to send care for those who are injured and replace the animals they've lost? Whatever can be done for them, we must do it."

"We shall see it done." The crofter got up and bowed deeply. "Beauty is our strength."

The king, queen and Ilishec echoed his words and Ian strode from the room. Laec and Ilishec excused themselves from the head table.

"Who is Bradburn?" Laec asked as he slid into his seat.

"Captain of the Guard, and Ian Peneçek has been the crofter for fifteen years now, or something like that. They don't always see eye to eye."

In their absence, their food had gotten cold. They ate it anyway.

"You didn't have to do that, by the way," Ilishec said around a mouthful. "The journey is rough, and Rahamlar isn't particularly hospitable. Why leave the comfort of the Scented Court if you don't have to?"

Laec shrugged. "I've always wanted to see the famous three-foot-thick walls and the twin rivers."

"Ah," Ilishec teased with an arched brow, a fried yam speared on the end of his fork. "Yes, the Tadylat and the Tamyrat. Who doesn't come from every corner of Ivryndi to bathe in their freezing depths?"

Laec took a bite of toast. "So far, all I see at the Scented Court is a lot of comfortable courtiers. The city is a wonder. It goes like the cogs of a clock. Everyone is polite, everyone knows the dances and smells like flowers. Elphame expects a report with something in it. The only sign of any trouble isn't here, it's in Rahamlar, so that's where I'll go."

"I suppose that makes sense," Ilishec acquiesced.

It did. It made perfect sense. The fact that a certain young widow was sure to be at this performance had nothing to do with it. Nothing at all.

Chapter Twenty-Five

Jessamine

JESSAMINE WAS CROSSING her room to slip under her quilt when a knock came at her door. Strange. It was after eleven and most of the Calyx were fast asleep already. She approached the door but didn't open it.

"Who is it?"

"It's Indigo."

Jessamine opened the door and peered out at one of the gardener's assistants. Indigo was a small, wiry man who was never seen without a hat on. Perfectly understandable, given that he worked in the gardens all hours of the day. Indigo was barefoot, as usual, and had dirty hands, as usual. Though this was usual during the day, it was not for this hour.

"Are you still working?" Jessamine opened the door wider.

"Just finishing up now, Miss Jessamine. There's some sprouts that like planting at night best," Indigo replied, picking at his thumbnail. "Ilishec requires you in his workshop. He apologizes for the hour, but it's important."

Jessamine's stomach gave a pinch of anxiety. "I'll change quickly and go right away."

She swapped her sleep clothes for the tunic and pants she'd worn for her afternoon classes, slid her feet into a pair of slippers and ghosted through the castle. She wondered what Ilishec had on his mind, and whether she might have an opportunity to ask him if she might take a day or two to go home. She had visions of him getting angry at her requesting time off when she'd only just started, but she was dying to get home to talk to Marion.

The lights had been turned down and the color glowing from the sconces had changed from pale rose to warm amber. Voices in conversation, pitched low, could be heard through a few doors as she made her way through the study to the back door of Ilishec's workshop. When she let herself in, Ilishec's head appeared from behind one of the thick wooden load-bearing beams which he liked to hang dried herbs on.

"Ah, you've arrived. Come. Come." He waved her to a place at one of his vast wooden tables where a few pots of empty soil had been laid out. "Were you asleep?"

"Just getting into bed. Indigo said it was important."

"Sorry. I'm short on time. Thank you for coming." Ilishec laid his hands on the table, leaning forward. He peered at her from under his brows. "I have a special assignment. An unusual assignment, one that requires me to put together a retinue of ten Calyx to perform for our grieving neighbor."

"Grieving neighbor?" Jessamine wracked her brains. The palace's only neighbors were lands for gardens, stables, outbuildings and storage, and an indoor riding stable for winter use. Beyond that and down a long, long slope, one would come to suburbs of Solana City where civilians lived.

Seeing her misunderstanding, he shook his head. "I mean our neighboring kingdom."

"Rahamlar?" Jessamine's curiosity and ears perked up. "What's happened?"

"The king-in-waiting passed away in a tragic accident." He shook his head. "It's a very sad state of affairs. He was thrown from a horse. He was young and much loved."

Jessamine's shivered, wishing she'd brought a shawl. "I'm sorry."

"Me too. King Osvitan—I am told—is not well and may not live another full year. Prince Ander was well groomed for the position. They are in mourning and King Agir and Queen Esha have arranged for us to show our solidarity by sending a retinue of Calyx to comfort them, along with mourning gifts. The first thing I have to do is put together a cast list. I have already spoken to several Calyx, which took a little longer than I expected it would. You're the last one I need to speak to, which is why it's so late. Do forgive me."

Jessamine was more intrigued now than tired. "That's okay."

"Let me get to the point. You have shown you can bring up *ipomoea*." He glanced at a notebook for reference. "Specifically, so far, you've conjured *coccinea*, *batatas* and *imperati*."

The gears of Jessamine's mind, which had shut down for the day, began to turn again at the sound of the species of moonflowers that she had been working with. *Coccinea* had tubular, red flowers and heart-shaped, three-lobed leaves. *Batatas* had edible tubers, ovate leaves with light green to deep purple leaves and pale, funnel-shaped flowers with a purple stain at the base. *Imperati* grew in sand and came in both white and a bright purple. As her imagination painted images of these flowers, her skin began to ooze perfume.

"Wait, wait." Ilishec said, seeing what she was doing. He picked up a small glass vial with a handwritten label. "It's a pale purple flower, softer in color than that of the *imperati*. I want you to scent this and see if you can bring it up." He unstopped the vial and handed it to her.

Jessamine closed her eyes and inhaled the undiluted scent. She could pin it as a member of the convolvulaceae family, but she was not skilled enough to identify the genus from scent alone. Still, she felt her body quicken, and when she focused on one of the pots of soil, it had already sprouted with green tendrils. They slithered outward, buds formed and brightened in color. Ilishec seemed to be holding his breath, and when they burst open with a pink-purple shade and a deeper red stain at the base, he smiled.

She left off growing the vine and it settled at her command. "That was easy."

He leaned a hip against the table and folded his arms. "I would like to offer you a place among the retinue that goes to Rahamlar."

Jessamine's heart swelled with pride. It was not necessarily an honor for a Calyx to be chosen to perform at a rural village, but to visit a neighboring nation to perform for another monarch, another court, this was usually reserved for Calyx in their prime. "Why me?"

"Because only you can conjure *ipomoea cordatotriloba*, which has a symbolic meaning of extinguished hopes. The presentation I am planning will not only be moving and beautiful, it will be layered with meaning. The other Calyx I chose can also produce blooms with relevant symbolic meaning. It is important to Queen Esha and King Agir that we put thought into this gift." Jessamine took a breath to say yes but Ilishec put up a hand. "You must understand that when the Calyx venture beyond our borders, there is always risk."

"What risk?"

"It comes in many forms, Jessamine. I haven't been to Rahamlar since the young prince himself was born. When you leave the safety and security of our land, you enter the unknown. The Calyx are valuable, this is well known, and every precaution is taken to keep you safe. We will have an armed escort and our coterie will be large enough to discourage thieves. The danger is only while we are traveling. Once within the walls of Rahamlar, we will be welcomed and honored as guests. It is a fine thing and a privilege to see how other kingdoms live, but I would be remiss if I did not warn you of the danger. It is my request that you come, but you have final say about the assignments you take. I do need an answer quickly, however. We are set to leave within a fortnight."

"I want to do it." Jessamine's hesitation had fallen away when Ilishec told her they'd have armed guards. Not only might she have an opportunity to observe the Fahyli, she would finally be able to see up close the kingdom she'd only glimpsed from a distance from the clifftops behind Dagevli, a smudge of cloud that she had gazed at since she was a young girl. With a performance in Rahamlar to prepare for, she definitely couldn't ask for time off to scamper home for a visit, but if she made him proud, maybe he'd give her a short break when the Calyx returned.

Ilishec smiled. "Good lady. Thank you. Now go to bed. You'll receive more instruction before we leave, but part of your charge will be to produce only this species when you are in Rahamlarin company. The meaning you express, alongside the rest of the coterie whose blooms will also speak of sympathy and solidarity, will touch their hearts and be a soothing balm to their wounded souls."

Jessamine blinked at this poetic speech.

Ilishec looked almost as startled, then smiled as he followed the pretty rhetoric with, "I think I should go to bed. Hazel has warned me many times that I become insufferably pompous when I am weary."

"It was nice," Jessamine replied. At the mention of Hazel's name, she recalled the incident with the brooch. "Can I ask you something about your wife?"

Ilishec listened while Jessamine told him about Rose's brooch. She left out nothing, not even Hazel's strange behavior. But Ilishec seemed more disturbed by her vision of the brooch's location than he was about Hazel, and questioned her about it.

"It was just as I told you," she explained. "I was bringing up species for a guest who had asked for me to show him. While I was doing so, I received a vision of the brooch's location and knew exactly where it was."

"But you were not with Rose when she lost it?"

"No. Beazle has shown me things before—"

"You see through Beazle's eyes?" The gardener's brows shot up.

"Sometimes, yes. But he controls it, I don't. And he's never sent me an image of something he saw in the past before. Nor has he ever gone out to find something for me."

Ilishec went thoughtful. "This is very interesting, Jessamine. You say you were conjuring *solidago* when it happened." He went to the bookshelves and traced a finger along several spines before pulling one down. It was a big square tome with hand-painted flowers on the cover but no title. Ilishec lay it on the worktable and began to hunt through the pages. "This book catalogs symbolic meanings. But it's also a litany for something else that I haven't paid much attention to, because in all my years as gardener, I've never seen a wisp of proof that its real: that of the folklore around different species."

Jess peered over Ilishec's shoulder and the illustrations in the book. "Folklore?"

"Yes, stories, fables, superstitions. I haven't the time or patience for pseudoscience, but I do remember something I read once about *solidago*. Here it is." Ilishec found an illustration of the yellow weed. He ran his hand down the page past a section entitled Symbolic Meaning to a section entitled Folklore.

"Wear or carry a nosegay of *solidago* for a full day and on the following morning, your true love will appear," Jessamine read aloud.

"Utter nonsense," Ilishec scoffed. "But look at this." He pointed at a sentence with a blunt finger.

Jessamine read out loud again: "*Solidago* is known to lead one in the direction of lost or hidden objects." She looked up at Ilishec in surprise. "So it's true, then?"

The gardener shrugged. "Something led you to the brooch, and it happened after you conjured *solidago*, so I would venture to say that perhaps not all folklore is rubbish, after all. But until we know more, I would like you to keep this event to yourself."

"That's what Hazel said."

Ilishec's look softened. "Yes, she has retained something of her old self."

"What do you mean?"

"My wife is suffering from something usually reserved for the elderly, a form of dementia. Her short-term memory is terrible, but her long-term memory and her recall of botanical trivia is second to none." He let out a long sigh, a weary sound, and rubbed at his eyes.

Jessamine wasn't sure what to say. "I am sorry," was all she could manage.

He blinked at her with red eyes. "Thank you. In spite of her suffering, she is mostly happy. I have wonderful memories of my quick-witted wife. I learned long ago not to correct her when she is confused or forgets where she is or why she came into a room. It only upsets her. Once in a while, I am reminded that she is still in there somewhere."

His words were hopeful, but his body expressed a heavy sadness. Jess wished she knew how to comfort him. She had no experience with this kind of suffering; she hardly had experience of any real suffering at all, she suddenly realized.

Ilishec gave her a tired smile. "You'd better go to bed. You'll need your sleep."

Jessamine thanked the gardener and returned to her room. But she restlessly tossed and turned as she thought about the deterioration of Hazel's mind. It had to be very difficult and painful to have a family member whose mind was breaking down. Ilishec only had Hazel, and Jess only had Marion. Marion had chronic pain in her hip and had to use a cane to get around, but her mother's mind was razor sharp. Jess had grown up being a support for her mother, getting things down from cupboards, doing the difficult work at harvest time, putting up and taking down the market stall. But now Jess saw how much more difficult life might have been if Marion's injury had been in her mind instead of in her body. She suddenly missed her mother, and fell asleep with gratitude for Marion in her heart, something she hadn't felt since she was a child.

Chapter Twenty-Six

Çifta

ÇIFTA WAS COMBING out her hair and preparing to braid it for the night when a soft knock made her lift her head. It was late, and she wasn't expecting visitors. Eda had left her more than fifteen minutes ago, after banking the fire for the night and setting a bedwarmer between Çifta's sheets. She stilled, wondering if it had just been someone in the neighboring room. When the knock came again, soft, yet with an urgency, she went to the door. Sliding open the judas window, she stretched up on tiptoe to look into the hall.

"Who is it?"

A young man peered back at her, his face cast in shadow. He gave her a polite smile as he held out a fist, showing the gold ring on his index finger. It had Serya's seal engraved into the flat circular face. "The queen-in-waiting bid me relay a message to you."

She opened the door and stepped back as he slipped inside, making her pulse jump. "They couldn't send a woman?"

"I was the only option, I'm

afraid," he whispered. His hair glinted with gold in the torchlight, and his skin was ruddy and tanned. There was no hint of fae about him, and he seemed tense with nervous energy. "Send a letter to your father. Dissolve the betrothal. Have him send men to escort you home as soon as possible."

Çifta was speechless for a moment. "Princess Serya suggests this?"

"Directly."

"But I've only just arrived. It's been little more than a week." And in all that time, she'd only seen Faraçek once, for the stroll in the garden. She no longer trusted her memory of the encounter: her trembly unease, his cool detachment, the strange kiss. But what else should she expect when meeting the person she was meant to spend her life with, to share her intimate thoughts with, her body and bed? He must have been as nervous as she, even if he did not show it. Her body tingled with caution, but logic bade her delay judgment. It was early. Far too early, and she was keen to see him again, hopeful that the next visit would be an improvement.

"I can only tell you what was given to me to say. It will go better for you if you heed this advice. Go home." He said it kindly. He opened the door and peered out, looking both ways down the hall. With a parting nod, he slipped through and was gone. It happened so quickly, she had no time to react. He hadn't even told her his name.

Çifta backed up until she met the bed and sat down.

Dissolving the betrothal so soon would be an insult, not only to Prince Faraçek but the entire kingdom. It would be embarrassing to repack the trunks she'd just unpacked, to call Endyr and his men back. Her mind spun. The queen-in-waiting herself had told her to do this, Prince Faraçek's own sister.

Did it have something to do with what she'd overheard a few nights ago?

The candle near her bed guttered before she realized how much time had passed. Not bothering to finish with her hair, she slid beneath the blankets, listening to horses whinny from distant paddocks. She resolved to visit Princess Serya early, before breakfast. She needed more information before she did something that couldn't be undone. Goodness knew, Kazery would expect an explanation.

Çifta threw her coverlet back at first light. Her room was cold. She was surprised that her fire had been allowed to go out. Every morning since she'd arrived, Eda had slipped into her room to put fresh wood on so that the room was less bracing when Çifta rose. She shivered as she took care of the fire herself, stirring the embers and erecting kindling into a small tent, the way her father had taught her when she was young. The ice-cold metal of the poker seared her hands and she was reminded about the cool kiss. The fire flared. She opened the shutters to peer into the courtyard. All was quiet save for the call of larks. The sky hinted at the coming day. She shivered again and changed into her mourning gown, not bothering with the cuffs or making the rear laces tight. She took a candle and stole down the hall toward Serya's suite, thankful it was not far.

The town crier called that it was six o'clock.

She came to Isabey's door first; it stood a few inches ajar. She knocked and waited. No answer. She pushed inside, calling softly and holding the candle aloft. Shadows congealed in corners and behind furniture. The princess's room was empty of life. The bed was unmade and the fire almost dead, a wisp of smoke drifted toward the chimney. No servants had been here either. Çifta's stomach knotted. Strange.

Çifta backed out of the room and went down the hall to Serya's chambers. Knocking, she waited impatiently, trying not to dance from one foot to the other. When no one answered, the knot in the pit of her stomach tightened. Was it possible both princesses were breakfasting early? She supposed so. She wasn't accustomed to the rhythm of life at Rahamlar yet. Perhaps there was no reason to be concerned, yet her instincts rebelled. Something was amiss.

On her way to the staircase leading down to the dining hall, she passed Eda.

"Oh, thank heaven." Çifta gave the maid a quivering smile.

"Good morning, milady. You're up early. How did you dress yourself?" Eda's eyes raked Çifta from head to foot. She dimpled. "Not very well, I see. If we return to your chamber, I can tighten the stays and help you with your sleeves."

Çifta allowed herself to be led back to her room where she stood impatiently to have her dress fitted properly. "Have you seen either of the princesses this morning?"

"No, but that's not unusual." Eda tugged on the laces at Çifta's wrist. She glanced at the window, measuring the light. "They don't rise for another hour, unless they've planned a ride."

Çifta's stomach relaxed a fraction. "That must be it. They're out for an early ride."

Eda stood back, examining Çifta's hair with a frown. She guided her to a chair, raking her fingers gently through her hair to untangle the knots. "No, milady. They only ride at weekends."

Çifta tried to remain still as Eda placed the hated veil over her hair. "But they're not in their rooms."

Eda's hands paused. "They must be."

Çifta shook her head. "Isabey's bed is unmade, her room empty. I didn't look in Princess Serya's chamber, but she didn't answer when I knocked."

"I'm sure there's an explanation, milady." Eda finished with Çifta's veil, positioning it over Çifta's forehead where it brushed annoyingly against her eyebrows.

Çifta immediately pushed the veil back. "It bothers me."

"It's the proper way, milady."

"Hang the proper way!" Çifta stood, flushing.

Eda blinked at her, startled.

Çifta sighed. "I'm sorry, Eda. I just—I had an exchange with… someone last night. It's put me on edge. It's important that I speak with the queen-in-waiting."

"What exchange?" Eda's forehead wrinkled.

"A young man. I don't know his name." Çifta put her fingertips to her brow. Why hadn't she asked him for his name?

"This is unseemly and improper, milady."

"Yes, I'm aware of that."

"It was wrong of him to see a lady in her rooms, alone, in the evening, when she's preparing to sleep."

"I'm not disputing—" Çifta sighed again. Eda seemed to have missed the point. She took the maid's hands and looked her in the eyes. "Would you please find Princess Serya for me? It's a matter of urgency."

"Right away, milady." Thus appealed to, Eda bobbed a curtsy, then sailed from the room with purpose.

Çifta paced and chewed her thumbnail. Was she really going to do this? She sat at her desk and drew ink and paper from its drawers. She stared at the blank page a long time. She could pen the letter now, then see what could be learned from Princess Serya afterward. She could burn the letter if she decided it wasn't prudent, or just leave it in her desk for later posting. There was no harm in having it prewritten.

The letter she penned was simple. Addressed to her father, it reported that her betrothed was unsuitable and—with regrets for the awkwardness she knew could not be avoided—she needed him to dissolve the agreement and send an escort as soon as possible. She would explain everything more thoroughly when she was home.

Home. Her city. Her kingdom. Boskaya.

Çifta's heart lifted to think of it: the sound of port activities coming in her windows, the smell of salt on the wind, the cool, bracing sea air lifting her locks and kissing her cheeks. Kirkik was so unlike Rahamlar. Here, the air was close and damp, a little too suffocating. It dragged into her chest and weighed down her clothing and hair. Kirkik was fresh and cool and open.

Now that she'd penned the letter, and the more she thought about going home, the better she felt. Perhaps it was the right thing, after all. She wondered what it would cost her father's business. Hopefully nothing. He wanted access to the twin rivers, but could that not be arranged without a wedding? Marriages were not the only way to form alliances. Prince Faraçek was odd but seemed reasonable. King Osvitan had agreed to the dissolution clause, so she was perfectly within her rights to invoke it. Faraçek would only want the right for himself as well, if he found Çifta to be unsatisfactory. The fact that he'd not sought out her company since their first encounter certainly pointed in that direction. Maybe he'd even be relieved, saving him from having to do it.

Çifta rolled the letter into a tight spiral and used the Unya family's smallest seal to close the tiny scroll. She would send it by the fastest bird the Rahamlar aviary offered and rose from her chair with a view to doing so immediately. Tucking the scroll into her sleeve where the cuff hugged her wrist, she left her suite. The activity boiling in the courtyard nearly brought a yelp to her lips as she emerged. In the short time it had taken to pen her letter, it seemed like every living being had awoken and leapt into the day's tasks.

Horses were led this way and that, their tack was adjusted as men mounted and dismounted. There were even some ladies among the group, dressed in riding trousers that no women in Boskaya would wear. Pageboys and stable hands ran amok carrying armor, weapons, tack or saddlebags. It was for a hunt. She wondered why she'd not been invited. She wasn't a huntress, but she loved to ride. She looked for the princesses among the bustle, thinking Eda must have been mistaken about them only riding on weekends, but didn't see them.

Skimming the outskirts of the courtyard, Çifta slid toward the aviary, keeping her eyes down. Guilt swarmed within her, but the remedy would be to see the message carried up and away. Once the bird took to the air, it could not be called back. She'd feel relieved, the decision having been irretrievably made. She reached the narrow staircase which ascended the exterior of the aviary tower. She lifted her heavy black skirts, already damp from the humidity, and began to climb.

"Lady Çifta!"

At the sound of Faraçek's voice, a cold hand gripped her throat. She gasped, feeling suddenly like she couldn't get enough air. He called a second time, closer now. Even someone hard of hearing couldn't miss his commanding tone. She couldn't pretend not to have heard him.

Handsome in black boiled leather and hunting trousers and boots, he stopped at the bottom of the steps. His dark eyes probed hers. “Is milady well?”

“Quite well.” She forced a smile, then gestured to the courtyard. “A lot of excitement this morning. What are you hunting?”

“A stag that was spotted yesterday. Normally, all hunts are suspended until our period of mourning has past, but this winter is sure to be a cold one. We must stock our larders when the opportunity presents itself, happy times or sad.” His look turned serious. “I was wondering if you have seen either of my sisters this morning?”

Relief made Çifta sag against the railing. It made sense that he would ask her this; after all, they shared her hallway. She found her strength and straightened. “No, my prince. I was looking for them myself. Are they to join the hunt?”

“Isabey usually does, but not Serya.” His lip curled with the faintest contempt. “She can ride, but not well, not with her deficiency.”

“If I see them, I will be sure to tell them that you seek them also.” She was eager to get her message sent, but etiquette said she should wait to be dismissed.

He put a hand on the stone railing and ascended a step. “What brings you to the aviary?”

Çifta’s stomach rolled like a log on the river. She suppressed a shiver as fear raked her heart, even as she pasted on a smile. His kiss had been strange, that was true, but he’d never been anything but nice to her. He’d even carried her to her room when she’d felt faint. Yet she felt like a mouse cowering under a bush. “I wish to send a letter to my father. Let him know that all is well and I am settling in.”

She could have kicked herself. Why was she lying? Was she so cowardly that she couldn't deliver the news herself?

Prince Faraçek's brows tightened. He took another step up, his face coming even with hers. "Did you not do so the day you arrived? I was told Eda showed you to the aviary."

Çifta put a hand over her eyes and gave a hollow laugh. "Yes, that's true. She did. But this letter is to reassure my father that I have met you, and… and…"

Prince Faraçek listened to her stutter for a moment, then offered a soft suggestion. "And I meet with your approval?"

"Yes." She smiled at him, hoping it looked sincere.

He caught her wrist in a strong grip, turning her hand palm up. She gasped as he took the scroll from under the fabric of her sleeve, like plucking the head of a daisy from its stem. He even guessed rightly which sleeve it had been tucked into.

"M-my prince—" She sucked in air and gripped the railing, feeling faint again. At the sound of her wax seal breaking beneath his thumb, her heart began to sprint. "Correspondence b-between me and my father is p-private."

Faraçek dropped off the stair and out of her reach. Her vision swam as she watched him unfold the scroll. This couldn't be happening.

He scanned the contents of the letter, then looked up, disbelief etched on his features. His voice was hushed with incredulity. "You would make a mockery of me?"

"No, I do not mock. I would never!" Her voice was high and hoarse. "I was afraid to say… but I suppose… it is b-better… now that you know."

Faraçek put his hands behind his back and when he presented them again, the scroll was gone. He flashed his teeth in a dazzling smile, then stepped up and grabbed her by the waist.

Her feet skipped over the steps as he pulled her onto the gravel of the courtyard, then forced his face into hers.

"Now that I know what, my love?" he asked with terrifying gaiety.

He put an arm firmly around her waist, then marched her across the courtyard, mumbling down at her, acting as though sharing some pleasantry with his betrothed. Her gentile breeding had made her so well behaved that she didn't know what to do. She didn't want to make a scene, but she'd never been manhandled like this. While she stiffened and tried to pull away, there was nothing that could break the hold he had on her. She was swiftly propelled back to her suite where he opened the door and threw her into her room. She stumbled over the corner of the carpet and cried out, landing painfully on her hands and knees, and biting her tongue for good measure. She rolled over onto her backside, her legs tangled in her skirts. She spider-crawled backward across the floor, looking up at him in terror, her mouth filling with blood.

Faraçek closed the door. With the same sleight of hand, he produced her scroll and threw it into the fire. There was a flare of light and the letter was reduced to ash.

"You will pen another."

Çifta's teeth began to chatter. She couldn't stop shaking. She put her forearm to her mouth to absorb some of the blood. "N-no."

Faraçek hauled her by one arm and her hair, making her cry out again. He slammed her into her chair, bruising her hip and the backs of her thighs. He placed such heavy hands on her shoulders that she felt her collarbones might snap, like the dried breastbone of last week's chicken.

She sucked in a sob, her knees knocking together. She'd never been so frightened.

"You shall write precisely what I say, every word, exactly as I dictate them." Prince Faraçek's voice was calm and icy, his consonants hard.

"No!" Tears filled her eyes, blurring her vision. They spilled down her cheeks and dropped off her jaw.

"Yes." His lips brushed against her ear. His breath smelled of mulch. "Or I shall break every finger on your pretty hands and you'll never write anything again."

With a trembling hand, Çifta Unya picked up her quill.

Chapter Twenty-Seven

Laec

Laec found Solanan military livery on his bed. Some servant had folded a dark blue tunic and leggings and lain a deep green boiled leather vest with matching vambraces beside the clothing. The vest had the wreathed lion's head embossed over the heart. A midnight-blue scabbard and belt held a short sword with a leather-wrapped handle. He hefted the sword, unsheathed it and admired it in the light. Not bad. Nice to have the one that had been stolen finally replaced. He buckled the sword at his waist. Laec wrinkled his nose as he held up the tunic. It was his size, but he'd feel weird in any gear but his own. He left it on a chair in the corner of his room and left, trying to remember how to get down to the training facilities. He'd spent most of his time in banquet halls and parlors so far. He had to ask a servant for directions, but he finally found the group selected to escort the Calyx to Rahamlar. They were standing around a table where the crofter had laid out several maps, both of countryside and of the Rahamlar fortress and city.

A zigzaggy topographical map showed the meandering route they'd take over a mountain called Vargon. When Laec saw it, he thought of Çifta, how he'd told her he'd have to get over the mountain in order to visit her. How ironic that this was exactly what he was about to do.

As Laec entered, a few of the soldiers looked up. Laec halted inside the door when he came face-to-face with a raccoon perched on the top of a woman's head. Both the woman and the raccoon looked at Laec with glittering black eyes.

"Sorry. Excuse me." He gave little curt nods as he moved closer to the table to get a view of the maps. There were several birds of prey sitting in the rafters, and a few dogs lying about. He realized there was a panther sleeping on the floor under the table and decided that he could see fine from a few feet back.

The crofter was saying, "Once we've crested and return below the tree line, Regalis, you can finish the rear sweep, while Kite continues to scout the head."

"Where is she?" someone asked.

"Doing an errand for me. She'll join us soon," the crofter said, then: "You've neglected your livery, soldier."

It took a few beats of silence before Laec realized the crofter was speaking to him. The soldiers and Fahyli were quiet, waiting for him to answer.

"Oh. I did find it in my room. Thank you. I'm more comfortable in my own clothing, but I do appreciate the sword." He patted the handle of the weapon hanging at his waist.

Ian frowned. Something huge moved in a far corner of the room, making Laec start. His heart gave a startled leap. Laec stepped back and trod on the foot of the soldier behind him. "Sorry. I assume we're all aware that there's a bear in the corner?"

The raccoon chittered. Laec was fairly certain he was being laughed at.

The crofter lifted his hands from the table, straightening to his considerable height. He pinned Laec with a glare. "You're under my headship for this assignment, Laec. While on this detail, you'll look and behave as one of us. You'll wear the livery."

"Fine." It wasn't a hill to die on. Plus, the livery was in better shape than the gear he'd brought from Stavarjak, which was feeling a little tight these days.

The crofter waited. No soldiers moved or made a sound. The bear lowered his head and whiffed at the floor, blowing up dust.

"Now?"

"Now."

"This meeting is important though, right? I don't want to miss anything."

"You should have thought of that before. Go dress properly and return. Ask someone to fill you in on what you missed. Any one of these soldiers will be able to confer to you my instructions word for word. Twice, if you need it. As I suspect you will." The crofter shifted the maps to unearth one that had laid beneath. "Now, as for the fortress, let's discuss the approach. We come north along the Tadylat here." He pointed a blunt finger where one of the rivers came alongside a road.

Laec chafed at the insult. He left the room, grumbling under his breath. He went all the way back to his suite and changed into the livery. It made him even grumpier that it was a perfect fit, and when he looked in the mirror, he liked the way his bright hair contrasted with the darkness of the green boiled leather. He looked fierce. He unsheathed the sword and pointed it at his reflection, swinging it with a few warm-up flourishes.

Plus, this livery smelled a bit like crushed rosemary, which was a step above his old boiled leather, which smelled like Grex. Let the old crofter have it his way.

Laec returned to the meeting room to find it empty. Even the bear had vacated the corner. He continued down the hall to find that it branched off in five directions. He took the hallway headed in the most westerly direction, since he was to train at the West Keep, and took the first door leading outside. A stable hand passed, leading a bay horse by the bit.

"Which way did the Fahyli go? Do you know?" Laec asked.

Without looking back, the stableboy lifted a hand and pointed. "Justicia Yard. Through the gate at the end."

Laec followed the trail where the keep's foundation met the dirt as it descended and rounded a turret. There, he found a closed wooden gate through which he could hear voices. He found it unlatched. A yard opened before him. There were animals, horses and soldiers everywhere, training in groups. Closest to Laec was the Fahyli he recognized as Regalis. Beside him stood a woman with long black hair tied back in a warrior's tail. Both were looking up. In the sky, a large hawk and another smaller raptor with a villainous-looking beak were doing aerobatics. They spun and spiraled in mock battle. Laec hooded his eyes with a hand and watched with admiration. The hawk gave a piercing cry and changed direction, going straight for the other. The smaller bird made a sharp turn and suddenly there were three birds in the sky, a hawk and two smaller raptors going different directions. The hawk seemed confused for a millisecond before it decided which one to pursue and slid smoothly down-sky. Laec blinked, wondering where the third bird had come from. In the sun's glare, Laec was half blind.

"Are you lost?"

Laec tore his eyes from the birds' play to see both Fahyli staring at him.

"I'm with the Rahamlar group."

The female soldier with the black hair looked around. "Where's your familiar?"

Regalis said with his eyes still on the sky, "He doesn't have one, Kite. He's not Fahyli."

Laec added, "I'm from Stavarjak."

"The foreign volunteer?"

"That's right."

"You're in the wrong place, mate," said Kite. "Next paddock over, you'll find the soldiers. It's called Heuchera Yard. Best not keep the crofter waiting or you'll find yourself assigned to serve tea or buff nails."

Regalis chuckled and lifted his arm to receive his hawk. The smaller raptor landed on Kite's forearm a moment later. The third bird had disappeared somewhere else.

"Oh." Disappointed that he wouldn't be able to watch the birds longer, or snoop on what else the Fahyli were up to here, Laec went back to the gate and continued on the path. He could still hear the Fahyli, but they were blocked from view behind a tall wooden fence. At the next gate, he heard men grunting and the scuffles of feet in the dirt. When he stepped through the gate, he saw a less unusual sight of human soldiers training much the same way they did everywhere. A pang hit Laec at the thought of his vacant magic and he sighed deeply. Back home, he was a force, one of the more capable members of Elphame's court… when he wasn't drinking and sulking. Here, he was ordinary, and didn't even qualify to get lumped in with other fae. He spotted one of the soldiers he'd seen in the room with the others and went over to find out what he'd missed.

Chapter Twenty-Eight

Jessamine

"It's important to the king and queen that the presentation we give to honor Prince Ander be as full of depth, meaning and emotion as we can make it." Ilishec strode through a set of double doors down the hall from one of the ballrooms where Jessamine and the other Calyx learned their choreography. The dissonant sound of instruments being tuned and tested grew loud as Jessamine followed Ilishec through a section of tall wooden cases.

"I get that." Jessamine ran a finger along the pretty embossed label marking one of the drawers with a capital letter P which had been entwined with vines and flowers. "What's in these drawers?"

"Sheet music."

"Right." She should have guessed.

They emerged where a group of musicians stood or sat about a room with music stands and chairs set in semi-circular rows. A woman holding a violin to her chin noticed Ilishec had come in.

"Gardener," she called, and the din ceased.

"Thank you, Lola." Ilishec gestured to Jessamine. "This is one of my newer members."

"Let me guess." A man holding a trumpet squinted one eye shut, peering at Jessamine with the other. "Honeysuckle? Or Honey?" Both eyes popped open. "Goldie, for goldenrod? I remember you from the banquet. Nice sprouts."

Jessamine flushed. "Thanks."

Ilishec chuckled. "Excellent guesses, but she goes by Jessamine."

The trumpet player smiled. "What can we do for you?"

"Jessamine will accompany us to Rahamlar. This will mark her first foreign presentation. I would like her to hear the music before I teach her how to conjure the mystics this afternoon. Just to give her an idea of what we're working with."

The musicians moved to their places. The trumpet player winked at Jessamine. "Too bad it'll be such a maudlin event. Hopefully your next one will be more cheerful."

"Thank you, Mr. Kinney, for your opinions." A tall slender woman with a sleek silver crop of hair entered from a side door. "Hello, Gardener."

Ilishec nodded at the woman. "Liese. I was just here to—"

"I heard." She clapped her hands and the musicians straightened, bringing their instruments to the ready. Liese lifted her hands. There was a collective breath, and the music began.

Slow, swelling and sad, the strains of a sentimental march swept over Jessamine like an inrush of water. The music softened, seeming to cradle her, then swelled again and lifted, carrying her along on waves of mournful melody. She closed her eyes and felt her sinuses tingle with emotion. She let go of her surroundings and pictured herself flying over the countryside of

Dagevli in slow, lazy circles. She could see the stooped figure of her mother pulling weeds in the squash patch behind their cottage. Butterflies drifted on downdrafts and fluttered in choreographed harmony as bees buzzed in minor keys, adding their own low-flying synchronization to the scene. She withdrew and drifted away, skimming over hills and valleys, winding rivers and sparkling bodies of water dimpled with raindrops. She imagined the twin rivers of Rahamlar, and as the march deepened and grew weighty, she pictured rows upon rows of people dressed in black, their heads covered and their faces downcast—some wept. Jessamine's eyes limned with moisture. She opened her eyes and a tear slipped down her cheek. She brushed it away, looking at the floor and pretending there was something in her eye.

Liese brought the music to its elegant, heartbreaking conclusion. As she let her arms down and turned, she caught sight of Jessamine's face. The corners of her lips turned up in a smug smile as she retrieved a kerchief from a pocket.

Jessamine sniffed and then laughed at herself.

Liese handed her the kerchief. "I would think we were doing something wrong if you didn't shed at least one tear."

Dabbing at her eyes, Jessamine noticed that the musicians looked pleased, and Ilishec's eyes were shining. "You have the emotional makeup of a Calyx, my girl. Never be ashamed of that. It's part of what will give our presentation such impact. A sadness shared is a sadness healed."

"And beauty is our strength," murmured Liese.

"Beauty is our strength," repeated the musicians and Ilishec. Jessamine managed to say "our strength" at the right moment.

"I'll leave you to your rehearsing." Ilishec led Jessamine the way they'd come.

Out in the gardens not far from the Perfumery, Calyx

worked in small groups to build up a sweat, or to review choreography. Lotus walked waist deep in pond water, conjuring stunning pink blooms in rapid succession, making symmetrical patterns, only to make them disappear again. The air smelled sweet and delightful.

Ilishec drew Jessamine over to a quiet corner with a garden of thick groundcover: a combination of creeping *phlox*, *alyssum* and flowering thyme. "You've mastered the art of conjuring your botanical matter, but today I'd like to teach you the art of the chromatype, less formally known as the mystic bloom."

"You mean the wispy blossoms that float in the air and leave a patch of perfume wherever they fall, like soap bubbles?" Jessamine had enjoyed the patch left on her skin at the festival for several hours before it faded away completely.

"Precisely. Before I can finalize the choreography, I need to make sure you can produce the blooms as needed and in sufficient quantity."

"Are they difficult to manifest?"

"No, though every Calyx varies in the quantity they can produce. Some manage only a few at a time and then need to rest before they can produce more, while others seem to have no end of energy for it." Ilishec kicked off his shoes and knelt in the *phlox*, patting the ground in front of him.

Jessamine toed off her shoes as well, sinking down beside the gardener. "Like Proteas? I remember his from the festival."

"Proteas is very clever with mystic blooms, yes. One of our stronger chromatypers, I'd say. Where's Beazle?"

"Sleeping in my hair. Should I wake him?"

Ilishec waved a hand. "No, no. As long as he's nearby."

Jessamine looked around for Greta before reminding herself that Greta's presence wasn't necessary for her magic to work.

A brief ache made Jessamine bring her hand to her heart. As if saying hello, the glasswing fluttered closer, flitting to the yellow heads of a thorny rosebush, not far from the pond where Lotus worked. Jessamine drew her attention back to Ilishec.

"The mystic blooms are a more esoteric matter than conjuring living botanicals, but of all the magic a flora fae possesses, chromatyping is the easiest of all. Most Calyx barely have to think about it, and the mystic blooms appear, as long as the humidity and temperature isn't too far outside the ideals needed for their species."

"So there's no science to it, then? No standing barefoot in dirt, or letting energy flow through my body."

"Exactly. The physical effort is minimal. Let me say it this way. If science is my right hand, and magic is my left"—Ilishec spread his hands wide—"the ability to bring up plant matter, which lies entirely in your genes, might best be placed to the right of center. Whereas chromatyping might live between center and my left hand. Does that make sense?"

"I guess." Jessamine wasn't sure it did, but conjuring the real thing was easy. Surely the image of the real would be even easier. "But what are the mystic blooms made of? My sweat?"

"A combination of water, light, and yes, your sweat. There is moisture on your body at this moment, a tiny fraction of which evaporates when you chromatype and then condenses in the air to form the desired image. As I'm sure you can imagine, flora fae can only produce images of the same living species that they can bring up, because that's what's in your blood. So, give it a go. It can help to close your eyes the first time. Imagine the air around you filled with blossoms."

Jessamine got comfortable and closed her eyes. She tilted her face back to let sunlight fall over her eyelids. A light breeze stirred the leaves, and she could hear little splashes from the pond where Lotus was. She imagined *nicotiana* buds spinning into transparent images in the air over her head, then opening to the sun and letting their fragrance spill out in a waterfall of silvery light. She opened her eyes a crack, certain she'd see the undersides of hundreds of flowering tobacco blossoms dancing on the breeze, but there was nothing.

Ilishec went from his knees into a cross-legged position, indicating that she should keep trying.

She closed her eyes and discarded the *nicotiana*. Instead, she thought of the tubular whisker-like blossoms of honeysuckle and pictured them exploding like embers from a bonfire as they ascended and arced overhead in a shower of fragrance to fall and kiss their faces and hair. The sweet scent of her *lonicera* swept around them and she inhaled deeply, certain that she'd done it. She opened her eyes in anticipation. There was still nothing there.

"I don't get it. What am I doing wrong?"

"Why don't you run a few laps and work up a sweat. Perhaps a little more moisture is needed." Ilishec began to deadhead the nearby plants, plucking off withered blossoms to make way for new ones.

Jessamine got up and went to the workout area where a flattened grass track wound its way around the back of the Perfumery, the nearest hothouse, and back again. She ran two laps, enough to make her pant. Her forehead and the bridge of her nose felt damp, then she returned to where Ilishec had finished deadheading everything within reach.

Jessamine repeated the process, imagining her species as mystic blossoms hanging in the air. After she'd imagined every single one of them and failed to conjure any of them, she huffed out a sharp frustrated breath. She expected Ilishec to comfort her, but when she saw the line between his eyes, her anxiety doubled. Her body was now lined with sweat and her clothes felt damp. It wasn't for lack of perspiration that she was failing. Something else was wrong.

When she asked Ilishec if there was some other technique she could try because imagining the blooms wasn't working, he told her to wake up Beazle and try again. When she poked him, he squeaked indignantly and nipped the end of her finger.

"Ow. Beeze!" She put her finger in her mouth. He never drew blood, but his sharp little teeth were painful.

He squeaked again as he dropped onto her shoulder and flapped away.

"Let's try some guided visualization," said Ilishec, drawing Jessamine up to standing and holding out his hands.

She put her hands in his. "But I've been visualizing this whole time."

"I believe you, but I can't see what's going on inside that head of yours. Maybe your imagination is insufficient."

Jess frowned. She thought her imagination was very vivid.

"Listen as I describe what I want you to type."

"Eyes closed or open?"

"Closed."

Jessamine shoved her mounting annoyance away and closed her eyes. Concentrating on the gardener's voice, she let her imagination follow his instructions. She could see them standing in the garden near the Perfumery as clearly as she'd been able to see her mother weeding in the squash patch. Ilishec's poetic descriptions of *datura* and *cestrum* filled her mind with a host of glorious plants and blossoms, all made of light and water and swirling with transparent rainbow colors. He described the bright, oblong and twining leaves of *cestrum*, and the spidery, pink-flushed flowers and spiny stems of *cleome* and the clusters and spikes of deep yellow columns of *solidago*. He told her where these mystic blooms had appeared, how high over their heads they were, and how they drifted on the wind.

Already smiling, Jessamine opened her eyes. Her smile faded. There was nothing. Not so much as a soap bubble shaped like a leaf. Her heart dropped. A distant titter drew her attention to a group of Calyx lingering near the Perfumery. She spotted Peony whispering something into Gardenia's ear. Both of them looked in her direction, then looked away again. Jessamine flushed. Were they talking about her? What if they knew that Jessamine was trying to do the "easiest magic of all" but was failing?

"Can we try this somewhere quieter?" Jess murmured.

Ilishec released Jessamine's hands, his expression concerned. "There's nothing wrong with you, Jess."

"Your face says something different. You said this was the easiest magic of all for a flora fae, but we've been at it for half an hour already. How long did it take you to produce your first mystic bloom?"

"That's… not relevant."

"Isn't it?"

"Perhaps I should pair you with one of your peers for this exercise." Ilishec rubbed his thumb across his lower lip thoughtfully as he weighed her with his eyes. "I lost the ability to chromatype many years ago. Perhaps I'm too out of touch with how it feels."

Jessamine frowned. He was making it his fault when she knew it was not. "Do other Calyx have to learn chromatyping from their peers?"

He hesitated before answering and that was all the answer she needed.

"So there is something wrong with me."

"Let's not assume anything. You've proven to be unusual in a few other ways, your prolificness, for one thing, and your mammal pollinator for another. Perhaps they are a factor. I am confident with the right key, we can unlock your mystic blooms, just as we were able to unlock your conjuring abilities by trying it at midnight."

"We don't have much time, though. We leave for Rahamlar in less than ten days. If I can't chromatype, are you still going to take me?"

Ilishec's brow relaxed. "Of course I am, Jessamine. Don't forget you're the only one who can conjure *cordatotriloba*. It's an important part of the presentation. You're in the retinue whether you can chromatype or not, but I'm sure your struggle has a simple fix."

Jessamine let out a long breath. "Okay. Let's try matching me up with someone, then. Maybe Rose or Aster will have time."

"I'll check their schedules." Ilishec glanced at the clock tower in front of the Perfumery. "Let's try again tomorrow. You'll be late for Nomenclature."

Jessamine called Beazle and headed for the palace. She almost called Greta, but she was sitting on one of Lotus's lily pads and Jessamine thought she might be sleeping. She didn't need Greta for any of her classes anyway, so she left the butterfly to her afternoon.

For her first perfume making class, Ilishec had Jessamine conjure nothing but honeysuckle until a section of previously tilled soil was bursting with fragrant shrubs. Once the magic of *lonicera* was running through her body, he had her change into the bralette and shorts Olinya had made for her workouts and do several loops of the circuit. When her skin was slick with moisture and dripping down the sides of her face, the gardener met her at the dome where her sweat would be harvested.

"Why do I feel so oily?" Jessamine ran a finger up her forearm and rubbed her fingertips together. What she'd produced didn't have the watery, salty feeling of normal sweat. What came off was thicker and slicker and, of course, richly fragrant.

"Plant oils." Ilishec took a small vial out of his pocket and pressed its edge to her skin until he'd collected several drops. "What you're producing is the raw material. We could get the same thing by extracting it from the plant, but it would take fields and fields as well as months of growing season to produce a fraction of what Calyx are able to produce in a matter of hours. Put yours arms out to the side. That's it, don't put them down until they're finished."

Insects and tiny fae converged upon her. A force of hundreds fluttered over the surface of her skin, collecting her sweat to carry it into the refinery. The featherlight touches all over Jessamine's body made her want to scratch. She shuddered and shifted from one foot to the other.

"Close your eyes and listen to the music," Ilishec told her as he put a stopper in the vial. "You won't even feel it."

"What music?" All Jessamine could hear was the sound

of Calyx grunting from the circuit, and birds twittering in the garden.

Ilishec just smiled. "I'll be back in twenty minutes. Enjoy."

Fighting the urge to rub at her shoulder where a butterfly was crawling, Jessamine closed her eyes and ignored the tickling sensations. After several deep breaths, she discovered what Ilishec had been talking about. It wasn't music, not exactly, but it was nice. It reminded her of the sound of crickets, only not so chirpy. It was a soothing harmony that rose and fell softly, filling the air around her. The sensation of being harvested didn't go away completely, but she was no longer irritated. It took her a few minutes of listening to realize that the music was coming from the insects and the fae, and that their songs were different from one another, though she couldn't tell which song belonged to which creature. There was a long low note beneath it all and high short chimes, as well as the sweet buzz of tiny wings. When she opened her eyes, the sound receded behind all other sounds. Smiling, she closed her eyes and let her mind drift away on the vibrations, her bare feet in the dirt.

When the music began to fade, Jess opened her eyes to see that the harvesters had gone and her skin was dry. All the moisture had been whisked neatly away, even from her scalp and hairline. She saw Anthurium waiting for his turn, sweat dripping down his forehead and arms. He smiled at her as she stepped out from under the dome.

Jessamine smiled back but folded her arms over her bare stomach, unaccustomed to having so much of her skin showing. It was especially disconcerting when there were good-looking males around, and all of the male Calyx were good looking. Anthurium had a blazing smile, dark skin and warm brown eyes. He wore only the white loincloth that the male Calyx wore during perfume making. His long body glistened with oil in the bright sunlight, his muscles prominent from working out.

"First time?" Anthurium asked as a droplet fell from the tip of his nose. She couldn't place his accent; in fact, she couldn't place anyone's accent unless it was Dagevlian, but listening to Anthurium gave her a pleasant shiver.

"How can you tell?" Jessamine poured herself water from the silver dispenser near the dome.

He grinned. "First-timers are always embarrassed. We haven't properly met. I'm Anthurium. I'd shake your hand but we're not supposed to cross-contaminate. Makes things harder for the refiners."

"Right. I'm Jessamine." Her face felt like it was in flames. She took a big gulp of water and almost choked. "Where are you from?"

"Sarnish. Ever heard of it?"

She shook her head.

"Don't worry, no one has. It's a small village in south Boskaya." He spotted something behind Jessamine and lifted a hand to say goodbye. "Nice to meet you. I'd better get inside. Gardener's here."

Anthurium stepped into the dome, leaving Jessamine with the fetching view of his bare back.

Ilishec beckoned Jessamine over to where he stood in the shade of a *jacaranda* tree. She drained her cup and put it in the tray with the used ones before joining him. She thought the gardener looked confused. He held a tube of paper in his hand, which he handed to her.

Jessamine unrolled the page and read a long list of strange words. Each one had a percentage beside it and a colored dot.

"There must be a hundred and fifty things listed here, and some of them are more numbers than letters."

"There's over two hundred. These are the scientific names of the chemicals you produced. It's the chemical profile of the *lonicera* raw material you produced." Ilishec pointed at the number beside each one. "This is the percentage of the whole that each one contributes, so altogether the numbers add up to one hundred. As you can see, they're listed from highest percentage to lowest. We keep this in your perfumery file. Over time, you can observe how the ratios might fluctuate according to your diet, your overall health, your hydration levels and other factors."

Jessamine got the feeling that Ilishec wasn't telling her something. "So, is this a good mix?"

"It's..." He tugged on his beard. "Well, it's different, but before I explain what makes it unusual, I'd like you to produce a few more batches."

"Of honeysuckle?" Jessamine was glad for the chance to work up another sweat. She was getting chilly standing around with her body mostly bare.

"Let's do *solidago*, *oenothera* and *cleome*. I'll take a sample each time and run the results. If what I'm seeing with the *lonicera* is a pattern, then we'll discuss it."

"Is something wrong?"

Ilishec took the scroll back. "Don't worry. Now, off to the gardens with you, and then to the circuit. *Solidago* first. While you're working up a sweat, I'll have an elixir prepared. You're going to need it."

By the time Jessamine had sweated out and stood for the last batch of raw material to be harvested, she left the dome on wobbly legs. She was beginning to comprehend why Rose's body was so springy and strong. Even the green tonic that Ms. Tierney had made, which she had drunk after her batch of primrose-scented sweat, had not fully recharged her. Tonight, she would sleep like a stone. She poured herself a glass of water and took it to the nearest bench where she collapsed.

The sounds of laughter and conversation drew her gaze over her shoulder toward the Perfumery where one of Ilishec's chemists had brought out a tray of vials. A group of Calyx had gathered there, which included Peony, Lotus, Nympha, Dianthus, Wisteria and Alstro, a male Calyx who conjured *alstroemeria*. They were taking turns inhaling the different perfumes, exclaiming over them and congratulating one another. Alstro put a drop from one of the vials onto a piece of sampling felt and waved it under his nose. His eyes rolled back in his head with obvious pleasure, then he drew Peony into a hug and kissed her on the cheek, making the other Calyx beg Alstro to wave the scented felt under their noses. They all expressed so much pleasure that Peony was glowing with pride. Peony must have felt Jessamine's gaze on her, because she looked over. Jessamine smiled at her, but Peony only looked away.

By the time Jessamine finished her glass of water, Ilishec had come across the lawn. She couldn't read the look on his face. He sat beside her, handing her three small scrolls. Jessamine unrolled each one, read the nomenclature at the top of the page for each of her species, then skimmed the long list of chemicals. Each was identified with a colored dot that corresponded to a legend tracking different groups, such as alcohols, aldehydes, ketones and esters. A bunch more were labeled volatile or miscellaneous.

"What am I supposed to understand from this?"

Ilishec put his arm over the back of the bench so he could

face her more easily. "Every species we conjure is made up of hundreds of different chemicals. Not all of them contribute to fragrance. For the purpose of perfume making, what we're after are the aromatic compounds that evaporate easily into the air, which can then be picked up by the nose. It's these we isolate for our perfume business. You might sweat out four ounces, but only one ounce is suitable. Some Calyx are exceptional at producing higher portions of the aromatic compounds—like Rose, for example. Her body and her magic know instinctively what we're after. Others have to work harder to get the same amount. We analyze your profiles early on, which helps us understand how you change, but it also helps us forecast."

"Forecast? Like… predict?"

"Exactly. The Perfumery is a significant source of income, but it fluctuates according to how productive the Calyx are that make up our roster from year to year. Doing these tests allows us to predict how much a given Calyx is expected to produce during their time with us. We have to use averages, but over the years, we've gotten it down to something of an art. We know that productivity follows a bell curve over a span of five to ten years, and we apply that to your analytics as well. The forecasting allows you to set goals for how much of the raw material you'd like to try and produce throughout the year, which informs your schedule, but it also allows the teams who manage our shops throughout Ivryndi to set the prices of our perfumes, which are sold by the ounce, and our treasurers to set budgets for future projects. If our shop managers know roughly how much Rose is capable of producing per season, they'll be able to set the prices according to supply and demand. Understand?"

"Sure." It was a little over her head, but Jessamine understood that profit was the overall goal, for both herself and the kingdom. Marion had taught her to keep track of the productivity of their squash patches as well as any costs that came up throughout the year to replace tools, purchase fertilizer and keep the cart in working order. Jessamine understood that the price of the squash had to fluctuate in order to make sure that they made more than they spent every year. The Solana Perfumery was the same, only on a grander, more complicated scale.

"You still have five species to produce an inaugural batch for, but we'll do those another day. I know you're tired. The four we have is enough to confirm that the pattern I told you I was going to watch for is there. It's one I've not seen before. Very simply, you produce less of the aromatic compounds that we are after, and more of… ones that are not useful to us."

Jessamine's shoulders drooped. "I have to work a lot harder than other Calyx to make the same amount of perfume?"

"It appears that way. There are things we can do to maximize your output, and every Calyx improves from where they start, so don't lose heart. We also don't know yet about the quality of the aromatic compounds that you produce. It may be that they are small in quantity, but of high quality, which may create a greater demand, which will allow us to price your perfume higher. There are things Ms. Tierney can add to your elixirs that might help, and we can also play with your schedule. For example, we know that some flowers are vespertine: they produce the strongest odor at night. If you're up for midnight workouts, then you might find that the profile of your output improves. We just don't know enough yet."

Jessamine couldn't shake the feeling that Ilishec was more disappointed than he was letting on, but she was too tired and too hungry to prod him. Also, she was going to be late for her dance class. She handed the scrolls back to Ilishec to put in her files and made her way to her room to change. She had five more species to sweat out. That was more than enough chances to buck the trend she'd made so far. She made a mental note to stop by the elixirs kitchen to ask Ms. Tierney what she might have up her sleeve to help. She'd also make sure to ask Rose or Aster for advice. As she was sliding her feet into her dancing slippers, the crowd of Calyx standing around the vials of perfume came into her mind. She frowned, then forced herself to smile as she left her room with Greta on her shoulder and Beazle in her hair. She could produce several highly fragrant and desirable scents with her magic; even the queen had expressed excitement at having *lonicera* and *cleome* as part of the retinue. Jessamine didn't care what it took, bitter elixirs, midnight sweat sessions, mud baths, whatever. She would make herself valuable or burn out trying.

Chapter Twenty-Nine

Çifta

At first, her door remained unlocked and unguarded. After coercing Çifta into writing a letter to Kazery falsely reporting that all was well, Faraçek took the paper, quill and ink from Çifta's room so she couldn't write another. He didn't know about her sketchbook and colored pencils, which she'd hidden under her mattress in case he sent someone to rifle through her trunks.

She'd already written another letter to her father and stashed it behind a loose stone in a quiet servant's stairwell in case her room was searched. But getting it to the aviary had been impossible because, since then, she'd grown a shadow she couldn't shake: a single unseelie soldier. He never approached her, but he was always there, no matter where she went—the dining hall, the parlor or for an outdoor stroll to visit Caramel—he lingered at the edges of her life, as far away as he could be without losing sight of her. He was big and armed, and had a scary face and unseelie talons, otherwise Çifta might have attempted to talk to him. As it was, she felt too terrified to even retrieve the letter, and had to write yet another. This one she'd stuffed in her pillowcase but its presence in her room was like that of something explosive.

She took comfort in sketching at her window, but the moment there was a noise in the hallway, she'd spring up and hide her art supplies, her heart flapping around like a caged bird.

When Eda came, she left the door propped open, never allowing it to close. When Çifta asked Eda if she was expected to change with the door open now, the maid just nodded, her gaze on the floor. So Çifta took to changing in her bathing room, the only place with a modicum of privacy. Eda now only spoke when asked a direct question and only with one-word answers.

One morning, while Çifta sat in front of her mirror and Eda was preparing to put Çifta's veil on, Çifta whispered, "Will you help me?"

The only sign that Eda heard her was the stilling of her hands, then she shook out the veil and set it on the vanity to pick up a hairbrush. Çifta's heart fell as Eda began to comb out her hair, not daring to meet Çifta's eyes in the mirror. When she was finished pinning Çifta's hair, she leaned forward and set the brush and remaining pins down.

"What can I do, milady?" the maid whispered, picking up the veil.

Çifta's heart bobbed like an apple in a barrel of water. "Will you send a letter for me?"

Eda blanched and still didn't look up. Even her lips lost their color. She settled the veil over Çifta's hair and pinned it in place.

"I wouldn't ask if I wasn't desperate," Çifta whispered.

"I know, milady." Eda's lips compressed and she glanced in

the mirror, not at Çifta but at the open door of the chamber. All was quiet in the hall, but they both knew that Çifta's shadow wasn't far away. "I could get in a lot of trouble."

"Could you pass it to someone else? Say it's yours?"

They both froze as footsteps came down the hall and passed by the doorway, not stopping. Eda grabbed the back of Çifta's chair. The girl was even more terrified than she was.

"I'm to be a princess, Eda, not a prisoner. Please."

When Eda gave the tiniest nod, Çifta found a shaky smile for her maid and grabbed her hand. Eda pulled away but squeezed Çifta's shoulder in passing.

"I make no promises," she whispered. "I must go. If I linger, I get questions."

Çifta went to her bed, rooted in the pillowcase and pulled out the folded note. She slipped it into Eda's hand and the maid tucked it up her sleeve, curtsied and left the room.

Çifta spent much of that day in the parlor that had the best view of the aviary, putting on a show that she was reading. A few courtiers made light conversation with her, giving no indication that they were aware of her situation. She didn't know any of them well enough to trust them, and there was a distant coolness in their eyes that did not invite confidence. Çifta longed for Princess Isabey's company. When she casually asked a courtier if they knew where Isabey might be found, they replied, "I heard the princesses have undertaken a tour of nearby villages to host memorial visitations for citizens who are unable to travel."

This answer threw Çifta into additional turmoil. Surely the princesses would have taken her with them had they done such a thing. She'd attended all the visitations that had taken place in the courtyard. And if Çifta wasn't welcome, surely the princesses would have told her before they left. Did the courtier believe what they were saying?

Çifta never saw Eda approach the aviary, but she saw other traffic go up and down the stairs of the tower, keeping hope alive within her breast. One of them might be an unknown friend to her.

That evening, after a lonely dinner in the hall where she felt surrounded by strangers who had no care about her suffering, Çifta withdrew to her room, hoping Eda would join her soon to stoke her fire and help her undress. She left her door open, knowing the maid would prop it open anyway. By evening, she felt like she was suffocating in her gown, suffocating in this room, suffocating in this fortress.

Eda didn't come, so Çifta made a ritual out of stoking the fire herself: raking up embers, selecting kindling and placing it strategically to light the wood. She was sitting on the floor when she felt a presence. Expecting Eda, she cast a smile toward the door, which faded as Faraçek came into her room.

"My lady." He came to stand by her.

Çifta looked into the fire, silent with mutiny and fear. She was tired of being afraid. She had done no wrong. If she could find the courage to stand up to him, maybe he would back down. Kazery had sometimes talked about dealing with bullies and those who liked to intimidate within the business community of Kirkik. He'd always said the way to deal with them is to never show it if they intimidate you, to stand your ground and speak your truth. Faraçek stood there, his foot close enough to her hip to kick her, if he wanted. Could he be reasoned with? What if she pushed back?

Çifta shifted the logs with a piece of kindling. Her iron poker had disappeared in the last few days. Now when Eda came to stoke the fire, she brought one with her. Did they think Çifta was going to use it to bash someone's head in? Or maybe do herself harm? Çifta clenched her jaw. She could be strong. She was an Unya. Adversity had never stopped her father from climbing from the bottom to the very top of society. She'd never marry Faraçek, and he couldn't force her. So what did he hope to gain by lying to Kazery?

"You never eat in the hall," Çifta said, poking at the embers, her voice as nonchalant as she could make it.

Faraçek took a long time to answer, and she didn't look up. Finally, he said, "Curious about my habits, are you?"

"Of course," she murmured, her gaze on the embers at the edge of the fireplace. "I don't understand you at all. Why are you treating me like a prisoner? I was meant to be your wife."

"And you shall be, in time."

Çifta scoffed.

Viselike, Faraçek's hands wrapped around her upper arms. He yanked her off the ground, tossed her up in the air and turned her, like a child, before catching her by the ribcage. She gasped as he held her off the ground, looking up at her.

She grasped at his upper arms. They felt like iron posts. "Put me down!"

"My wife will be obedient above all." His dark eyes drilled into her. His teeth gleamed, and his irises seemed to be expanding, the whites shrinking. "When you break a filly, you first must show her who is in charge. Women are no different. We can butt heads for as long as you want. When you figure out your place, things will get a lot nicer around here for you." He lowered her a little, her face coming closer to his, but very slowly.

Under her hands, his arms moved like machinery, evenly,

slowly, with not a hint of tremor or fatigue from holding her weight over the floor. Çifta wasn't a large woman, but she was no waif either, and she was strong from riding. She had swung a foot back to kick at his thighs when he gently breathed into her face. A plume of mist enshrouded her head, rich with the scent of rotted leaves, decayed bark and rich dark earth. Her legs went limp, her hands where they clutched at his sleeves relaxed… even her heart slowed a little. Her tongue and jaw felt slack, and the skin on her face felt torpid. Her sinuses tingled, like she needed a sneeze that never came. The feeling was maddening.

Faraçek carried her to where the long oval mirror stood, turning her semi-limp form in his arms until she was facing the glass. He lowered her until the soles of her shoes hit the floor, then a little further. Her knees buckled.

"Oops. A little too much." He raised her again. "You can stand on your own, my lady."

Strength came back into her legs, just enough for her to hold herself upright. Her thoughts were laborious, confused. What had he done to her? Somewhere deep inside, alarm bells rang with high, frightened peals on a nonstop loop.

"Look in the mirror," Faraçek said beside her ear.

She did. Her expression was vacant, her eyes appeared almost lifeless. It felt difficult to close her mouth because her jaw wanted to sag. Faraçek gazed at her. He moved his hands from her waist to her hair, where he began to unpin her veil.

"I never liked mourning veils," he said conversationally. He removed one pin at a time, gently and efficiently, like he'd done it for her every evening. When the veil came away, he dropped it on the floor and ran his fingers through her hair in admiration. He drew her hair back over her shoulders, his blunt fingertips grazing her neck.

"I need to ask you something very important." He held her gaze in the mirror as he continued to stroke his fingertips from the front of her neck to the back.

She wanted to shudder, to squirm away, but she couldn't. She felt like even her mind was not entirely her own anymore.

He went on stroking her neck from front to back, front to back, getting slower each time. When something sharp grazed across her neck, her gaze dropped to his hands, where long dark talons had sprouted. Somewhere deep inside, where the bells were tolling, she wanted to duck away, to scream, to call for help. In another section of her mind, she admired how his hands had changed, thinking how interesting, how clever, how droll. What other skills was her betrothed hiding?

She exhaled a whisper. "What?"

His mouth beside her ear, blowing his leafy breath across her cheekbone, he asked, "Where are my sisters?"

She inhaled. Her room smelled like a swampy forest.

"I don't know," she managed.

He straightened. The intense musty, peaty smell diminished. She couldn't tell if he believed her or not.

"You'll see, Lady Çifta." He looked the way he had when she'd first met him: calm, serious, a little melancholy. His talons were gone. "You don't trust me yet, but you will."

He left her standing there and wandered to the fire where he added another couple of logs. She watched him from where she stood, her horror growing by the second as her intellect and self-mastery returned.

"You will." He straightened, wiping his hands. He went to her door, then turned back. "Oh, one last thing. Don't expect little Eda any longer. When you show me you can be trusted, you may have her back."

He closed the door.

Çifta stood rooted to the floor for a long time. As the smell in the air cleared, she began to shake. She felt so cold, so shocked. She stumbled to her bed, not bothering to take off her wretched mourning gown, and crawled beneath the quilt. She lay there quivering, with tears leaking from the corners of her eyes. Maybe he had the power to make her marry him, after all.

Chapter Thirty

Jessamine

Jessamine barely noticed when Snap appeared beside her at the Perfumery lab where Jess was sifting through vials of raw material she'd produced over the past week. "How are the rehearsals going?"

She looked up from squinting at the label of the seventh vial of *cleome*-scented sweat. "What?"

"The rehearsals for Rahamlar." Snap had a towel stained with pale green splotches around his neck and was rubbing his face. His curls were damp and even tighter than usual. He wore the white workout bottoms, but they had greenish stains as well. His pale body practically gleamed in the late-afternoon light.

"Okay, I guess." She put the *cleome* vial back in the holder. "I know all the choreography and the music by heart, I know the symbolic meanings behind every botanical we conjure and I can tell you exactly when and where the chromatyping comes in, but I still can't conjure any mystic blooms myself. No matter what I do. Neither Rose nor Aster could help me because they can't describe how they chromatype. They can just do it. It seems like that part of my flora magic is either shut down or I never had it to begin with. Ilishec is disappointed. To make things worse, I'm still only sweating out puny amounts of aromatics, even when I work out in the middle of the night. I'm tired, and I can't tell you how many weird-tasting elixirs I've drunk in the past week. None of it has worked." She sighed. "I'd hang upside down from the hothouse rafters, like Beazle, if I thought it would help."

Snap squeezed her shoulder. "I don't think stressing about it is going to help either, Jess. Give it time and don't give up."

"I don't have time. We leave for Rahamlar in two days. I'm supposed to chromatype *cordatotriloba*, right in front of Rahamlar's head table, because it has the most significant meaning. Ilishec says that Queen Esha wants to give a bottle of perfume made from every bloom that appears in the presentation to King Osvitan. Mine will be the only one that's missing." The thought made Jessamine wither. She watched Greta float over from a rose blossom to perch on her shoulder.

"You've still got a little time, Jess. Have a good sleep, and try again tomorrow."

She felt torn between hugging Snap and pinching him. She settled for a bitter smile. "You're always so optimistic."

"It's one of my powers. *Antirrhinum* supposedly deflects negativity, if you want to believe the fables." He ran his towel over his scalp, making his curls jump. "I've always been like this, though, so I don't think it has anything to do with my flowers. But cheer up. Most snapdragon species aren't very fragrant, so I'm not expected to make much for the Perfumery, but I can produce a green dye, which is almost worthless, so things are looking up. You, on the other hand, have great prospects."

"That explains the stains on your towel and your… loincloth."

He reddened. "They're shorts."

"Looks like a loincloth to me."

"Point is, you have a lot of botanicals, which means your possibilities are through the roof. Maybe that's why it's hard. Your magic has to sort through all the stuff it can do. Maybe it's just gotten itself mixed up a little."

"You think?"

Before Snap could answer, Peony and Nympha came into the Perfumery. They went to the bell jars, beneath which sat the latest batches of perfumes from the refinery. The chemists put samples under individual glass lids etched with the names of the Calyx for them to analyze. Each sample was labeled. Beneath Peony's lids were three tiny perfume bottles. Each bottle had a frosted glass stopper in the shape of a different kind of peony blossom. Jessamine wanted so badly to find these exquisite perfume bottles sitting beneath a glass lid with her name etched into it. She wanted to see her botanicals formed in glass, cradling delicate perfume bottles full of liquid gold. She swallowed as she watched Nympha lift the lid and expose what had to be nearly a dozen beautiful perfume bottles, each with its own stopper in the shape of a unique variety of water lily. Each bottle had calligraphy etched into the side with names like attraction, fire crest and blue beauty. The amount of work Nympha had to do to produce this much fragrance was enough to make Jess feel faint.

Nympha noticed Jess and Snap watching.

"Would you like to scent these with me?" Her voice was soft and soothing, like wind chimes.

Peony shot Nympha a hard look, but then drew her gaze away as Jess and Snap came over.

"I would love to." Jess's raw materials were put into simple, generic vials and labeled with stuck-on paper labels. It wasn't until the sweat was processed that these perfume bottles were custom made.

"May I?" Snap gestured to a perfume bottle.

"Please." Nympha made an inviting gesture. Jess thought there was more grace in that single movement than Jessamine had in her entire body. Was *nymphaea* being a water plant the reason she moved like she was a liquid?

Snap read the label. "*Nymphaea lucida.*" Gingerly, he unstopped the lid. He held it under his nose and inhaled. His eyes widened. "Wow. That's… I can't even describe… Smell this, Jess."

Jess took a whiff. She drew back, concentrating on the pleasant sensations in her nose. "It's sweet and warm and citrusy, all at once." Nympha was watching her, shy, expectant. Jessamine took another inhale. "It smells like… dancing under a starry sky in your bare feet with someone you just met but really want to kiss."

"Oh, nice. Let me try." Snap picked up another. "This one is called *nymphaea odorata var minor.*" He gave Nympha a dubious look.

She laughed. "If it makes it to market, that won't be its brand name, don't worry. That's just the varietas. It's from a minor subdivision of my species."

He swept off the lid and lifted the bottle to his nose, holding his pinky in the air. He made a show of waving the mouth of the bottle and inhaling the smell, letting his eyes roll up into his head and his eyelids close. "Ahhhhh. This one smells of… warm birch candy fresh from the oven on a cold winter morning."

Nympha giggled. "I like that."

"Oh, please." Peony rolled her eyes. "You two haven't the faintest idea what makes a winning fragrance, or how to sell it."

"And you do?" Snap put the stopper back in the bottle and set it down.

Peony's tone became passionate, her features animated as she talked with her hands. Her usually severe expression softened. "Of course. I was born for this. I come from nine generations of flora fae. If you want to make a little money, you make solo note extracts, like Nympha has done. If you're lucky, unrefined customers with money will like them. If you want to win awards or set the market on fire, you have to make a symphony of scent-sual experience, a sublime olfactory harmony. A perfume needs to be unique and original, it needs character and longevity. You need at least twelve different notes. You need to make something that will haunt the imagination, trigger emotional memories. A valuable fragrance is experienced in the mind, not the nose."

Jess and Snap exchanged a look. She was secretly impressed, even if Peony was insufferably snobbish. She'd been initiated the same time as Jess and Snap, but Peony sounded like a teacher, not a fresh initiate.

"That's… kind of what they were saying when they put words to my fragrances," Nympha replied.

"With banal, uninspired poetry that has nothing to do with what they were scenting. Pure extracts are the building blocks of a great perfume. But alone they're incomplete, one-dimensional, embryonic, like a single note hanging in the air. Is it nice on its own? Sure. Is it a song? Not even close. Can you describe what strikes first, what develops and then what lingers afterward and when the notes change? No. You can't. Why? Because you don't understand the first thing about it. Perfecting fragrance takes years. Some of my father's best concoctions took decades."

"Your father is a perfumer?" Nympha studied Peony with interest.

"He was one of the best." Peony sniffed. When she spoke again, her voice was lower, calmer. "Years ago, when he was a teenager, he was Calyx, but when he lost his powers, he loved the business of perfumes so much that he learned how to do it the old-fashioned way. It takes a lot longer and a lot more work than the Calyx way, but our family has the only fragrance business in Ivryndi that can compete with Solana. I grew up around fragrance. It's the only thing I have ever cared about… or been good at."

Jess was taken aback. Peony walked around like everyone else was beneath her. She still sounded like that, but Jess could see now that Peony was a connoisseur. She was the kind of being who devoted their whole life to perfecting one practice, one skill, one art. Jess never expected her to admit to not being good at anything else.

"I'm sure that's not true," Jessamine said.

Peony's gaze sharpened on Jess. "I overheard Ilishec and Hazel talking about you."

"Peony, don't." Nympha put a hand out.

"Don't what?" Jess looked from one Calyx to the other. "What is it that you both know that I don't?"

Peony pressed her lips together and crossed her arms. She looked away.

"What did you overhear?" Jess pressed.

"He said that for the first time in the history of the Calyx..."

"Oh boy," muttered Snap under his breath.

"He might have to admit to making a mistake."

"Peony," Nympha murmured, her tone full of disappointment and reproach. "That's very unkind."

"Well, someone has to tell her. It's for her own good. I don't want to watch her killing herself day and night trying to do something she'd not capable of doing. No one wants to watch that. But I'm the only one honest enough to say it to her." Peony looked at Jess. "You have to face the truth at some point, Jessica. You don't belong here."

Jess felt as though Peony had slid a letter opener between her ribs. She put a hand on the table for support as she opened her mouth to defend herself, but fear seemed to have frozen her lips. What if Peony was right? What if Jess was killing herself day after day for no reason? What if Ilishec just didn't want to break the news that Jess didn't have what it took to be Calyx? Was he even now debating with Hazel, or worse, King Agir and Queen Esha about the problematic Calyx they'd initiated?

Jessamine felt Snap put a hand on her back. "Don't listen to anything Peony says. Come on, Jess."

Peony turned back to her extracts, flinging words like they were stones. "The gardener doesn't have the stomach to tell her the truth, and you think *I'm* the cruel one?"

Jess let Snap lead her away from the Perfumery. She felt rattled, mowed over, deflated. Her first thought was that if she lost her place here, she'd have no choice but to go back to Dagevli. Something inside her began to shrivel. She barely noticed as Snap led her to a bench and made her sit while he went and got her a glass of water. Beazle gave a sympathetic squeak and crawled out of her hair to nestle in the crook above her collarbone. Greta fluttered from Jessamine's shoulder to her cheekbone, kissing her. She put her hand up and let the glasswing crawl onto her knuckle. She was staring sightlessly at Greta and distantly aware of someone joining Snap at the tap, but too lost in her own doubts to look up.

She was trailing her colleagues. Was she fatally behind, as Peony made it sound? Maybe. Maybe not. But she was behind her fellow Calyx for sure, probably even last.

A fat bumblebee droned past as Rose sat down beside her. "Snap told me what Peony said. You mustn't listen to that nonsense, Jessamine. Peony is just jealous."

Jess lifted her gaze to Rose's concerned face. "Jealous of what? I haven't managed to produce more than an ounce of usable raw material, and Ilishec thinks taking me on was a mistake."

"Just because she said it doesn't make it true."

"Lying is an offense that could lose Peony her position here. Do you really think she'd risk that?"

"What I mean is, Peony might not even know what she heard. Ilishec could have been talking about anything, to anyone." Rose gripped her hand. "You're not to give up. You're a wide Calyx. That means you'll have to work a little harder to get your magic straight than someone who is deep, but don't you realize that that means you have even greater potential than we do?"

"That's exactly what I was trying to say," added Snap.

Rose nodded. "Peony knows it too, and she just wants to sabotage your growth. I know her type. She's competitive, she sees opponents wherever she looks. The most important thing to her is being the best, even when Ilishec says over and over again that there is no competition between Calyx. She invents rivalries in her head. Don't let her bait you into her way of thinking."

Snap handed Jess a glass of water. "Exactly. Just be you. Learn what you are capable of and forget about whatever pushy Peony thinks."

Jess took the water and sipped it. She appreciated their support, but she could also hear the sinister ringing of a gong, deep in her gut, bonging away incessantly, echoing Peony's words: *You don't belong, you don't belong.* Did Ilishec regret bringing her into the Calyx? Was he even now trying to think of a way of letting Jessamine down gently? Would it happen after Rahamlar? That would be the most likely time because, before then, he needed her. It was too late to switch her out with another Calyx, and she could still conjure the *cordatotriloba* plants, she just couldn't chromatype them. If she were the gardener, she'd wait until after Rahamlar before letting the axe fall.

Chapter Thirty-One

Jessamine

As the tops of Rahamlar's fortress peeked from above thick foliage, Jessamine took a few deep breaths. They were nearly there. Her hips and thighs were aching and she reminded herself to sit up straight in her saddle. The Calyx were to maintain bodily awareness and self-possession, to be beautiful to look upon at all times, weariness notwithstanding.

The road between Solana and Rahamlar began through a pretty valley, but soon turned to switchbacks that seemed like they would never end as they meandered back and forth across the mountain sitting between the two castles. Up and up and up the retinue climbed, gaining scant meters even though they traversed many kilometers. They spotted wild boar, a stag with enormous antlers and many fallow deer. The temperature dropped as the elevation rose. Halfway up the mountain, they stopped to stretch and snack and give the animals a rest. One of the soldiers carried a small canister of ether, which produced a flame. He heated up tea and the Calyx stood around blowing the steam off their cups and sipping to warm themselves. The Fahyli were spaced out, even invisible part of the time, as they spread before and behind. Twenty minutes' break and they were back on the switchbacks. The view might have been beautiful, but the forest closed in around them.

Above the tree line, the road was a loose, boulder-strewn nightmare of exposed double-track. It was windy, snowy and bitterly cold and there was no animal life anywhere. The train had to stop so everyone could pull out jackets, gloves, scarves, hats and blankets. The more fragile familiars, including Greta, were put inside an insulated box with many small compartments so they would be protected from the wind. Beazle stayed snuggled against Jess's neck, beneath her scarf. A view briefly opened up of other mountaintops and one of the great rivers. Snow dusted the tops of the highest peaks, and Jess overheard one of the soldiers saying that this snow never melted.

Then they began the long descent of even more laborious switchbacks. It was tough going for both mounts and riders. They left before dawn and traveled—with brief stops to eat and stretch—until just before sunset, but they had finally arrived.

Jess lifted her chin and squared her shoulders as she noticed the Calyx in front of her doing the same. Palpable relief swept through the retinue. Conversations struck up, punctuated by laughter, as they observed the clear depths of the famous Tadylat river. The road descended around a bend to run parallel with the water, beneath overarching trees. The air grew humid. Bright mosses coated nearly everything on the ground. Large fish darted about in the depths of the Tadylat. Jess could see why the river was famous. It was a gorgeous, clear turquoise blue, and very deep. Bit by bit, the train came to a halt as those riding in front reached the outer gates. They waited for several minutes before moving again.

Jess had been expecting something similar to Solana with its pretty spires, glinting marble and wide streets, but Rahamlar was entirely different. If there was a city behind the fortress walls, none of it was visible save for a few spindly towers piercing the canopy. These towers seemed hardly wide enough to enclose a staircase. The blocks of stone were huge and crudely cut. Passing through the outer gate revealed a gap between the outer and inner walls the length of four horses placed nose to tail. To the right climbed steep, boulder-strewn ground that disappeared into the forest and blocked out the sunlight. To the left, the terrain followed the gentle curve of the wall as it descended. The sound of trickling water filled the air, and algae clung to the bars of lower windows.

Guards patrolled the ramparts. Three stopped to observe them from above, helmeted heads backlit with evening light. It was impossible to see their faces. When Proteas saw where Jessamine was looking, he smiled and waved at the men. Several of the Calyx joined. If the guards smiled, Jess couldn't tell. None of them returned the wave. A moment later, they found themselves in a large courtyard. It was cooler than it had been on the road, since there was no canopy holding the humidity down. Overlooked by rustic balconies, towers and the shoulder of the main keep, the courtyard was open to the sky.

An unseelie soldier with long sharp ears, wearing brown boiled leather with a small bird stamped over the heart, came out to meet with the crofter. The crofter dismounted, and they clasped one another by the forearm. Pages and stable boys materialized to help the retinue dismount. The cobblestones here were raised in places where the earth beneath had shifted, making the courtyard a bit treacherous. The Calyx dismounted and stretched their legs.

The Solanans were only to stay for two nights, but they brought costumes, gifts, warm clothing and layers for the journey, shoes for dancing, overnight things and supplies for the animals and familiars. In Solana, unloading was done by the palace staff. When help was not immediate, Asclepias started to unload, and the rest of the Calyx followed. Eventually, Rahamlar servants moved to help until everything was unloaded and the horses were led away.

Jessamine exchanged an uneasy look with Aster. It wasn't much of a welcome, at least not so far. The Calyx stood in a listless group, their belongings sitting in piles on the ground, while the crofter conversed with the Rahamlar captain. Jessamine spotted Laec, but he was busy consuming the layout of the courtyard, studying every guard and servant as though he meant to memorize everything and everyone.

The crofter and the captain approached the Calyx. "The kingdom of Rahamlar welcomes you. I am Captain Yorin. Please follow me inside. Your rooms have been prepared and your things will be brought up."

They were escorted into the belly of the fortress through a narrow doorway that Proteas and Asclepias had to duck under. A single-file journey through dimly lit stone passageways began, none of which had been built in straight lines. A couple of stairs here, a landing there, a few more steps going down, around a hairpin corner, up another set of stairs. By the time they arrived in a parlor with two fireplaces and high narrow windows, Jessamine would not have been able to find her way back to the courtyard. The parlor smelled like vegetable stew, and the Calyx sniffed appreciatively. A large cauldron sat in one of the fireplaces, simmering and steaming. Through a doorway by the fireplace, three servants appeared.

"Behind me is our guest wing," Yorin said. "We've enough space to accommodate two persons to a room. These servants will see to all of your needs. This entire wing is yours. We will leave it to you to sort out how you divide up the rooms. I'm sure you're very tired after your journey. Once you've settled in, you can return to this room for a hot meal."

Then he swept past them, and it became clear that this was all the instruction they were going to receive.

Jessamine paired with Aster as the Calyx claimed rooms for the night. Their room had one large bed, a small fireplace, a bowl and washstand and a threadbare tapestry with a frightful image: what might have been dancing ladies in a moonlit glade at one time but now looked like frolicking ghosts in a swamp. The colors had faded, but at least it lent some warmth to the cold room. There was no firewood in the hearth or beside it. While it had been muggy outside, inside it felt cool. Jessamine pulled her cloak around herself as she sat on the bed. Aster stood at the doorway hoping to get the attention of one of the staff. It became apparent that some of the rooms had firewood and others didn't, so Aster went next door to pilfer wood from Vanda.

Celebrating her release from her insulated box, Greta fluttered to the tapestry and began to crawl around. Beazle was still a warm lump in Jess's hair. He'd slept for the majority of the journey, but he'd be wanting to hunt soon.

Aster blew on the tender flame and watched as the damp kindling struggled and smoked. When Ilishec popped by to check in on them, they didn't complain. The gardener went from their room to the next, noting where every Calyx was staying.

"It's not what I was expecting." Jessamine shivered. As she

held her hands to the fire, Beazle woke up and fluttered to the window. She opened the narrow shutters to let him out.

Aster straightened and stretched, tossing the matches back on the mantle. "Me either. There is definitely a gloom hanging over this place. They're a kingdom in mourning so I suppose we can forgive them."

A pageboy appeared in their open doorway, a small cedar chest in his hands. "Vanda?"

"Next door." Aster smiled at him. "We're Aster and Jessamine."

"Okay. Your things are coming. Hot stew and fresh bread in the parlor in twenty minutes."

Soon their own trunks arrived. Jessamine's stomach tightened when she thought about their performance the next day. Would the courtiers notice all the subtle nuances that Ilishec had woven into the production? Still unable to chromatype, Jess was assigned to produce many vines and blooms of *cordatotriloba* for the head table. She wouldn't be able to shake her nerves off fully until her part of the presentation was over.

As the fire beat back some of the chill, they busied themselves with organizing their costumes and accessories. They'd been taught by Olinya's team how the female nobility in Rahamlar did their hair and wore their clothes for mourning, and Ilishec had choreographed their performance with Rahamlarin folk dances in mind. Tonight, they would sleep until they woke up naturally. Tomorrow, they would rehearse in the banquet hall after lunch. They were set to perform in the evening before the banquet began.

Aster and Jessamine gathered with the other Calyx in the parlor where a buffet had been laid out. Servants ladled and served as the Calyx sat at the table or stood near one of the fireplaces, letting the flames chase off the chill of the day. The

Calyx were quiet as they ate the steaming stew and bread. When Jessamine went for a second helping, Alstro, Proteas and Vanda followed. Everyone was hungry.

Jess handed her bowl to the serving girl. The girl looked so morose, she wished there was something she could do to cheer her. "The stew and bread are delicious. Thank you."

"You're welcome, miss," the girl said softly, handing Jess another full bowl.

Jess took it. "What's your name?'

"Eda, miss. What's yours?"

"Jessamine."

"Would you like another slice of bread, Jessamine?"

"Yes, please. Did you make this food?"

"No, miss. I'm a lady's maid. But my lady is… Well, I've joined the kitchen staff temporarily." Eda cut a slice of bread for Jess.

Proteas handed her his bowl. "We're all very sorry about Prince Ander."

Alstro added sympathetically: "Yes, such a tragedy. Was he as lovely as they say?"

Eda's lower lip wobbled and her eyes misted. She nodded. "Even more lovely."

The Calyx shared looks of dismay as tears tracked down the girl's cheeks. She sniffed and brushed them away. No wonder Queen Esha and King Agir had sent them. If the courtiers were as miserable as the staff, then the Calyx had their work cut out for them.

"Does Ilishec know the foreign dances of the entire continent?" Jessamine asked the following evening as Aster was pinning her locks into place. The mourning style was to pin the hair into a square bun at the nape of the neck, capture it in a black net, then lay a black veil over everything.

"I'm sure he doesn't keep them all in his memory, but yes, he knows a lot of them." Aster stood behind Jessamine, frowning into the mirror. Jess's bun looked saggy. Aster took out the pins to redo it. "He has a researcher he contracts when it's needed. I don't think he's used them in a while. Not since Prince Ander was born, I think. There. That looks… not bad."

Jessamine thought she looked dowdy, but it didn't matter. It was more important to get the presentation right. "It'll be covered anyway. Ready for the net?" She held up the flimsy black string.

After the net, Aster fixed the mourning veil over Jessamine's hair and arranged the lace so it lay at her eyebrows. The girls switched places and the process started over, only, wrestling Aster's thick, tightly coiled curls into place required more patience. Next were their gowns. Every gown was mostly black, but Olinya had found a way to include some jewel tone into the costume. For Aster it was deep maroon cuffs laced along her inner forearms. For Jessamine it was a deep green stomacher with a black lace overlay. The female Calyx had been given identical earrings: simple black beads with a gemstone matching the shade of their colored item.

They inspected each other from head to foot. They'd worn practice veils for the rehearsal in the hall earlier in the day because the performance veils were delicately beaded and the lace was fragile. Even with all the pretty beadwork, Jessamine thought Aster looked older and paler with all the black fabric framing her face. When she looked at herself in the mirror, she frowned, but she supposed it had the desired maudlin effect.

The trill of the flutes sounded in the hall. It was time to assemble.

The Calyx made their way through their wing to line up silently outside the great hall. The double doors were still closed. With only brief slashes of jewel tones, and the women's hair veiled and black bands hugging the men's foreheads, they looked like well-dressed wraiths. The sounds of the crowd reached them through the doors and Jessamine wondered just how many people they'd be performing for. When the scent of cooked meat reached her nose, her head came up sharply and she looked at Aster who stood directly behind her in line.

"Food?" Aster mouthed, eyes wide.

Jessamine winced. The scent of meat must have accidentally leaked into the hall from nearby kitchens.

When the slow, sweet music began and the doors swept open, the Calyx at the head of the line began to enter, sweeping in with low graceful movements. The entrance took a long time as the Calyx took two steps back for every four steps forward.

The smell of food grew strong as Jessamine entered the banquet hall, moving in time with the music. A cold feeling filled her stomach. The smell of meat was not accidental. Ilishec's request to keep food out of the hall until the performance was over had been ignored. Some people were already eating.

Pots and trellises of soil had been placed throughout the room as requested, but they were not where they'd been during the rehearsal. They were meant to line the center of each table and the floor along the aisles and walls. But in order to make room for the food, they'd been moved to the floors beneath or beside the tables.

The gardener had drilled into every Calyx that if anything went amiss during a performance that they were to ignore it, to continue on as if nothing was wrong. If something directly impacted their choreography, they were to improvise around it. So Jessamine did her best to ignore the smell of meat and the sounds of people chewing and utensils clacking against plates. Her feet moved across the floor in time with the symphony as chromatyped blooms began to appear, drifting through the air. Mystic blooms of *armeria*, *asclepias*, *proteas*, *aster*, *cupressus* and others floated over the heads of the guests as the music swelled.

Some of the guests put down their utensils. A few caught the mystic blooms and sniffed where they dissolved against their skin. Some, but not all, conversation ceased. The Calyx reached their position in front of the head table, elegantly and mournfully executing the steps with the music while conjuring their meaningful blossoms. The familiars fluttered in the air, adding depth and life to the chromatypes which festooned the hall. Guests admired the insects, pointing out brightly colored butterflies to other guests, such as Aster's Trea, and Vanda's Thorne, a beautiful hairstreak butterfly. The musicians sat in a front corner of the room. A few who played smaller instruments like flutes and violins strolled slowly along the outer walls.

The smell in the room grew strange as the food scents mingled with the perfume of flowers and soil.

Jessamine stole glances at the citizens of Rahamlar and saw a mix of expressions. The majority of those watching were women. One of the men glanced around, made a show of sniffing the air, made a face, then shoved a large hunk of gravy-soaked bread into his mouth. Blood flushed Jessamine's face.

Struggling for focus, Jessamine put her gaze to the floor and moved her way toward the head table. She was to reach the front dais, perform sixteen bars of choreography and fill the trough of soil on the head table so that it was overflowing with *cordatotriloba*. She spotted Ilishec near the musicians. As the Calyx took turns dancing in front of the head table, filling the air with their chromatypes, he began to commentate, speaking through an instrument he'd brought that magnified and deepened his voice. The Calyx did their best to honor the choreography as the gardener poetically narrated the symbolism: *armeria* for sympathy, *asclepias* for hope in misery, *cupressus* for mourning and sorrow, *proteas* for courage and so on.

Unable to change the positions of the pots, the Calyx had to bring up their botanicals wherever they could. Jessamine's *ipomoea cordatotriloba* was a long, creeping vine with pretty trumpet-shaped blossoms. She was supposed to grow them in a trough on the head table, but the trough had been moved to the floor, so her vines expanded beneath the table, winding around the feet of those seated. Jess's face heated as she saw a woman gave a start, then peeked beneath the table at the mass of greenery and flowers now taking up foot space. The woman nudged the man beside her and he lifted the tablecloth to look beneath. They began to pluck blossoms from the vines to toss to their neighbors, put in their hair. Someone dropped blossoms onto a neighbor's plate as a joke.

A moment before Jessamine had to perform a turn, she caught sight of a woman seated at the end of the head table. There was something wrong with her face, but Jessamine couldn't get a good look. Her *cordatotriloba* wrapped itself around and up the table legs. It crawled across the top of the table, sprouting moonflowers as it weaved around goblets and platters of food.

A man in the center of those at the head table caught Jessamine's attention like a fishhook at her cheek. This had to be Prince Faraçek, one of the royals Ilishec had highlighted.

Everything about him was as sharp as knives. A severe hairline, glossy black hair and long sharp ears made him frightening to look at. With another half turn, Jessamine was able to get a better look at the woman at the end. She had a bruise high on her cheekbone and half encircling her eye. There was a split on her lower lip and a mound of swelling beneath it. She was beautiful, even with one eye swollen nearly shut. Her other eye was bright blue and lucid, but misery stole much of her beauty. She had pulled her chair away from the man seated beside her, and her body was partially visible at the table's end, like she wanted to escape.

Another half turn and Jessamine caught sight of Laec against the wall, standing with other Solanan guards. He wore a helmet over his bright hair and was dressed in the Solanan livery. He seemed to be craning his neck, looking toward the head table, his expression thunderous. It was strange to see him looking angry after she'd had such fun with him at the initiation ball. Jess lost sight of him as she dipped and turned.

Vanda, the one who conjured orchids, took her turn dancing and conjuring blooms near the head table. Her familiar, Thorne, fluttered prettily overhead, circling like a bird on an updraft. Vanda's face was a mask of serenity, showing none of the embarrassment that Jessamine was feeling. Jess took strength from Vanda. She beckoned Greta to her and the glass-wing fluttered closer, swirling around Jessamine's waist, then up into the air over the head table. Greta was not as well trained as Thorne, but she understood that this was a performance, and her job was to add beauty and charm.

The denouement began. Jess was relieved that it was nearly over. She couldn't wait to leave the hall. She finished growing her *cordatotriloba*. The open blossoms and leaves settled into stillness. After the performance was over, the troughs of flowers would be taken to decorate other rooms, or taken out to public buildings where the citizens could enjoy them.

Prince Faraçek's expression was dark and closed as he leaned back in his seat, one elbow resting on the arm of his chair. He stroked at his black goatee and his eyes glittered as he watched. He neither frowned nor smiled, and yet somehow oozed disapproval.

Perhaps wanting to cheer him, Vanda's familiar fluttered toward the prince, swooping prettily overtop the head table. He was bright and big and drew every eye. He landed on the side of a wine bottle, where he flexed his wings, showing off. One of the young women leaned forward, admiring the pretty markings.

Jessamine noted the effect that Thorne was having and sent Greta to join him. Thorne took off again. He approached the prince, fluttering close to offer Rahamlar's royalty a good look. Prince Faraçek's dark eyes followed the hairstreak, though the expression in his face never changed. Greta followed Thorne, banking around the items on the table, floating and drifting. Other butterflies had followed suit and the air above the head table was full of color and life. Rose's fat bumblebee landed on one of Jess's blossoms. He buzzed his wings in time to the music. Greta fluttered behind the prince's head, then came around, swooping close to his face. The prince startled and recoiled, smacking his head on the back of his chair. He snarled and, with a swift motion, waved a hand, batting Greta away.

She fell to the tablecloth, fluttered her wings a couple of times, then lay still.

Jessamine froze.

There was a high-pitched squeak from the rafters. The

music disharmonized, then halted. A woman gave an inarticulate cry of dismay.

Jessamine sprang toward the table, almost tripping over her skirt. She reached the dais and stepped up on the front of it, reaching over the food and *ipomoea*. Her throat closed up as she gently scooped Greta into her hand, careful not to touch her wings. Her heart thundered so loud that she could hardly hear anything else. She felt commotion all around her but had eyes only for the glasswing.

"Greta?" she whispered. "You're okay, you're just dazed. Come on, love. Wake up."

Greta didn't move.

Jess felt strong hands on her waist, lifting her backward off the dais. Greta lay so still in her hand, Jess cupped her other hand over Greta to protect her as she was half carried through the hall, her slippers skimming over the flagstones. Beazle landed on her shoulder and clung to the fabric.

"Please," Jess whispered. "Greta. Please. Wake up, dearest. Don't leave me."

But she could feel in her spirit what her heart and mind refused to accept: Greta was dead. With one careless sweep of his hand, the prince had ended her life. A sob rose in Jessamine's throat.

She was surrounded, a crowd of Calyx and Solanan guards escorting her back to the main doors. The music had begun again, but very poorly, then it stopped again. Voices raised in anger, but Jessamine couldn't understand what was being said. Her senses deadened to everything but Greta.

Beazle crawled down her arm as they were rushed from the ballroom. When he reached Greta, he nudged the butterfly with his nose. He looked up at Jess with big liquid eyes, then gave a sorrowful squeak and drew himself inward, wrapping his wings around himself. Like a scared turtle, he retreated from the world and lay in Jessamine's palm like a tiny furry acorn.

"Greta? Love?" Jessamine blew gently on the glasswing, hoping against hope that the butterfly's favorite game would rouse her. Greta's body only shifted in her palm, her wings already stiffening. Hot tears filled Jess's eyes, then overflowed down her cheeks.

There were louder shouts from the banquet hall, but they were distant now as Jessamine was ushered toward the guest wing. She thought she could hear Ilishec, but she barely recognized him. She'd never heard him sound like that before.

Jessamine was guided into the room she shared with Aster. There were Calyx everywhere, swarming, whispering, some were crying and hugging one another. The smell in the room was sour. Jessamine felt that her body's perfume had changed. She smelled like flowers that had begun to molder, and so did the rest of the Calyx. Every face was drawn and stressed. Every familiar was close to their Calyx, on their head or shoulder, or sitting in the palm of a hand. Wings and antennae drooped with sadness and shock. Everyone looked traumatized.

"Drink this, Jess." Aster put an arm around Jess's shoulders, holding a cup of something fragrant. Trea crawled over Aster's curls toward her face where he reached a tiny foreleg out to touch her cheek. His wings drooped pathetically.

Cradling Greta and Beazle in her cupped palms, Jess shook her head. "I can't."

"It'll help you sleep. Here. Let me." Aster brought the cup to Jess's lips and stroked her hair as she tilted the liquid into her mouth. Jess took a few swallows of the nectar. The cool, sweet liquid soothed her throat.

Ilishec swept into the room with a face like an earthquake.

"All of you, to your rooms. Let her be. I know you want to comfort her, but she needs privacy right now."

"I'm not leaving her." Rose sat beside Jessamine. She'd taken off her veil and Bombini was sitting on the top of her head, cradled in the folds of her hair.

Aster tightened her arm around Jessamine. "Me either."

Ilishec ran his hands through his hair, flustered. "Fine. The rest of you, shoo. Please. I know you're upset, but you need to pack your things. We aren't staying the night."

Rose put a hand on Jess's back. "She isn't fit to travel tonight, Gardener. Surely. That road is bad enough in the day-time. What will it be like up there when we can't see?"

"And it'll be freezing at the top," Aster added.

The gardener put a hand over his eyes. "Of course. I wasn't thinking. I'm not… thinking straight. This is a nightmare."

Rose's voice was calm. "Let her rest. She's in shock. We can leave at first light. How about that?"

If Jess hadn't been so miserable, she would have felt proud of her friend for her self-possession. The Calyx clustered in the doorway, reluctant to leave. They murmured their agreement.

"Very well. But everyone be ready at dawn and not a moment later." Ilishec spat into the fire. "Damn this kingdom!"

The Calyx departed, leaving Rose and Aster sitting either side of Jessamine, still cradling her familiars. Ilishec paced a bit, then disappeared, then reappeared minutes later holding a small treasure box. He knelt in front of Jessamine, holding the open box. It was lined with velvet. "Put her in here, Jessamine. We'll bury her in the palace gardens, where she was so happy."

Jess resisted, pulling Greta and Beazle back toward her heart. Her head felt heavy. Her heart was burning in her chest. She'd always thought grief was purely an emotional pain. She hadn't known until now that loss could also be physically painful. The thought of putting Greta in a box was abhorrent.

"She's gone, dearest, and we are so sorry," Rose whispered. She unpinned Jess's veil and took it off. "But you can't hold her all night."

Jessamine tried to protest but now her tongue felt heavy too. The room tilted. She had to let Rose transfer Greta's body to the box or she'd drop her. Rose did it gently, and Ilishec closed the tiny coffin. Beazle roused himself enough to crawl up Jess's arm and bury himself in her hair. With a sorrowful whistle, he fell silent and still.

Aster took off Jessamine's dancing slippers while Rose unlaced Jess's costume. When she was down to her slip, they helped her get beneath the quilt. The bed already smelled of her body's sadness. Jess closed her eyes and found she was unable to open them again. With her eyes closed, her friends were easier to hear.

"She was murdered," Aster hissed as she put wood on the fire. "I can't believe what I just witnessed. Why did our guards not do anything?"

"Do what?" Rose whispered from the window where she drew the drapes closed. "It happened so fast. We can hardly arrest him for murder."

"Why not? That's what it was."

"To us it was murder, yes. To the citizens of Rahamlar, Greta was a bug. A pretty one, but nothing more. How do you punish the monarch of another kingdom for accidentally killing an insect? I'm sure he didn't intend for it to happen. She startled him. Didn't you see?"

Mutinous silence met this question.

It's not real, Jess thought. *It's a bad dream. When I wake up, she'll be alive. She'll be fine.*

With the warm lump of Beazle snuggled in her neck, Jess fell asleep to the sound of her friends quietly packing, hot tears soaking the pillow beneath her cheek.

Chapter Thirty-Two

Laec

When Prince Faraçek had batted away the insect, Laec had had his eyes on Çifta. The moment Laec had recognized her behind the bruises and swollen lip, everything else was inconsequential.

At first, he wasn't certain that she was the same woman he'd met in Syrgana. *That* woman was flush-cheeked, bright-eyed and bold. This woman was thin, taciturn and defeated. It took him several minutes to decide that yes, it was her. Laec was against the wall with the rest of the Solanan guards. He hoped she'd look over, but she hardly looked up, and when she did it was to stare straight ahead. Even if she had looked over, she might not have recognized him. He looked the same as everyone else in the Solanan livery and helmet.

Then Laec's peripheral vision caught the prince's hand move, and everything froze. Even the insects who had been fluttering around the room landed on the nearest object. Çifta had gasped and recoiled, her gaze focused on the table in front of the prince. It was the first emotion she'd displayed aside from apathy. When Jessamine bolted for the dais, Laec felt the Solanan guards tense, watching the crofter for a command.

"What happened?" Laec whispered to the guard beside him. Then he saw the tips of Greta's wings poking up from Jessamine's cupped hands. His heart dropped into his stomach. Was the little butterfly dead?

The guards shifted around, unsettled. The crofter barked, "Be still," and Laec had to agree with the man's decision, even though it left a bad taste in his mouth. Any threatening moves they made would only inflame the situation.

Ilishec yelled obscenities and the crofter had two soldiers hold the gardener back. Laec leapt onto an empty space on a bench between two guests, lifting his arm in an attempt to get Çifta's attention, but she used the disturbance to withdraw from the room. Laec watched helplessly as Çifta slipped through a door at the back of the hall, followed by two Rahamlarin guards.

Meanwhile, Regalis pulled Jessamine off the dais. She hardly seemed to notice what was happening. She cradled her familiar in her hands as Calyx crowded around her, trying to see if Greta was okay. Jessamine's little bat zipped into the midst of it all.

As Regalis escorted Jessamine to the big doors, Ferrugin swooped silently from the rafters, over the crowd and through the open door. The musicians trailed after the Calyx. The gardener was dragged out, shouting oaths the entire time, his face flushed and his forehead gleaming. It was strange to see such a gentle being lose control over his temper so completely.

Prince Faraçek watched the chain of events he'd unleashed with cold contempt, as though it was all childish melodrama.

He might not have intended to kill Greta, but the fact that he displayed no remorse was like pouring vinegar into a cut.

With a final glance at the door Çifta had slipped through, Laec joined the tail end of the Solanan retinue along with Kite, who looked like she was ready to behead someone… anyone. Her raptor swooped over the head table and gave a scream that bounced off the stone walls. Some of the guests flinched and covered their ears. Prince Faraçek got to his feet in one swift motion, glaring at the bird.

"Kite!" the crofter barked.

The raptor shot obediently to Kite's shoulder, but Laec heard her uttering curses under her breath.

Hushed conversation among the guests resumed as the Calyx left the hall. There was even some nervous laughter. Laughter!

Laec slipped to the crofter's side as they went down the hall. "What are you going to do?"

The crofter glanced down. "Who are you again?"

Laec glared at him.

"Not that I owe you any explanation"—the crofter looked straight ahead—"but nothing. We will do nothing. It was a tragic accident. The creature should not have ventured so close to the prince."

When the crofter picked up his pace, Laec didn't try to keep up with him. He fell back and let the upset Calyx and musicians continue to their wing. He found the passage used by servants to bring food into the hall. Staff passed carrying dirty platters, but they paid little attention to him as long as he stayed out of their way. He reached the side door that opened into the back of the hall. Another passage branched off. This had to be the hall Çifta had gone down. He began an exploration of the warren-like halls. When he spied the guards who'd followed Çifta from the hall, he backpedaled, hoping they hadn't spotted him. He was still in Solanan livery. He peeked around the corner and noted that they stood either side of a closed door, guarding it. Was this Çifta's room? Laec chewed his lip, his heart thudding heavily in his chest. From the looks of things, Çifta was in trouble.

Laec returned to the soldiers' barracks below the guest wing. The room he shared with three other guards was empty. He changed into a plain black tunic and leggings, then checked himself in the mirror. There were times when he wished his hair wasn't quite so bright. It made it hard to blend in. Some of the male guests wore dress hats with feathers while others were bare headed but wore their hair tied back. Laec snooped in the bags his fellow guards had brought but didn't find any hat suitable for a banquet, so the best he could do was tidy his tail.

He returned to the banquet hall, where the Rahamlar musicians had struck up lively music and all tables had been cleared away to make room for dancing. There was no sign of Prince Faraçek. Perhaps he'd gone to bed. A few of the guests had left, and Laec wondered if it was because they were sad at what had transpired. He hoped that was the case, otherwise the general reaction made the Rahamlar nobility appear very callous. Those not dancing stood around talking or walked laps around the perimeter arm in arm with a friend or lover.

Laec sauntered the perimeter like the others, plucking a glass of wine from a passing tray and sipping it as he eavesdropped on conversations. When a woman wearing an embroidered belt over her mourning dress going in the opposite direction asked someone where the princesses had gone, Laec did a graceful turn and tailed them, keeping his eyes on the dancing but his ears on the ladies.

The companion hooked her hand around the woman's forearm. "I heard that Princess Isabey is suffering from one of her headaches, and Princess Serya, well… she doesn't exactly excel at dancing."

"I heard they haven't been seen in quite a few days," the lady in the belt mused.

The other shrugged. "They are in mourning. I would expect them to want to spend time alone."

"When did Lady Çifta leave? Did you see?"

The other looked toward the head table, her gaze skimming over Laec. He buried his face in his goblet.

"After Prince Faraçek killed the bug, she probably thought no one noticed." She gave an exaggerated shiver. "What a miserable girl. Maybe if she smiled once in a while, Prince Faraçek would seat her beside him, instead of making her sit where she half falls of the dais."

Laec resisted the urge to spill wine down the back of her gown.

The belted one said, "Honestly, I hope the dowry was worth it. We've inherited a rich Boskayan cow, but for what? She's not even a lesser noble." She laughed.

To Laec, her laughter sounded about as genuine as a wool toupee.

"What led King Osvitan to make such a match?"

"Money, of course. Do you not know of Kazery Unya's wealth?"

"What do I care for the riches of a foreigner?"

"Oh, my dear." Her tone turned patronizing. "King Osvitan has always had ambitions he was unable to fulfill. Expand our borders, acquire more farmland, make a coastal ally. I've forgotten more ambitions than I remember. An alliance with the merchant brings him closer to all that." She glanced over her shoulder, her gaze skimming over Laec.

He headed for the door. He'd heard enough to confirm that Çifta was not respected or known here. It also sounded like the princesses were hiding themselves from court life. Mourning was a good reason for that, except… wouldn't they want to attend a performance given by the Calyx in honor of their deceased brother?

Laec rubbed his forehead in irritation. Who had bruised Çifta's face and why? Why was she guarded? Since Prince Ander was dead, why wasn't she on her way back home? She hadn't been here long enough to forge strong relationships. She was either waiting until after the Calyx performance was over, or she was being prevented from leaving. The guards posted at her door supported the latter. Laec considered going straight to the room that was being guarded and presenting himself as a friend of Çifta's, but then they'd take note of his appearance, and he didn't want that. There had to be a less risky way to learn more.

Laec found the gardener in the parlor, talking with Proteas and Asclepias in low voices.

Ilishec looked up when Laec entered. "Where have you been?"

"How is Jessamine?"

Ilishec shook his head, his eyes glassy. "Devastated, of course. In shock. We all are. I still can't believe it. Aster gave her a sleeping draft."

"Has anyone from Rahamlar apologized or addressed what happened directly?"

Ilishec's lips tightened. "Captain Yorin unofficially expressed regret, but from the royal family there has been nothing yet. I doubt King Osvitan has even been told."

Laec nodded. The longer Rahamlar waited to address the incident, the worse the insult was. "Did you happen to notice the woman at the end of the dais?"

"Lady Çifta?"

Laec was surprised. "You know her?"

"Only of her. Queen Esha gave me a list of the more important nobles and courtiers that would be here. There were a few she wanted to give gifts to. Lady Çifta wasn't one of them, at least not yet, but after she marries the prince, Queen Esha will arrange a more opulent gift for them."

"After she—"

A puzzle piece fell into place. Laec had been operating on the assumption that Çifta was to wed Prince Ander, but it was Faraçek she was betrothed to. Laec's stomach did a slow, sickening slide.

The gardener, not noticing Laec's shock, looked at the floor and rubbed his temples. "I don't know what Queen Esha will do now. If King Osvitan had been in attendance, I know he would have handled this nightmare with humility. In fact, it wouldn't have happened at all. Who swings at a familiar? It's… loathsome. Monstrous."

"I met her," said Laec suddenly.

Ilishec looked up, confused. "Who?"

"Lady Çifta."

"Oh." Ilishec was too preoccupied to probe.

"We met in Syrgana," Laec added. "Her soldiers helped me when I got into trouble."

"That was nice of them."

Laec lowered his voice. "More than nice. Listen. I think she's in trouble."

"Did she say something to you? I can't imagine when there was time for that."

"No, we haven't spoken, but didn't you notice her misery?"

Ilishec looked annoyed. "I was a little distracted with other matters. I'm sure she'll settle into her new home soon. These things can take time."

He stared at his uncle, horrified. "Someone beat her."

"Why do you assume so?"

"Did you not see her face?"

"I've had similar bruises from being bucked off a horse."

Laec's expression turned skeptical.

Ilishec eyed him suspiciously. "Are you attached to the prince's betrothed in some way?"

Laec's heart skipped a beat. "No. Of course not."

He laid a hand on Laec's shoulder. "Then forget the girl, Laec. We have enough trouble, and what could you do anyway? If you're concerned, write to her family, though I don't see why she couldn't have done so herself if she is unhappy. Make sure you're ready to ride at dawn. We can't leave this place soon enough, as far as I'm concerned."

Ilishec returned to his group of Calyx, encouraging them to go to bed.

While Laec could see why the crofter and the gardener would stay out of it, sworn as they were to Solana, Laec was not bound by any such oath. Learning more about Çifta's situation might even be what Elphame expected of him. What of the matters the two gossips had been discussing? The acquiring of farmland, the expansion of borders? Which borders? Solana and Rahamlar shared hundreds of kilometers of borders. What if Prince Faraçek had his eyes on Solanan lands? Surely that was something Queen Elphame and Queen Esha would want to know.

He turned the situation over in his mind. He couldn't leave Rahamlar without trying to talk to Çifta herself. He needed to find out what she'd done to deserve being treated like a prisoner. Maybe she was a shrew, a terror, or behaved like a spoiled child. It was possible; she'd grown up with enormous wealth. But Laec didn't believe it. He'd met her, and she was sweet. More than sweet. Whoever had done it hadn't even bothered to aim for body parts that would be concealed beneath clothing. They'd damaged her face. That spoke of a lack of shame as well as a lack of fear of being caught.

As Laec slipped outside, the night crier alerted the city that it was midnight. A mist hung low and thick over the stones, creeping from the riverbank. Guards moved along battlements but the courtyard itself was empty and quiet, the inner gates closed. Staying off the gravel and keeping to the shadows, Laec's gaze skimmed over the fortress walls for windows most likely to belong to Çifta's room, but to get a view he'd have to climb a steep and slippery bank of grass, which would raise him into the moonlight, where he'd likely be spotted.

The familiar cry of a bird made him pause.

"It's just me." Her voice came from across the courtyard. "Kite."

Laec spotted her squatting in the shadows. Her raptor swooped past the moon and landed on her forearm.

Kite stood as Laec went to her. "What are you doing out here?"

She stroked her familiar's plumage. "I needed to… cool off. You?"

Laec considered her and the bird. "He's male, right? All familiars are of the opposite gender of their fae."

"Some kind of genius, are you?"

He ignored her sarcasm. "What's his name?"

"Erasmus. I know it bucks the convention, but I'm a patriot."

"What convention?"

"To choose a name inspired by the binomial nomenclature. Linnaeus can pound sand, as far as I'm concerned."

Laec didn't know who Linnaeus was, but he didn't care because he was getting an idea. "How well trained is Erasmus, exactly?"

Chapter Thirty-Three

Çifta

Çifta was dreaming she was at home in her own bed when a sound broke through her sleep. Her body tensed and she was swallowed by the disappointment. Still stuck in Rahamlar. She sat up, listening. The fire had burned low to a bank of flickering coals. All was quiet save for some distant voices as guests left the banquet hall and headed for their rooms. She heard some high female laughter and the low tones of men, then all went quiet again. She put a hand to her cheekbone and winced at the soreness there. In a few days, it would be healed. She shouldered her way into the mattress and pulled the quilt up to her ear as the sound came again. A fluttering sound. It came from the window. Her heart picked up speed when she heard tapping on the windowpane. She got up and padded to the window to peer through the warped glass. A gray bird with black-tipped wings perched on the ledge. It cocked its head, looking at her with one dark eye. It was the size of a small cat and had a sharp hooked beak. It tapped on the window again, then blinked at her. She'd helped birds who had accidentally flown in through an open window back in the Unya's summer home, but never had she seen a bird knock to get in before.

"Aren't you a handsome one." Çifta unlatched the window. "What do you want?"

The bird swooped into the room the moment she opened the pane, making her step back with a gasp. It perched on the top of a bed post and looked down at her, ruffling its feathers. There was something familiar about it.

"You were in the hall." Çifta recalled. "You're someone's pet, right? You're from Solana."

It turned its head this way and that, seeming to take in the room, and Çifta herself, before swooping out through the open window. She looked for it, but the bird had disappeared into the darkness.

Shrugging, she went back to bed. It must have just been curious.

She had drifted off again when the sound returned, the same flutter of a bird's wings. This time, the sound was more insistent. She sat up, a little annoyed. Sleep was her only escape from this hell she was trapped in. And having watched Faraçek kill a special fae insect was another memory she wanted to avoid.

She went back to the window to see that this time it had something in its beak.

She let it in, and as before, it zipped into the room the moment the window opened wide enough. Landing on the top of her chair, it dropped the something onto the carpet. Before it could roll under the bed, Çifta caught it up in her hand. Her heart climbed up inside her throat. It was a message cylinder. She took it to the moonlight and popped the cap open. Hair sprang out of the open end. It looked blood red in the moonlight, but in the daylight, she was sure it would be very bright. Pulse racing, Çifta pulled the hair out of the cylinder. It unraveled into a long lock, the right length to have belonged to…

"Laec." She lay the lock of hair over her palm. Black thread had been tied around both ends, keeping the long strands together. In the middle of the strand, tied with the same black thread, was a little rolled-up scroll. With trembling fingers, she untied the note.

A simple question written in tiny lettering made her let out a shocked breath of laughter: *Need help?*

The hair on the back of her neck rose and she shivered. Laec had to have come with the Calyx. She went to the window and looked out, straining for some glimpse of him, but she caught sight of a guard and retreated. She dug out a dark blue pencil and scratched an answer on the paper.

She hesitated; how was Laec planning to help? Was he alone? She didn't want him to put himself at risk, but she wasn't getting offers of help from anyone else, so… She stuffed the message into the cylinder, wishing she had a knife so she could include a lock of her own hair. She had brought sewing shears from home, but along with her quill, ink, writing paper and poker, Faraçek had removed anything sharp.

She closed the cylinder and looked at the raptor, who tilted his head but made no sound. She held it up, inching closer and closer. The bird snatched it out of her hand and shot out the window, a high-speed projectile. Çifta waited at the window until she got cold, then slipped back to her bed, leaving the window open. What would happen now?

The bird returned a third time, with another message. This one said only: *I'll think of something.*

Çifta stared at the words with mixed feelings. She wanted out now, but Laec didn't have a plan. She supposed that if he'd only just found out about her imprisonment, then he couldn't possibly have come up with a strategy to get her out in so little time. But he knew she was here now, and that was a huge improvement on her situation.

Çifta went to the box she kept cosmetics in. She put colored balm on her lips and pressed a kiss to the paper. She didn't care if it was improper or forward. Rolling up the stain she'd left, she tucked it into the cylinder and the raptor took it out into the night. Çifta left the window open in case the bird came back, even though it made her room cold and damp. She returned to bed and fell asleep with Laec's hair clutched in her fist.

Part Three

Chapter Thirty-Four

Jessamine

Jessamine swayed back and forth in the saddle, her eyes fixed sightlessly on the road. The clopping of horses' hooves had lulled her into a state of near hypnosis. She felt like she'd swallowed a sack of rocks. In her mind's eye, the prince made his careless gesture over and over. Greta flopped against the tablecloth and fell still over and over. She couldn't stop it, couldn't run away from it. She was a prisoner of her own mind.

They could have been on the road for three hours, or seven, she couldn't tell. At some point, the cold had stung her face and made her lips dry. She didn't care. When someone, she didn't know who, draped a blanket around her shoulders, she barely held it in place. She deserved to freeze to death. She had sent Greta fluttering around that head table after Thorne. Why hadn't it occurred to her that Greta might not know that she should stay out of the reach of strangers? She was so vulnerable, so helpless and trusting. Jessamine should have kept Greta close the whole performance. It was her fault. Hers, and the prince, of course. The lack of remorse on his face, his contempt for

Greta's life and the devastation it would obviously cause… it was like a serrated blade sawing across Jess's heart.

"Jessamine?" Laec pulled his big black horse alongside hers.

Jess blinked and looked around. They were on a flat traverse, heading straight across the side of the mountain, through thick trees. She couldn't tell if they were on a climb or a descent. The canopy kept out much of the sky. She looked behind where Aster and Rose kept pace with her. They brightened when they saw Jessamine looking back.

"Are you hungry?" Aster asked. "We have—"

"I'm fine. Thank you." She faced front, but not before she saw Aster and Rose exchange a worried look. "Where are we?"

"We'll be home in three hours." Laec's unearthly gaze seemed to go right through her. "I'm not going to ask if you're okay, because that would be a stupid question. But, are you okay?"

"I'm…" Jessamine gave a start as their proximity to home sank in. Shame burned her face. "Beazle hasn't eaten all day."

Putting a hand to the warm lump inside her hair, she felt Beazle's tiny warm body. His pulse thrummed under her touch as he sleepily wrapped himself around her finger. She pulled him out and put him against her cheek, feeling his velvety coat against her face. She closed her eyes.

"Neither have you," murmured Laec, "in case you hadn't noticed. Not at breakfast or at lunch."

Beazle squeaked as she looked down at him. "Do you have any fruit?" she asked Laec.

"Here." Rose nudged her horse alongside Jess's other side. She held out an apple. "I have bread, cheese and raisins for you as well. If you want."

Jessamine took the apple, bit off a piece and gave it to

Beazle. He sniffed at it and looked away. "Come on, Beeze. You're tiny, you can't get away with not eating. Please?"

He sniffed the apple again and took a tentative bite. She let out a sigh as he bit off a piece and mashed it between his teeth.

As Beazle ate, Jess looked behind and ahead, noting the sprinkling of guards, the morose musicians and the Fahyli. There was no sign of Regalis. Ferrugin and Kite's birds would be scouting somewhere overhead. Ilishec was behind Rose and Aster while the crofter led the rest of the Calyx in front. Everyone's faces were drawn, solemn. It took a minute to sink in that everyone was sad for her sake, even the guards who didn't know her and the Fahyli, whose birds might have eaten Greta in the wild. She faced front, feeling a little comforted.

"I'm okay, only…"

Laec gave her a minute, then prompted her. "Only?"

"Did you know that if a pollinator dies, flora fae get a new familiar soon after? Sometimes only weeks later. Whenever they're over the worst of the grief. I overheard Proteas talking about it. As long as they're young enough, they'll attract a new familiar and a fresh bond will form, because a flora fae in their youth always needs a familiar to make the magic flow. You never forget the old one, of course, but the new one is drawn by the need for healing. The magic does it. It's a defense mechanism, I guess. A survival strategy."

Laec's expression lifted a little. "So, you could have a new pollinator in a few weeks?"

Jess shook her head and took a shaky breath. "She wasn't my true familiar, even though she felt like one. She belonged to my twin. Greta is all I had of him, my only connection, and now she's gone. She'll never be replaced, not that she could, even if another familiar came along."

Laec's mount slowed as they took a steep downhill hairpin, and Jess's horse stayed alongside. As the road flattened, Laec asked, "What happened to him, your twin?"

"I'm guessing he died at birth, but I don't know for sure. My mother owes me an explanation. I wonder how she'll feel when I tell her Greta is gone. She never really liked my butterfly."

"Who doesn't like a butterfly?" Laec looked shocked, then seemed to realize he was openly criticizing Jess's mother. He wiped his expression clean. "I mean… why not?"

Jess shrugged, biting off another piece of apple for Beazle. "Probably because Greta reminded her of him, my brother. I'll find out. She won't be allowed to keep secrets from me anymore. It's not right. It doesn't matter how painful it is for her to talk about it. Not knowing is worse. Don't you think so?"

"I guess it depends what it is." At her look, Laec amended again. "I mean, yes. Of course, you're right. So when are you going to talk to her?"

"She won't come to the palace, or even the city, so I have to go home. I wasn't going to ask Ilishec for time off because I haven't been Calyx for very long, but now… I don't think I can wait." Jess didn't think she'd be able to conjure so much as a sprout for a while. And surely, in this emotional state, her sweat would only smell foul.

"I'm sure he would want you to go," Laec said. "You just lost one of your best friends."

Jess nodded. "Just because she wasn't my true familiar, doesn't mean I didn't love her like one." Beazle squeaked. "And Beazle loved her too."

"Going home will make you feel better."

"I doubt it." Jess lifted Beazle back to her hair. He crawled inside and snuggled against her scalp. "But at least I'll get some answers."

"What would make you feel better? Is there anything that would help?"

She looked at the bitten apple, feeling like she had a bone stuck in her throat. She threw it into the woods as hard as she could. "Something I can never have."

Laec's gaze followed the apple as it sailed into the trees and bounced off a trunk. "And that is?"

Jess turned hard eyes on him. "Justice."

Chapter Thirty-Five

Laec

The floor around the desk in Laec's room was littered with crunched-up discarded letters. Laec jammed his quill into the ink bottle in disgust and shoved himself away from the desk. He began to pace in front of the windows. He'd started a dozen reports to Queen Elphame, each one seeming more idiotic than the last. Reporting what he'd overheard in Rahamlar was no problem, but what he really wanted was to get Elphame to care about Çifta. If Laec had never met her, he wouldn't even devote a single sentence to mention her in his report. He might not have even noticed her suffering. But he *had* met her, and he *did* know she was suffering. He couldn't close his eyes to her need, and for his own self-respect, he needed to free her. He didn't just owe Çifta for helping him in Syrgana, he owed his own heart that. But if he wrote to Elphame asking for advice or help, he already knew what the response would be: *Stand down, don't get involved.* He'd be lucky if she didn't address her return correspondence with "*Dear*

Moron." And if he received that kind of response, he was under oath to obey it.

Abruptly, he stopped pacing.

What if he reported the situation to Queen Esha? By now she'd already heard from the crofter and the gardener about what a disaster the performance had been, and the tragic death of Jessamine's familiar. She was the most likely of the two queens to lend him support, support he needed if he wanted a chance of freeing Çifta.

He glanced at the sky. At this time, courtiers gathered in the queen's parlor to have tea and socialize, play games or read books. He pulled boots over his stockings, wormed into a vest and straightened his hair. He still looked frazzled, but he was too impatient to take the time to bathe and primp.

He made a beeline for the queen's parlor, hope burgeoning in his chest like a bubble.

Queen Esha was seated in the same place she'd been when he first met her, but Princess Kara wasn't with her, and neither was the little dog. She was reading by the fire with a glass of wine and a carafe at her elbow, while a group of courtiers played games in an alcove. Laec kept his distance but moved into her line of sight. He needed to be invited to approach her.

She looked up. "Laec! Hello."

He bowed his head. "Ma'am. I hesitate to interrupt but there is something I would like to ask you."

She lowered the book. "If you promise not to gossip about my drinking alone so early in the day, then I promise to give my full attention to your question, even if I don't have an answer."

He flashed his teeth. "If you knew how many bottles of wine I've murdered before five, you wouldn't worry so much."

She laughed and gestured to a nearby chair. A servant girl rushed up and offered Laec a drink.

"I'll have whatever she's having," he said.

Queen Esha put her chin in her hand, waiting while a goblet was brought for Laec.

Laec took a grateful sip of the wine. For better or worse, he needed the fortification. "I assume you've had a full report about what transpired at Rahamlar?"

She raised her head from her hand, her gaze heavy. "A sorry business. That poor girl. We are very disappointed, as you can imagine."

"That was not the only disappointment, Ma'am." Laec proceeded to tell her about Çifta, how she had rescued him in Syrgana and offered him shelter afterward, who she was and that she was betrothed to Prince Faraçek. "In no way is she being treated as his betrothed, though. She is a prisoner, and a mishandled one at that. She needs help."

Esha's brows knit together. "What of her family?"

Laec frowned. "Her father is the one who got her into this mess. Clearly, he doesn't care."

Queen Esha considered this. "It is unfortunate. I feel for Lady Çifta, but we cannot be overly surprised."

"No?"

"There is a saying in Solana that 'unseelie is unseemly.' As queen, I can never be overheard using such a phrase, but many believe it to be rooted in truth."

Laec knew this well. Not all unseelie fae had the malevolent streak they'd become known for, some could even be mistaken for seelie, but many conflicts had been started by unseelie courts and their reasons often seemed petty to seelie fae and humans. Laec had more than once tangled with unseelie on the outskirts of Stavarjak where they liked to dispute the borders and even the ownership of useless swampland.

"But Rahamlar is not an unseelie kingdom," said Laec. "King Osvitan is human."

Queen Esha nodded. "Yes, but his wife Queen Daryli was unseelie and King Osvitan's days are numbered. Did you see him while you were there?"

Laec shook his head.

She sat back. "He was too unwell to hold court. Between you and me, I am surprised that King Osvitan didn't pass the moment he heard of Prince Ander's death." She studied Laec's face, measuring him. "Were you surprised when, rather than dealing with the skirmish at the border with violence, we elected to send a retinue of Calyx as a gift instead?"

Laec hesitated. "It's not my place to judge."

"I welcome honesty."

He chewed his cheek before answering. Queen Esha was so approachable, so transparent, so unlike Queen Elphame. Criticizing Elphame was a dangerous pastime, but Esha seemed almost to want it. "I did think it was an odd choice, yes."

She nodded, satisfied. "Then allow me to explain, because I think I know where you're going with this."

"You do?"

"You want me to give you men, to help you rescue this young woman." Laec brightened, but she put up a hand. "Before I answer, you must understand a little of our history."

"Okay." Laec would listen to the entire history if it meant Esha would help him.

"Six hundred years ago, Rahamlar was a kingdom much like ours, consisting of a mixed population of humans and seelie. The land that our kingdom now sits upon was wilderness and part of Rahamlarin territory. The reigning monarchs—both seelie at that time—gave birth to twin boys: Erasmus and Iskandar."

"The Erasmus that Kite named her familiar after?"

"That's right." Esha smiled. "Kite is a patriot and wants everyone to know it. Anyway, back to the story. Tradition said that the eldest prince, Erasmus, should inherit the crown, but the king and queen loved Iskandar better, so they passed the crown to him."

"That must have been quite a blow." Laec took a drink and settled into his chair, feeling more relaxed. Esha was so easy to talk to. He understood better now why Ilishec hadn't returned to Stavarjak. It wasn't just for the gardens. This approachable style of ruling that Esha had was very appealing.

"If he were the usual sort, yes. But Erasmus wasn't like other royals. He was not interested in power. He wasn't a good rider or swordsman, but he loved everything that was beautiful: flowers and trees, music, art and fine food. Lucky for Erasmus, Iskandar loved him and sought to share the kingdom with him. He set what are now the borders of Solana and gave the land to Erasmus to do with as he liked, suggesting that he attempt to make it worth something. The land was inhospitable mountainside and heavily forested at the time, without any byways better than goat tracks. It was also full of wild boar." She waved a hand, her rings glinting with the amber light from the sconces. "Well, you know. You've been through some of it."

"Yes, I have" said Laec. "Even with the double-track road, it remains inhospitable, steep and forested."

"Precisely. Undiscouraged, Erasmus contracted a famous fae architect named Patosy to design this palace in which we now live. He is credited with inventing the ingenious features which capture energy from the ether to give us light and power, but some say he stole the idea and brought it back to Ivryndi from unknown lands across the Ivryndian Sea."

Laec scratched his chin, comparing the two structures in his mind's eye. The Solana Palace was a wedding cake to Rahamlar's bran loaf. "One can only imagine how surprised Iskandar might have been with his brother's cleverness."

Queen Esha folded her hands in her lap with an elegant shrug. "It isn't written whether Iskandar was proud or jealous, but it is recorded that he married a young fae woman named Toryan. History puts her at seventeen when she married Iskandar, who was in his early thirties. She looked seelie—there are portraits that confirm this, if they can be trusted to be accurate—but it was later learned that she'd kept it secret that her blood was unseelie."

"Iskandar didn't question her bloodline?"

"Or perhaps he knew but he didn't care. He was in love. Toryan—not quickly, mind you, but slowly, over the course of decades—brought more and more unseelie into the Rahamlar population from other courts. By the time the humans and the seelie realized they were outnumbered, it was too late to stop it. Dissension grew quickly as they realized it had all been orchestrated by Toryan. She was a flora fae, by the way. Not many know that."

"I didn't realize unseelie could be flora fae."

She looked surprised. "Of course they can. Some have even attended Discovery. We've never invited any to join the Calyx, though. Their botanicals are interesting, but less desirable from an aesthetic perspective. Anyhow, things escalated, and in one horrible night unseelie soldiers removed all humans and seelie from Rahamlar fortress save for the king himself and the royal children."

"Removed?"

Queen Esha fingered the base of her goblet. "Killed or chased off. We have a tapestry in one of our lesser-used parlors that depicts the event, if you care to see it. It's called *Toryan's Massacre*."

Laec shivered. "And the survivors fled to Solana?" He was beginning to see how Erasmus had become an iconic figure here.

She dipped her head. "That's exactly what they did. It was the nearest safe haven. After that night, humans living in the villages of Rahamlar, fearing they would be hunted down by unseelie soldiers, fled to Solana as well. It became a sanctuary city and the population, in turn, protected it most passionately. My husband, King Agir, is a descendant of Erasmus."

"What about King Iskandar?"

"He died from a hunting injury in his mid-fifties, leaving Queen Toryan to rule Rahamlar. Naturally, the relationship between her and Prince Erasmus crumbled. He sent a document announcing the emancipation of Solana from Rahamlar, which enraged her. She wanted the kingdom put back the way it had been, the borders dissolved. She should have been happy that she was left to sit on the throne, for it belonged rightfully to Erasmus. He had every right to take the throne back after Iskandar's death, but it was all he could do to repel the unseelie raids. Nonetheless, every attack was thwarted. Thanks to natural features in the land, Rahamlar could never take Solana, although both sides suffered casualties and both sides took prisoners. The unseelie liked to make fun of Solana; the city full of flowers and butterflies, music and art, but our beautiful kingdom was stronger than they expected, which inspired our motto and sigil."

Laec had seen it written in the stained glass of windows

and etched along the stems of silver utensils and crystal wine glasses. "Beauty is our strength."

Queen Esha dimpled. "The lion plays a part as well, but that's another matter. We sent our Calyx as a show of empathy. We've held a tenuous peace for a long time, thanks to a queen of Solana named Nella, who reigned long after Toryan's death."

"She ended the strife?"

"Exactly. Sick of the constant conflict, Nella offered Rahamlar an exchange: human and seelie slaves for unseelie prisoners. She wanted peaceful trade at border towns and no threat to citizens of either side. This way, she proposed, both kingdoms could renew the wealth they'd once enjoyed. She was successful, and a treaty was signed. Nella's treaty has stood for nearly three hundred and fifty years. We have a…"

"Let me guess," Laec interjected, "you have a portrait of her in one of the dining halls."

Queen Esha smiled. "It's in the Oleander Parlor, but yes. I suppose the story has changed some as it's been passed down, but that is how I learned it. Around one hundred and fifty years ago, a Rahamlar monarch invited humans to fully return to the kingdom, and to improve this relationship, he married a human queen. Through the resistance of the bloodlines to mix, destiny had a human king return to the throne. After that, it became law that the throne would always go to the eldest human male, to keep the kingdom in the hands of humans. It was a sneaky bit of legislation and upset the unseelie population, so in consolation, the king also decreed that the human king must always marry an unseelie queen to keep the unseelie citizens represented. It's a law that holds true today. King Osvitan is human with two human children and two unseelie children. That's why Prince Ander's death is doubly tragic. Ander was his only human boy. I asked one of our lawyers to verify that the throne of Rahamlar must pass to the next human child, Princess Serya, and they have confirmed that, but I am also certain it will make the unseelie population restless. Did you see Princess Serya while you were there?"

"No, and that's the other thing you should know. I overheard a conversation between two courtiers. One suggested that the princesses hadn't been seen in some time."

"Did she say how long?"

Laec shook his head. "Her companion thought they'd withdrawn to mourn, but still, one would assume they'd want to attend a requiem for their brother."

Queen Esha rolled her goblet between her palms. "Did you see the prince?"

"Yes. Faraçek, to whom Lady Çifta is betrothed," Laec reminded her, "was seated at the center of the head table."

Queen Esha cocked an eyebrow. "Çifta is an Unya, a wealthy merchant's daughter, and about to become a princess. There are many ambitious young ladies who would endure a few beatings here and there in exchange for such a position. How do you know she wants to be saved?"

Laec fought to keep his expression neutral. Esha had shocked him a little. Was *she* the type who wouldn't mind enduring a few beatings in exchange for position? She was a sweet, tiny woman, but perhaps flintier than she appeared. He said, "I just know."

Queen Esha's gaze burned through him. "You love this woman."

Laec was shocked twice in as many seconds. If he'd had wine in his mouth, he would have sprayed it all over the queen.

She laughed at his expression. "It doesn't matter if you're

human or fae, the males of the species always underestimate how transparent their motivations are when it comes to love."

His heart beat faster and he stifled his instinct to jump to a denial because he wasn't entirely sure she was wrong. Better to dodge the subject, in classic Laec style. "You sound sympathetic."

Her smile faded. "I am always on the side of love. I love my own husband, after all. But I cannot give permission where I know he would not. It would be foolish to risk ruffling Rahamlarin feathers for the sake of this Boskayan woman. Even if you were a Solanan citizen, he would never agree. I am sorry. Peace and freedom cannot be taken for granted. Our people sleep well precisely because my husband and I often do not. I'm sure you understand."

Laec felt like a punctured bubble. He was going to have to do something on his own, though without any allies and without any magic, it was a fool's errand. Yet he couldn't do nothing.

"However…" Queen Esha began, then stopped.

A servant materialized to fetch their empty goblets and the mostly-empty carafe. She gave the queen an inquisitive look.

"Just water, please. You?" Esha raised her brows at Laec.

"Same." Laec smiled at the girl. "Thank you."

The queen waited until the servant girl retreated. She stole a glance at the Calyx and courtiers playing games in the alcove. All appeared to be absorbed in their fun, even if the Calyx were more subdued than usual. Esha lowered her voice and leaned closer.

"I cannot give you soldiers. However, if I wanted to help unofficially, I would tell you that long ago, during construction of this palace, a tunnel was dug through the mountain such that the transport of timbers and other building materials could be more easily managed."

Laec almost slipped off the front of his seat. A secret passageway between the fortress and the palace?

Her bright eyes reflected the firelight. "This underground passage was also used as an escape during the conflict, but the entrances were closed soon after Solana divided itself from Rahamlar, and the whereabouts of them were lost to time. Most people don't know about this passageway, and many who do believe it's just a myth."

It was like a beam of sunlight shooting through thunderheads. It was a sign. Even without the assistance of soldiers, with a secret approach that led right into the fortress, the odds of getting Çifta out of there improved by orders of magnitude. It would be dangerous, of course, but when had danger ever stopped Laec before? And if there was a chance…

He and the queen scooted back in their seats as the girl returned with water and clean goblets. As the girl poured, the queen said in a conversational tone: "I understand you enjoy ancient maps."

Laec didn't miss a beat. "Yes, I'm fond of the old cartograms and gazetteers. They're very quaint."

The serving girl bobbed a curtsy and left.

"We have quite a collection here," Queen Esha said airily. "I couldn't say whether any of our maps predate construction of the palace, but your uncle might know."

Laec gazed at the queen, his fondness for her inching higher. "My uncle, you say?"

Chapter Thirty-Six

Jessamine

Jessamine looked at the items spread across her bed, holding Beazle in her hand. He'd been clingy since the incident, hardly leaving Jess long enough to go hunting. He'd eaten some of the berries Snap had dropped off for Jess, but she hadn't taken in anything more than an elixir since the retinue had returned the evening before.

Since Jessamine had become Calyx, her number of personal items had increased. Olinya's team had made her several new outfits for daily wear: tunics, leggings, dresses, vests and several pairs of shoes and boots. She had hair accessories, belts, scarves and jewelry. She'd also been given little bottles of perfume to take home for Marion from Rose, Aster and Nympha, as well as a pot of green paint from Snap. She had a small book of drawings that Auvo had given her that morning, of gardenscapes and flowers. At the end of the sketchbook, she'd found a beautiful color drawing of Greta perched on a frond of wisteria blossoms, which Jess wanted to have framed. But she hadn't acquired a new carpet bag along with all these things, and she couldn't fit her clothes, shoes and all the gifts into the one she'd brought from Dagevli. She'd been staring at the pile trying to find the will to deal with the problem for… ever?

She sat on the bed, stroking Beazle with her fingertips. "Maybe Aster or Rose will have something I can borrow."

"For what?"

Peony stood in the open doorway. Her dark hair was piled into a huge bun on the top of her head and decorated with a fresh white peony. She wore a flowing white gown belted with a peony-pink sash. Her skin glimmered, and the dark circles that had once marred her eyes were gone. Her neck seemed longer, her cheekbones rounder and her eyes larger. Peony's fragrance drifted into the room, a scent that Jess was beginning to associate with feeling bad about herself. Envy and dislike burned in Jess's gut like acid. They had been at the palace for the same amount of time, but already the magic had improved Peony's appearance. Jess hadn't changed a bit, and now, on top of that, her eyes were red and watery.

"What do you care?"

Peony's jaw flexed. She leaned casually on the doorjamb. Her digger wasp crawled around to the front of her dress from the back, then began to climb up Peony's body. "I suppose I deserve that."

Jessamine raised an eyebrow. "Is that an apology?"

"Maybe."

Jess snorted.

Peony scratched the back of one hand. The gesture looked weird on her, self-conscious. "Listen. I am sorry about Greta. She was… Well, I never met another familiar like her, with wings like that. I'm really sad about it. If anything happened to Sphex…" Her wasp buzzed its wings and she lifted him to her shoulder. Her voice hardened. "The prince is a beast."

"Yes, he is," Jess replied—slowly, cautiously. "Was there anything else you wanted to say?" Would Peony retract what she'd told Jess that day in the Perfumery?

Peony looked thoughtful. "Nothing else comes to mind."

Jess looked away, unsurprised. Lying was grounds for dismissal, and Peony valued her position here too much to have concocted such a statement just to hurt Jess. "Fine. Thank you for your sympathy. You can go now."

Peony didn't move. "Are you going home? I heard that you are."

Jess glared at her.

She put up her palms. "I'm just saying… I would. Even though my mother is a harpy, I would want to be with my family. There's nowhere like home when you're sad."

Jess wondered if Peony had been told that Greta had belonged to Jessamine's twin, and waited, half expecting her to bring it up. Peony just glanced at the things on Jess's bed, and the small empty carpet bag sitting on the floor at Jess's feet.

"Ask Ilishec for a bigger bag. Hazel used to collect them."

Jess looked up in surprise.

"See you when you get back." With that, Peony was gone, her perfume lingering in the air.

Jess got up, bemused. "Not the worst interaction we've ever had with her, eh, Beeze?"

She trekked through the gardens toward Ilishec's workshop. Gardeners and arborists were hard at work, weeding, watering, pruning. It was nearing the time when Ilishec took his half-hour break. As Jess approached the workshop, she could hear voices drifting from the open door. She paused just outside, wondering if she should interrupt. She wasn't sure who Ilishec was with—it might be someone important.

"Most of these are maps and plans of the gardens and grounds," Ilishec said. "But nothing I have is older than one hundred years, which is far too young to be helpful to you. Most believe there was never a tunnel, that it's just a story that parents and nursemaids made up to keep children in their beds at night." There was the sound of rustling papers and a cardboard tube being dropped, the kind Ilishec kept large botanical sketches in that couldn't be folded. A tube was opened with a pop.

"You mean they told kids that some nasty fae would come from underground and kidnap them?" Jessamine recognized Laec's voice. He wouldn't mind if she interrupted. She took another step when the gardener said:

"Something like that. Either way, your quest is as good as impossible. You can ask Beyaz for older maps but it's doubtful you'll find anything earlier than three hundred years. Keep in mind that if there ever was a tunnel linking us, it probably collapsed a long time ago."

Jessamine blinked. A lost tunnel?

"Perhaps, but Queen Esha believes it was real or she wouldn't have mentioned it. It makes sense. How else did they get all the supplies they needed to build this place? A lot of these stones are from a quarry on the other side of Rahamlar. Getting them over the mountain would have been a nightmare."

Jessamine's heart picked up speed. A secret passage between kingdoms? Could it be true? She moved to the patch of flowers beside the walkway and crouched there as though weeding. Beazle licked her earlobe, then fluttered away. She watched him go as she listened, happy that he had the will to go hunting, even if the timing of his appetite was all off.

"Really? How do you know that?" Some of the doubt had gone from Ilishec's voice.

"I asked around. According to Esha, the tunnel is what saved so many people during Toryan's Massacre. What if it hasn't collapsed? And what if Rahamlar found the entrance on their end? Such an advantage could be dangerous. No peace lasts forever. Has the king never thought to search for it?"

"I wouldn't know that, Laec. Why are you so interested anyway?"

Silence met this question. Jessamine strained her ears.

"Come now, lad," Ilishec pressed. "The look on your face suggests you are up to no good."

"My face always looks like this."

Jess pinched her lips together to keep from snorting.

Ilishec gave a half-amused grunt. "Need I remind you that you are not in Stavarjak anymore? We're running an organized civilization here, an efficient society that adheres to the rule of law. No offense to Elphame, but fae mischief is less well tolerated here."

"What fae mischief? I'm only researching a rumor, because what else do I have to do? If such a passage exists, do you not think it better that Solana knows of it? Between the skirmish at the border and the murder of a familiar, it is clear they are not concerned about insulting Solana. They as good as spat in your face."

Jessamine almost smiled. She could hear how easily Laec manipulated his uncle, even if Ilishec could not. Bringing up Greta's murder immediately made Ilishec upset and took his mind off Laec.

"The dumb brutes," the gardener growled. "I never thought I'd see the day when a visit from the Calyx would be treated as something to be endured. It's insufferable."

"Exactly. I don't trust them. If there *is* a tunnel and we don't at least try to ferret out its location, then we deserve to be invaded."

"Don't say such things," the gardener snapped.

"You are not naturally suspicious." Laec sounded unbothered by Ilishec's rebuke. "You don't think like me. If I didn't think about this, no one else would." And then, as though it just occurred to him: "Perhaps this is why Elphame sent me."

Ilishec let out a long breath. He sounded weary of the topic now. "Whatever the reason, my boy, these are all I can provide by way of maps. I'm telling you you'll find nothing suggesting a tunnel here. See Beyaz, he'll have older maps, although I think you're chasing vapor. Erasmus wiped away all the evidence of the passageways after the emancipation. It was too risky not to. He may have even bought long-lasting magical protection to ensure no one ever found them."

"You're probably right."

Jessamine heard them moving toward the door. She straightened as Laec emerged.

"Pardon me." He brushed past her, his arms brimming with tubes and folded parchment. One of the tubes fell and, as he halted, he recognized her. "Hello, Jess. I thought you'd gone home."

"Tomorrow." She picked up the tube and put it in his overstuffed arms.

Ilishec emerged a moment later. "Jessamine. What are you doing here?"

"I came to see if you might have a bag I could borrow. Mine is too small."

The gardener gave her a tired smile. "Of course I do. Come with me, dear."

"See you when you get back." Laec waggled his fingers at Jess, showing his incisors. He reminded her of a fox when he grinned like that.

"See you." She watched Laec as he carried his collection toward the palace, musing about what she'd overheard.

"Jess? You coming?" Ilishec was already on his way to the cottage he shared with Hazel.

She caught up. "Did you ask the crofter about my escort?"

"Not yet. I've been distracted. I'm sorry. I can do it tonight."

"No, I'm glad you haven't bothered him. I'd rather go home alone, if it's all the same to you."

He shook his head. "Calyx traveling alone can be a target for… deplorables."

"Yes, but I don't look like a Calyx. I'm the same as when I arrived. Even Auvo has commented on how my appearance hasn't changed. If I cover my ears, no one can even tell I'm fae. The road between Solana and Dagevli is busy and safe for humans. I could do with the alone time."

Ilishec frowned. "You should have at least one companion."

Jessamine thought about the Fahyli who had been there when Greta had been killed. Whose company could she best tolerate? She'd recalled the feeling of Regalis's strong hands pulling her off the dais, guiding her protectively out of the hall. "I'll ask Regalis."

"Regalis is a good choice. He'll be quiet and vigilant." Ilishec put his arm around her. "I know it hurts, but it'll get easier. You'll see. One day, you'll cherish the memories you have of Greta. The bad memories will fade. They always do."

She put her arm around the gardener's waist. "You mean one day I won't continuously replay the moment the prince knocked the life out of Greta right in front of me? One day, I'll think about something other than strangling him with a violin string? Or stabbing him with a red-hot poker? Or dumping a bucket of flaming cow shit on his head?"

Ilishec looked down at her, alarmed.

"Sorry," Jessamine mumbled. "I'm not myself."

He squeezed her to his side. "Quite alright, my dear. Quite alright."

Chapter Thirty-Seven

Jessamine

The bag Ilishec and Hazel had loaned Jessamine was packed. The sun was still above the horizon and the Calyx would be gathering in the hall for dinner, but she wasn't hungry. The conversation she'd overheard between Laec and Ilishec had gone round and round in her mind. She instinctively knew Laec hadn't been transparent with the gardener, and something had convinced Laec that this lost tunnel existed. Jess was set to go home, but she couldn't shake the idea that had been gnawing at her like a squirrel gnaws a nut. Would it work? It had worked with Rose's heirloom and she hadn't even been trying. Might it work for something much larger, something that she was actively seeking?

Beazle hung upside down, clinging to one of the wooden beams overhead.

She looked up. "Psst."

His little head emerged from beneath a wing.

She crooked a finger. Beazle squeaked and dropped from the ceiling. He swooped into her hair, and they left the room.

She emerged in the gardens and found what she was looking for: a patch of empty soil, in the shade of a copse of fae silvertrees. Crouching there, Jessamine drew up *solidago*, just like she had for the gentleman at the ball. She inhaled the scent as it grew, asking the lost passageway to reveal itself. Beazle gave a squeak, and then crawled out of her hair and took off into the sky. She quested after Beazle gently, in anticipation, watching the fronds of the *solidago* unfurl and the little yellow blooms come to maturity.

A vision engulfed her like an enormous wave.

She fell on her bottom in the dirt as her sight changed. She was flying over Solana City, free, lifted on drafts of warm air. She could still feel the solidity of the earth beneath her hips, but it was a distant sensation. The scent of the *solidago* was strong as the city expanded below her. Elegant spires glittered and evening sunlight reflected off marble tiles, sending stark shadows across the grounds behind the East Keep. Over stables and storehouses she flew. She recognized the cooper's workshop, the stretch of forges, the training grounds, the stone wall she and Snap had peered over. She flew over another stone wall, then a field of flax. Beyond the waving stalks, a rocky cliff dropped away to another field. There she slowed and banked, turning one hundred eighty degrees. Now she could see the cliff face. It reminded her a little of the cliffs behind Dagevli, with blueish-gray stone and shelves sprouting grasses. Beazle took her into a thick copse of silvertrees. She passed through the mirrored leaves, so bright they temporarily blinded her, then dropped closer to the earth. Ivy lay in a thick mat across the face of the cliff. The ivy rippled as though baking in a wave of intense heat, then shimmered and became transparent. There, beneath the tangle of overgrowth was a human-made cylindrical shape with a flat top. It was a well.

Jessamine felt an unpleasant jolt at the form the entrance

had taken. An old well was not exactly inviting, but there was no doubt in her mind: this led to the underground passage that Laec was searching for. It was real.

"What are you doing down there?"

Her sight returned and she blinked up at Snap. He held a hand out and she let him pull her to her feet.

"Are you okay? Did you fall?"

She put a hand to her forehead, feeling a wave of vertigo as blood rushed down through her body. She put her head between her knees.

Snap touched her lower back. "Jess? You're scaring me. Do you need a healer?"

She straightened and put a hand on his shoulder. "No, I just stood up too fast. I'm alright. There's something I have to do. I'll talk to you later."

"But—"

Without waiting for a reply, Jessamine hurried around the palace to the entrance near the herb garden. She waited there impatiently until Beazle returned, then she made a beeline for the wing where nobility stayed. When she passed a servant carrying a pile of rumpled bedsheets, she made straight for her, startling the girl.

"I'm looking for a courtier named Laec. Do you know where I can find him?"

The girl shook her head shyly. "I'm new here. Sorry."

Jessamine went up the steps and came to a set of arches. Another servant came along, carrying folded livery. This one looked senior and wore his long hair in a low tail tied with a blue bow.

Jess stepped in front of him. "Excuse me, I'm looking for a guest named Laec."

The man stopped, the corners of his eyes crinkling. "You're one of the new Calyx. I recognize you from the ball. Honeysuckle is my favorite fragrance. I'm terribly sorry about Greta. What an awful thing."

Jessamine felt winded. Was there anyone in the palace who hadn't heard what had happened? "Th-thank you," she stuttered.

"I'm Hob. Whom did you say you seek?" His brow furrowed.

"Laec. He has red hair, and—"

But Hob was already pointing. "You'll find him in the library. Straight down that hall, at the end."

She thanked him and carried on until she came to a set of double arches, through which she could see hardwood floors and shelves full of books. Inside, she was struck by the musty smell of paper and leather. Jessamine passed through one section of stacks before finding Laec in a study area.

His fire-bright hair hung over his shoulders as he leaned on his elbows, squinting nearsightedly at a large map. Stacks of books and tubes, some of which she recognized as the colored ones he'd taken from Ilishec's workshop, lay clustered around him. Jessamine stopped at his elbow.

He tucked his hair behind an ear and blinked at her, bleary-eyed. "Hello, again."

"I know where it is." She was unable to keep smugness out of her voice.

"You know where what is?" Laec straightened, rubbing his eyes.

"The entrance to the tunnel that links Rahamlar with Solana. It's real." She took immense pleasure watching him lower his fists as her words sank in.

He looked startled. "What?"

"I'm the only person who knows its location."

Laec cocked a brow. "And how do you come by such precious knowledge?"

"I can't tell you that." She leaned close. "But I'll show you where it is."

He stared at her for several long moments, then began folding up the map. "You'll forgive my natural skepticism, given that I have been combing these records for hours and have found no sign of such a passageway, even in the oldest documents. I'm not sure my eyes will ever fully recover. So to believe that a wee flora fae barely out of puberty—who probably got lost on her way to this library—knows the location of a feature that is supposed to be mythical is beyond extraordinary and quite improbable."

Jessamine opened her mouth to retort, but Laec held up a finger. "However… I'm from Stavarjak. A kingdom with more magic in its blades of grass than Solana has in its entirety. I don't have to understand *how* you know to believe that you might. Rescue has come from less likely places. So, you lead, little faeling, and I follow."

"First—" Jessamine held up a hand.

Laec ran a hand over his face. "I knew it. What do you want?"

"Why are you looking for it?"

Laec blanched. "You don't want to know."

"But I do want to know, and in exchange, I'll take you straight to what you seek."

"It's safer for you if you don't know."

"Why? Is what you're doing unlawful?"

"No." He didn't meet her gaze. "Not exactly."

It was Jessamine's turn to narrow her eyes. Laec was a foreigner. She liked him, but could she trust him? "Give me a reason not to take my knowledge to Ilishec instead, or to the king himself." Jessamine wasn't about to go near the king, but Laec didn't need to know that.

"It's for a good cause."

"What cause?"

A librarian poked her head from around a bookshelf. "Shhh!"

"Sorry," Laec whispered.

Leaving the maps on the table, he hooked his arm through Jessamine's and walked her through the stacks toward the arches. On their way out, they passed a gentleman with an arm full of books.

"May I leave my maps out for a little while?" Laec asked.

The man looked up. "Of course, sir. I'll put them away if you haven't come back by nine."

"Thank you." Laec led her to a quiet alcove where he faced her, holding her by the upper arms. "There is a young woman being held against her will in that damp, smelly place."

Jessamine let this sink in. "The lady with the fat lip and the bruises?"

He released her arms in surprise. "You noticed?"

"I was near the front. I saw her. Who is she?"

Laec's eyes flashed with fury. "She's supposed to marry the brute that murdered Greta."

Jessamine let this news wash over her. The woman was the prince's betrothed. "You want to get her out?"

Laec nodded.

"You can't do it alone."

"I have to. No one will go against the crofter's command."

Jess was shocked. The crofter struck her as being more granite than living soul. "You asked *him* for help?"

Laec's eyes glittered. "I didn't have to. He's already said that no one is to take any retributive action for what happened during the performance. If he won't avenge one of Solana's own, why would he take a risk for a foreigner?"

A new kind of hunger flared in Jessamine's gut. It was crazy, what Laec wanted to do. At the same time, it was an opportunity for retribution, the only one she was ever going to get. Before she thought about it too hard, the words surged to her lips. "I'll help you."

She'd hardly finished saying them and Laec was hissing. "Absolutely not. Ilishec would kill me—"

"You don't have a choice," she replied calmly.

They paused their impassioned conversation as a couple strolled by, arm in arm. The man said something and the lady laughed throatily. Their footfalls fell away as Laec and Jessamine glared at one another. She stoutly held his gaze and felt no small amount of satisfaction when Laec's expression took on an edge of pleading.

"Please, don't get involved. Show me the passage and then pretend we never had this conversation. It will be better for you in the long run."

"Everyone thinks I'm going home. No one expects me back for several days."

"Don't you have an escort waiting?"

"I haven't asked him yet."

Laec growled in his throat.

"Listen." Jess pitched her voice low. "I know you don't like it, but think about it from my perspective. I'll never get true justice for Greta. I need this." She swallowed down the lump in her throat as Faraçek's fist swung in her mind's eye. Greta flopped against the tablecloth, then went still, never to move again. Never to sip nectar, or kiss Jess's cheek, or ride on Beazle's back just for the fun of it. She took a breath, telling herself to focus. She could get what she wanted by helping Laec get what he wanted. "Together, we can use the secret passage to free Lady—"

"Çifta," Laec supplied.

"Çifta. Then, when we get back, I'll slip away. I'm already packed. No one will be the wiser."

Laec closed his eyes for a long moment before looking at her again. "You don't know the risks you're taking. We could be captured, held hostage. Anything could go wrong."

Jessamine made a face. "The worst has already happened."

Laec paused. "I understand that. I do…"

"Okay, then."

"We don't know if the tunnel is even passable."

"At least we will have tried."

Laec considered her. "Alright, prodigy, since you know so much about this secret entrance. Tell me, can we ride horses down there?"

She shook her head. "We'll have to walk. How far is Rahamlar as the crow flies?"

"About fourteen miles."

"We're fit. If we walk fast it'll take us, what, five hours. Six? We'll have to take food and water… and… weapons." She didn't mention that she was more effective with a gardening trowel than with a knife or a bow. It wouldn't exactly instill confidence.

"It'll be dark, stale, dirty, full of bugs."

She put out a hand as if meeting him for the first time. "Hello. I'm a flora fae with a bat familiar. I like the dark, dirt and bugs." After several moments with her hand sitting out in space, she added, "And I'm very stubborn."

Laec rolled his eyes. "Thank you for stating the obvious. Fine. It's your life. I won't be held responsible for the consequences to your person or your career if we are caught, if we even make it back here with Lady Çifta in one piece. You have to do as I say. I'm in charge. Got it?"

"I understand." Jessamine was so excited that her blood felt like sparkling wine. She could already picture the fury of being thwarted twisting Faraçek's features when he discovered his betrothed missing. The only thing that would make it more satisfying was if he knew that it was the Calyx whose familiar he had killed who had served him such a bitter pill. But she'd settle for knowing she'd humiliated him and freed a woman in misery.

"Before we do anything else… show me the entrance," said Laec. "Then we'll make a plan."

But Jess shook her head. She wouldn't risk showing him the way, then him sneaking away without her. "No way. We do this tonight. Whatever we think we'll need, we pack it, then I show you. That's the deal."

Laec considered her. "And here I thought you were all honeysuckles and primroses. You're a bit scary, you know that?"

"You must be joking." Laec's gaze flicked up as he bored a disbelieving hole through her. "I'm all for practical jokes but I'm having trouble seeing the humor in this one."

Dusk had leached color from the world, and crickets blanketed them with their chirruping song. They were scratched and sliced from brambles, burrs stuck to their clothes and hair. Jessamine was bleeding from a score along her leg.

"It's not a joke." Jessamine pushed back her hood. She had one foot against the wall and the other half buried in prickly deadfall. Branches jabbed into her ribs and hips as she held a tangled mat of ivy out of the way so she could see Laec. "I know it's not pretty, but I'm telling you, this is it."

"Not pretty," Laec mumbled, pulling long strings of ivy and ropes of stranglebush away from the old well.

As he pulled away the plants, the well cap appeared: a disk made of thick beams held together with wooden dowels. Three more dowels pierced straight down into the sides of the well, probably anchored in the stone with mortar. The wood was so old, it was mushy. She couldn't even tell what kind of tree it had come from.

He shifted the shoulder straps of the backpack containing their food and water, frowning. He seemed to be deciding between turning back or figuring out a way to open the well so he could throw Jessamine down it.

She gingerly brushed aside prickly growth to give herself room to squat. Groping at the place where the wood met the stone, she searched for a grip. Laec positioned himself on the other side, swearing under his breath. They got their fingers under the wooden covering and with a look of agreement, tried to budge the cap together.

It didn't move.

But a big chunk of rotten wood with a texture like sponge came away in Jessamine's hand, exposing part of a dowel. Getting the same idea, they clawed away at the cap, tearing the rotten wood off in chunks. Around the dowels, the wood broke apart easily. A few minutes of ripping and tearing and the entire cap lay scattered around them in pieces. They stared into the well.

Laec made a sound of disgust.

Jessamine looked up. "It's a trick. Just an enchantment, or something."

"I'm not going in there!" Laec spluttered, indicating the ink-like water about twelve feet down.

Jessamine gave him a sour look. "This whole thing was your idea."

Laec jabbed a finger straight down at the villainous-looking liquid. "*This* was not my idea."

"Yes it was. This is the entrance to the tunnel." Jessamine straightened her legs, ignoring the burning sensation in her calf and the desire to scratch at her lower back.

"How do you *know* it's the entrance?" Laec's nostrils flared.

"I can't explain it, I just know. Beazle showed me. It's part of our… flora… magic. Which you're not supposed to know about, so keep it to yourself." Jessamine directed Laec to move the light so they could see the interior of the well better. Beazle climbed out of her hair to cling to the fabric at her shoulder. He looked down, giving a dubious squeak.

"Flora fae make flowers. They don't locate secret passageways," Laec mumbled.

Jess ignored his grousing, seeing something new. "Look. You see the way these stones are positioned, the way they've been chipped at. They're handholds."

"Handholds leading to death by drowning?"

Jessamine sniffed the air over the well. "Smell that?"

Laec sniffed. "I don't smell anything."

"Exactly. If this was stagnant water, it would stink. But it doesn't smell like anything at all. It's not normal water. I'm telling you, it's magic." Jessamine felt desperate to transfer her confidence to Laec. Every fiber in her being knew this was the lost passage.

Laec rolled his eyes. "You want a prize for that? This is stupid. I'm sorry I trusted you. Deal's off. I'll figure out another way." Laec turned away and immediately got tangled in brambles. "Blast these… augh!"

Jessamine threw a leg over the side of the well. The wooden cap was rotten, but there was nothing wrong with the stonework. She positioned herself with her feet dangling down the inner wall, then found toeholds. She tested them with her weight. They felt sturdy.

"Are you mad? Come out of there." Laec hissed as a thorny vine caught at his sleeve.

Jessamine inched down past the mouth of the well, her heart pounding more from excitement than fear. There was something here. She was determined to discover it. She climbed down using the inbuilt holds until she reached the liquid.

"Don't touch that water, Jess," Laec warned, his voice echoing around her.

She lowered herself into a crouch. "Move the lantern, please."

In spite of himself, Laec shifted the light. The water was completely opaque and as blue-black as ink. She lowered her hand.

"Don't—" Laec warned again.

Jessamine touched the cool liquid with a fingertip. Nothing happened. It felt like water, but when she withdrew her finger and lifted it to the light, it wasn't wet. She held her finger up so Laec could see it. "You see that? It's not water. At least, not normal water."

"All the more reason not to touch it."

But Jessamine immersed her entire hand. When she pulled it out, it was completely dry. Beazle dropped from her shoulder to her hand to sniff at it. She showed Laec, unable to keep triumph from her face.

"Should've let me go down first," he grumbled.

Jessamine scooped a palmful of the liquid, marveling at how opaque it was, the way it stayed together instead of running into the folds and wrinkles in her skin. Definitely not water. She let the inky stuff run back into the well and thought the sound it made when it struck itself was prettier than simple droplets of water. It was almost musical. She lowered her boot to the water's surface, dipped it in, then lifted it out. She tried to get a look at her sole, but as she did, her supporting foot twisted… and she fell.

Grasping at the toeholds with her fingers, she gasped as the liquid swallowed her up to the neck. She tried to tread water but her legs kicked and flailed as if in midair. Only her body from her hips to her neck felt wet. Beazle—who had taken to the air the moment she'd fallen—clung to a stone. He squeaked, and then hopped onto the top of her head.

"You alright?" Laec called.

She looked up at him with wide, enlightened eyes. "There's air beneath the liquid!"

The sensation of her upper body floating but her legs dangling in space was the strangest she'd ever experienced, and a little scary. She didn't know how far down this well went, or what was below the air.

She felt around until her feet found the holds, then lowered herself down. The liquid came over her chin. "Hold your breath, Beeze."

The liquid filled her ears, then closed over her head. Beazle's claws clung to her hair as they went down. Her waist emerged from the underside, then her chest, and finally her head. The liquid ran up her chin and over her face, it trickled out of her ears, then wrung itself out of her hair.

She lowered herself another step and looked up for Laec, but she could see nothing but the ink. It looked the same as it did from the other side, only it was much darker down here. She called Laec's name. It echoed. Maybe sound couldn't come through?

Then she heard a muffled response: "I'm coming!"

She felt Beazle shake himself, out of habit. She wasn't wet in the least, so neither was he.

A faint light source came from nowhere and everywhere. She descended, emerging from the bottom of the well. The handholds continued down. Faintly, she could make out a rock-strewn dirt floor.

A splashing sound drew her gaze up. She grinned to see the bottom of Laec's foot as he felt around for a toehold. The lantern appeared, held by a disembodied hand, illuminating the drop to the floor and the earthen wall of stacked rubble on one side. Jess took the lantern, hooking it over her forearm, and climbed down further, giving Laec room to come through. His legs emerged up to the hips, then he paused, bracing to put his head under. That had been the hardest part. After a moment, his torso appeared, then the rest of him. He looked down at Jess, amazed.

"You were right, Jessamine," Jessamine mimicked Laec's Stavarjakian accent. "Yes, I know I was, Laec. Thanks for believing me."

"Alright, alright. No need to rub it in my face."

But she couldn't resist another jab. "What happened to: I'm from Stavarjak, we have more magic in one blade of grass…"

"Shush and climb down, child."

Hand under hand, foot under foot, they reached the floor. She dropped onto uneven ground littered with rocks and pebbles, then moved out of the way. Unhooking the lantern, she lifted it so Laec could see the floor.

He dropped into a squat, then straightened and took the lantern.

"Where is the blue light coming from?" Her gaze skimmed the wide passage that wound off into the darkness in one direction. Behind them lay a pile of compact rubble, blocking the way that Jess assumed would return to the palace.

"SubTerranean worms." Laec brushed himself off, plucked thorns and burrs from his clothing and straightened his sword. He pointed out the fissures and deep cracks between the layers of sediment. "They live in the cracks. We have them in Stavarjak, only ours glow purple."

They walked, being careful because it would be easy to roll an ankle. Many of the rocks were not stable, as they'd fallen from the walls or ceiling over time. But the rubble soon thinned and the way became hard-packed earth. It was a tall passage, and six men with their hands stretched out palm to palm could reach across it. The air smelled heavily of dirt and minerals, and it was warm. Laec rooted in the pocket of his tunic and produced a small, shiny object.

"What are you doing?"

"Checking to see if this compass works down here, mine would have but it was stolen. I borrowed this one from Ilishec." Laec rubbed a thumb over its face and held it near the light.

Jess didn't bother to inquire whether Laec had gotten Ilishec's permission before taking the compass. "And does it work?"

"Yes."

"And we are headed toward Rahamlar?"

Laec tucked the compass away. "Yes. Only six or seven hours to go, if it's this flat and straight the whole way, which it should be. It was built to bring timbers and stone under the mountain."

"I know."

Laec shot her a bemused look. "How do you know so much?" He froze momentarily. "You were eavesdropping on Ilishec and me."

Jess shrugged. "It was a happy accident."

Beazle launched himself into the air, landing near a crack in the wall. He sniffed at it, then crawled inside. He soon emerged chomping on a tiny glowing thing. He followed Laec and Jessamine down the passage feasting on glow worms the entire way, until he grew full and came to rest in Jessamine's hood.

They hiked along the even surface, following the amber glow from the lantern. It cast a circle of light around their feet and made their faces look eerie. When the novelty and the self-congratulations wore off, Jessamine began to feel anxious. How many tons of rock were sitting over their heads? It was too still down here, and Laec was actually not that talkative.

Jessamine spoke for the first time in an hour. "You're quieter than I thought you'd be."

"I'm respecting your right to grieve in silence."

"Oh. Thank you. I'm okay to talk, though. It'll help pass the time."

"Okay." But Laec fell silent again.

"So, what brings you to Solana?"

"Queen Elphame sent me."

"Why?"

"She and Queen Esha are cousins. She wanted me to make myself useful to Esha, and to keep an eye out for trouble."

"What kind of trouble?"

Laec shot her an exasperated look. "How should I know?"

"Why *wouldn't* you know? You're the one who was sent here for it."

Laec switched the lantern from one hand to the other. He was quiet for a long time before answering. "Elphame gets premonitions. But what she sees isn't always clear."

"She had a premonition about Esha?"

"I'm not sure if it was just about Esha. It's possible it was for your whole kingdom." Laec dodged a collection of fallen rocks.

"But you're only one person."

"And?"

"Well, it can't be that big of trouble, or she would have sent more than you. Right?"

"I'm just supposed to be her eyes, for now." A look crossed Laec's face. Jessamine tried to identify it and settled on uncertainty. He'd been sent to keep an eye on Solana but he was involving himself in Rahamlar's affairs. He couldn't very well keep an eye on the happenings at Solana when he wasn't even there. Jessamine almost asked him if what he was doing would upset his queen but changed her mind. She didn't want Laec to have second thoughts. He might turn around, and Jessamine would have no choice but follow him home.

"Are there flora fae in Stavarjak?" Jessamine watched as Beazle flew from her hood and disappeared into another crack. He backed out quickly with an audible squeak. Maybe he'd run into a worm that was bigger than he was.

"There are some in Elphame's court, but they're not organized the way the Calyx are." He chuckled. "Nothing in Stavarjak is as organized as here."

"Are you friends with any of them?"

"Not really." Laec shot her a sly look. "I'm friends with a couple of Wise, though."

"Wise what?"

"You know, earth elementals? Wise?"

Jessamine shook her head. She'd never heard the term.

Laec looked surprised. "They're pretty rare, but you should know about them. As flora fae, you're related."

"Really?"

Laec adjusted his packsack. "You're connected to a specific kind of plant, right? A Wise is connected to all plants, and the ground too. They're the ultimate in earth magic. They can do a lot more than a flora fae can."

Jessamine crept to the edge of disbelief. "Like what?"

Laec gestured around them. "Making a tunnel like this wouldn't be a problem, not for the most powerful Wise I know. All she'd have to do is wave her hand."

Jessamine laughed, sure he was kidding. Laec shot her a lopsided smile that she couldn't read.

"Hungry?"

"A little."

"Another hour and we eat?"

Jessamine agreed, and on they walked, consuming the miles between them and Rahamlar, one step at a time.

Chapter Thirty-Eight

Jessamine

They ate, rested for fifteen minutes, then continued on. Jessamine asked Laec about life in Stavarjak. When he asked her about where she grew up, she deflected the topic back to him. She didn't want to think about her childhood. She didn't want to go back over the days when Greta was alive. It was too soon. Jessamine got lost in Laec's storytelling and time passed quickly. He stopped her suddenly and pointed at a wall of dirt straight ahead, looming in the dim blue glow.

"There's the end."

Jessamine shifted her shoulders; the skin of her back was warm and damp. She wondered how Laec felt—he was the one carrying their supplies. She needed to give her feet a rest, and she couldn't wait to breathe fresh air. "The ceiling is a lot higher here. Is that… stairs?"

They approached a very tall, very narrow set of wooden steps leading up and up and up. Every dozen steps, there was a wooden landing. The next set of steps made a left-hand turn and then continued up, making a tall, squared-off spiral staircase. The whole thing was fastened to the wall with wooden beams that had been pounded into the soil. At the very top, which seemed a long way off, was a small circular opening: the underside of a shaft.

She pointed it out. "It's just like the one at Solana."

Laec scanned the platforms. "This will be as rotten as the cap was at the other end."

Her heart fell as she looked for toeholds like the ones at the other end and failed to see even one. "There's no other way up. Let's hope they hold."

While Beazle fluttered around exploring the glowing nooks and crannies, they tested the first set of steps. To say they were soft was an understatement. Laec's boot left an imprint an inch deep. The second step groaned and one side tore away from the rusty nails with a horrible sound. But instead of dropping to the ground, Laec scooted up further. Reaching the first landing, he looked back. "Just hop over those first few steps. These ones are okay."

She joined him, hating the soggy feeling of the wood under her feet. When she put her hand on the banister, she yanked it back fast. The wood felt slimy.

Laec ascended ahead of her, one landing at a time. He tested the steps and warned her which ones to avoid. Up and up they climbed, her heart pounding in her ears. The ground soon looked very far away. She thought of her mother, then of Clair, then of Ilishec and Snap, Rose and Aster. What would they think of what she was doing? What would they say? She relegated these thoughts to a rear shelf and focused on not looking at the floor. She was doing this for Greta.

The bottom of the well loomed close.

Near the top, the beam holding the landing to the wall

came apart like it was made of bread instead of wood. The whole platform swayed sickeningly. Jessamine gripped the railing as she swallowed a scream.

"You're alright," Laec called from the next landing. "You're alright. Almost there. There are handholds here. Thank heaven."

Heart in her throat, Jessamine reached the topmost landing as Laec climbed toward the shaft using the handholds. Jessamine was relieved to get off this wreck of a staircase, and thankful that stone never rotted. Jessamine called Beazle, her voice swallowed by the cavernous space. The bat appeared and clung to her hair as she climbed after Laec, refusing to look down.

Laec disappeared fully into the stone cylinder. His voice echoed low and quiet. They didn't know where this well emerged. For all they knew, it could come up in a dungeon beneath the fortress. "Here's the inky stuff. It looks the same. I'm going through, and I'm putting out the lantern."

"Okay," she whispered.

Jessamine gripped the handholds, then took a breath, trying to relax. As the sound of Laec passing through the liquid faded, Jess followed him up. When her head emerged in utter darkness, Laec shushed her.

Halfway out and half still submerged, she froze, hearing voices in casual conversation, and muffled footsteps. They weren't very close, but still too close for comfort. They remained still until the voices receded completely. Laec climbed further, giving Jessamine room to emerge. Now Laec's boot heels were in her face. Though she couldn't see them in the darkness, she could hear grit being crushed beneath his soles. She wished there were glow worms inside the well. Beazle crawled up her hair to perch on the top of her head.

The well was filled with the sound of Laec's clothing rustling and soft grunts as he applied pressure to the cap. Then came the sound of rotten wood breaking apart. Debris fell in Jessamine's hair and splashed into the ink below her. Her muscles were burning now from clinging to the holds. She wanted to ask Laec how it was going but she was afraid to make more noise than he was already making. He had to stop twice as distant voices went by again.

Jessamine's arms ached and her toes were starting to cramp. Just when she wondered how much longer she could hang on, a sliver of light appeared over her head. Moonlight flooded the well, silhouetting Laec. She wanted to keep looking up, but when she did, she got dirt in her eyes, so she looked down and watched the rind of moonlight reflecting in the ink as it got bigger and bigger. Laec's success gave her the strength to hold on. Bit by bit, Laec shifted the well cap until what remained of it landed with a *thunk* on the ground outside. He ascended, first just poking his head up to look around. After that, he moved fast. Heaving his bulk out of the well, he turned and helped Jessamine. They collapsed on the ground in a blanket of thick ivy. Jessamine was thankful it wasn't prickly.

The air was cool and humid and felt heavenly to breathe after the stale air in the tunnel. Crickets chirped, an owl hooted. The sky was dark and smudged with banks of low-hanging clouds. Beazle immediately fluttered off to explore the new territory.

As they took sips of water, they saluted one another in silence, celebrating that they'd made it this far. Jessamine felt some of the ache going out of her body as they rested, though her feet were sore from hours of hiking. She gazed at the sky through a mesh of branches.

Laec got to his feet, then helped her up. "We're near a graveyard."

She winced at the soreness in the soles of her feet, looking around. The moon sent diffused light through the canopy, illuminating a collection of crooked headstones and worn statuary. Roots had heaved the earth over time and every headstone was tilted, some severely, like bad teeth. Squat oaks with gnarled trunks and branches held the whole place together, while ivy had a chokehold on everything. They needed to figure out where they were in relation to the fortress and mark this place so they could find it again. Wrapping themselves in their cloaks and pulling their hoods over their heads, they crawled from the tangle of undergrowth to find a footpath snaking its way between the trees. It brought them to a clearing where they had a view.

Jessamine was the first to spot the distinctive aviary tower which marked the main courtyard. It was a narrow spike backlit by stars. They'd emerged behind the fortress, within the walls encircling the village and terraced fields behind the city. A cluster of cottages were scattered over the uneven landscape, and beyond them, the twinkle of torchlight from the city.

Jessamine whistled Beazle to her before they went any further. He swooped out of the darkness and burrowed under her hood and into her hair. They followed the path to a wider double-track road sprinkled with rocks. As the track curved around the edge of the forest, city lights came more clearly into view.

The double-track angled down and the sound of flowing water increased. The trees grew thick again and humidity engulfed them, making their skin sticky and their cloaks damp. The clouds drifted overhead like shredded fabric. The double-track became a gravel road which ran parallel to a very steep riverbank. One wrong step and one would tumble hopelessly into fast-flowing and deep water.

An open gate came into view. The gate was open, but a guard stood nearby, head bent over something as he leaned against a pillar. Moonlight reflected off the open book in his hand. Two torches burned on either side of the entrance to the city. Laec drew Jessamine closer, whispering: "You have women's troubles. Leave the talking to me."

Heart in her throat and stomach roiling with nerves, Jessamine didn't have to try very hard to look unwell. She wrapped her arms over her stomach and slouched, stealing peeks from underneath her hood.

The guard looked up as they neared. He was human and looked like he should have been retired with his feet up and grandchildren sprawled around him, not guarding a gate. How he could read in the torchlight was a marvel.

"Who goes?" He straightened away from the wall and the book disappeared into a pocket. Jessamine cringed with her hands cradling her lower belly and made a low moan.

"We seek a healer," Laec explained calmly in a totally different accent than his own. He sounded like the maid who had served the Calyx soup and been emotional about Prince Ander.

"What's the trouble?" The guard seemed more concerned than suspicious. Jess doubted that the guards at the outer gates were anything like this one. They'd be big, burly unseelie fae and well armed. The reason for posting a retired human soldier was obvious: if a person was inside the city walls at this time of night, they were either a citizen or a guest of a citizen who had been allowed in during the day, while the flow of traffic in and out of Rahamlar was more closely monitored. Guards of interior gates were just there to keep an eye on things, or to be of service if it was needed.

"Cramps," Laec said simply. "She gets them bad sometimes."

The guard waved them by. “My wife had them something awful too. I wish you swiftly better, miss.”

“Thank you,” Laec replied, and they walked through the gate.

As they entered the village, everything changed. No longer were they fenced in by trees but by tall walls. Narrow passageways shot off in every direction. It was late but some houses still had life in them. They were not completely alone on the street. Rahamlarin citizens went about in twos or threes. They passed a few pubs, several parks, and crossed a sturdy bridge leading over a canal. They kept up the pretense that they were a couple as they wound closer and closer to the fortress. It became a huge bulk looming over the city, blocking out the night sky. When they reached a familiar courtyard, the one the Calyx had been led into from the front gates, Laec pulled Jessamine toward a horse trough.

She drew Beazle from her hair as Laec produced the hollow capsule which contained the short message he'd prepared for Çifta. Laec watched their surroundings while Jessamine tried to fasten the capsule to Beazle's leg by a tiny belt. Beazle nipped at her fingers. She tried again and he bit her harder.

She shook her finger. “How are you going to carry it, then?”

Beazle picked it up in his mouth, showing off the flexibility in his jaws. She was impressed. A weight fastened to one leg might throw off his flying, but held in his mouth, he'd be balanced.

She looked up at the fortress walls. “Which window is hers?”

“Fourth from the right. Can he count?”

Beazle gave an indignant squeak around the capsule.

“He's smarter than your average bat.” Jessamine kissed Beazle and tossed him into the sky. He flapped silently around the courtyard, then disappeared in the shadows. Jessamine caught his tiny form as he crawled up the stone to the ledge of Çifta's window, then disappeared from sight. Her heart swelled with love and she waited breathlessly for his safe return, hoping Lady Çifta wasn't afraid of bats.

Chapter Thirty-Nine

Çifta

Çifta was dreaming. She was on the swing her father had built behind their summer home in the lowlands near Boskaya City. She could feel the bristly rope beneath her hands, the wind flowing through her hair, the wooden plank beneath her hips. Strong hands pushed her from behind, her father's hands. She couldn't see him but his touch was unmistakable. She kept trying to turn to talk to him but every time she did, he would push her and the swing would go so high that she had to face front so as not to twist in the air. She was laughing but she was also frightened. It was exhilarating, a breathless kind of fear that was also fun. She wanted to beg him to stop but she was laughing and breathing too hard to get the words out. Her squeals only encouraged Kazery to push harder. It was incredibly frustrating. She needed to tell him that she was being held against her will!

The rope squeaked where it cut into the tree branch above her head. A louder squeak drew her consciousness toward the surface of the dream. As the sensation of swinging faded into the background, another squeak jarred her fully awake. Her body jerked, her hands clenching at the coverlet. Her heart skittered around in her chest. She felt out of breath just lying there, remembering where she was. She was both thankful to be woken as well as disappointed. She missed her father so bad she could taste it.

Çifta turned under the covers and tucked a fold between her legs to cushion her knees. She closed her eyes and snuggled into her pillow, hoping for a less frustrating dream this time.

A clear and insistent squeak came from her window, which she'd left open a crack every night since the raptor's visit.

Her eyes flew open and she sat up. The covers bunched around her and her hair draped over her shoulders. A moment later, the squeak came again, and this time it came from her desk. Heart racing, she threw back the covers and slid to the edge of the mattress. She groped around on her bedside table for the matchbox and lit the lamp.

Another squeak brought her to the desktop. She lifted the lantern, casting the desktop in amber light.

In the middle of the desk sat a tiny furred thing. It took her a moment to identify it as a very small bat. Çifta didn't like bats much, but seeing this one close up, its black eyes looking up at her with an almost pleading expression softened her heart. It was cute.

"I was expecting a bird, but I suppose you'll do." She moved to the window and looked outside, but the courtyard was swathed in black.

The bat dropped something which rolled around on the desk like a marble weighted on one side. Hope took off in Çifta's breast. This capsule had a stamp on it, a lion's head wreathed with flowers. Solana's crest. With trembling fingers, she pulled out the folded note and opened it in the light of the lantern.

Be dressed and ready to travel light. Act ill after the four o'clock crier. Give them a reason to open your door. Burn this. -L

Her heart began to sprint. Her brain stalled, then chugged back to life as she processed the command. The crier called at one, four, and seven a.m. She wondered what time it was. The night sky was a wash of broken clouds against velvet.

Be dressed and ready…

Çifta looked around her room in a daze, then shook herself into action. Being in her nightclothes was not very ready. She chewed her lip, reading the note a few more times, memorizing it, then threw it in the fire.

Çifta went through her things. Her heart ached at the wealth of finery she'd have to leave behind. She told herself that her father would send men to retrieve it. He had to. She'd not only brought many beautiful and expensive gowns, but also all the jewelry she owned. She realized with a stab of annoyance that the best thing she could wear was the mourning gown. It covered her completely and had large pockets. She could even pin the veil over her face. She got herself into the gown and laced it up as well as she was able on her own. She drew the veil over her loose hair and made sure the fringe covered her forehead. Pinning the veil over her face, she looked in the mirror. A pair of frightened eyes peeked out. She unpinned it and draped it over her headboard, then rifled through her chests. She stuffed what valuables she could into the deep pockets of her skirts, along with her sketchbook and her favorite letters from her sisters.

She slipped gold coins inside the lining of her traveling cloak where thin walls of fabric kept the coins from clinking against one another. She filled her riding water skin with water from the ewer. She slung it over her body and tightened it so it wouldn't bounce around while on horseback. She hoped Laec would have an empty saddlebag or two for her. Between her sketchbook, the jewelry, the letters, the gold coins, the set of brass Unya seals and the water skin, she was weighed down. She put on her boots, wrapped her cloak around herself and went to the window to listen, her heart straining with hope.

She drooped with her elbow on her desk, her chin in her hand and her eyes closed when the crier's voice came drifting through the bars.

"Oyez, oyez, oyez! Four o'clock and all's well!"

Her eyes burned with tiredness and she felt like she'd been waiting for a long time. Of course, it was probably only half an hour. She went to the bed, her heartbeat whispering past her eardrums.

She got beneath her quilt, shifting her jewels aside so they didn't jab into her, and lay her head on the pillow, cringing at the idea of the dirty soles of her boots against her clean sheets. She began to moan as if in pain. At first there was no response, but when she got louder, she heard the guards exchanging words through her door. One of them thumped on the wood as if telling her to shut up.

"I need a healer. I'm in pain!" She made her voice breathy but as agonized as possible. "Please!"

The judas window slid open. "Go to sleep!" It slammed shut again.

She moaned louder and began to beg. "You don't know

what it feels like, you brutish louts!" she wailed. "You wouldn't keep a healer from your own sister, would you? I need herbs!"

Words were exchanged. She couldn't hear them well but thought they were arguing. She moaned again but resisted the urge to wail. It wouldn't do to wake those sleeping down the hall. Finally, the heavy beam was moved back and set aside. She waited, her body tense, her brow damp. The door opened and torchlight flickered into her room. Kutrin came in, holding a torch aloft, his expression full of thunder. It took him a moment to notice the black collar of her mourning dress at her throat.

"What the devil—"

There was a thud. His eyes rolled up in his head and he pitched forward. He hit the side of her bed and flopped onto the floor. Laec, wearing Rahamlar livery, lowered the beam used to bar the door.

Snatching up her veil and fixing it over her hair, she followed him from the room. Laec shut the unconscious guard into her room and slid the beam back into place. He led her to a set of narrow servant's stairs. As they reached the next level down, the smell of baking bread made her mouth water, though her stomach was too tied up in knots to eat. They passed kitchens and came out in a courtyard with a herb garden. A collection of wicker baskets full of fruit sat on the cobbles.

A narrow shadow materialized from behind the gate. Çifta almost screamed. Laec squeezed her hand and the shadow lifted her hood. It was a young woman, and she looked vaguely familiar. She put a finger to her lips. She pulled the hood of Çifta's traveling cloak up over her veil and set it to shadow her face, then she picked up a basket of pears and shoved them into Çifta's arms. When Çifta turned to find Laec, he was no longer there. She shot the girl a panicked look. She reinforced that Çifta was to be quiet, then beckoned her to follow.

They carried the baskets of fruit past the garden and out through the open gate. They went by a couple of men having an intense conversation, then silently swept out into the street. There were a few signs of early-morning life along the street: the distant sound of drunken laughter, the crunch of wooden wheels on cobbles. Çifta kept tight to the girl as she fell in step behind a man rolling a wheelbarrow full of small kegs of ale up the street. A courtyard opened before them and the man stopped in front of an alehouse. The women kept walking. They meandered through the village, going in the direction of the terraced crops Çifta had only caught sight of from the top of the aviary. The girl seemed to know where she was going and walked through the passages, courtyards and open marketplaces as though she had every right to be there. Çifta tried to emulate her.

Finally, the girl spoke quietly, her face deep inside her hood. "I'm Jessamine."

"I'm—" Çifta cut herself off as they passed a man seated outside the door of a pub with a giggling woman on his lap.

"I know who you are," Jessamine whispered.

Çifta realized with a jump that a man had come up behind them. She glanced at her rescuer, alarmed. Jessamine expressed no change of emotion, nor did she acknowledge that they were being followed. Çifta stole a glance behind, her heart banging against her breastbone. It was Laec. He'd changed out of the Rahamlar livery and looked like an everyday villager in a navy surcoat, leggings and boots. A sword swung at his hip and the straps of a pack hugged his shoulders. He gave a shake of his head and she faced front.

An angry shout went up behind them. They'd been able to put some distance between them and the fortress, but they didn't appear to be anywhere near an exit. She recognized nothing—she didn't even know how big the city was. Jess picked up the pace. Weighed down, it was all Çifta could do to keep up. The basket of pears was getting unbearably heavy. She was sweating and panting.

When Jessamine ducked into a rear alley overhung with strings of laundry, Çifta followed, and Laec followed her. Jessamine put her basket of fruit down and Çifta was relieved to be able to do the same. Leaving their props in the alley, the trio skimmed through a passage wide enough only for one person at a time. Ducking beneath sheets, they ascended a set of stairs. Someone opened a window and emptied a bucket of dirty water into the street. It splashed against Çifta's hem.

They came to a landing where a thick wall of hops overhung the stone wall on one side. Jessamine began to climb the trellis as Laec kept watch. She moved like a cat, quickly and almost silently. When she reached the top, she signaled Çifta to come up.

Her pulse sprinting, Çifta hiked her skirts and hooked her fingers into the trellis. It shifted as it took her weight, coming away from the wall. She swallowed a cry and froze, but the trellis held. The weight of her valuables strained the fabric at her waist and shoulders. Uncomfortably hot, she wished she could throw her hood back and rip the veil off her head. Her nose filled with the smell of hops. She couldn't see well with her hood on, and it seemed an eternity before she reached the top. Jessamine helped her into a gully between two tiled roofs. Without waiting for Laec, Jessamine led her along this valley between houses. By the time they reached the next alley, which they used a rickety chimneysweep's walkway to cross, Laec had caught up to them.

Zigzagging along the roofs and the beams connecting the houses, a canopy of trees appeared where the rooftops abruptly ended. They'd reached the village wall, marked by a long drop into a wooded glade. Looking down, Çifta's courage nearly failed her. She watched, wide eyed, as Jessamine grasped a branch that didn't look strong enough to hold a child, but it held as she pulled herself up. She shimmied until she could pull herself on top of the branch, then looked back at Çifta expectantly.

Laec was right next to her. He put a hand against her back.

She gulped. "I can't do this."

Laec's breath was warm next to her ear. "Yes, you can. Give me your cloak."

She untied the cloak with shaking fingers and passed it to him. When he felt the weight of it, he shot her a look of surprise. "Anything else weighing you down?" He rolled it up and fastened it to the bottom of the pack he wore.

She hesitated. Laec and Jessamine had risked everything to help her. He wasn't about to run off with her jewels. She retrieved the heaviest of her valuables, passing them to Laec. If he was shocked by the wealth, he kept it hidden, tucking her items into his pack and pockets.

When Çifta got a hold on the branch, she felt Laec's hands at her waist. Together, they got her into the tree, though how Laec managed to see anything all with her skirts billowing everywhere was beyond her. Hand over hand she went, dangling like some overgrown sloth. She tried not to think about how far down the forest floor was, or how many huge stones were probably jutting upward, waiting for her body to break against them. Jessamine helped her get on top of the branch and then let her recover before they moved to larger, steadier boughs. By the time they reached the trunk and leaned against it, Laec was with them, looking unfazed.

The sound of horseshoes striking against cobblestones made them huddle together, hidden in the canopy. Horses burst from an exit, thundering off through the forest—her search party.

"Now what?" Çifta hoped these two had horses stashed somewhere, because every muscle in her body was burning.

Laec pointed into the forest. "We have a half-hour hike."

Çifta found a watery smile. "At least we are outside the city walls."

Laec and Jessamine exchanged a look she couldn't read.

"What is it?"

"We're not outside the city walls," Jessamine explained on a low breath. "We're just outside the village."

Çifta absorbed this in silence. This forest would soon be crawling with soldiers. She'd been discovered missing now. Villagers would soon know as it passed from mouth to mouth. By the time the sun broke through the darkness, everyone in Rahamlar would probably know that the prince's betrothed had run away.

In spite of the dangers, a tidal wave of gratitude broke over her heart. She'd been taught not to bite a gift of coin in the presence of the giver. Fresh determination hurried her heartbeat. With a whispered prayer, she followed her rescuers as they melted into the woods.

Chapter Forty

Jessamine

THE MOON FLOATED low behind fleecy clouds, like a bright coin, throwing its glow through the canopy in patches. They stuck to the darkest of shadows, zigzagging from tree to boulder, scrambling over steep slabs of stone laced with roots and navigating thickets of brambles that snagged their clothes and scratched their hands. Twenty-five minutes after leaving the tree and slinking into the forest, Jessamine was convinced they were going to make it back without detection. Çifta had not once complained, not when she stumbled over roots or hollows in the dark, not when Laec and Jessamine pushed her until the breath whistled through her throat, not when they yanked her down to lay flat out on her back in the mulch and rocks as horses galloped by.

Jessamine's body thrummed with energy. The feeling of doing something, of acting, made Greta's loss a little less painful.

I love this. The thought was unexpected, but clear and coherent, and couldn't be denied or explained away. She felt infused by a bright delirium, like the possibility that she could live forever and yet also be killed on the spot converged in her heart to foam up like a mix of baking soda and vinegar. Her own emotional state surprised her. She was unafraid, determined, empowered. The moment Jessamine had seen Çifta's pale, frightened face she had been overcome by a righteous fire. Any and all doubt about what they were doing burned away in the heat and storm of her conviction that they were doing the right thing. That alone made her sure they would prevail, even against the best of Rahamlar's soldiers, because they were restoring balance to an unjust situation. The passion Jessamine felt did not diminish as the trio eeled their way toward the well. She hoped the actions she and Laec had taken would mystify the enemy to the point of superstitious fright. Çifta would disappear without a trace. One woman will have appeared to have taken on all of Rahamlar and won.

Jessamine took Çifta by the hand and whispered: "You see the headstones?"

Çifta put a hand over her heart as she sucked in air, her eyes gleaming with terror. "Yes."

"On the other side of them—"

Something moved in the trees behind Laec as he crested the rooty climb. Jessamine yanked Çifta into a crouch. There was more than one something moving out there. Laec had seen them too, and unsheathed his sword. He didn't bother trying to hide; the soldiers had seen them too and were closing in. Jessamine counted four bulky shadows.

Did they run for the well and give away its location? Her hopes of disappearing Çifta as if by magic dissolved. Unless they killed the soldiers—and killing was not an option, she hadn't signed up for murder—then they'd have to trade the secret for their freedom. If Laec could hold these guards off, then she could see Çifta safely into the well. It was well hidden behind headstones and trees and buried in ivy, so there was still a chance no one would see where they'd gone.

Laec hefted his blade with confidence. Etched into his fae features was the same steely determination she felt, no hint of terror or doubt. It fueled her with fresh energy—she felt like a live wire, a struck lightning rod. She felt Çifta's hand tremble and she squeezed it.

Laec positioned himself on the even ground at the edge of the short bank between the women and the soldiers.

Three guardsmen, all with unseelie ears slicing up along their helmets, closed in on Laec, swords lifted. As Jessamine and Çifta sprinted for the graveyard, the fourth guard, a human, cut away from the others to dash after them.

The clash of steel and grunts of combat faded as Jessamine pulled Çifta past the first of the statuary. Weaving through headstones, Jessamine strained to locate their pursuer. Beazle swooped by her head, giving a squeak.

A vision flashed before her eyes, blocking out the graveyard. Çifta kept her up when she stumbled as Beazle delivered an overhead view from his vantage point. The terrain zoomed beneath him in shades of gray. The tops of the headstones and statues were pale ovals, trees were smudges of charcoal. There was the soldier, slowing as he approached the graveyard, a blob of reddish-black, like a shape seared on the retina after a flash of bright light.

Disoriented, Jessamine pulled Çifta into the hollow between a fat gnarled trunk and a granite block. She never would have made such a choice if Beazle hadn't showed her what he was seeing. This hiding place would keep them from view for a short time.

Çifta pressed her back against the tree. Jessamine could hear the fear in her breathing. She put a finger to her lips. The soft footfalls of their pursuer crunched over dry leaves, moving slower now. Beyond them were the sounds of Laec doing battle, broken by stretches of silence which were more terrifying than the fighting.

A moment later, her vision flashed again. This time she was ready for it and received the information without losing her balance. Their pursuer stood in the aisle beyond the monument they were huddled behind, waiting for them to give themselves away. He took a step in their direction, then another, and another. He need only lunge past the monument and he would see them. They held their breath.

If they didn't move, they'd be trapped in this hollow, and this soldier wouldn't be alone for long. How long could Laec keep three guards busy? Jessamine shifted forward, preparing to run. Çifta mimicked her. A leaf crackled as Jessamine's vision flashed.

Half-blinded by the overhead view, Jessamine launched herself from the hollow, low, and straight at his legs. He sprawled backward with a cry. His sword fell from his grip as the breath was knocked from his lungs. Jessamine scrambled past him, stepping right on his chest. Çifta was behind her, but she went around the man and that gave him time to register what was happening. Even as he gasped, trying to suck in air, he scrambled after Çifta. She went down with a cry, tripped. She landed in a heap of billowing fabric, rebounding to one knee and both hands. She clambered forward but was yanked back by her ankle.

The soldier tried to yell but the words came out on a wheezy, near inaudible gasp. "I've got her, she's here!"

Çifta rolled over and swiped her free foot at the soldier's face, delivering a glancing blow to his mouth. He did not let go, even as his lip split and blood dribbled down his chin. He reached for his sword with his other hand, lying half obscured by deadfall, just beyond his reach.

Jessamine grabbed Çifta's hand, pulling as hard as she could to free her, but she couldn't compete with the soldier's strength. She felt Çifta being pulled toward him, stretched. Çifta squealed as Jess dug her heels in and pulled with everything she had, her jaw clenched. The solder's fingers inched closer to the handle of his sword. Çifta gave another cry as her body was stretched in opposite directions.

The soldier's hand closed around the blade.

"No!" Jessamine screamed. As she released her cry, she expelled a pulse of desperate magic. It was so violent that the fabric of Çifta's dress billowed with it. Like a thousand tiny snakes shooting through dry grass, vines sprang from the earth and wrapped around the soldier's body, pinning his limbs down. He gave a cry of horror and released Çifta as his body was swallowed by thickening vines.

Çifta scrambled to her feet, staring at the leafy, man-shaped tangle of *ipomoea*. He glared at them, wide eyed and petrified, even as his face was swallowed by leaves. One bulging, terrified eye stared out at them, then it too disappeared. Buds sprouted from the vines, maturing and bursting into full bloom with little puffs of pollen.

"Are you okay?" Jess put an arm around Çifta.

Çifta nodded, face pale.

The solder's struggles only allowed the binding weed to tighten further, holding him fast to the ground by hundreds of thousands of roots. Purple-white moonflowers bloomed all along his body in the hundreds, until nothing of him could be seen.

The women stared, amazed, at the mass of flowers and leaves. They could hear him struggling, shaking the leaves with his efforts. He tried to call out but the weed tightened and his cries were strangled then cut off. Incredulous about what she'd done, the terrible speed and efficiency of it, Jessamine lifted a hand and the weeds loosened a fraction. She heard a gasp as he sucked in air. He tried to shout but only wheezed.

Down the hill, footsteps crunched on leaves and broke twigs.

Jess pulled Çifta through the graveyard at a run. It was much bigger than she'd first realized. Beazle shadowed them as they snaked between trees and stones, through thick grasses and patches of ivy. Çifta tripped and Jessamine yanked her to her feet as they reached the well. Jessamine indicated that Çifta had to go down it. The woman stared at her, shocked.

"It's just an enchantment," Jess whispered, stealing a glance through the cemetery. "There's only a few feet of liquid, after that there's stairs."

Çifta's expression shifted to wonder. "You're not coming?"

Jessamine put her hand under Çifta's elbow. "Hurry. I'll follow you as soon as I can. I can't leave Laec."

Çifta sat on the well and drew her legs over. Jessamine pointed out the handholds. Hand under hand, Çifta descended, pausing only when the ink had reached her neck. She looked up, her eyes huge in her face. Jessamine nodded. Çifta took an audible breath, then disappeared beneath the opaque surface.

Jessamine moved away from the well and into the trees near the road, listening for sounds of combat. All was quiet save for the chirrup of insects and, distantly, frogs.

Skirting the graveyard, she went toward the last place she'd seen Laec, sticking to shadows. When she received no images from Beazle, she guessed there was nothing to see. She had to trust that if Beazle saw some danger from overhead, he would show it to her.

She passed the end of the graveyard and cut across the rough terrain toward the stone slab.

The sound of a grunt and fast footfalls from the other side of the road reached her ears and she headed toward it, not bothering to go from trunk to trunk and shadow to shadow in her hurry. Çifta was saved, no one saw her go into the well—all that remained was for Laec and Jessamine to follow, undetected, and they would have won.

As she stepped into the long grass in the ditch beside the road, Jess received a flash of Beazle's overhead view. Half blind, Jess misjudged the depth of the ditch and fell. Beazle showed her four horses down the road a short distance. As she got to her feet and turned to dive back into the forest, horses thundered up beside her. She ran for the trees, but a horse went through the ditch and cut in front of her.

"Where do you think you're going?" A rough voice growled.

Horseflesh blocked every way she turned. She looked up at the nearest figure, the moon directly behind his head, giving him a soft blue-white corona. Beazle fluttered around the rider's head, squeaking furiously. The man waved a hand at his little tormentor and Jess's heart iced over.

Stay back, Jess thought at Beazle. *I can't lose you too.*

Beazle seemed to listen, although they'd never been able to hear one another's thoughts. Perhaps he felt her concern.

When a gap appeared between two of the horses, Jess went for it.

"Not so fast." A rider lashed out, latching onto the fabric at her shoulder. She twisted away and a loud rip split the air as the stitches at her shoulder gave. She yanked again and the whole sleeve came off but caught at her wrist, trapping her hand. Horses closed around her as the men laughed. Jess struggled to free her hand, but the guard lifted her off the ground. Her shoulder protested as her feet kicked. She spun and dangled for a few seconds before the fabric gave way. She dropped, just catching herself from collapsing. The soldier lifted the fabric of her sleeve to his nose and inhaled.

"What are you doing?" the largest of them barked.

"Smell this." He held it out.

"You idiot. Give it here."

Without sniffing it, the leader crunched it into a ball and threw it away.

Beazle squeaked again from somewhere overhead, distressed. Jessamine watched the horse's legs, preparing to take advantage of an opening beneath the black destrier with feathered fetlocks. The largest guard leaned forward, cocking back a mailed fist. A burst of pain exploded in her head, then all went sweetly black.

Chapter Forty-One

Laec

As the women made a run for the graveyard, Laec raised his sword to receive the soldiers. They were big, they were trained, and two of them were clearly used to operating as a team. Laec spun away from the pair at the last moment, slashing to evade them as he leapt toward the single. One of the duo grunted in surprise as he deflected Laec's passing thrust. The single soldier shuffled to the side to where the roots were less prominent. In a flurry of offensive thrusts and aggressive forward motion, Laec attacked, manipulating the soldier to shuffle sideways until he came between the trained pair and Laec. When a vicious clash of swords brought Laec and the soldier eye to eye, Laec shoved him backward so he tripped over a root and sprawled into his fellows, giving Laec precious seconds to sprint into the forest.

He had to buy time for the women. Already, he could hear the soldiers splitting up for the chase. Laec wove between the trees, moving toward the road. He recalled how deep the ditches were, how the thick line of overgrowth and the trunks of old oaks made huge dark shadows.

He thought he heard a cry coming from the direction of the graveyard, but it was a male sound, so he didn't veer off course. Weaving through the thickening trees, Laec dodged into the shadow behind a trunk. He worked hard to breathe quietly. A soldier ran past, then another, but further downhill. He slowed, then stopped. Where the third was, Laec couldn't tell. He looked up but the nearest boughs were too high to leap for, and if he was spotted going up, he would be trapped.

The sound of a blade parting air made him duck instinctively. A sword struck the trunk where his neck had been. Laec slid into a roll, bruising his back as the items in his backpack pressed into him, and came to his feet. The soldier bared his teeth, yanking at his blade where it stuck in the wood, giving Laec precious seconds. Laec could have finished the unarmed man then and there, but he clung to his original hope that they would get out of there without killing. A rescue was one thing; deaths were another.

Jessamine and Çifta were surely at the well by now. They would be waiting, hopefully at the bottom of the stairs. He'd told Jessamine that if they were to get separated, she was to return to the point of exit and hide for one hour. If he did not join her in one hour, she was to go back to Solana with Çifta.

He drove the soldier back over the uneven ground until he could deliver a punch to the jaw with the fist that held his sword. The soldier flopped backward and settled into a hollow. He left the man's sword wedged in the tree trunk. Leaving it there would be seen as restraint.

Putting distance between himself and the other two soldiers, Laec dropped into the long grass filling the ditch. He waited until all became silent and the insects around him resumed their night songs. Just as he made to crawl from the ditch, the sound of hoofbeats came thundering along the road. He lay flat until they passed, lifting his head for a glimpse at their backs.

What he saw froze his blood. In front of one rider, just visible beside his shoulder, was the drooped head of a woman who was either unconscious or dead. Flying well over the tops of the soldiers and keeping pace with them, was the tiny silhouette of a bat.

Chapter Forty-Two

Jessamine

A sharp pain in her neck roused Jessamine to consciousness. She was swaying side to side and there was something tight closed around her ribcage, keeping her from breathing fully. Her legs dangled with no support. She was on a horse, slouched forward. She tried to lift her head and move her arms, wincing as the back of her neck spasmed. Her hands were tied behind her back. A crawling sensation filled her stomach, like she'd swallowed a nest of baby snakes. She was well and truly caught. A muscled arm clamped around her waist kept her from sliding off the mount. Her vision was full of sparks, but after a few shallow breaths, it cleared. It was dark and humid, which meant they were down by the river under thick canopy, headed back to the fortress. The sky was a little lighter than it had been before she'd been struck. She couldn't have been out for more than five minutes.

Jessamine rode in front of one of the guards. His saddle had no pommel; only a smooth ridge of leather hugged the horse's withers. As the guard felt life come back into her body, he loosened his grip a little. She had to squeeze the horse with her legs to keep upright, loath to press her back against his chest. She wanted to touch him as little as possible. She could feel the heat of him against her hands. It made her want to gag.

"Beazle?" she croaked. Her heart threw itself against her sternum. She couldn't feel him in her hair, and she couldn't see him flying around anywhere. Had something happened to him while she was unconscious?

"What's that?" someone said.

"She's awake," her captor told the others.

Wrinkling her nose at the sour smell of sweat and dirty boiled leather, she used her elbows to keep distance between them. But that was awkward and exhausting. Her head and neck throbbed, her heart was racing, she was uncomfortably warm and she was desperately worried about Beazle.

"Good morning." The guard gave a nasty laugh and ran a hand down her bare arm. "What's the matter, little sprite?"

"You reek," she croaked.

He laughed even louder. "You hear that, fellas? She thinks I stink."

"She's right," someone replied.

Her guard raised his hand to his nose. She heard him inhale the scent of her. He let out an exaggerated sigh and then buried his nose in her neck. "Well, you stink too, but I kind of like it. Go figure."

Jessamine turned her head to get away from him. The taste in her mouth was bitter, and there was a savage burning sensation in the back of her throat. She needed a drink. She hated to ask for anything, but the state of her mouth and throat was unbearable.

"I need water," she rasped.

"I don't care what you need," he snarled.

"Give her water, Sulpak," another said. "She has to be well enough to explain herself to the prince."

Her guard uncapped a water skin, which appeared in front of her face. He pressed it to her mouth too hard, making her push back against him to keep the rim from cutting her lips. He tilted the skin into her mouth, and water sloshed over her chin and the front of her tunic. He lowered the angle and she had to backwash or she'd choke. The water smelled swampy, but she finally managed to swallow enough to clear the taste from her mouth. She tried not to think about the fact that she'd just had her lips on something that her captor put his lips on all the time. She shuddered and had to squeeze her thighs to keep herself upright as the horse moved around. The muscles in her legs quivered, her face felt hot and the hair at her brow and neck felt damp. The early-morning air licked at the skin of her bare arm, cooling her a little.

After she drank, the guard took a swig of the water skin, capped it and put it away, clearing his throat. Moments later, he cleared his throat again. Then he horked and spat off to the side. His weight suddenly canted forward, leaning heavily on her. She shoved back at him but he only leaned on her more. One of the others looked over and saw how Jessamine was being crammed up the horse's neck. He laughed as she shoved hard against her captor's weight, out of breath from using all her strength yet still not budging him. Sweat dripped between her breasts and down the side of her face. Her hands were being crushed between his torso and her lower back.

"Get off me," she panted. His weight was becoming unbearable.

In answer, he leaned forward even more. She cried out as the sensitive skin of her inner thighs got pinched. Then the guard canted to one side.

"Sulpak?" someone asked.

With the slow, boneless weight of an unconscious person, he fell from the saddle and landed with a thump in the steep ditch. Jessamine straightened and watched, wide eyed, as the guard rolled into the long grass, disappearing from view. A soldier leapt from his horse. Tossing his reins to a comrade, he went into the ditch, yelling. Sulpak was headed for the river, and fast. The ditch was long and steep. Sulpak's body made the grasses sway maniacally back and forth.

"What did you do to him?"

Jessamine blinked at the guard holding his comrade's horse. His face was half in shadow, but she could see enough to know that he was angry.

There was a yell and a splash, followed by another splash.

"N-nothing. I didn't do anything." She'd only just registered that the big man behind her hadn't been intentionally trying to crush her. There had been something wrong with him.

"Sulpak? Perrin?" the two remaining guards called from the edge of the road. The canopy overhanging the river's edge was so thick that it was impossible to see the water itself. Someone responded, but the voice was already downriver.

"Dammit," one of them cursed. "Now what? Should I ride to the bridge? See if I can get there first?"

"You'll never make it, the currents are—"

As the guards engaged in their debate, Jessamine realized she was sitting atop a mount alone. Her hands and legs were tied, but now was the best opportunity she'd have. She shimmied her butt back into the saddle and kicked the horse hard with one foot as she pressed with the other, trying to tell him which way to run. He tossed his head and whinnied as he jumped forward, which almost unseated her. He pranced in a half-circle, then cantered down the road before slowing to a walk.

"Get her, you oaf!" The voice was half alarmed, half amused, like he didn't believe Jessamine would actually get away.

She had to admit, the odds were poor. If she could only free her hands. Jessamine kicked harder, leaning forward and squeezing with her knees. The horse jolted forward again. Her body jerked back and forth as she fought for balance, but her mount finally got the idea. Reins swinging in the air, he began to trot. He was going in the wrong direction, but Jessamine wasn't about to be picky. She struggled at her bonds.

The soldiers exchanged commands and cuss words, but one of them actually laughed. The sound made Jessamine's insides go cold. It was funny for them; an exhausted, injured, bound girl trying to outride two trained soldiers. It was impossible, no matter how big and powerful her mount was. The ground seemed like a long way down and the rocks were many. She dreaded urging the horse to go faster. She couldn't get her feet in the stirrups while they were swinging around. She'd fall off for sure if she kicked him into a gallop.

Hoofbeats came up behind, overtaking her easily. A powerful hand clamped around the sweaty flesh of her upper arm. She was violently hauled over the front of his saddle, landing like a sack of grain. She struggled to suck in air as she jounced against the horse's withers. Her ass was slapped so hard that tears sprang to her eyes.

"What did you do to him?" The guard struck her behind—hard—again, and again. "What did you do to Sulpak? Tell me!"

Her head felt like it would burst. Her cheeks were hot and she couldn't breathe. Humiliation and rage built as he continued to strike her backside. She finally got air into her lungs, enough to give a loud and lusty scream.

"Shut up," he snarled.

But the guard quit beating her so he could grab the reins of the horse she'd just been yanked from. Turning them around, he walked both horses back to the guard who'd stayed behind.

Hot tears poured down Jessamine's cheeks, as much from shame as from the pain of the beating. She was rudely shoved off the horse, landing hard on the stones on her back with a yelp. The back of her head struck a rock. Pain sliced across her skull and her vision went black, yet she could still hear the horse's hooves against the rocks near her head. Her vision slowly cleared, but the world looked blurry.

The soldier peered down at her from atop his mount, expression hidden in shadow. He dismounted and stood beside her, then kicked her half-heartedly in the thigh. She bent around the blow in soundless agony, the muscles in her leg cramping. She heard him sniff as he stood over her, as though deciding how to inflict further punishment. He sneezed, then sniffed again. She managed to glare up at him. He wiped his hand across his nose and then spat. She turned her face and it landed in her hair.

"Where's the prince's betrothed?" he grated, his words slurring.

"What's wrong with *you*?" his companion asked from near the ditch.

The guard standing over her swayed, as though undecided about delivering another kick. Then he fell, landing in a heap right at her head, facedown. There was foam at his lips, and a strange smell wafted over her when he fell. She stared at him, her mind racing as she tried to assemble her thoughts through a haze of pain.

"Rys." The last soldier hadn't moved from his place by the ditch. He sounded annoyed. "Quit playing around."

Like the rays of morning light crawling over the horizon, Jessamine had a realization. Her body ached, but with renewed energy. That awful bitterness was back, filling her mouth and coating her tongue.

Her body was making poison.

Her memory flashed back to when Ilishec showed her the chemical profile of her sweat. He hadn't told her that what she was producing was toxic, he'd only said they were less desirable compounds, yet it was the only explanation. Jess closed her eyes, tuning in to her body and the magic swirling through her blood. *Datura stramonium* and *atropa belladonna*, that's what was coming through her skin. Without her realizing it, her body was defending itself. Jess's eyes popped open, her arms covered in goosebumps. Her pulse surged as she struggled to her feet.

She planted one foot over the unconscious guard and faced his comrade, forcing herself to hold his frightening gaze. He was all sharp angles and shiny teeth. She ignored the pain in her back and bottom, the throb at the back of her skull, her fear. She felt something hot and wet trickle down the back of her neck. It was either blood or sweat—either way, it was toxic.

"Let me go, or you'll share his fate."

The guard's eyes widened. Then a tiny winged figure swooped silently around his head. He ducked, startled.

Beazle landed on the front of Jessamine's tunic. She felt like shouting for joy, like a yoke had lifted from her shoulders. Even the pain of her bruises bothered her less now that her bat had found her.

The guard unsheathed his sword. "You can tell the prince your story in hell, demon," he snarled.

Jessamine braced herself, drawing as much spit into her mouth as she could manage.

Blowing like an angry bull, he ran at her, sword drawn back. She tensed, heart thundering, ready to spring. Beazle launched himself from her chest and flew straight into the man's face, squeaking and scratching. The guard faltered. Bolting forward, straight into danger as his sword lifted, Jess spat, aiming for his face. The huge gob landed in one eye with a splat.

He gave a disgusted cry. The handle of his sword hit her on the top of her shoulder, making her arm go numb. He clawed at his face, screaming and cursing her in a foreign tongue. He took a step toward her but crumpled to his knee.

Jessamine scampered out of his reach. Both his eyes had a milky coating, not just the one she'd spit into. He made a gagging sound, vomited, then collapsed onto his face.

She stared at his limp form, panting. Beazle landed on the front of her tunic and crawled up to her neck, where he burrowed himself beneath her hair.

"I'm okay," she whispered. "We're okay, Beeze. You are so brave. You saved my life, little love. Thank you."

She sucked in a breath and surveyed the damage. Two bodies lay unconscious in the road, big mean soldiers, both facedown. How much time did she have before they woke up? Four horses grazed in the ditches, munching away without concern. The river trickled merrily by in the early-morning light. Frogs sang. A lark warbled, welcoming the dawn.

When she felt steady enough, she lay on her back and looped her legs through her arms so her bound wrists were in front. Bracing the blade of her attacker's sword between her knees, she sawed the rope against the blade. Her bonds parted. She threw the rope off and rubbed at her wrists.

She didn't have long to think about what to do next because someone was coming. She grabbed the sword and dashed into the trees, her heart in her throat.

Chapter Forty-Three

Laec

Laec caught a glimpse of a horse's tail as it swished at its hind legs. He froze, straining to make out the details of those occupying the road up ahead. A second horse had its head down in the ditch, clipping grass. Both were saddled but without riders. He got closer, sword at the ready. Two more saddled horses grazed further up the road. Dark shadows that looked like bodies lay in the road, unmoving. Laec's foot brushed against pebbles. One of the horses lifted its head and whickered. It chewed as it watched him ghost his way toward them, listening and watching the bodies for signs of life. When he got closer, he could see no visible wounds, and no blood. One of them had a sword still in its scabbard, while the other's scabbard was empty. He checked for a pulse on one, then the other, noting the foam at his lips. The smell of vomit tainted the air. A chill swept over Laec. Both of these soldiers were dead.

A twig snapped in the forest as he crouched by a body. He braced himself for an ambush, tightening his grip on his sword.

There was a rustle of leaves. Then a whisper: "Laec?"

Jessamine materialized from the shadows, her face a colorless moon, her eyes just two sparks of light in the darkness of her hood. She was missing a sleeve and there were red welts visible on her wrist.

Laec straightened, opening his arms.

She started for his embrace but then halted. "You'd better not touch me, not yet."

"Are you okay?"

She nodded. "Just a little bruised. I'm sorry, Laec. I was really stupid."

"Yes, you were. But here you are, alive, and without any broken bones."

"Are you angry?"

He led her away from the bodies toward the horses. "Anger doesn't serve well in this situation. Besides, I've been in worse trouble. Where did the other riders go?"

"Downriver. I'll explain later." Jessamine took the reins of one animal. "How did you find me?"

"Beazle."

She nodded. "Let's get out of here, before they wake up."

Laec was about to tell her they didn't need to worry about that when an angry yell shattered the quiet: "Halt! You're under arrest!"

Laec vaulted into a saddle. Jessamine bounced around trying to get her foot in the stirrup, finally hauling herself laboriously up. Their horses wheeled as they hissed them into a gallop. As they thundered down the road, the silhouette of the guard who had yelled appeared beneath the trees. He had his sword unsheathed but he was on foot and alone.

"Go straight for him," Laec called.

Jessamine nodded and bent low along her mount's neck as they urged the horses faster.

The man assumed a fighting stance, lifting his sword. Laec braced himself as Jessamine's horse drew alongside his, neck for neck. The soldier backpedaled as they bore down upon him, yelling for them to stop. He gave a cry and dropped into a crouch, his sword clattering on the stones. Jessamine's mount sailed by him as Laec's horse leaped over the guard's head.

They climbed away from the riverbank, winding through dense trees. Mulch and hard-packed earth replaced the slippery stones, their hoofbeats turning from sharp strikes to soft thuds. Laec considered whether they might risk going cross-country. Horses had decent night vision and excellent footing, even on rough terrain, although this was some of the roughest boulder-strewn land he'd ever seen. He glanced behind. They were not being followed, so he slowed to a canter and Jess kept pace.

"How far?" Jessamine asked. Her complexion was almost gray.

"Ten minutes at this pace. Are you sure you're alright?"

She rubbed a hand at the base of her scalp, wincing. When she withdrew it, Laec saw congealed blood on her fingertips. "I might be concussed." Jessamine tugged her cloak around her and pulled her hood forward.

"How are you going to explain your injuries to the healers at the palace?"

Jess glanced behind them. "I don't need a healer. Let's just get home."

Laec shivered when he thought of the soldiers' bodies in the road. What had happened back there? He ducked his head to avoid a tree branch, deciding to ask her about it later. They needed to get to Çifta.

Voices and hoofbeats drifted up behind them on a breeze. They exchanged an uneasy glance. Then came a sound that made Laec's stomach go cold: a hound.

Jessamine's horse gave a half buck of surprise at the piercing wail. She dropped close to his neck, her eyes wide and frightened.

More hounds joined the chorus.

There'd be no losing bloodhounds over any terrain. Their best friend was speed. They put their boots to their mounts, eating up the road. Galloping through the forest, Laec noted how low the canopy was up ahead.

"We have to get as far ahead as we can," Laec called, pointing up, "then cut off our scent."

A glance at Jess made his heart jump into his mouth. She was bouncing around white-faced, barely keeping upright, her butt thumping hard against the saddle. Her feet were jammed too far through the stirrups.

"Jess!" he called.

She looked over, clearly terrified.

"Lean forward and use your legs," he said, raising his voice just enough to be heard over the hoofbeats. He let go of the reins with one hand to point at his own backside, showing her how he hovered over the saddle, not touching. Then he pointed to his feet. "Look where I am in the stirrups."

It took her several awkward strides but she got her weight forward and the balls of her feet on the stirrups so she could post, flexing her thighs to keep her butt off the saddle. She shot him a wobbly smile of triumph.

Up the steep, winding and treacherous road through dark forest they flew. Their mounts flicked their ears around, listening to the baying of the hounds.

Ahead, the road passed through a section of open land. Beyond it, boughs hung low over the road. They slowed to a canter, passing through the open section and under the low-hanging trees. Laec halted, his mount snorting and tossing his head. The horses bellowed air as they danced in place.

The riders were coming, the dogs baying like lunatics. The bends in the road kept them from view, but they had moments only.

Laec took Jessamine's reins so she could climb up and balance on her feet on the saddle. She grabbed the nearest bough and hauled herself up into the canopy where she was swallowed by the leaves. Laec released her mount and climbed on top of his own saddle, balancing as his horse danced in place. He dropped the reins, leaping up into the branches, swinging a leg over until he lay along the rough bark on his stomach. His horse stood beneath, looking back down the hill with his ears flicking. Laec unsheathed his sword and stretched out an arm as far as he could to whack the horse on the buttock with the flat of the blade. He was too far away to hit very hard, but at the same time, he loosed a predatory snarl.

His horse bolted, and Jessamine's wheeled and followed. Their hoofbeats faded as the sounds of the search party grew loud.

zCatching two riderless horses would be easy, as the horses would run out of steam and forget why they were running in the first place. The search party would soon be back.

Stowing their cloaks, they moved toward the graveyard, staying in the canopy and listening for their pursuers. At the cemetery, the trees were too far apart to be used as a road. They had to go on foot.

Laec dropped out of the trees and Jess followed, falling to her side and almost knocking her head against a headstone. He heaved her to her feet and they sprinted for the well, trying to keep from being tangled in the ivy. Laec made Jess go in first, hoping what they'd done would be enough. Even if the dogs sniffed around the well, who would think they'd gone into an old well full of dark water? He smiled grimly as he passed through the liquid. It hadn't been enough to keep Jessamine from trying it. He had developed a grudging respect for the young woman's courage and curiosity. Hopefully, Rahamlarin soldiers lacked these qualities.

The moment his head broke free beneath the liquid, Jessamine whispered for him to wait. He craned his neck, looking for her below him in the darkness, and could just see the top of her head. She stood on the platform at the stop of the stairs, her hands out for balance. Though she herself was as still as the statuary over their heads, her whole body swayed back and forth. He saw the problem immediately: the stairs had come away from the wall. He felt sick, and his thoughts flew to Çifta. Had she fallen? Was she even now lying on the dirt below, with broken limbs, or dead? He couldn't yell in case the well was within hearing range of the dogs.

"I'm sorry." Çifta's voice echoed up from way below. Laec let out a long breath. She sounded okay. He made a shushing sound. Çifta must have heard him because she didn't say anything else.

Jessamine began to move, very slowly, closer to the wall. She reached for a shelf of rock, getting enough of a grip on it to pull the steps back toward the bracers that had rotted away.

They had no choice but to risk the rotten stairs. Several steps that had been intact when they'd climbed up had broken when Çifta had descended. He felt nauseous thinking of her facing this obstacle alone. She must have been utterly terrified.

Jessamine moved down the steps, keeping as close to the

wall as possible. But when she reached the next landing down, she would have no choice but to move away from the wall.

Laec lowered himself down the handholds, stopping just above the first platform. As Jessamine moved away from the wall, the platform shifted. He settled his weight on the landing, hoping it would be enough to counterbalance Jessamine's weight and keep the staircase upright.

In the corner of his eye, Laec caught a flash of Beazle as he fluttered around in the air, following Jessamine's progress.

When Jessamine hit the second landing and headed back toward the wall, Laec began to descend. The swaying motion made his stomach turn over. As Jessamine came back toward the wall, he headed away from it, doing the best they could to keep the whole thing from toppling over.

But as Laec hit the next landing, the steps swayed away from the wall and didn't sway back. Jessamine just wasn't heavy enough to offset him. He grabbed the railing, holding his breath. Jessamine scrabbled for something to grab, but there was nothing within her reach. The entire construction leaned, drawing Jessamine's reaching hand away from the wall. They were going over. Laec saw Jessamine's fingers spread out, grasping desperately at nothing. His stomach lurched up and out through the top of his head as the world tilted. His body seemed to turn in slow motion as the landing tipped him off into space. Flipping over the banister, he flailed and grasped at the post holding the banister to the steps. The post broke off with a crack, and then he was in freefall.

From these heights, they had no chance. Though his limbs were flailing through the air, his mind was coldly calm as he hoped that Çifta had gotten out of the way.

A scream echoed around him, then morphed into a cacophony of squeaks and screeches.

Laec was suddenly buffeted by flying forms, thousands of them. Wings battered his face and body. Claws gripped his clothing, puncturing and ripping, even as he plummeted toward the ground. He was consumed by the smell of animal. There was fur in his mouth, in his eyes. His momentum arrested as he became caught in the air by his clothing, suspended a few feet over the floor and skimming along like a dragonfly.

He was alive, being carried by… bats.

Hundreds of them.

There was a soggy crash and the crunch of breaking wood as the stairs hit the ground. His ears rang with the immensity of the sound. Dust and debris blew through the air. Laec hardly felt it, surrounded and insulated by winged creatures. Some were only a little bigger than Beazle, others were enormous, with massive sharp teeth glinting in the dim light. One of them had wingbeats that struck the floor with every downstroke.

Only after the echo of the collapse was gone did Laec's winged saviors settle him to the floor. One by one they released their claws from his clothing. Some had to rip themselves loose. Laec rolled over, panting and feeling nearly hysterical with relief as he looked for Jessamine. She was on the floor too, not far away, her face as white as a cotton sheet, her eyes huge caves of shock. They crawled toward each other, confirming that they were both indeed still alive.

The staircase had become a long heap of ruined wood, scattered down the tunnel as far as they could see. Laec got up, his limbs weak and shaky with adrenaline. They looked up.

Bats filled the cave with shadows and the soft sound of their wingbeats. Then they vanished like cockroaches frightened by sudden light, moving too quickly to see where they went. Into the cracks in the walls, Laec guessed. That was the only place they could go, but they were gone. All of them. Except for Beazle, who fluttered down to perch on the very top of Jessamine's head. The little bat crawled down her hair and disappeared into her neck. Jessamine closed her eyes and put her hand to her familiar. Laec mirrored her relief and amazement.

Çifta came stumbling along the edge of the tunnel, stepping over rubble, shock imprinted on her features.

"I've never seen anything like that in my entire life." She came up to Laec and patted his arms, his face, as though trying to make sure he was real.

He took her hands. "I'm okay."

She let out a shaky sigh and looked at Jessamine. "Friends of yours? All those bats, I mean?"

Jessamine shook her head.

"Friends of Beazle's?" Laec guessed. "Who among us could call on an army of bats?"

Jessamine kept one hand in the hair at her neck where she had Beazle cradled and looked around, mystified. "He's never summoned a bunch of bats before."

"But have you ever come so close to death before?" Laec asked.

"No. Never. I really thought we were finished."

Laec dusted himself off. "I think you just discovered another capability of your flora magic."

"And handy magic it was. How do you say 'thank you' in bat?" Çifta released another shaky laugh, her gaze skimming the ceiling.

Laec scanned the darkness above, the walls, the ceiling. There were no bats in sight. "They came out of nowhere, out of everywhere. There were *so many* of them. You'd think there'd be a few stragglers at least."

Very distantly, a hunting dog bayed.

Jessamine shivered. "Come on. Let's get out of here."

Chapter Forty-Four

Jessamine

By the time they emerged from the well at the other end, very grateful there was no rotten staircase to deal with, Jess was moving like she'd aged fifty years. She resisted Laec's help, not wanting him to touch her. She could feel that her body had stopped producing poison, but she was paranoid the residue of her sweat might hurt him.

They had walked the underground passage in almost complete silence, stopping often to rest. Jess had never felt so weary. They ran out of water halfway home and spent all the hours of daylight underground. The sun had been coming up when they dropped into the well on Rahamlar's end, and it was going down when they emerged. They were dirty, bruised, pale and worn, but triumphant.

"The Calyx will be at dinner," Jess said as they climbed the slope to the base of the West Keep. "If any of them see me, they'll hyperventilate." Her clothing was torn and filthy, there was blood crusted on the back of her head and she was limping, favoring her right foot.

"What are the odds you'll run into them on the way to your room?" Laec asked as they navigated the furrows between rows of flax.

"Pretty high. They don't all eat at the same time. There's usually a few roaming the halls at this hour." Jess winced as the heel of her boot pressed against a blister. Going uphill was a lot more painful than the flat of the passage.

"You can bathe in my suite and I'll ask a servant for some extra women's clothing for Çifta so you'll have something to wear. They don't need to know who it's for."

Jess agreed and the weary group closed the last of the distance between them and home. As they followed the fence along the training ground, the shadow of a bird trailed them. Laec glanced up and frowned.

"What's wrong?" Çifta asked.

"We've been spotted. That's Kite's familiar, Erasmus. I was hoping to avoid being seen, but I should have known better, not with all the animals around here."

"What are you going to tell people?"

They reached a side door. Laec pushed it open. "The truth."

"I'm desperate to take these boots off." Jess slid down the wall to the floor and pulled off her footwear. Her feet felt swollen and hot. She rolled her head and put her fingers to her scalp where she'd struck the stone. It was going to sting when she washed it, and maybe bleed. Aching everywhere, she used the wall to get to her feet, and carried her boots.

Laec led them to the courtiers wing. As they reached the top of the stairs, Kite stood in the middle of the hall, her bird perched on her shoulder. Her keen gaze went from Laec, to Jess, to Çifta, noting their dirty clothes, tired expressions and Jess's stockinged feet. Her expression was of thinly veiled amazement. "Where have you been?"

Laec found a smile for her. "It's a long story, Kite. Are you going to let us pass?"

Erasmus gave a squawk. "I can't do that, I'm afraid. Besides, it's too late. The crofter is on his way." Kite focused on Çifta. "Are you alright?"

Çifta lifted her chin. "Thanks to these two."

Kite shook her head slowly, and with a scoff. "I don't get how you pulled it off. We only just got back from Rahamlar, there hasn't been enough time for you to return—"

"They'll tell it to the king," thundered a deep voice.

The crofter strode toward them, his dark eyes flashing. Panther was with him, and behind him padded the huge black cat.

Çifta backed up when she saw the feline. As the crofter and Panther came to a stop in the hallway, the cat held her head low, her tail switching back and forth. Her yellow eyes were trained on Jess, Çifta and Laec, and she panted with just the tip of her tongue poking out of her mouth.

"You're being detained," the crofter said formally.

Kite stepped behind them, her hand on the pommel of the sword at her waist. Erasmus gave another piercing shriek.

"Shut him up, Kite," snapped the crofter.

"Sorry," murmured Kite. "Come on." She herded them forward. "No trouble from you three. Erasmus can tear out eyeballs before you even see him coming."

"I'm a little more concerned about the cat, to be honest," murmured Laec, then added conversationally, "No offense. Erasmus is also very impressive."

Jess shot him a look of incredulity. How could he sound so calm and collected? They were being arrested.

"Çifta had nothing to do with our plan," Jess croaked. "At least let her go."

"Save it." The crofter strode down the hall.

As Kite herded them forward, Panther and his familiar slipped in behind them. Panther's thoughts were hidden behind an expressionless face. He and Jess looked at one another.

"I remember you from the ball," she rasped from a dry throat. Was he friend or foe, sympathetic or indifferent?

"I don't remember you." His tone was not unkind, but neither was it warm.

Jess faced front. The black feline stalking them exhaled little puffs of air that made shivers run up and down her spine.

Carrying her boots, she limped between Çifta and Laec as they were escorted to an area of the palace she'd never seen before. They were made to stand outside a set of large double doors. Jess's feet were cold against the stone floor. Arching over the doorway was a carving of a pride of lions with a large central figure of a male with an impressive mane. Either side of him were six females, and between their legs they sheltered many small cubs. To distract herself from her thundering heart, Jessamine tried to count the cubs. It didn't work very well. What would the king think? What would he do? After ten minutes of standing in front of these doors, Jess bent to put her boots on or her feet were going to freeze. She tried to pull them on but found that her feet were too swollen. She was sitting on the floor when the doors swung open. Laboriously, she got up, wishing she could move faster.

King Agir was pacing near a set of windows, his hands behind his back. He wore a black dressing gown with a fur collar. He wore no crown. Queen Esha looked pale and serious, seated in a chair in front of a fireplace. She was swaddled by a soft yellow shawl and wore a thin coronet. The room was spartan, with only a few chairs and one table littered with papers and books.

Laec, Çifta and Jessamine were herded into the room and made to stand in the center. Laec bowed while Jess and Çifta curtsied. For a second, Jess was worried that she might not be able to straighten.

"Tell me this is a joke. You're having a lark." The king looked at them directly, moving from one set of eyes to the next. "Are you— Have you really kidnapped a member of the Rahamlar royal family?"

"I am not a member of the Rahamlar royal family, sire." Çifta's voice trembled only a little. "Until early this morning, I was a prisoner of Prince Faraçek. Jessamine and Laec risked much to rescue me."

"You are Prince Faraçek's betrothed, yes? You agreed to marry him, you went there with that understanding, of your own free will?" The king stood by the table, the fingertips of one hand tented on the wood beside a piece of parchment.

"Yes, Sire." Çifta swallowed. "But we had an agreement with terms. King Osvitan and my father, Kazery Unya, agreed that if I or Prince Faraçek were unhappy with the betrothal within eight weeks of my arrival, the contract could be legally annulled."

"And you were unhappy?"

"Most unhappy. I tried to write to my father to dissolve the agreement, but the prince burned my letter in front of me and forced me to write another, telling my father lies, that all was well and that he should arrange to deliver my bride price."

The king and queen exchanged a look.

Emboldened, Çifta went on. "Please, don't punish them. I'll pay a fine on their behalf, if you'll accept it?"

The king sighed. "You don't understand. We cannot have citizens of our kingdom, let alone members of our court, running amok within the borders of our neighboring kingdom. I have to take responsibility for the actions of my people. I am sorry for your situation, but there are a great many more lives that may be adversely affected by what they've done than just yours. We have to send you back, I hope you understand. This is not the way. Now that you are here, you are free to write to your father and tell him what has transpired, but you must go back, and your father and King Osvitan must decide what to do next."

Jess shook her head, her heart darting around inside her ribcage like a frightened jackrabbit. After all they'd been through, Agir would send Çifta back to prison?

"Can't it be resolved without her having to—" Laec began.

The king shot Laec a hard look. "You are the worst offender of all. You come into my kingdom posing as a friend, and this is the thanks we receive for our hospitality? Taking the law into your own hands? How does what transpired in Rahamlar even concern you, pray tell? The dungeon will be your home until I've decided what to do with you."

Queen Esha came to her feet. "My love, let us not make any decisions until we've heard the story in its entirety. All we know is that they were discovered entering the castle with Lady Çifta. There are many questions that need answering."

The king rubbed his temples. "Go to the beginning, then, and don't leave anything out."

A fist hammered against the double doors hard and repeatedly, making Çifta jump.

When Ian opened the door, Ilishec shoved his way through. He was panting and puffing, sweat dripping down his temples.

"I beg your pardon, my king, my queen." He gave a flustered

bow, his words coming out between deep inhales and exhales. "I only just heard that one of my Calyx has been involved in a crime. Jessamine, can this be true? And my nephew, Laec? What have you done, my lad?"

"Hello, Uncle," Laec said, marveling Jess once again with his reserved calm. Did anything ruffle him?

Esha beckoned. "Come sit by me, Gardener. Calm yourself."

Ilishec moved to Esha's side, giving the cat a wide berth. "Forgive me. I'm in a state of shock."

"We all are, believe me," mumbled the king. "I want to hear from Jessamine first. You are a subject of Solana, while they are foreigners. You will begin."

Jess felt like wilting, her head was pounding and she was parched. She spotted a decanter of water near Esha's elbow. "May I have a drink, please?"

Esha poured the water into a goblet and carried it to Jess. Jessamine guzzled it in one go. Queen Esha gave her the tiniest smile. It gave Jess the strength she needed.

"I overheard a conversation between Laec and Ilishec about a passageway that was supposed to exist long ago, and I believed I could find it."

The king's eyes grew round. "A passageway… *the* passageway?"

"Yes, Sire."

Queen Esha looked delighted. "You knew you could find it… *how*?"

Jessamine shot a questioning look at the gardener.

Ilishec waved a hand in permission, smiling weakly. "Go ahead, child."

"Part of my flora magic seems to be the ability to locate lost or stolen items," said Jessamine. "I've done it twice now. The first was by accident."

King Agir and the crofter exchanged a weighty look. "When did you first discover this ability?"

"At the initiation ball. Rose lost something important to her. When a guest asked me to conjure some of my botanicals for their entertainment, one of the plants I brought up was *solidago*. As I made it grow, Rose walked by and I thought of her lost heirloom. Beazle flew away, and moments later, I understood where it was. I could see it through Beazle's eyes."

The king squinted. "Your… bat?"

"Yes."

Agir looked at Ilishec. "Did you know about this?"

"Yes. In folklore, *solidago* is fabled to have this meaning. You know how I feel about the fables. I wanted her to keep it a secret until I could categorize her better."

Jess thought the gardener looked guilty as he said this, but she couldn't imagine why he would feel that way.

The crofter harrumphed and shook his head. Jess wasn't sure exactly what he was upset about, but it was clear that something displeased him.

"Let's keep to the topic at hand," Queen Esha prompted. "You used this ability to find the lost entrance to the passageway, my dear?"

"Yes, Ma'am."

Esha shook her head. "Incredible. What has been lost for centuries, you found in a matter of… what? Hours?"

"It took a few minutes, Ma'am."

The crofter and the king again exchanged a look. That look made Jess very uncomfortable, but she was up to her neck already. There was no going back, no matter the consequences.

"I understood that Laec wanted to help Çifta, and I wanted

justice for Greta. I knew no one was going to do anything about the murder of my familiar—"

"Tread lightly," the king murmured.

Jess cleared her throat. "Yes, Sire… so Laec and I conspired to use the passageway to get Çifta out. At first, it was easy…"

Jessamine launched into the sequence of events that had transpired in Rahamlar, keeping her description short and as simple as possible. When it came to the poisoning of the guards, the air was palpable with astonishment.

When she described the huge cauldron of bats, and how they saved her and Laec, the king loosed an unkingly oath, but seemed more amazed than upset. The crofter rubbed at his jaw, and Queen Esha gasped audibly. Even Panther and Kite reacted. They were out of Jess's view but she heard them shuffling around behind her. When she was finished, she needed another drink.

"Had that ever happened to you before? The duplicates?"

Jess cocked her head. "Duplicates?"

"Of Beazle."

Jess almost laughed, but she was too tired, and the situation was too serious. "They weren't duplicates, Sire. They were all different shapes and sizes. And no, Sire. That's never happened before."

The king and the crofter swapped another impenetrable look. After a long silence, the king said, "It beggars belief, but the evidence is right in front of me. Lady Çifta is here, looking battered and tired. You and Laec look like you've been in a series of bar fights, and I daresay that if I keep you here much longer, you'll collapse before my eyes. I must decide what to do with you, yet there is no precedent. Further, this is all greatly complicated by a letter we received from King Osvitan yesterday, while you were conspiring to entangle my kingdom with them." The king retrieved the parchment and held it up. "King Osvitan writes to ask if we have had any correspondence with, or know the whereabouts of, both or either of his daughters. It seems they are missing."

The room was quiet as the king scanned the letter, then read aloud: "I ask as your neighbor and, I hope, as a friend. I am aggrieved about my eldest son. I am ashamed of the attack on your border and swear that I did not sanction or command such, and now my daughters are missing. I am sure you understand what a serious predicament Rahamlar is in with our queen-in-waiting unaccounted for, and also the beloved and tender Princess Isabey. My kingdom will be in upheaval until we install the rightful heiress. If you can illuminate me, I will be most grateful and generous. Wherever we discover foul play, our wrath and retribution will be swift and savage. We look to our long-time neighbor for assistance in bringing any and all culprits to justice." The king lowered the letter. "I trust I do not need to emphasize the threat King Osvitan has woven into these lines."

"I don't know anything about the princesses' whereabouts, sire," said Jess.

"Me neither," added Laec.

"I can offer something." Çifta put up a finger.

The king set his shoulders. "Please—"

Çifta cleared her throat. "In my first week at Rahamlar, before I was imprisoned, I happened upon the princesses whispering together. They sounded frightened. The queen-in-waiting had been walking in one of the gardens when a stone fell from a rampart and crashed to the ground, mere steps from where she walked. She believed it was pushed. The walls at Rahamlar are very sturdy, stones and mortar do not simply come loose, she said. She told her sister to remember what she'd taught her, what question she should always ask: *cui bono*."

"Who benefits," murmured the queen.

"Yes, Ma'am. When I approached them, they tried to hide their concern. That was the last time I saw the queen-in-waiting in person, but two evenings later, she sent a soldier to my room in possession of her seal. He told me she wanted me to dissolve the betrothal. But I had only been there for one week, and I didn't want to humiliate the prince. This was before I learned how bellicose he really is. I wanted to understand why the princess had given me such advice, but the next morning, I couldn't find either of the princesses. When I tried to mail the letter to my father was when Prince Faraçek caught me, burned the letter and imprisoned me."

"Did the prince say anything about his sisters?" Queen Esha asked.

"Only to ask if I had seen them." Çifta paused, then added: "His inquiry seemed… genuine."

"Your story is compelling, Lady Çifta," said King Agir. "I will report your incarceration to King Osvitan, and your knowledge."

Çifta sucked in a breath and blurted, "Please don't send me back there, sire."

The king nodded. "You are welcome at the Scented Court, and you'll be safe in our halls. You may use the royal aviary to send a letter to your father. It will be for Kazery and Osvitan to decide what must come next for you."

Çifta sounded immensely relieved. "Thank you."

"As for you"—the king turned his gaze to Jessamine—"tomorrow, first thing, you will show the crofter to the passageway. After that, you may go home to your family, as you had planned. Please know that we are very sorry for your loss. You may linger at home as long as you need, and your escorts will remain with you until you're ready to return. When you want to return, send us a letter ahead of your departure by post. The gardener and I will make a decision about your future with the Calyx so that you will not have long to wait."

"Yes, Sire." Jessamine managed a small bend at the knees. Allowed to go home and return, but to what? To be dismissed? Would they consider what she had done as treasonous? Her heart felt small and heavy. Peony's voice seemed to ooze out of the air: *You don't belong here.* This would be the excuse Ilishec needed if he really did believe he'd made a mistake. She felt Beazle move against her scalp, snuggling behind her ear. She could almost hear him saying, *As long as we are together, we'll be alright.*

"Laec," the king's voice hardened, "I regret having allowed you into our court. You'll be escorted to the dungeon where you will await—"

Queen Esha put a hand on her husband's forearm. She leaned in close and whispered something to him. King Agir listened, whispered back, listened again as Esha spoke in his ear.

Jess wondered if it would be inappropriate to sit on the floor until she was dismissed.

The king looked up. "I amend. Laec, you'll be confined to the palace until further notice. It is because of our respect for Queen Elphame that you will not be directly incarcerated, but you'll be under constant supervision, whether you can tell you're being watched or not. Remember that our Fahyli have gifts that regular soldiers do not have."

Laec dipped his chin. "Yes, Sire. Will you allow me to make my report to Elphame? She is expecting one, and there is much to convey."

"Yes, but I or Queen Esha will read it before you send it. Your behavior has marked you, so for now, all communications will be monitored. You've lost the privileges of a courtier."

Laec bowed his head. “I understand.”

“You’re dismissed.” King Agir waved his hand.

Jess looked at Ilishec. He would have words for her, of that she was certain. But would he give them now?

“I’ll speak to you tomorrow morning, Jess,” Ilishec said. “You clearly need to rest.”

“Thank you, Gardener.” As Jessamine turned to go, she caught the queen exchanging a subtle nod with Laec. What was that about?

After the doors had been pulled shut, leaving the gardener and the crofter in private conversation with the king and queen, Çifta turned to Jess. “I can’t thank you enough for what you did for me, a stranger.”

“We’re not strangers anymore.” Jess smiled at Çifta, then turned to Laec. “Looks like you got the worst of it.”

He flashed those foxlike incisors. “I’ve been in worse trouble.”

“Move,” Panther said to Laec and Çifta, his tone flat. “To the courtiers wing, both of you.”

His black cat gave a chirping bark.

“May I touch her?” Laec asked. “She looks as soft as a duckling.”

“It’s up to her. She’s not a pet,” Panther replied. “But I doubt it, she’s a professional.”

Laec slowly put a hand out toward the big cat’s head. The cat gave a low rumble in her throat and flattened her ears. Laec withdrew his hand. “Maybe another day.”

“What’s her name?” Jess asked as Kite moved to her side.

“Tulliana, but she answers to Tully,” he replied. “And I’m sorry about Greta.”

Surprise rocked Jess, making her forget briefly about her pain and exhaustion. It seemed like everyone had heard about what had happened to her familiar. Her body flushed with warmth. Why it mattered what Panther thought, she didn't know, but somehow his words made her feel lighter. "Thank you."

Panther escorted Laec and Çifta toward the courtiers wing, while Kite stayed with Jessamine until they reached her room. Erasmus sat perched on Kite's shoulder, darting his head this way and that, but the raptor was quiet.

"Don't tell anyone I said this," Kite said as they paused at Jess's door, "but I would have done something similar in your shoes. Have a good rest. I hope when you come back to us, that you feel better."

Without waiting for an answer, Kite stalked off down the hall. Erasmus turned around on Kite's shoulder to look back at Jess. Kite turned her head, as if communicating something silently to her bird. Just before the pair disappeared around the corner, he gave a piercing cry and took to the air. He swooped down the hall and through Jess's open door, landing on the top of the chair near her desk.

Jess found that someone had filled her tub with hot water and lit a fire in the fireplace. She almost burst into tears. She was home. She stripped off her filthy, poison-crusted clothing and shoved it into a basket to deal with later. She let out a groan of pleasure as she sank to her neck in hot, fragrant water. Gingerly, she cleaned her scalp and washed her hair. Beazle hung upside down from the rafter over her head, wrapped up in his wings. When she got out, she scrubbed her skin raw, put some ointment on her blisters, and crawled into bed with wet hair. Beazle flapped over to her headboard and hung upside down near her head, not wanting to be too far away from her.

Sleep dragged Jess under as Erasmus watched over them.

Epilogue

Captain Yorin squatted by the body in the graveyard. The man's arm was outstretched, his fingertips grazing the handle of a sword. He'd been reaching for it when he died. He lay between the headstones, cradled in a patch of ferns and ivy. But there was something strange about his clothing, something Yorin couldn't make out very well in the dim light of morning. He suspected that even at high noon, this derelict graveyard lay choked in shadows. No one had trimmed the grass or managed the once decorative shrubs in decades.

"Bring a torch," Yorin bellowed to one of the soldiers milling about the hillside, tramping over evidence with their boots. The lot had grown sloppy and Yorin had no one to blame but himself. He too had grown too soft around the middle. Extensive times of peace made for slothful, dull soldiers, no matter how much he forced them to train.

One of the men brought a torch and Yorin took it, bringing the body into better view. Dogs yelped in the background. Someone cursed at them, but it didn't stop the baying.

"Shall I put him on the cart, Captain?" The soldier gestured to the wagon sitting on the road, already holding three other bodies. Bodies the captain hadn't yet examined.

"What do you make of these?" Yorin looked up at the soldier. "Cardak, was it?"

"Yes, sir." The man knelt, moving his sword out of the way. He peered at the strange marks pressed into the fabric of the victim's trousers and the soft sleeves of his shirt. "Looks like he was wrapped in bailing twine."

"Very good," Yorin replied thoughtfully, gaze never leaving the man's clothing. "I suspect if his vest were not of boiled leather, we would see its marks there as well. It is remarkable."

"Is it, sir?" The soldier looked doubtful.

"Well, yes. Where is the twine now? Why is there no debris left behind? Twine is brittle and messy. And is that what killed him? I see no other evidence of injury, do you?"

"No, sir."

"Why wrap him in layers of twine, or perhaps very slender rope, only to remove it again? It passes peculiar. Do the other victims' clothing have these markings?"

"No, sir. If you ask me, them was poisoned."

Yorin looked up. "What makes you say that?"

"The vomit, sir."

"Do the bodies have puncture wounds or cuts?"

Cardak hesitated. "Not that I saw."

"Then how was the poison administered? I have a difficult time imagining that it was delivered in their supper. We all ate the same stew, the same bread. Drank the same ale."

"Yes, sir. I couldn't say how, sir. Only, I had a cousin who mistook some fae berries for moireberries and we found him in the field, like them, with puke on his lips."

Yorin considered this. It did sound as if poison was the most likely weapon used on the bodies in the wagon, as weird and impossible as it seemed. But the body lying here in the graveyard was different. The face was blue, which supported the theory that someone had wrapped him in twine until he couldn't draw breath. But what an unusual and troublesome way to kill someone. It made little sense.

Yorin bade Cardak put the body on the wagon with the others and then went to join the soldiers on the road. A dog bayed from the other side of the graveyard. Most of the hunting dogs had been returned to the kennel, but a few had been kept out in case a trail was picked up, which was highly doubtful. If there was a trail, they'd have found it long ago. It was as if their quarry had vanished into thin air. One moment they were seen galloping through the forest at a speed to break necks, and the next those same horses were riderless and grazing in the ditch. Yorin felt a grudging respect for whoever it was who had helped Lady Çifta escape, but along with it came a thorny irritation: they'd been outsmarted. They were being outsmarted still. Made fools of, and little irked him more than being made a fool of. He and Prince Faraçek agreed upon this. It was one of the reasons Yorin had risen to captaincy. This had the feeling of a charade, a show. In spite of his annoyance, he knew that all it took to discover a magician's trick was to view things from a different angle.

A houndsman came to the wagon with two unruly dogs on a leash, fighting him every step. He bound them to the wagon and stalked away to retrieve another pup, still baying from the graveyard.

"What's got them excited?" Yorin asked.

"Naught, sir, I'm sorry to say. These young ones are green. How I miss my old bitches. Nothing escaped them, even with nothing to scent 'aforehand. W'out a smell, these pups don't know their own arses from the trail."

"So why are they baying?"

The houndsman shrugged. "Come see for yourself, if you can spare the time."

Yorin followed the houndsman to the other end of the graveyard where three dogs circled some odd lumpy bit of stone half buried in privet and ivy. One of the dogs had his paws up on it and his nose stretched out, sniffing at the stones. He lifted his head and bayed again, hurting Yorin's ears. The houndsman grabbed the dog by the collar, pulling him back to fix him to the others.

"They're all excited over some animal what's fallen into an old well and died, I'm sure. Should have had a cap fixed over it a long time ago." The houndsman pulled his dogs away, leaving Yorin standing there in the ivy.

He sniffed but couldn't smell anything, not a rotting carcass, nor even stagnant water. Picking closer to the well, he held his torch aloft and peered into it. Embers fell and hissed out in the water. Yorin could make out nothing but his own puzzled reflection. The water was extremely dark, oddly so. Even the stone walls of the well itself disappeared utterly beneath the surface. Yorin looked around and found a small piece of loose mortar, which he chucked into the well. It made a musical splash and disappeared, the ripples quieting almost right away. It was the strangest water Yorin had ever seen. He'd suspect it of being foul if only there'd been a smell. He plucked a leaf from the nearest stem and dropped that in too, watching as it drifted down and landed on the water's surface. What he saw made his pulse jump. A bit of the water leaked over the edge of the leaf and pooled in the tiny reservoir it made, but the pool was not clear or transparent at all, but as black as ink. He squinted, wondering if his eyesight was deteriorating. He was the age for it, but also, torchlight was not great to see by, even for young people.

One of the men called a question to him but the captain was so focused he didn't acknowledge it. Yorin turned. "Bring me the longest branch you can find, will you? Has to be at least thirteen or fourteen feet."

"Aye, sir."

The soldier returned a short while later carrying a long slender branch with the leaves and twigs stripped away. Seeing Yorin peering into the well, he'd divined what the captain wanted it for. He handed it over. If he thought Yorin was up to something strange, he didn't let it show on his face.

"Hold this over so we can see." Yorin traded the torch for the branch. He lowered the branch into the well as the soldier held the torch aloft. When the branch hit the water, Yorin looked for it beneath the surface, but there was nothing, only opaque black liquid swallowing all. He lowered it further, not really expecting it to encounter any resistance but utilizing the full length of the branch because, well, why not? When he came to the end of the branch, he stirred the water, watching as it lapped over the wood.

"Do you see that?" he asked the soldier holding the torch.

"Sir?"

Yorin pulled the branch up to look at the end of it. There was something to this, he knew it now, but the well had not yet given up its secrets. "Look."

The soldier did see. "It's not wet!"

"Exactly." Captain Yorin lowered the branch into the water again and stirred more vigorously to gain a second witness to this bizarre feature. The pressure the water exerted against the branch was also strange, lighter than it should be. The sensation demanded further exploration.

"What's your name, soldier?"

"Mert, sir."

"Mert." Yorin withdrew the branch and tossed it aside. "How do you feel about climbing into this well?"

To Mert's credit, he didn't flinch. "I'm yours to command, Captain."

He patted Mert on the back. "Good lad. You're no craven. Fetch some rope, quickly now."

"There's handholds, sir. Do you see?" The soldier moved the torch so the light fell along the inside of the well. He pointed out the flattened indentations between the stones.

"Oh, clever." Yorin breathed.

"It'll take time to bring rope up from the fortress. I don't mind using the handholds, they look solid enough." The young soldier spoke stoutly. "I'm a good swimmer. Should I happen to fall in, I'll just climb out again."

"Good lad," Yorin repeated. "I suspect this well played a part in the escape of our quarry. If they passed this way, as preposterous as it might be, then we can too."

"Yes, sir." Mert handed Yorin the torch and slung a leg over the side of the well. He positioned himself in the handholds and lowered himself down. As his head disappeared below the rim, two more soldiers came over to watch. By the time Mert's foot made ripples on the inky surface of the water, there were six soldiers in addition to Captain Yorin, elbowing each other for a view.

Mert looked up, a question in his young face, though he was not afraid. *What next?*

"Do the handholds continue down?" Yorin asked.

Mert felt around in the water with a booted foot. "Yes, sir. I believe they do." He took another step down, and another, and another. With the water nearly to his waist, he paused. He put a hand in the water and brought it out again. He held it up for them to see. "Dry!"

The soldiers murmured, amazed. Someone called over more of their party.

Mert took two more steps down, now up to his shoulders in the black liquid and completely invisible below it. He looked up, astonishment on his face.

"What is it, lad?" Yorin held the torch to the side so it didn't drop embers on Mert's head.

"There's air!" Mert's eyes were as big as eggs. The inky stuff sloshed against his chest and shoulders as he felt around, leaving no stains on the fabric of his uniform.

"This is it, we've discovered their trick," Yorin said. "Are you willing to go further?"

"Yes, sir." Mert was eager. Those watching the drama unfold were clearly impressed with Mert's bravery. The young soldier wasn't about to retreat now. He took a breath and disappeared below the surface. The ripples he left behind diminished and the water was left glassy and undisturbed.

They waited.

The waited some more.

They grew restless. A few of the soldiers yawned, and a few of them returned to the road where others were asking why they were still there. Yorin could hear the story being explained.

Mert did not return.

They began to imagine the worst. That it was a trap, or that there had to be some creature inside the well who'd made a meal of the young man.

Finally, Yorin admitted failure. Mert was gone. No one could hold their breath that long, and whatever air was down there had clearly not been of a quality to sustain life. He cursed. He sent the other soldiers away while he took out the little tin of tobacco he kept in his chest pocket and rolled himself a cigarette. He smoked it furiously, taking courage from the drug. He called one soldier back and bade him to hold the torch over the well.

"Hold it steady." Yorin put his legs over and found the holds.

"Are you sure—"

"Do you want to go in after him?" Yorin snapped.

The soldier didn't reply.

"I sent him down there. I have to explain to his family what happened. We can't see him, but we know he's there. If I can't reach him, I'll come back up."

"At least wait for someone to fetch a rope."

"Mert didn't have a rope," Yorin growled, and lowered himself into the well.

"What if it was what they said? A monster or the like."

"Do you really believe that?" Yorin's head was below the lip of the well now, his voice echoing.

Again, the soldier didn't reply.

The truth was, Yorin felt terrified, but he was more enraged than afraid. He'd be damned if he let anyone else go after the lad other than himself. He was responsible. Their quarry *had* vanished somehow, and this was not a normal well. Mert had felt air, or some other gas. Yorin could not shake the feeling that Mert might yet be alright, that if Lady Çifta had taken this route to escape, then an escape it provided.

He experienced wonder all over again as he submerged to the waist and rose up again to see the strange liquid leave no stains on his uniform. Another foot down and he was able to feel the air. There was no body to be felt below the surface, only more free and open handholds.

Before he changed his mind, Yorin held his breath and took the plunge, squeezing his eyes shut as he climbed down until his head was free again. He gasped and opened his eyes. A dim blue glow drew his gaze straight down to a circular opening.

"Mert?"

The air was quite breathable. Descending, he looked up to see the underside of the black liquid looking exactly as it did from the top, completely opaque.

Down through the rest of the well he went until it finished on a great wide and poorly lit emptiness. There was no visible light source, yet the huge space did have light, a soft illumination emanating from cracks in the walls. He lowered himself another step but had to catch himself when the handholds suddenly ended and his toe scraped against solid earth. He craned a look around and could make out only a very, very long drop. At the bottom appeared to be a pile of rubble, like a disastrous shipwreck. Directly below Yorin lay Mert's body, small and broken, hardly distinguishable from the debris around him.

That was why the lad had not returned.

Yorin could feel weariness growing in his heart, but also in his hands and feet as he clung to the last handholds, quietly astounded by what he'd discovered. He climbed back up the holds and into the bottom of the well. Passing through the liquid, he was greeted with great relief by several soldiers, who helped him out of the well.

"Where is Mert?" One asked.

"I couldn't retrieve him. There is nothing below the liquid. A few more holds and then a very long drop. He fell," replied Yorin, stepping away from the stonework. He nearly tripped when his heel hooked on something solid. Staggering, he righted himself and then bent to part the ivy and take a look at what he'd tripped over. A heavy piece of rotten wood lay hidden in the greenery. With effort, because it was very solid, he propped it on its side.

One of the soldiers moved the torch to light it better. "The well cap."

It was crumbling and mushy, but Yorin lifted it and—with the soldiers' help—placed it over the mouth of the well. It didn't cover the hole entirely anymore, having several chunks missing, but it would serve its purpose until Yorin could give a full report to Prince Faraçek.

On his way to the mount he'd left grazing in the ditch, Yorin discovered that the wagon with the bodies had been taken back to the fortress, along with the dogs and most of the soldiers. A few stayed behind to wait for him. Yorin told them to return to the fortress and took his horse by the bridle. His mind was a whirlwind at what he'd discovered.

A soldier on horseback came cantering up the double-track. He pulled his horse up. "We found this further down the road." He pulled a ratty bit of fabric from beneath his belt and handed it to Yorin. "Looks like a sleeve. It's not big enough to be a man's, and didn't one of the party say the girl had a bare arm?"

"They did." Yorin took the sleeve and stretched it out. The threads were torn where it had been ripped from the torso of a dress or a tunic. There were sweat stains beneath the arm. A whiff of something floral drifted past his nose. Unmindful and uncaring of how it might look to his men, he brought the sleeve to his face and inhaled.

The epic fable continues with

A MEMORY OF NIGHTSHADE.

The Scented Court, book 2.

www.ingramcontent.com/pod-product-compliance
Lightning Source LLC
Chambersburg PA
CBHW020522310726
48979CB00014B/2174/J

* 9 7 8 1 9 8 9 3 3 8 4 6 9 *